KICKERS

a novel of the
Secret War

Patrick Lee

This is a work of fiction. Names, characters, places and events are either products of the author's imagination or are used in a fictitious manner.

Cover photograph of Laos airdrop by smokejumper Larry Moore.

Laos map by Keely Eliason, graphic designer, Business As Usual, Ketchum, ID

ISBN: 1492911038
ISBN 13: 9781492911036

Library of Congress Control Number: 2013923817
CreateSpace Independent Publishing Platform,
North Charleston, South Carolina

for Tex and Yogi

—keep 'er into the wind, boys

CHINA
NORTH VIETNAM
Dien Bien Phu
URMA
Ha Noi
LAOS
Luangprabang
Long Tieng
Gulf of Tonkin
Vientiane
Mekong River
Savannakhet
Ho Chi Minh Trail
THAILAND
Mekong River
Bangkok
CAMBODIA
SOUTH
VIETNAM
Saigon

PROLOGUE

A buzzer went off.

They stood and hooked their static lines to an overhead cable. An American CIA agent and twenty French soldiers, half without parachute training, jumped into a drop zone named "Natasha," a red dirt airstrip two hundred meters north of the village of Dien Bien Phu on the Laos/Tonkin border. The agent and the French replacements for the dead fell through most of six hundred feet, then drifted briefly when their chutes opened, oscillating in darkness and cold rain.

Natasha was under Viet Minh fire as they came in, machine guns and antiaircraft guns lighting the night air but not the ground. The American did not see the ground and struck it hard, his parachute swinging him sideways into the packed surface. The blow broke ribs and knocked the wind from him. Bullets from raking machine gun fire began to strike the ground near him. The Viet Minh knew where the airstrip was despite the dark.

As if on signal the Viet Minh guns stopped. Night's silence was broken by sporadic gunshots of sentries and snipers. The American, bearing a false identity, rose and walked in the dark, back against the direction of the drop, standard paratrooper rendezvous. He sought the field hospital near the village.

He almost missed the sound. Hearing it, he did not mistake it. Rifle bolt being thrown. He began talking immediately, talked slowly, more loudly than the intimacy of silence and close quarters required.

He started to say why he was there, realized he did not know who he was talking to, stopped. Trying to compose himself he said to the darkness "You sonsabitches need considerably more help than me."

The CIA agent worked in the Company's branch for Southeast Asia, covert operations. Others had conceived his one-man mission to the middle of a battlefield. Standing in the dark, he retraced in silence what they had said. *"The arithmetic of the French dead sums at ninety thousand. If the French withdraw, National Security Council thinks the Communists will have a walkover in Laos, Vietnam, and Cambodia, all the way to India and Europe. It's the 'domino theory.' Our analysts say it's bullshit, but it's religion at NSC. I need someone on the ground saying it's bullshit."*

He thought he heard a laugh, then voices in a language he did not recognize. It did not sound like Vietnamese or Lao. Algerian colonials he guessed. Rough hands took him to the French commanding officer.

They were underground in a room of log walls that leaked sand and water. There was smell of sewer and decaying flesh. The floor was inches of mud. The room seemed to tremble, on the verge of collapse in the monsoon rain. With effort the American shook the hand of the clean, well-dressed commanding officer and explained who he was.

"How is the chef at the Metropole in Hanoi? If you have not brought your own wine you will be disappointed here." The commanding officer stopped the greeting and asked "Are you in pain?"

"A little. Haven't done the night stuff in a while."

The commanding officer began a sympathetic response. A junior officer interrupted without ceremony, bristling command presence, lines of exhaustion creasing his sunburnt face. He addressed the agent in mixed English and French, ignored his commanding officer.

"I will introduce you in the morning to the artillery group at strongpoint Isabelle. They fight exposed and under attack. They are the key and they are fucked and they know it. Their commanding officer committed suicide within twenty-four hours of commencement of the battle. As soon as he realized *c'est bordélique complètement*. Herve was not stupid.

"One visit to Isabelle will tell all. You could leave then. But I will take you on patrol tomorrow night. Washington will want details of *la agonie*. Paris will expect you to acknowledge our *hêroïsme* and *habilité*. When you dine with me you will understand all elements of the supply situation, another key." The junior officer, commander of one of the paratroop battalions, ran a hand through his short brush-cut hair. He sighed, a talker but tired of it. "I will take you now to the hospital. But I warn you, the nurses will think you *la malade imaginaire*. So will you once you have stood in the blood pools of the surgery."

The hospital was a single room, underground. The air was filled with the stench of dead and dying men. The smell entered the nose, the mouth, overriding all other impressions.

Maggots moved atop open wounds on naked limbs and bellies. One of the nurses flicked a maggot to the floor. She covered the crushed leg of a boy as he hissed in rage and pain.

"The worms come through the walls," she said. "From the graves outside. So many die they are buried everywhere, on top of one another."

The nurses were borrowed from the mobile field brothel. They were efficient, tender, and teased the CIA agent with exaggerated grimaces of pain. His nurse, an African tribal, spoke in a croon of sympathy and he understood nothing of what she said. As he left the hospital room the girl pinched his butt and winked at him. He grinned and threw a kiss with his bad arm.

In the predawn he ate with the battalion commander in a sagging dugout, dark disguising the food. "Is this your regular rations?"

"No, of course not. We are on half rations. We have run completely out of food several times. It is the antiaircraft guns. The planes have to fly too high to drop accurately. The Viet Minh collect our parachutes and eat our rations, drink our wine, and shoot our artillery shells. We will run out of ammunition in the final attack. Let us go to Isabelle so you can see what supply does to them."

They drove on a rutted, shell-pocked road five miles south to strongpoint Isabelle. They reached Isabelle as the morning fog lifted. Shelling from the line of hills looking down on French positions began immediately. Isabelle was afloat in muddy water and unburied dead from both sides. The French began counter-battery fire at half the rate of the Viet Minh fire, and then slowed, conserving ammunition. The battalion paratroop commander brought out the lieutenant in charge of Isabelle artillery. The artilleryman was black with dirt and the work of firing cannon.

The CIA agent began scribbling notes as the lieutenant talked without reaction to the surrounding howitzer fire and explosions. He spoke of the four to one artillery advantage of the Viet Minh, the trickle of French ammunition supply. The only inflection was an occasional shrug of the shoulders.

The French paratroop commander pulled a flask of cognac from a pocket and held it out to the lieutenant. The lieutenant opened it and drank. "*Merci.*"

They drove from Isabelle in silence, as if recalling a sermon while returning from church. The road to the village was exploding.

The agent crouched near the command center, seeking cover from intermittent shelling and rifle fire. The fetid stink of rotting bodies, exhumed and shredded daily by Viet Minh artillery fired into the sand and clay of strongpoint Elaine across the river from him, seeped into his hair and clothes. He blew his nose, tried to cough and spit the encrusted reek away, imagined he tasted it.

"We are going there tonight." The paratroop commander stood over him, disregarding the lethal sounds of battle. He pointed at Elaine, a slightly higher rubble heap than the village, equally barren. "You will hear the sounds of Viet Minh digging their trenches toward us. We will go through our wire to kill their sappers." The Frenchman offered a cigarette. "Maybe you will kill one, too. Eh? Does the CIA permit you that?"

He wanted to stay crouched, safe from explosion and the odds of whining bullets. He could not and rose to take the offered cigarette. He ignored the Frenchman's question. He had been sent to witness. "*Is this going to become our Indochina war? That's the point, why I asked you to come in. Are we their default position?*"

"When do we go?" he asked the battalion commander. He wanted to get it over with.

"After dark, when the fog comes. Now you should go in the hospital and sleep." The Frenchman threw his cigarette away and left.

The French officer woke him and handed him a bowl of rice and a fistful of Benzedrine tablets. "We will leave in half an hour. Make sure your watch is correct. It is 0100." The paratrooper was all business as he prepared his small patrol.

Pain from his ribs and shoulder joined Benzedrine in keeping the CIA agent wide-eyed but blind in the foggy dark. The patrol stopped moving whenever flares suffused the fog with vague light.

He knew they were close to the fortifications of Elaine. Increasing intensity of the carrion smell told him where he was. They reached sentries, exchanged sign and countersign in Breton and Arabic. The patrol stopped at the strongpoint and listened to whispered instructions for passing through the barbed wire, moving to Viet Minh approach trenches, and the task when they got there.

The agent rested as the patrol talked in hushed voices. He could make out the top edge of the strongpoint revetment. Curious to see what lay beyond their protecting embankment he grabbed the edge to pull himself up. The wet material gave way, fell in on him. He leapt back, startled, then shocked at the corpse insinuating itself down the front of him. In his own mind he screamed. The only sound was a stifled "Unh!"

He stared at the embankment. Lumpy irregular layers. He looked away. The entire revetment was dead and decaying soldiers. French and Viet Minh. The fortification had once been logs and sand bags. Artillery had crushed those materials until they did not exist. He shivered when he realized the nature of the fighting at Elaine. He wanted to cry out and run. He saw the French officer watching him.

"We are going through the wire, paying a visit to a Viet Minh forward bunker. I invite you to come. It is up to you," the Frenchman said. The American would have walked naked and unarmed to the Viet Minh bunker, anything to leave the revetments of Elaine.

The patrol spent the next half hour crawling in sewage-filled trenches, silently murdering teenage sentries, distracting bunkered machine gunners with rifle fire, and burying explosive at a Viet Minh bunker wall. With the flick of a switch a small current of electricity ran from a battery in a backpack down a wire to the plastic explosive at the base of the bunker. It detonated with a bright flash and loud boom, the light of the explosion capturing for a moment the flight of logs, guns, and bodies. That was followed by larger secondary explosions roaring from the site of the bunker.

No one in the squad spoke until they were back at the strongpoint. There the French officer slapped the CIA agent on his sore shoulder. "Congratulations. You helped buy Elaine twenty-four hours. Viet Minh would have concentrated at the bunker and attacked with ten to one advantage. Now they will have to put their attack together without supporting fire of machine guns in the bunker."

The agent followed the patrol away from Elaine, crossed the chest-high Nam Yum River and returned to the village, once again under bombardment from Viet Minh artillery in the surrounding hills. He felt no joy, separated himself from the men of the patrol as soon as he could. If they did not die tomorrow, they would die in some last battle only weeks from now.

That morning he said goodbye to some of the French paratroops. The battalion commander pulled out his flask of cognac and offered it. "It will help you keep up with the Meo who will lead you out. If you don't, well, maybe we can go once more to Elaine." The agent drank and handed the flask back.

The Frenchman saluted, stepped forward and embraced him. Holding him, he whispered "Tell them we are worthy. Ask for our relief, but do not beg."

The agent left under cover of monsoon fog, following the Meo *maquis* as they disappeared into the jungle of northern Laos.

CHAPTER ONE

They came from China. In old times, on the Yellow River, some had blue eyes and blond hair, though not now. Legends say their homeland is somewhere else, beyond China, and tell of migration.

Migration was a survival way for the Meo. One migration, generations before, brought them to the mountains of Laos.

Why their history is full of last resort, of fleeing eradication, is a mystery. Observers count the Meo a people of virtue, and they cherish children.

Thua Ly, a descendant of migrants and headman of a Meo village, knelt and scraped the soil near the path. He pinched the dirt he had loosened, placed the pinch in his mouth, chewed it, stirred it with his tongue, tasting. Once again he had sought and found the sweet limestone of northern Laos.

He sat in the forest and felt the rhythms of the growing season, feeling more than recalling. As headman he had chosen the new field, an hour walk from the village, the closest ground not exhausted by planting poppy. He would call the women to cut the underbrush with knives and machetes, the men to cut the trees with iron axes. He would gather them again months later, when the slash had dried to fuel. The young men of the village would run down the mountain setting fire to the dead remains of the forest, an excitement now centuries old for the Meo. The new village farm would be created in ash.

As he sat feeling his life, comfortable that he knew the future, he was joined in the mountain shade by the youngest of his wives. May had brought him lunch. Thua was dark haired with a narrow, ruddy-brown face. Even though he was thirty-five and nearing old age, his three wives considered him handsome and lusty. Teenage May excited him and he found ways to have her near him. He thought they would have a child.

Thua and May squatted on the forest floor. He played a few notes on a small bamboo flute he carried in his loose clothing. He had made it as a young man, had courted his first wife with it. Notes he played now were love talk, and made her smile. They spoke about plans for the new field and building the field houses, raised bamboo pallets under thatch roofs for resting when the time and effort to return to the village was too great. Even that talk was musical, meaning carried in song tones.

"When will be best for a child?" He put a hand on her stomach, moved to touch her between the legs.

She enjoyed the touching. She focused on the ground beside her in order to leave the sensations of her body, think what her answer was. She had to reckon growth within her against life rotating through the field.

She told him "When the poppy blooms." After the petals fell from the seed pod, she would be strong enough for the work of cutting incisions in the poppy bulb and collecting the congealed sap. She could carry the infant in a sling on her back. "If she is a girl we will call her May Ying—Opium Poppy."

He nodded, said "Yes," pulled her to the ground beside him and made love to his wife. She cried out, her eyes open but not seeing, the forest canopy rising above her from the ground soon to be a field. They walked back to the village hand in hand.

Thua did not hurry though he had a meeting with other tribal leaders that afternoon. They were the opium brokers in Xieng Khouang province and they were meeting to discuss who would represent them with the buyers from the Corsican syndicate.

The men would discuss other matters, as they often did now. Things were changing. The *fackee,* the French colonials, had left after their defeat, except for the Corsicans. The Corsicans made no demand except to buy opium.

The change the tribal leaders discussed was the Pathet Lao, the communist political movement. Communists seek land reform, insist on it. That was no fit for slash and burn farming. Pathet Lao were filled, too, with reprisal for Meo assistance to the French in the Indochina war. They confiscated Meo opium to trade to Chinese merchants for weapons. They split the Meo by stoking old feuds between the Ly and Lo clans.

The threat of the Pathet Lao to march on the administrative capitol, Vientiane, through the Plain of Jars, would bring armies to fight in their midst.

Thua Ly, with other elders, resisted the Pathet Lao. When he did he tried to keep a cool heart, hold his anger in check. He did not take orders. He was not persuadable to any belief not received directly from his ancestors. His politeness was infuriating. The Pathet Lao began to see him as a cause of their failure to convert the Meo to communism. They looked for ways to end his opposition.

Later that evening Thua Ly told his family he had been chosen agent for brokering the year's sales to the Corsicans. They were not surprised. Thua and his father had a long history in the French opium trade. Xieng Khouang province, home of the Ly clan, was the principal opium production area, the town of Phong Savan on the Plain of Jars the principal buying and collection point.

Wealthy merchants among the French colonists of Indochina had built Phong Savan as a highland retreat. It was nothing other than a French hilltop village, complete with two-story stone residences. Air Laos Commerciale, a charter airline operating twin engine Beech aircraft, flew almost daily from the faux French town. Most of its flights were to parachute drop sites. The small airline was owned by Corsican gangster Alain Vecchio.

Vecchio also owned the inn at Phong Savan, the Château de la Vallée Bleue. The stone chateau was where he entertained Lao and Vietnamese government officials, syndicate friends, competitors, Nung mercenaries, French expatriates, and itinerant whores. It was business.

The business associate he liked most was illiterate Thua Ly. Thua sometimes played his flute, the *raj*, when Vecchio asked. Thua mimicked melancholy tunes picked out on a piano by Vecchio.

Thua walked to the inn at Phong Savan several days after his meeting with the Meo leaders. He was immediately taken to Vecchio's table in the courtyard of the inn. Vecchio rose and shook Thua's hand.

Vecchio looked for it but did not see the small flute. He gave a shrug. They were busy. They were going to negotiate.

They negotiated through lunch. Price was never mentioned. They knew there was no talk in a number. Instead they spoke vividly about how bandits and weather and army generals had impaired the market. Or refuted such explanations. In the end, by their custom, Vecchio counted out Lao kip in the amount he was willing to pay for a kilo of opium. If Thua accepted that price, he swept the money from the table and produced a kilo of opium, wrapped in banana leaf, from a woven bag he carried for the purpose. If he rejected the proposed price Thua played on his flute a Chopin polonaise copied from Vecchio that sounded like angry cats. The ritual always made Vecchio laugh, though it did not today.

At the close of the day's successful negotiation Vecchio said "Let's celebrate then. I want to show you the business, where your opium goes. A short airplane ride. It won't take long. You've never been up have you. C'mon."

There were no wheeled vehicles in any Meo village. A ride in Vecchio's airplane was beyond belief. Thua quickly accepted.

They walked the short distance to the airstrip and watched two of Vecchio's men load pallets into the side door of a Twin Beech. Vecchio stepped up and through the door, turned and extended his hand to Thua. The Meo headman entered his first airplane ever.

Thua and Vecchio sat in passenger seats forward of the side door and cargo. Thua twisted and leaned seeking the airborne views of his country through the plane's small windows. Vecchio was tour guide, explaining the operation of the aircraft, pointing out rivers and mountains that Thua had known since childhood. He described how the parachutes on the cargo bundles would open. "You probably sold it to us. We are delivering it to Vietnamese river bandits."

An hour had passed before the captivated Thua realized he must be far from his village. The Beech was fast and it was, in fact, far from home. The plane circled and the two men handling Vecchio's cargo, now in parachute harness, repositioned the pallets, attaching the static lines of cargo parachutes to a cable inside the plane, making the cargo ready to push out the door. Vecchio walked back toward the pallets of opium, inspecting. He motioned Thua to join him.

Vecchio pointed to the hills below. He said "Vietnam," and stepped back to allow Thua to look. Standing behind Thua he grasped his own left wrist with his right hand, released it, and pointed at the Meo. He walked away to his seat.

The two men in parachute packs quickly overpowered Thua, twisted both his arms behind him. Thua kicked the side of the plane with his feet, pounded his head on the floor. His offended shouts and sounds of resistance were muffled, carried away by the smothering rush of air over the Beech.

The plane continued to circle. As it passed again over the drop zone Vecchio nodded to the two men kneeling on Thua and watching for a signal. They threw the writhing Meo from the plane, a small contorted thing. Easy to do, really. They pushed the bundles out the side door, retrieved the static lines, and watched the slow descent of the cargo chutes.

Vecchio looked straight ahead, hands on his knees. *It is what it is. Price of doing business. Can't imagine why the Pathet Lao were afraid of the little bastard.*

He heard the sound of bamboo rolling on the metal floor of the airplane. He turned and saw the flute, picked it up, about to throw it out the door into the jungle below. He stuck it in a jacket pocket. *It is what it is.*

May Ly tried over many weeks to find out what had happened to her husband. She walked to Phong Savan and talked to people there. No one had seen him, which seemed strange. Not even the man he had gone to see about the price of opium knew anything.

As she left, walking barefoot through the tiled reception area of the Château de la Vallée Bleue, her eyes continuing the vain search, she saw it. His flute hanging among other musical instruments carved and fitted by Meo men, turned to graceful decoration on the inn walls. She told herself not to stop, not to cry out or stagger, to change nothing in her bearing. She walked on to her village, bitter pain filling her arms and belly as she climbed the familiar path. When she reached the village, she asked for opium. Then she asked to see the *txiv neeb,* the shaman.

When the shaman came he asked what illness she wanted cured. "Where is the pain?"

"It is not for pain. There is nothing to cure. The prayer I want is that a child not be born to me. My husband's soul is lost to the *farang,* the foreigner, since he last came to me."

The shaman knew Thua Ly, was aware he dealt with the foreigners and had disappeared. He considered for a moment and thought he understood. He sacrificed a young dog in barter for the souls of the mother and the unwanted child. The shaman shook a hoop hung with metal discs, making the rhythmic sound of hoof beats, the sound of the spirit horse he rode in search of the soul of the unborn child. Finding that soul, he chanted and danced in a frenzy, on and on, sweating, a black hood over his face, arms and legs flogging the air. When the child spirit understood it was not wanted and assured the shaman it would not stay the dance ended. His final arrangement with the spirit world was to place around May's neck a ring like those used to attach a newborn child's soul safely to the mother. He cut the neck ring.

In most respects the ritual was like that used by every Meo shaman for every pain and illness. Cutting the neck ring was something new, introduced on inspiration, by what agent the shaman did not know.

That night May Ly bled a non-viable fetus through the bamboo pallet on which she slept. Within months of the shaman's visit she joined the people of her village as a refugee from war, walking rough mountain paths, the broken neck ring and other possessions at the bottom of a woven bag.

M.I.A.

The two men wore silk top hats and dark overcoats. The POW thought about the look of the hats, solemn and silly. Some said the hat was the younger man's idea, so he could remove it and speak for a "new generation."

"Now the trumpet summons us again," the young president said. The prisoner remembered how cold it had been. He was cold now and shivering with fever.

Remembering was his way out of the bamboo cage. Remembering and fantasies and whatever came in the night dreams. He remembered the president, at a news conference just months after the inaugural, saying "all Southeast Asia will be endangered if Laos is lost." He could not remember the words exactly. He did not pay attention to things then, not like he did now.

Quick as Jack and Jill went up the hill, they send us to Lay-os and don't tell anybody. He laughed at how Kennedy would say "Lay-os," the O sound that of someone ordering cod.

He looked around to see if they were watching him. He did not want the guards to see him laughing.

Jesus, I was a schnook. I worked for them six months before I realized it was CIA. How can you miss that? Because the checks said Intermountain Aviation? I guess. But I shoulda figured it out. Wasn't payin' attention.

Jungle prison had made him introspective. Not a lot, but enough that he felt uneasy once in a while. When that happened, he escaped to a memory of adventure or pleasure or vindication. He felt uneasy about missing something as obvious as who he worked for. He avoided the feeling by remembering the day he went dove hunting at Long Thanh. Walter Cronkite talked him into telling the story again.

I didn't go to Laos right away, Walter. See, the Customer—a name we call the Agency sometimes—sent me to Vietnam to train dinks in tree jumpin'. We were insertin' 'em in the North. It was a Lansdale idea so everybody thought it was brilliant. But I was workin' these guys every day and seein' things. I sized it up. I thought it was goin' to go over like a lead balloon. I told Saigon what I thought and they more or less told me to mind my business. Now, of course, we know I was right.

Anyhow, I had some time on my hands. The dinks had stolen every last inch of parachute cord off the jump tower. I ordered up more but it was slow showin' up at Tan Son Nhut air base so I had time to kill before everything was back in workin' order. I had some buddies were from Texas. You couldn't be in smoke jumpin' and not have buddies from Texas. They talked about how great dove huntin' was. I'd never been dove huntin'. You start shootin' pigeons in my town the black 'n' whites would be all over your ass.

I noticed there were doves around the air strip at Long Thanh. It was red and orange dirt with a lot of little gravel in it, kind of like caliche the Texas boys say. Anyway, the doves would walk around peckin' at the gravel. So I had this idea I would finally go dove huntin'. Like I was on a private huntin' preserve, you know.

I checked out a twelve-gauge sawed-off shotgun from Saigon. I asked a buddy who did dove huntin' what he shot doves with and he recommended number eight shot.

When I was all set to go bird huntin' it was too hot to be walkin' around in the sun. I got the ARVN Marvin worked for me to drive a jeep while I sat on the hood with my scattergun and a six-pack. Comfortable. I turned out to be pretty good at shootin' doves. Got ten of 'em and had the kitchen cook 'em up for the next bunch of dink trainees.

Goin' down to see my buddies in Lampasas soon as I get out of here. Goin' dove huntin' and rattlesnake shootin' with 'em.

Stand at ease, Mr. Cronkite.

The POW pulled his thin blanket tighter to him. The temperature in the cave in the mountains was that of a mild day in Chicago winter and he was not dressed for it. He blamed that, too, on not paying attention.

CHAPTER TWO

It was a time of ideology and hubris. Atrocity became the ordinary in life. Escape was calculated and laid off daily in every mind. Some fled on footpaths, some on ships, others hid. Whatever would serve escape.

The ragged plan of Thanasis Mavros and his uncle Ilias for escaping Greece was little more than a list. His uncle had hidden Thanasis with mountain sheepherders, just another difficult herder neither side would want. When the fighting between Communist and king seeped into the mountains, a villager warned Ilias. "The Communists are taking the sheepherders, all of the mountain people, for the fighting. They will not overlook a big boy like Thanasis. What are you going to do with him?"

By nightfall they were on a mountain path, Thanasis following his uncle. Thanasis was focused by the challenge of fleeing in the night. The narrow path, invisible in the dark, seemed illuminated. He stepped between rocks without sound.

The dark, once again, brought Thanasis to his father's death. He said nothing to Ilias as the lurid figures formed in his head. They came in familiar sequence. It began with the gunshot. The shot was loud, as always. It knocked his father to the ground. He thought of their play at wrestling as he watched his father struggle to get to his feet.

Their neighbor, standing next to the man with the gun, shouted and struck his father with a shovel. Thanasis cried as the shovel cut through the skin and bone of his father's face. He was enveloped by blunt cracking sounds. His father groaned, sound pushing through the blood filling his throat, moustache flying away in pieces.

Thanasis hid his face in his hands. The sound of the shovel made him sick. He vomited. He fainted and fell in his vomit.

Thanasis stumbled on the mountain path. The dark images fled as he regained his footing. As always the phantasm filled him with grief and shame. He stopped on the path, then hurried on.

He daily fantasized rescuing his father, tearing the shovel from the neighbor's hands, knocking the pistol from the gunman, making the group of men disperse. Daily he judged his inaction and fainting against the fantasy of rescue. *I didn't try.* He cringed at the recurring thought, became disassociated in the face of it. He walked in silence with Ilias.

Ilias left his own fear unspoken. *God, let there be a ship. Otherwise he will join his parents in the graves of the war.* The last entry in their thesaurus of flight was a steamer leaving a port in Greece bound for anywhere else. By the grace of God and Greek shipping, that part of the worn plan worked. The ship's roundabout destination was the port of Baltimore, Maryland.

Thousands of miles later they landed in an American city that reminded Thanasis of nothing so much as a port in Greece. That Baltimore looked like Greece did not surprise him. For all he knew, the rest of the world looked like Greece.

They found work. Collecting garbage, washing dishes, sweeping and mopping bars. Ilias wanted something more for Thanasis. Thanasis wanted only to be in the mountains he had fled, but said nothing. He worked alongside his uncle and tried to read every poster, billboard, and street sign in Baltimore.

Looking out from a Baltimore park bench on a summer weekend, Ilias had an idea. He was watching two men straightening from under the hood of a car, talking to each other, pointing at the car. One directed the other into the driver's seat, reached under the hood, and the car started. *That easily,* Ilias thought, and the idea came. *Thanasis can do this. It will get him out of the garbage.*

The next day Thanasis followed his uncle through the door of a building in which they sold and repaired cars. He knew this was not a good idea, but it was what his mother's brother wanted. He shrugged.

Ilias had shaved for the occasion and was wearing suit and tie, his shoes polished. He asked for and was taken to the manager. He explained in broken English that Thanasis was hardworking and wanted a job fixing cars and later, of course, selling them.

The manager wore glasses that sat far down his nose and he looked over them at Ilias, the sleeves of his white shirt rolled up. He looked busy, in charge. He began dealing with the job applicants, seeking and organizing the information he needed.

"Where you guys from?"

"Greece."

"Not Communist sons of bitches are you?"

"No!" Starting to spit on the floor, Ilias stopped himself.

"He speak English?" Without waiting for an answer the car dealer turned to Thanasis.

He looked directly at Thanasis and said nothing, a practiced first step in his homemade interview process. He was surprised when the young man did not drop his eyes or look away. The quiet face was alert, waiting. The manager saw brown eyes, black short-cropped hair, olive skin, a swarthy look. Though youthful, it was clear he shaved his dark cheeks and needed to. The manager's usual reaction to dark visage was imagined threat. The boy's demeanor kept the manager's customary feeling at bay. The dark eyes were calming.

"Where you from, son?"

"Mt. Smolikas. I lived with them." Thanasis began a slow-paced explanation of what had happened to his family, dead in the Greek civil war, and what he had been doing hiding in the Pindos mountains.

In spite of himself, the manager stopped looking at his watch and became interested. The Cold War was afoot and not everybody felt bad about that. He concluded that the youngster could speak English, was respectful, hated Communists, liked mountains, and, if you believed him, knew a hell of a lot about herding sheep. He decided to cut through it with a few more questions. The answers he got confirmed that Thanasis knew nothing about cars.

"I like you and your uncle here. But I don't have anything for you. I doubt if anybody does. Unless you want to keep cleaning up other people's shit, you have to get out of here. You know sheep, I guess, and mountains. That's where you might find something with sheep. Do you know where that is, how far that is? Two thousand miles. That's where sheep and mountains are. Montana, Idaho, Nevada. And Mt. Smolikas, of course!"

The manager could tell from their expressions that Thanasis and Ilias were not registering the geography he was introducing. He said "Here let me show you," and got down a road atlas from a shelf.

An hour later Thanasis owned the atlas they had been studying, a gift from the car dealer. He knew where Boise, Idaho was. The highway going there from Baltimore was marked with a thick line of pencil. He had hitchhiked before. Now he had an American word for it and assurance from the car dealer that lots of Americans did it. He and Ilias left the car dealership with the atlas and a need to talk.

Thanasis was bursting. He was going to the mountains. Usually silent, he could not stop talking.

"If we roll our things in a blanket, one for each of us, we just have a sling on the back. It is easy to walk like that." Thanasis was measuring and tying imagined blanket rolls, shaping them in the air with his hands, walking rapidly as he did. "Then we take the smaller road, the blue one. You remember." He was gesturing as if the atlas lay before them. "We will get a ride on that road, probably all the way to the Lincoln Highway, the red one, the major highway." He was using the car dealer's words describing their route.

Ilias listened without offering his thoughts. They were painful and he was torn, but he had made his decision. *I will stay behind. One can hitchhike faster than two.* He could no longer work as hard as Thanasis, could not live and work in the mountains. He would just hold Thanasis back. He dropped behind the pace Thanasis was setting even now, walking on the imagined highway.

The talk between them that night was loud. A stranger overhearing it would think they were angry, near blows. It was the sound, however, of Greek words charged with love, loss, the parting of survivors. There was disagreement about the need for the separation, the timing and purpose of it, and then argument about the disagreement, but those were only details that scattered before the emotions. They both wept, in front of each other and then separately.

Early the next morning, Ilias fixed coffee for Thanasis. He hugged him and kissed him goodbye. He reached into his pocket and took out his red and black worry beads. He gave them to Thanasis, closing his nephew's hand over them. "Remember me and comfort yourself with them."

Obedient to his uncle, Thanasis left, walking alone. He was still deep in the night's conflict when he thumbed his first ride. He stared at the road through the windshield of the first car, sunk in the pain of separation. The emotions subsided with the miles and talk of succeeding drivers. His enthusiasm for the journey returned and grew.

In two weeks Thanasis reached Boise. He approached town late at night driving a powder blue Cadillac through sagebrush desert at seventy miles an hour, confident in his new driving skills. He could not believe the luxury. He liked its owner and told the man all about himself. The owner was a large black man who sang a strange song over and over as he drank from a silver flask.

"Beautiful streamer
open for me.
Blue sky above me
and no canopy."

The black man said his name was Biggie Brown, that he was a magazine salesman. "Who made the most sales in the United States last year? I did. Biggie Brown. Sold 478 magazine subscriptions in one year." He continued singing his song, drinking, and asking Thanasis about the mountains he came from.

There were few lights on in the town of Boise. Biggie told him to drive until they found some lights. The first they found spelled out BAR GERNIKA. Biggie told Thanasis to stop. He got out of the car and went in the place, trailed by his driver. Biggie ordered a sloe gin fizz. He looked at Thanasis and then asked the bartender if he had food. "Feed this boy a sandwich." He looked at Thanasis again and added "And a glass of milk. Help his night vision." Biggie laughed and wheezed.

Out of the bartender's hearing Biggie said to Thanasis "I'm goin' to talk to this man about sheepherding jobs. Let me handle this. I don't know anything about sheep, but watch and learn. There is nothing I can't sell, includin' you." When the food came Biggie began telling the bartender what a hard worker Thanasis was, what a careful sheepherder he was, not afraid of bears and wolves, never lost a sheep. "Any of that kind of work around here?"

The bartender finished drying a glass. "Could be. He Basque?"

Biggie looked at the dark haired Thanasis. "You know, he sure looks like a Basco. Has that long nose. Eyebrows clear over his nose. Could be. Thing is, though, what a Basco knows is fish. They all fisherman. I *been* to San Sebastian. No sheep there. Just fishin' boats. This boy knows sheep better than most Bascoes. I'm tellin' you, he never lost a single sheep in the hairiest mountains you ever seen. Pindos mountains. You ever been there?"

When the bartender confessed he had no knowledge of the Pindos, Biggie moved his sales pitch on Thanasis up a notch. "Pindos mountain people be the best sheep men in the world. Been doin' it for a thousand years. Kind of invented it. They been known to double the production of a herd. Swear. I *been* to the Pindos."

He touched his empty glass and the bartender made him another drink. He leaned forward and asked "Can you put this hard workin' fella in touch with a real sheep man, somebody knows what he is doin' and can use a good hand? Fella don't want to waste his time with somebody don't know the business. Know what I mean?"

The bartender thought a minute, cleaning behind the bar. "Why don't you bring him around early tomorrow morning. I think I know somebody might need a herder to take a fella's place, at least for awhile, until he recovers from a car running into his sheep wagon."

CHAPTER THREE

Charlie Mazzarelli thought he should have been named captain of the cross-country team. It was his senior year. He was the fastest on his team. He had lettered every year. He was counting on it, had told a girl at Holy Name he was captain.

Brother Paul, the track coach, named the McCarthy kid captain. Charlie was not going to ask why and give Brother Paul the satisfaction of telling him.

"He's an outstanding brown nose is why," Charlie told his father.

His father adjusted the newspaper with a snap. "Charlie, when are you going to stop talking out of both sides of your mouth. Life is not nearly as unfair as you think. You screwed up and you're lying to me. Or you're dumb as your grades suggest. First thing you do, find out why. Then fix it."

The Carmelite priests and brothers of Chicago are not indirect or secretive. Brother Paul told Charlie why he was not captain. "You want to smoke? Fine. You just can't do it at school and you can't be captain of the cross-country team as long as you're doing it. The captain has to train, abide by the rules, and lead by example. All require discipline. You have talent, Charlie, but no discipline. I don't know what your parents do at home, but we're not going to kiss your ass here at Mount Carmel. Not smart to cross me. I'm holding all the cards."

Late the next morning Charlie was on the cross-country course and he was flying. He was going to win easily. His points would assure Mount Carmel High School won its opening cross-country meet.

Thirty yards from the finish line he stopped. He did not slow down. He just stopped, and walked to the side of the course where his pals had gathered. They did their homemade South Side cheer, Charlie doing the counting.

"One—two—three." A silent beat. "Shiiiit!"

He took a cigarette from them, took a drag, and jogged toward the finish line. Two runners from St. George passed him.

Brother Paul walked up to Charlie. "Here's a piece of information you're going to need in order to understand why this is your last day at Mount Carmel. There's a world of difference, Charlie, between scratching your ass and tearing it all to pieces."

When his father learned that Charlie had been thrown out of the private Catholic school he yelled for twenty minutes, mostly about wasted tuition, gave him five minutes to pack his things, and threw Charlie and his small bag onto the lawn. Then he kicked him in the butt and pushed him down again. Charlie rolled to avoid another kick, jumped up and ran. His mother cried while she prepared dinner for her husband that evening.

Charlie began hitchhiking the next morning. Like most of his relatives he was a hothead. He had talked himself into a rage. He tried to hide it and look cool, so drivers would stop. Faking cool turned his self-orchestrated rage into depression, which was painful. He went back to rage. By noon he had punched the only two drivers that had picked him up. One because he made a homosexual pass. The other because he made disparaging remarks about Joe DiMaggio. Both were serious offenses in Charlie's world.

He did not know how to think about the first offense. So he did not. *That's just the way it is in Chi Town, asshole.*

But DiMaggio. Charlie knew everything there was to know about DiMaggio. There was not much in Charlie's small bag, but five minutes had been enough to scoop up his DiMaggio stuff. An autographed baseball. A copy of a magazine article about the great man's hitting streak signed by the Yankee Clipper himself. A pin-striped flannel baseball shirt with the number 5 on the back. DiMaggio baseball cards. A signed Yankee team photograph saying, at Charlie's request, "For The Dago—With Respect, Joe DiMaggio". Charlie had read that DiMaggio's teammates called their center fielder The Dago, and did it with respect. Charlie had insisted that his baseball buddies call him The Dago. They did not know why. They thought Charlie was just being goofy and obliged. It was as good as wop or guinea.

The driver had made some jokes about Italian women, had slapped his forehead and used a foreign accent, said "goomba." None of it bothered Charlie until the guy started in on DiMaggio. The driver offered a few slurs—calzone, meatball—referred to DiMaggio as "Giuseppe" and argued the superiority of Hank Greenberg.

"Pull over and let me out."

The driver looked across at Charlie. "Sure. Nothing here but cornfields. Know what you're doing?"

Charlie reached over and got his bag from the back seat, leaned across the front seat toward the driver as if to say something and threw a straight right, pivoting on his butt, pushing off his right foot. He connected solidly with the chin of the unsuspecting Greenberg fan. He got out of the car.

Coldcocked him. He bounced on his toes, hands up. He felt really good. He looked into the front of the car. The driver was slumped over the steering wheel. *Aw shit.*

Charlie started thinking about his options. They included run, wait, and worry. He waited, peeked in. He waited until his hand began to hurt and depression returned. It took a few seconds beyond that for the driver of the car to recover enough to look around, see his attacker, lock the car door, and drive off. The driver was thinking *mental patient.*

Charlie thought about the DiMaggio stuff in his bag. *Hank Greenberg! Give me a break.*

Charlie was a good looking guy, black hair meticulously cut and combed into a "ducktail"—a DA in the schoolyard, large aquiline nose broken a couple of times in the schoolyard, lean and athletic. He sought the look of the South Side hood, dark and threatening, because it seemed to attract girls, even Holy Name girls. It was not working.

Charlie entered Idaho nodding in the narcotic of sexual fantasy. The fantasy involved a girl from Holy Name who thought he was captain of the Mount Carmel cross-country team. In spite of the disconnect between his fantasy and current circumstances, which included riding in an empty potato truck, Charlie moved toward Boise with an increasing optimism about his life and a growing store of information, facts available only on the road, ride after ride.

Seeking work, he was directed to the nearest Forest Service office in Boise. The government agency was in fact hiring brush crews for the summer to clean up behind Brown Tie and Lumber Company loggers cutting trees on the Payette National Forest.

Charlie hired on the Camp Creek brush crew. The job involved the use of axes, a competence foreign to most of Chicago. The foreman of the crew tried hard. He lectured and demonstrated. "Charlie, keep the log you're limbing between you and your axe. And cut forward where your feet are so you won't be swinging into yourself." He watched Charlie as much as he could. What he saw at the end of the first day gave him no comfort.

Charlie stood on the truck bed, ready for the ride back to Camp Creek and supper. The foreman looked down at Charlie's boots. They were new and unremarkable, except that the toes were cross-hatched with axe cuts, some completely through the leather.

The foreman shook his head. He had a clear picture of the coming accident. It arrived at the end of the second week of work.

Charlie sat on a bunkhouse bed looking at his bloody foot. He was pale and staring. His foot rested on top of a wooden stool, in a gel of blood. There was a wedge shaped hole in the instep.

A timber cruiser marking trees to be cut came in from work, saw the blood, and asked "What happened?"

A member of the brush crew explained while he bandaged Charlie's foot. "Charlie gets bored easy. He stopped payin' attention to what he was doin'. God knows the axe was sharp enough. Every time we got to a work site Charlie would jump off the truck and start filin' on his axe. He sharpened it more than he used it. He figured the foreman wouldn't complain if he showed respect for his equipment and spent all mornin' keepin' his axe sharp." He pumped his fist up and down in front of his crotch.

Charlie did not respond.

His caretaker finished putting a pressure bandage on Charlie's foot. "Super clean cut. It will heal so fast Charlie won't be in McCall long enough to get laid. But he couldn't get laid if he had all summer." He carried Charlie to a truck as he talked about him.

Charlie began to take offense at the account of the accident and the notion he could not get laid, but kept quiet. The tires of the pickup truck kicked gravel into the raised wheel wells as the boys hurried onto Lick Creek Road for their ride to the McCall hospital, and a beer if they hurried.

Ranger Bill Dobbindick was watching the departing truck, talking to his brush crew foreman. They were talking about the injured man being driven to McCall.

Dobbindick was animated. “Sonofabitch. He’s worked two weeks and laid himself up for the rest of the summer. Run my medicals up and my safety record down to hell before we even get started. I’ll spend the evening filling out reports on him. Last hitchhiking Chicago dago I hire. Ever. I swear to God. And the nerve of the little sonofabitch, making jokes about my name, even where he knew I could hear.”

“He’s just a kid. A little lazy, a little bit of a con man. My fault for hiring him, really. I’ll fill out the report forms on the accident. He’ll probably be back to work soon. I’ll watch him.” The foreman walked away. *Hell, the Forest Supervisor calls you “Horsecock.”*

M.I.A.

The interrogation went well, he thought, right up until they clipped the wires to his testicles and pulled the starter cord on the little generator. After that the POW told them everything he knew. They seemed to know most of it anyway.

The interrogator was Vietnamese and wore an army uniform without insignia. When the POW was cooperative the man was warm and talked about himself. His name was Vinh. He was from Hanoi. He had a brother named Minh. That was because, he said, his "mother thought it was easier that way." He did not beat or threaten to beat the POW. After the first time with the generator, whenever the prisoner resisted the interrogator smiled and directed the guards to pour water on the ground until there was a puddle. He stood the dirty, barefoot prisoner in the puddle next to the little machine. That was enough.

"Tell me about being a CIA case officer," Vinh said.

"I'm not a CIA case officer."

"Did I say you were? What agency of the United States government do you work for?"

"Aerial Delivery Service Research and Development."

"The titles of bureaucracies are so opaque. Help me. That is an office within CIA Air Branch isn't it?"

"Yes."

"So, tell me about being a CIA case officer," Vinh said.

The POW thought a minute and said. "From what I could see the whole thing about being a case officer is you have to be able to talk people into doing things. That's what they do. They don't know squat about aerial delivery."

The Vietnamese lit a cigarette and smoked it for a few minutes in silence. When he spoke again he said "I will accept that. But break it down for me. Does talking people into doing things include training them for guerilla warfare and parachute jumping?"

The prisoner thought about it and said "Yes."

"Are some of the CIA training camps where that is done in Laos?"

"Yes."

"Are some of those camps in Thailand?"

"Yes."

"Have you personally taught parachute jumping in Laos and Thailand for the CIA?"

"Yes."

"Where in Laos?"

"Place called Savannakhet."

"How about at Long Tieng."

"Yeh, Long Tieng."

"Try not to leave anything out."

"OK."

"Where in Thailand?"

"Hua Hin by the king's summer palace was the first. That was south, on the gulf. Then there was Takhli. The last one I know is Phitsanoulok, north of Bangkok. It's new."

"Who did you train in those places? The Meo of course?"

"Yeh, the Meo."

"And?"

"Some Lao Theung. And the Thai, most of them PARU."

"How much are you paid for doing these things?"

"I'm a GS-13."

The interrogator thought. "About an army major's pay?"

The POW thought. "I guess. Don't really know that."

"You did it just because you enjoy war? Don't care what you get paid?"

The question made the POW think again. It took a long silence to form an answer. "I enjoy what I do and I had buddies here."

"Who is the chief of the CIA Far East Division?"

"Desmond FitzGerald, I think. Least he was."

"Does he know what you do in Laos?"

"I imagine so."

"Does he know you are a prisoner of war?"

"I haven't had any mail from him sayin' so. Haven't had any mail at all, come to think of it."

"We will hold your mail until the end of the war. If you get any." The interrogator paused and continued. "You do understand that the United States is waging war in Laos."

"We are helping the people of Laos fight a war against communism."

"You understand the rules of warfare and the treatment of prisoners."

"I been instructed on that."

"One more question and we will end today's meeting. Where are the prison camps located in which Pathet Lao and Vietnamese prisoners of war are held?"

"I don't know that." The question bothered the POW.

"Do you know what happens to those prisoners?"

The POW knew, and he decided it would take a whole lot more of the little generator before he would talk about it. There were no prison camps for captured Pathet Lao or Vietnamese. *Not goin' there.*

CHAPTER FOUR

They left the McEvoy ranch in late May, Thanasis and an older man, trailing two thousand sheep. The older man was Julio Goitiandia, a Basque sheepherder. Black and white herd dogs moved the sheep quietly. Two horses, one black and one brown, pulled a wagon with wood-spoke wheels and a canvas top. The iron at the wheel rims ground against the gravel of the road, resonating sound through the wood and metal.

They were trailing sheep to the summer grazing allotment on Forest Service land, a hundred miles away in the mountains of central Idaho. After two weeks of walking they passed the last village before the mountains and brought the band of sheep over Gladiator pass into the Sawtooth Valley.

As Thanasis walked along a ridge through stands of fir trees and aspen he realized that he missed Ilias, that he might never see him again. He felt alone as he touched the worry beads. The feeling haunted his night and he longed for morning.

The morning sun relieved the solitariness of night and lit the peaks of the valley's western ridges. Well before any sunlight reached the valley floor Thanasis and Julio stood looking into their morning campfire. Julio began instructing him, as he did each morning, on preparation of breakfast, the coffeeola.

"Remember, you wait until the coffee is boiling fast. Then you put the eggs in the coffee pot, two for each of us. After you pour in a quart of milk you break up the bread and put it in the coffee pot. Don't forget the dog."

"I know. I know," Thanasis said impatiently. Then he grinned. "I always forget to put your dog in the coffee pot."

Julio grinned in turn at the picture of his favorite herd dog added to the coffeeola. The sheepherder's dog got the first piece of each loaf of bread Julio made, a piece with the sign of the cross baked into its crust. After two weeks on the sheep trail Julio knew it was not necessary to remind Thanasis about the piece of bread, but the dog came first. So he reminded Thanasis and together they suffered the morning recitation.

Julio called the dog Joe Stalin. "Because he is the boss of the sheep and has a black mustache. He gets the bread with the holy cross so maybe he will convert and be a good Catholic. We pray to our Lady of Fatima for Joe Stalin."

Moving the sheep through the valley, Thanasis walked at a steady pace, the sheep more slowly. The presence of the sheep, hard to see in the tall sagebrush, was marked by dust and the flat sound of sheep bells. He whistled the herd dogs to their feet. One-eyed or otherwise scarred by teeth of the larger Pyrenees guard dogs, always over stolen scraps of food, the black and white herd dogs were homely, dull-looking, listless in the sun. At Thanasis' whistles, the homeliest became handsome, the most laggard quick as they ran over and around the sheep. The band of sheep gathered and moved forward behind bellwethers.

Thanasis dropped back toward the last camp. He found Julio preparing to move the wagon.

"There is no grass for the next miles. Just sagebrush. I am moving them faster. Is it better at the creek we are going to?"

"We are going to fix this problem," Julio said, pointing at a thousand acres of sagebrush running off toward the north.

"Say it again."

"Mister McEvoy knows this problem. He said we are supposed to fix it."

"How are we supposed to fix two miles of sagebrush?"

"Mister McEvoy told me to burn it. Then in the spring the little grass grows. The lambs stay fat. You do not have to run the sheep so fast next time."

"What if the ranger sees us. Or the cowboys. The Forest Service might take the sheep."

"I will show you how they don't see us." Julio took charge, not explaining. "We do not tell them. You say 'yes' to me now. Or you go back to the ranch and tell Mister McEvoy why you are leaving."

Thanasis looked closely at Julio. He saw certainty and resolve in the sun-browned face. He felt neither of those things. He thought there were questions to ask but he did not know what they were. He chose quickly.

"When do we do it?"

"At the end of the summer, just before we leave the valley," Julio said as he completed hitching the horses to the wagon. "Now we go up Champion Creek to the lakes in the White Cloud Peaks. Do you have a fishing license?"

Thanasis laughed at what he understood was a sheepherder joke. He laughed with relief at putting off arson and settling again into the certainties of herding sheep.

The summer took on the measured pace of unremarkable, recurring events. The lambs went out. The rams came in. Grazing in the summer ranges came to an end.

It was time to burn two miles of sagebrush before trailing the sheep to the McEvoy ranch.

They worked through the night, coaxing flame out of a campfire at the edge of the woods near Champion Creek, spotting fire into the sagebrush as if done by pine cones rolling down the slope. By the time the sun rose, smoke lay in the valley bottom. Their evidence of the source of the fire in place, the sheepherders rested. The fire grew hotter in the morning sun and smoke lifted above the nearby woods. They went back to work digging fire line in a mime of firefighters, waiting for the morning wind to come up and burn out two miles of sagebrush.

Thanasis was bent over his shovel at the edge of the smoking fire when he heard the drone of airplane engines. He looked up and saw a three-engine airplane approaching. It came toward the fire slowly, deliberately. When it had finally crossed the valley it circled the fire. Thanasis thought he saw someone waving at them from an open door in the side of the airplane. He hesitated, waved back. The figure in the doorway threw out a small parachute. It drifted slightly south as the airplane circled again. The morning wind had not yet come.

Watching, Thanasis realized that the airplane was bringing firefighters in parachutes. He saw two figures fall out of the doorway on the side of the airplane, one after the other. He held his breath. He heard the airplane engines backfire and become silent. Two parachutes opened into rounds of white silk, making a slapping sound as they did. Power and sound returned to the engines of the plane. He breathed.

Voices came from the men in the parachutes, shouts to each other. They sounded like they were on holiday. The parachutes swung and turned above Thanasis. The descent of the chutes lasted only a minute or two before the two men hit the ground, one after the other, and rolled, sending dry summer dust into the air. The sound of the landing was violent, the hollow thump of a street fight, surprising after the quiet of the parachutes in the sky.

The two men who had parachuted from the airplane stood in the sagebrush taking off leather helmets, disconnecting harness from the parachutes. They removed brown canvas jumpsuits and laid orange streamers on the ground.

The airplane had circled and was passing over them again. Once more the engines backfired. Two more men fell from the doorway. In seconds their parachutes opened. Thanasis watched the men suspended in the air above the fire. His chest filled and he held his breath again. He grinned, hands shoved deep in his pockets. He exhaled and shouted like the men he was watching.

As he watched, he felt the first push of the up-valley wind. It snapped across his face. Then it rushed at the face of the fire. It did not hesitate or gather itself. It forced oxygen into the heat and the fire exploded.

Thanasis fell out of his love song, stopped shouting. His face reflected the heat, the orange flame. The spotter in the airplane quietly said "oh shit" as he watched the second stick of smokejumpers sweep by the jump spot, caught in the wind, carrying far south of the fire.

In minutes the fire destroyed two miles of sagebrush. Then it stopped, out of fuel at the broad fire line dug by Thanasis and Julio.

One of the jumpers walked up to them, extended his hand. "Ray Mansisador, McCall smokejumpers," he said. He shook their hands, pumping with a big grin and farmer muscles. "You guys did a hell of a job. Smart. Professional. You stopped it with your fire line. If you hadn't done that the sonofabitch would have run to the other end of the valley. And then it would have come back down the other side this afternoon. It was like you planned the whole thing. We'll help you mop up and look for spot fires. But we're out of here today. It's done."

Julio and the smokejumper scouted the smoldering perimeter of the dying fire together, gossiping in the native Basque of their families. They agreed on the cause of the fire, a careless camper. Julio was generous, crediting Thanasis with the fire fighting strategy.

Thanasis talked to the smokejumpers, obvious in his questions. "How do I get in the smokejumpers?"

"Best thing you could do for yourself is get another Forest Service job. Work your ass off for some district ranger, a guy will put your name up for the jumpers. Get yourself some more fire experience with a Forest Service summer job."

Thanasis thanked him and asked what kind of Forest Service job would get him fire experience.

"There's lots of things. Trail crew, fire lookout, guard station, brush crew. Get your sheepman boss to put in a word for you. You can bet he has friends in the Forest Service. You make your move, you tell me. I'll remember your name. Thanasis the firefighter." The big farmer grin had not stopped all day.

Julio and Thanasis spent another night at the burn making sure there was nothing left of their fire to flare up. Thanasis imagined himself a smokejumper in an airplane, guarding the forest.

CHAPTER FIVE

At first Charles Stewart Parnell Touhey's mother had worried about her small son. He was healthy, smart, and happy, both at home and school, but he seemed to bruise easily. Watching him at roughhouse play, however, it became clear that he did not bruise easily at all. Just a lot. The problem turned out to be a matter of deportment.

When Mrs. Touhey discussed the failing grade in "Deportment" with her son's teachers she learned that the recurring injuries were the result of fighting. Asked what could be done the teachers advised "He's small and has a sharp tongue. He needs to shut up and walk away when bigger boys tease him." Mrs. Touhey knew that was not going to work.

"What do they tease him about?"

"The usual stuff. His name, for example. He uses his full name, Charles Stewart Parnell Touhey. The worse the teasing, the more he insists on his full name. They say it's twice as big as he is. He says 'go shit in your hat'."

She took the matter up with her husband. "Can't you teach him how to defend himself or something."

"I've already bought him boxing gloves and taught him how to box. His problem is a complete inability to judge what weight class he's in. Picking him up at school I've seen him jump up in the air to hit another boy. That's how much bigger the other kid was. I don't know, honey, don't worry about this. It will stop when he is elected President of the United States. Secret Service will be all over it."

Thanks. No wonder people punch your son. "Thanks. Maybe I'll work on the name thing."

She had chosen her son's name, not out of regard for Charles Stewart Parnell the "un-crowned King of Ireland," but because she idolized Clark Gable. Gable had played the part of Parnell in a movie about the notable man.

After visiting with teachers and husband to no avail, she tried encouraging her son to not use his full name. She began calling him Chuck. He ignored the name. She tried another approach. She asked if his friends had nicknames and did he have one. It turned out he did.

"The kids at school used to call me Doggie because I'm little. Like 'Here, little doggie.' But I made 'em stop. Now they call me Dog."

"How did you do that?"

"I bit a kid on the leg when he hit me with a stick he was tryin' to make me fetch."

She hated the nickname Dog, but the cuts, scrapes, and bruises declined. Not only was the name cool among his friends, it signified a change in tactics that reduced the number of schoolmates interested in fighting the freckle-faced boy.

The next and last time anyone in school heard the name Charles Stewart Parnell was years later in high school when Dog read his report on *Finnegan's Wake* to the class and discussed the significance of the fact that the main character in the book was based on Parnell.

His performance in school was a source of pride and relief to his parents. Good grades came without effort. A college scholarship, important for a family living on a Forest Service salary, seemed likely. His academic prospects and constant reading did not keep his mother from yelling at him to turn out the lights at two a.m. Casting about for a rationale she came up only with the specter of Aunt Ellen, a reader of tarot cards, Nostradamus, and Karl Marx. "Stop reading or you'll turn out just like her." Other events assured that he did not.

As graduation approached, he took a plan for summer employment to his father. He had read, in a book discussing antique scientific instruments, about the alidade, an instrument the Forest Service had adapted for use in fire lookouts to establish the directional bearing of wilderness fires, locating them for firefighters. Working on a fire lookout captured his interest. It had everything. He would run his own life in his own forest cabin—a high altitude Walden. He would locate fires with the alidade and alert fire crews—science in the service of adventure.

He would experience the challenge and risk of fighting fires by himself when there were no crews available. He would be alone with his books through long days and nights. He would get a cold beer now and again if he was clever about it all.

His father was enthusiastic, though he did not know the entire plan. "You mean the Osborne Fire Finder. William Bushnell Osborne, Jr., inventor. I knew Bush, not well, but we would run into each other. Longtime Forest Service man over in Oregon. What do you want me to do?"

There were nearly a thousand Forest Service fire lookouts in Idaho available for summer work. With his father's intercession, Dog was hired to man one of them in the Idaho Primitive Area. In early June he and his parents drove the first leg of the trip to his new job in a holiday mood. Still celebratory, his parents dropped him off at the Krassel Ranger District on the South Fork of the Salmon River. He was to stay at the Camp Creek barracks a day or two until a packer showed up with mules to take him and his belongings to Skunk Camp lookout on top of an unnamed nine thousand-foot mountain. He waved goodbye to his parents and stepped into the barracks.

His entry was almost blocked by a small circle of young men near one of the bunks. A familiar feeling washed over him. *Wrong place, wrong time.*

One of the group, looking surprised and fearful, lay back across the bunk, one arm in the air as if to deflect a blow. The anticipated blow was about to be delivered with a piece of firewood held like a baseball bat by a red-faced man, coiled and shaking with rage next to the bunk. The watching group was silent, looked concerned.

Dog stepped through the circle and stood between the two men, an arm outstretched toward each of them like a referee about to announce a ruling. "Look at me!" He was speaking to the man holding the firewood club. He said it again, and the man looked up. Disappointed and furious at feeling the rage leave him, the red-faced man threw the club to the floor and pushed his way out of the circle around him. The circle fell away to other bunks, parts of it staying to welcome the new man to Camp Creek.

"Way to go, man. Singlejack is flat mean. He would have killed Bill."

Dog was puzzled. "Looked like it. Why wasn't anybody stopping it?"

"Like I said, he's flat mean."

"What was it about?"

"Bill teased him about the Civil War. Said burnin' Atlanta would be easier now that we all had cigarette lighters. That was all it took. Singlejack is from Georgia."

Dog began looking forward to a summer alone.

The packer arrived as planned and drove Dog and the mules in a truck for half a day, beyond the small town of Yellow Pine, until the rough dirt road became stock chutes and a turn-around. The final five miles to Skunk Camp lookout was roadless, the Forest Service-declared nature of all of central Idaho, and the mules earned their keep on the steep trail. The packer marveled at how much books weighed and at how many Dog carried with him.

Like most other fire lookouts in Idaho, Dog's summer home was a fourteen-by-fourteen one-room whitewashed wooden structure with a catwalk on all sides. There was a knee-high lodgepole rail around the catwalk. Its four walls were window glass from waist to ceiling and corner to corner, the large area of glass framed into small panes by slim wood muntins. Green wooden shutters could be propped up as awnings. The building design was designated the L-4, and that became Dog's name for his new home.

"Damn near charming," he said to the packer.

As soon as the packer and mules left, rather than attend to the housekeeping chores of moving in, Dog went immediately to the Osborne Fire Finder. It sat on a chest-high stand in the middle of the room. Inspecting, he saw that the system included a topographic map of the mountain wilderness that lay before him outside the windows. The map was oriented to true north, centered and mounted permanently on the horizontal top of the stand. It was surrounded by a metal ring laid flat on and bolted to the stand. The ring was marked with degrees and minutes of arc and calibrated to the map. Two vertical sighting apertures, slits in metal vanes, were mounted opposite each other on a movable metal ring which sat on the same plane as and just above the map, within the arc of the ring fixed to the top of the stand.

He reached out and touched the sighting slits. They moved, rotating around the arc of the fixed metal ring. Dog looked through the sighting slit nearest him and lined it up with the far sight. He lined them both up with an imagined fire on a peak miles away. He noted the degrees and minutes of arc on the metal ring to which the alignment of sights pointed.

"Azimuth. Now put the food away before the rats get it."

He was amazed at how much time housekeeping chores took. Splitting firewood, carrying water, tending the fire, cleaning, cooking. "I will remember your birthday, Mom."

He was equally amazed at how little time his official duties took. It was a nine-to-five job with little in between beginning and end. He reported the weather each morning to McCall Dispatch Headquarters. He reported any smokes. He answered the hand-cranked telephone when it rang. He relayed messages to other lookouts or to McCall. He scanned the surrounding mountains every half hour for fire. No job required more than minutes.

Nothing took his time except reading, hiking, fishing, thinking, and practicing rolling cigarettes with one hand.

He had wondered before he came to Skunk Camp how he would do at being alone. Could he bear it? After a month he thought he had it figured out. "Being alone is painful only if you have things you regret. Regrets take over when you are alone for long periods." Did he regret? "Not so you would notice. Nope." He knew for sure he was OK with being alone when he felt dismay at the approach of his first visitors, wilderness hikers looking for company.

He became aware of new habits he had acquired because of being alone. He talked out loud to himself and he bathed infrequently. "I'll have to change back at the end of the summer," he said aloud.

Two developments about himself that summer surprised him. He was never able to fully analyze them. The first was the longing for fire. Maybe he just wanted a little excitement, he thought. *I'm a man of action.* Or maybe he just wanted to feel needed, his job essential. He was there on the mountaintop to stop fire, but how could he do that if there was no fire. *We all want to feel worthwhile, needed.* In the end, he thought it was something deeper, darker. *An appetite for flame and destruction*? Dog left it there.

The other development that puzzled him was his pleasure at the lightning that struck "Little L-4." He had always been afraid of lightning, avoided being out in it. Now lightning was pure joy as he sat inside the lookout and watched. He liked the warnings lightning gave as it approached, the sizzling in the guy wires and telephone line just before it hit, all four corners of the building turning blue. A more personal warning was when his hair stood straight up. Without a haircut it was standing higher and higher with each new storm. He checked the behavior of his hair in a hand held mirror.

Best of all was the loud crack and the shaking of the building and everything in it and blue light running everywhere in the room when lightning struck the lookout.

He did not feel weird about the pleasure he took in lightning. After all the Forest Service and his father had assured him that the building was grounded with a copper wire, all the way down to bedrock. It was safe. But why had they told him he should sit in his high swivel chair during lightning storms because it had glass insulators on the bottom of its legs or get into bed because it was similarly fitted with insulated casters? *And can't a hundred million volts of electricity melt copper wire? I'll need some more science courses if I'm going to med school.*

Late in what he realized was a slow fire season, storms of dry lightning rushed through the Primitive Area for an entire week. Black and flat at the bottom, without rain, the twenty-thousand-foot cumulonimbus clouds set fires throughout the region. His own unnamed mountain exploded in small fires. In between making calls for smokejumpers, slurry tankers, and ground crews for the numerous fires he was spotting, he went out with shovel, Pulaski, and daypack to build fire line on his mountain to save Little L-4.

Near the end of the week of storms he put in a call for smokejumpers to handle a fire that he had planned to hike to and take care of. It was growing too fast and he was too busy in the lookout to build fire line. McCall Dispatch ordered jumpers for first light the next day.

Dog was up at dawn and watched four two-man sticks of jumpers exit a Ford Trimotor flying below him and descend into the forest near the base of his mountain. By the time he watched the last parachute disappear behind a small ridge in slow dream-like fall, he had decided on next summer's job. A few days later an August snow storm ended the year's fire season and Dog left L-4 for good. He left knowing he loved silk canopy as much as lightning, and for much the same reason.

M.I.A.

The POW woke in the bamboo cage. For the first time in months, as soon as he opened his eyes, he felt like going on. No fever. No swelling or pain in his feet. No diarrhea. He had not fully tested the last notion but that is how things felt as he lay waiting for the guards. They would release the rope around his throat that kept him in one position through the night. The rope pressed against his airway just enough to suggest the terror of suffocation. This morning he avoided the image of his constricted windpipe by recalling buddies. He thought he would introduce some of them to Chet Huntley and David Brinkley. *Hell, why have famous friends if you can't introduce your buddies to 'em.* He was scrupulous about details he gave his interviewers, today Chet and David.

> Good morning, fellas. Today I would like to introduce you to a couple of guys.
>
> One is Thanasis Mavros. He is my best friend, though I don't think he liked me much at first. Well, likewise for me. In the smokejumpers we called him Black Man. As we all know, there is a dark side to him. There is that.
>
> When he first came into Camp Creek to work on the brush crew I wasn't there. They tell me everything he was wearin' was brand new, right down to his underwear. Man could hardly move. And it was all blue—blue shirt, blue jeans, blue socks—'cause that's how he

thought a woodsman would dress. It was a guess. Had never seen one, you see. He thought he had to prove he was a woodsman in order to get into the smokejumpers and that is the only thing he wanted.

Now Thanasis is kind of a direct, stubborn boy. For example, you would think that when our foreman entertained us at lunch break with stories about all the sex he got in Hollywood during the war you would just shut up and listen. Not Thanasis. He wants evidence. He asks "Ed, do you get this stuff out of movie magazines?" He's respectful when he asks. Nobody wanted the lunch break stories to end. It wasn't so much a challenge of Ed's material as it was a request for validation, so he could say later over a beer "No, it's a true story."

Ed brought a lot of Hollywood celebrities to the Salmon River mountains that summer, to the logged over area between Cougar Creek and Buckhorn Creek.

Thanasis stopped asking questions and *I never* questioned Ed.

The other guy you would have liked to know, particularly if you needed someone to cover your back in a situation, is Dog Touhey. Picture a prematurely balding third-grader with freckles. He had to eat five pounds of bananas right before weigh-in so he could meet the 125-pound minimum for smokejumpers. Not very impressive, you say. Well, listen up.

Dog had two ambitions. One was to be seen as toughest man in the room. The other was to actually be the smartest man in the room.

He may not have won any fights, but he never walked away from one. The guy who won the fight seldom enjoyed it and Dog didn't have to cover the same territory twice. He was a biter and most guys don't care for somebody bitin' 'em on the leg while they're tryin' to stomp them.

As for smart, well, smokejumper IQ has never been measured, but solvin' all of life's problems alone in the wilderness with nothing but a lady shovel, a Pulaski, and a roll of toilet paper is nothin' short of genius.

What's that? See, you don't even know what they are. I'll tell you what they are. Lady shovel is a short-handled shovel with a small blade, about two and one-half inches narrower than a True Temper No. 2 shovel. Pulaski is a single-bit axe with an adze on the back of the axe blade.

Jumping out of an airplane to fight a fire on a wilderness mountainside takes a high level of intelligence and lots of optimism. Dog had all that. His plan was medical school and then run for political office so he could shape public health policy. Ambitious little fucker.

He could be charming. This whole prisoner deal would go a lot better with Dog here. Any jumper bein' here would help.

The fact there isn't any other smokejumper prisoners is the final argument in support of elevated smokejumper intelligence. How many smokejumpers have they captured? One. Big fuckin' deal. We're too smart, and Dog was the smartest. I bet you a night in Hong Kong I escape this illegally operated establishment within a week. Dog would have been out of here a year ago.

The prisoner was untied by the guards, told to come with them to empty his waste bucket. He was wrong, it turned out, about the diarrhea, and the fever had returned. Being wrong was a large part of life in Tha Pa Chon Village Prison. The POW had escaped it for part of a day.

CHAPTER SIX

It was late afternoon when Thanasis stepped into the Camp Creek barracks. Young men were opening mail in the thin privacy of their bunks. Thanasis introduced himself to the nearest occupant of a bunk.

"You're in the deep dark woods, Mr. Mavros. My name is Big Gravy. They caught me by settin' out food to lure me in. What you doin' here? What you gonna do to *get out*?"

Thanasis held silliness and cutting up in high regard. Mostly because he was not good at it and would have given a lot to be. He was about to show he appreciated the quality of the greeting, but remembered he was a new government hire and decided to be literal, serious.

"I hired on a Forest Service brush crew. I'm trying to find the Krassel District Ranger and report in."

With pointing and a few words of direction from Big Gravy, Thanasis found the District Ranger "down there." The Ranger was talking to another man in an outbuilding filled with fire packs, shovels, saws, and Pulaskis. Thanasis almost reached out to touch the clean, sharp equipment, an explorer arrived in the new-found land of fire fighting.

The Ranger made a brief speech of welcome. It sounded like government-sponsored promotion of clean forests and self-realization. The speech ended with "Your job is vital to the Forest Service mission. Ed Moyles here is your foreman. He will line you out."

Thanasis worked hard for Ed Moyles that summer. If he impressed his foreman, he thought, he would get picked for chasing fires. He would get the experience that the smokejumpers wanted to see in job applicants.

The fires would come, Ed assured him. The forest was drying. Summer heat was cracking open dead trees and logs, drying the stiff underbrush into tinder. Moisture was leaving ground, grass, and trees by the hour. The smell of resin filled every forest space. Fuel was being made.

Fires came to the South Fork of the Salmon in early August. Ed Moyles called Thanasis and Charlie down to the barn filled with fire packs. Charlie was recovered and back on the brush crew. The two "brush apes" had worked together for about a month piling logging slash. They were different enough from each other that they were still trying to figure each other out. They shared their excitement, however, over the possibility of a first fire.

"That's the only reason he would call us down here," Charlie said as they walked toward the barn.

"Unless he just wanted to chew our ass in private," Thanasis said.

"He wouldn't dare."

"What you mean wouldn't dare? He's the boss."

"Thanasis, buddy, let me tell you about leverage. We saw him shoot the bear . . . when he was drunk. Then he sent the whole camp bear hunting for a wounded bear, without a single gun between us."

"And we found the damn bear."

They started to giggle at the memory. "The bear ran to beat hell." Charlie was nearly shouting.

"But not as fast as you, Charlie."

"If the bear is chasin' us I only have to outrun you, Thanasis. Easy."

"Got me there. Wanna try rasslin'? Hold it, there's Ed."

Their foreman was all business. "We have a lightning strike on the Secesh," Ed told them. "The lookout says the smoke is small. We'll drive in as far as we can on the logging road, then walk. I've got the fire tools in the truck. Let's go."

Ed stopped the truck at the end of the abandoned logging road. Standing at the back of the truck collecting fire tools, Thanasis could smell the smoke. Charlie lifted his nose and sniffed the air.

"I can smell overtime on this one, Mr. Mavros," Charlie whispered. They both grinned.

The fire was burning in grass and brush, spreading out from remains of a snag blasted by lightning during the night.

The foreman watched as Thanasis and Charlie scratched a line around the fire with Pulaskis and lady shovels, cooled the broken stump of the snag with dirt, then chopped and grubbed the smoking roots out of the ground. In three hours they were soaked with sweat and filthy. Their first fire was contained, nearly out.

"I'm going back to Camp Creek for the night," Ed said. "You need to stay on the fire overnight, cold track it, make sure there's no heat left in it. I'll pick you up tomorrow morning where we walked in from. There's a spring in the next draw over."

Lying out overnight next to the burn sounded fine to Thanasis and Charlie, even though they were without sleeping bags. Cold tracking their fire was not as appealing. They began immediately, to get it over with. They felt through the acre of ash with their bare hands, searching for heat. When they found it, they dug it out and cooled it with the little dirt they could find. After two more hours they appeared to be lost and dying members of a strange mountain tribe, black skin streaked with pink lines edged with white, drying salt. Without a word they turned away from the burn and walked to the spring Ed Moyles had found.

The clear night without sleeping bags left them cold and sleepless. "Thanasis, you're not my best friend, but if you move any closer you will be." Thanasis did not think anything was funny anymore. He laughed anyway, threw an elbow at Charlie, and shivered.

They were glad to return to Camp Creek even though it meant returning as well to cutting and piling brush.

A succession of small fires interrupted the dull job of cleaning up logging slash. Late in August, Thanasis and Charlie were flown, along with other firefighters, from a grass and sagebrush mountain airstrip near Camp Creek across Idaho. They flew in a three-engine plane made of corrugated sheet metal. It was Thanasis' first ride in an airplane. He wondered if it was the same one he had seen the smokejumpers parachute from. He told himself it was.

When they landed, the firefighters were trucked to an open mountain ridge. Across a steep canyon was a forest fire, exploding in the shape of a mushroom cloud. As they removed their gear from the truck the cloud of smoke and gas and embers rose ten thousand feet above the creek flowing in the canyon below, a place called Bull Creek.

Thanasis and Charlie watched the fire. It was hundreds of times bigger than the fires they had worked on. It was roaring and rumbling.

"Sounds like a cash register, if you know what I mean," Charlie said.

"I think you're right. Bet the only thing that's gonna work with this is diggin' fire line at night. Remember Ed telling us we would be doin' a lot of our fire fighting at night? We'll be rich by the time you go back to college."

"I don't go to college, buddy. So I'll be really rich. First fifty cents I'm gonna buy us beers for findin' this gold mine."

Thanasis was surprised at the news that Charlie did not go to college. He still assumed everybody in America except the sheepherders did. The disclosure made him feel a little closer to the guy that kept calling him buddy.

Before they left Camp Creek for their flight across Idaho, Ed Moyles had taken them aside. "Been one man killed on this fire already. It's a dangerous one. Lot of wind, just coming up out of nowhere. Be careful."

That a man had been killed on the fire surprised Thanasis. Dying while he dug fire line had never entered his thoughts.

"What happened, Ed?" He wanted to know what he and Charlie should look out for.

"An Indian by the name of Dan Big Bull got killed yesterday. He was on one of the Indian hotshot crews out of Montana. They're experienced firefighters. They don't die easy. It just tells you this is a dangerous business. What I heard is he was working on a roll trench at the bottom of the fire. It is steep country up on the Nez Perce where you're going. Either a snag fell or a down log broke loose and it rolled over him, crushed him. Go ahead and work hard like you do, but keep looking around. Heads up all the time. Both of you."

"Just yesterday? What have they done with the dead man?"

Ed Moyles had wondered if Thanasis was unnerved by the fire death. "Smokejumper came in and took him out on a mule. Night was blacker than the inside of a cow. Followed all the way by packs of coyotes wantin' to eat the dead man. Smokejumpers are stout as a bear's breath, Thanasis. You'll like it." Focused on the unexpected death, Thanasis missed Ed's comment about smokejumpers, missed being told he would get his wish to be one.

Death on the fireground obscured everything else and would not leave Thanasis even as he stood on the ridge watching the exploding fire.

As he watched, a foreman told Thanasis to pick up his tools and get on the helicopter. He had seen the helicopter when they arrived but had not associated it with himself. The helicopter was a Plexiglass bubble sitting under rotor blades. It carried a pilot with space for one passenger. Charlie was told to follow Thanasis on the next flight.

The helicopter pilot reached across Thanasis to check the door latch. "Don't want you fallin' in the creek." The pilot turned to the black panel of instruments in front of him and began flipping toggle switches, casually, not looking at the panel. He was watching the fire cloud across the canyon.

The engine roared and the helicopter rose from the ground. Almost immediately the pilot moved the stick between his knees forward and the helicopter nosed down, diving into the canyon. The choreography existed at an ever-changing center somewhere inside the pilot.

The pilot addressed his passenger. "Welcome to Johnson Flying Service. We don't hand out wings or coffee. When we set down there will be a fella' standin' right there in a hardhat says 'Sector Boss' on it. Tell him who you are and he will tell you where to go.

"Walk away from the helicopter at the side, at two o'clock." The pilot pointed. "Don't go toward the tail rotor at all. Don't cut yourself gettin' outa my bird, and don't cut the bird either."

Thanasis stepped down from the helicopter, ducking at the sound of rotor blades thrashing the air above him. In a crouch, tools in both hands, holding the Pulaski away from him, he scuttled from the helicopter toward two figures shielding their faces from the dust and debris raised by the whirling rotor blades. The helicopter powered up. Engine roaring, blades spinning to invisibility, it rose immediately and moved quickly to the edge of the meadow, diving once again into the canyon, seeking speed and purchase in the high mountain air.

The roar of the aircraft was replaced by a muted roar of wind and fire receding up the face of Bull Creek Ridge, away from the meadow and the two men standing in front of Thanasis.

"I'm Thanasis Mavros. I was told to report to you."

Thanasis was speaking to the man with SECTOR BOSS written on a piece of adhesive tape stuck to the front of his aluminum hardhat. The man next to him wore an identical hardhat, a similar piece of hand-lettered tape stating a title.

"Good," the Sector Boss said. "You'll be working with Max, here. He's squad leader of a bunch of smokejumpers on my section of the fire and has agreed to add you to their exclusive company for a couple of days. Don't pick up any bad habits."

Thanasis nodded at Max and started to say something in greeting. Then he saw the title on Max's hardhat. SHIT COOLIE.

Thanasis felt as lighthearted as Max's title. He began looking forward to another smokejumper experience.

It took an hour of helicopter shuttle to transfer the ground crew and its equipment to the meadow where the "FNG" were told to gather. That was their unit name now. It stood for "Fucking New Guy." Max had put Thanasis and Charlie to work writing the acronym on pieces of adhesive tape. Max slapped the pieces of tape on the side of the hardhat of each young firefighter exiting the helicopter. Some bristled at the intrusion on their sense of extreme masculinity. Max chatted them up without seeming to. By the time he led them up the fire line bordering the burn they were willing followers.

At a knoll where up-canyon winds kept the worst of the smoke away from them, Max stopped his ground crew for a breather and instructions. The already sweating crew sat quietly. Max instructed. "You're going to take over from the smokejumpers diggin' this fire line. Don't rush it. There's enough to last the rest of the day and most of the night. You are diggin' this line to the top of the mountain. The jumper chain saw crew is goin' to stay with you. They will clear the snags. They will be cutting inside the burn. I don't want you inside the burn. Especially at night. Check your headlamp batteries. Any questions?"

Charlie spoke up. "Where are the smokejumpers goin'? Are they goin' to sit it out while we dig?"

Max squinted at Charlie in silence. Thanasis shifted his feet, embarrassed, wanted to tell his buddy to shut up. Thanasis thought Max might not answer Charlie's questions at all. When he did answer his eyes were merry again. "This crew of smokejumpers has worked twenty hours straight. Smokejumper regulations say that after twenty hours of building fire line a smokejumper gets to stop and bugger a hot knot hole." The giggling and hooting of the crew brought Charlie to his feet, glaring but not looking at anyone.

"Mazzarelli, only me and the fire boss get to worry about what my smokejumpers do. You don't get paid enough to take that on. You all line up ten feet apart and start scrapin' fire line. Show the jumpers how to do it.

"Mazzarelli, lead the way. You all follow Mazzarelli and bump the next man up ten feet when you have finished your ten." Max watched. Satisfied they could build line, he left to give his smokejumper crew its assignments.

The FNG worked through the night, pushing the fire line up the mountain in the dark. Their progress was marked by bobbing headlamps and the *clink* of their tools in the stone-filled mountain soil.

At a break Thanasis and Charlie doused their headlamps and smoked a cigarette in the dark. "How the hell you know where you're going, Charlie."

"Gravity is tellin' me which way is up. That's all there is to it. And my natural leadership skills."

Thanasis laughed. "Yeh, Max sure has an eye for born leaders."

Charlie opened a can of spaghetti and meatballs, offered some to Thanasis. "Can you believe him?" He spoke to no one in particular. He felt good about Max, thought of him as patron. Max was. Max specialized in rescuing those who could not or would not do.

M.I.A.

The POW had been isolated for more than a year, from everyone except guards that had beaten or ignored him. He had not dreamed for an entire year. It was not that he did not remember his dreams. He remembered everything. He just did not dream. *I even remember the CIA psychologist's friggin' lecture about dreams. And I'm not any crazier than he is.*

He did think his brain was slowly dying. He could remember, but he had trouble planning, projecting events into the future. When he would go blank while planning an escape he would panic. He would scream for the guards, for anyone, a presence he could talk to about anything, whether they listened or not. Talk became a daily wish.

The wish was granted one day in the form of two U.S. Navy lieutenants who had been shot down on a bombing mission over the Ho Chi Minh Trail. The Pathet Lao could not have cared less about the Trail, though it ran mostly through their country. The Vietnamese, on the other hand, relentlessly punished captured pilots shot down over the Trail.

NVA soldiers at the prison hung the two pilots upside down in a tree beside the creek where the POW emptied his waste bucket. They were suspended so their heads touched an ant hill mounded above the ground. The soldiers kicked the nest into activity and the pilots were quickly covered with furious ants.

The POW watched. He got a guard's attention and told him he had to empty his waste bucket. The guard took him to the creek, across from the pilots, and ignored him. The guards had long before stopped watching his stupor. Nothing there for them. The entertainment for the moment was the two men writhing above the biting ants.

When he had emptied his waste bucket, the POW walked through the small creek and up to the pilots. He brushed ants from the newly captured men, making soothing noises, saying "It's OK, guys." One of them had passed out. The other was still spitting ants and crying.

The guards noticed and removed him back across the creek, beating him with rifle butts. It was a short beating, mostly because no one else had seen they had been lax, and beatings took a lot of energy in the heat. They stuffed the POW into his cage.

The guards cut the pilots down, tied the two men together, and staked their ropes to the ground near the bamboo cage. They watched the prisoners from a shaded area, paying little attention, stealing naps.

The pilots, exhausted and disoriented, were silent as the prisoner in the cage talked and talked. His voice was a rapid, unpunctuated whisper. Listening to him was like standing under a spillway. They began, finally, to take assurance from his advice on prison life. They in turn assured him the Navy and the Air Force were bombing North Vietnam and the Ho Chi Minh Trail "into the stone age." No, they told him, "nobody back home knows there's a war on in Laos." No, they said, "we haven't been cut loose to bomb in Laos. Except the Trail. But don't worry. This isn't going to last long."

That night, without explanation, the POW was moved out of the bamboo cage to a log hut. The logs were vertical, posts planted in a trench and backfilled. There were four prisoners locked in the hut, the Navy pilots, an Air America pilot, and the smokejumper POW. The hut was one of several in a compound surrounded by barbwire. Just the thought of talk and companions every day left him feeling restored and ready to plan the next escape. He even dreamed. He dreamed an exciting jumble of people and events.

> An Air America H-34 helicopter carries him toward a smoking ruin. He is the only passenger and he asks the pilot why he is being taken there. The pilot's skin is blackened, smoke seeping through pores, and he does not answer or move as the helicopter approaches the smoking landing zone at a high rate of speed. The speed

of the descent alarms the POW. He grabs a parachute and jumps from the helicopter. There is no time for the chute to open. He lands on his feet, executes a perfect Allen roll, the smokejumper landing. He gets up and stands at attention in front of a man wearing pince-nez and a white lab coat. The man is smiling, he looks like Max the smokejumper. He removes the pince-nez and says "You did a perfect Allen roll."

The POW feels proud. He says "Reporting for duty, sir," and whistles a happy tune.

The man in the white coat, who now looks like his father, no longer smiles. He says "Only queers and bos'n mates whistle, and I don't see any stripes on you. Get over there and dig fire line. That's all you're good for."

He joins a fire crew, all of them dressed in orange uniforms of a chain gang. The man behind him pokes him as he bends over his lady shovel.

"Don't touch me," he yells at the man. "Keep your queer fucking hands to yourself."

"Then listen up dumb shit," the man yells back. "When I say 'bump up' that is what you do. You don't stand there scratchin' your ass. I poked you to get your attention. You are daydreamin' so hard you don't listen to other guys in the line. And you by-god don't build any line."

Somebody yells "Fight!"

Another man on the fire crew steps between them, grabs the POW by the shirt and spins him away. "Don't say a thing. You are about two seconds away from Max giving up on you."

He feels threatened by the possibility. "Do you think he will?"

"Let's go see."

The firefighters in prison uniforms find Max at the top of thc mountain. Max looks at the sky and says "I don't like the looks of that sky. The problem is gonna be the wind shift. If we don't get our jumper crews out of there they are gonna have two miles of fire blowin' right at 'em. I need a runner. Who's the runner here?"

Max is looking directly at the POW, who has changed out of prison clothes into track shorts and is doing leg stretches. The POW stops stretching and says "I am. I ran cross-country last year."

Max says "I need someone to go find that saw crew and get them back up here. We have to get snags cut where we are goin' to hunker down. We can't be in the black with wind blowin' snags on top of us."

"I'm on it." The POW runs off into the smoking woods. An hour later he leads all of the jumper fire crew to safety. The figure dressed in the clean white lab coat, leads the fire crew in cheering the runner. The figure in the lab coat does not look like Max anymore. It is Buddha, though the smile is surely Max's.

When he woke from the dream the escape plan came to the POW clear and whole. They would begin by pissing on the posts of the log hut wall.

CHAPTER SEVEN

Thanasis and Charlie slid from side to side on the bench seats of the bus from Boise, watching the river. Thanasis could not take his eyes off the whitewater of the spring runoff. He saw himself in it, deafened, falling, thrown under, riding. He thought how he would do it, survive its roll-rock tumbling. He left out altogether that he might not survive.

Charlie was fighting motion sickness. Before he could throw up the bus left the canyon, its course straightening through a broad valley. The driver jockeyed more speed and noise from the rebuilt engine. Charlie's nausea passed and he felt better. He was not sure he felt any better about his destination, the McCall smokejumper camp. All week long, bus ticket in hand, his feelings had swung between chest-thumping glory and a spooked fear of falling through space. He sweated with that fear now.

The bus pulled into a Texaco station on the edge of McCall, Idaho. McCall was a logging town, its largest employer Brown Tie and Lumber Company. Brown's loggers cut yellow pine and fir in the surrounding forest. Drivers, paid by the load, raced logging trucks, sixteen feet high, ten feet wide, thirty feet long and loaded beyond capacity, to the Brown sawmill, a sprawl of kilns and saw pits at the edge of town. There they spilled their loads into Payette Lake. Gears slamming, engine pitch rising, they roared back into the forest, the dust of the logging roads never quite settling.

When he stepped off the bus Thanasis smelled McCall. It was the first of many times. It would, like many other firsts, remain the best. "That's a really great smell, Charlie. Pine trees and water and fresh cut wood. It's neat. Don't ya think?"

"Hell's afire, Thanasis. It smells like Camp Creek. It smells like Brown's loggin' trucks. It's diesel. Get real."

"No, no!" Thanasis, swept along by nose and eyes, was astounded by little McCall. He searched for words to resist Charlie seeing it as ordinary. "It's like a movie." Thanasis had seen only two movies, one about Tarzan and one set in a place he thought like McCall. "It's like Canada, like the lake and the forest in the mounted police movie we saw. Look at it, Charlie." They saw a town of lake cottages, small houses with dark clapboard siding on wooded lots, dark screened porches, small docks, no one around, inviting mysteries.

"OK. You win. It gives you a tingle. But you can bet nobody in a red coat and a Smokey Bear hat is gonna ride in here on a horse. Let's find out where this smokejumper base is and see when they start feedin' us."

They got directions from the gas station attendant and began walking down the short main street of McCall. Shoreline, on the other side of storefronts and bars lining the street, paralleled their route. Thanasis was in love with McCall. His eyes sought the lake. He breathed the pine-saturated air in gulps.

"Thanasis, you got fuckin' asthma? I can hear you breathin'."

"Look, Charlie, I like the smell of this place. You got a problem?" Thanasis sometimes grew tired of daily Charlie. "Tell me again how you got in the smokejumpers. Just dumb luck?"

"Same way you did, Greek. Somebody put in a word for me. I followed your good example, teacher."

"You know as well as I do that nobody at Krassel would put in a word for you. You pissed off Dobbindick. You shit on Ed. Who put in a word?"

"I impressed a guy last summer. You were there. Remember the wind comin' up on the fire? Max told me he owed me one for chasing down his jumpers. He said if I hadn't done that they wouldn't have had any place to run when the fire blew up. Said somethin' about hero. Now you remember? So I called him on it this winter. Said I wanted in the smokejumpers. So I could go to the movies with you. He said, again, he owed me one and would put in a word. When the Shit Coolie speaks the Forest Service listens!"

A two-tone red and white '55 Chevy Bel Air convertible with bright red seat covers stopped in the street opposite them. The driver waved. She checked her short dark hair in the car's mirror as she spoke to them. "You going to the smokejumper camp? Hop in. I'll give you brave boys a ride." She arranged her hair with a flip and a pat, ran the tip of her tongue quickly over bright red lips. She was not looking at the brave boys.

They had not moved from the curb.

She turned toward them. "C'mon. I won't bite." She bit her lower lip as she looked at them over the top of her sunglasses. Eye contact and they were in the street. She stepped out of the car to open the trunk for their bags. She was wearing capri pants, a tube top, strapless heels. Thanasis and Charlie jockeyed for seating position. "No pushing boys. One of you in the back."

It was a short ride to the jumper base. She told them she lived with her mother, she loved dancing at the Shore Lodge, the Green Lantern—"they call it the Green Latrine, by the way"—had Michelob on tap, she water skied. "Do you guys water ski? Well, here we are. I'm sure I'll see you on the lake. Say hello to Dooley when you run into him. Jumper friend of mine." She wrinkled her nose and hunched her shoulders, recalling some past good time.

Thanasis and Charlie stood by the side of the road, watching the red and white convertible drive away. Each shook his head.

"Yes she will. She will bite," Thanasis said.

"You think?"

"Better learn how to water ski, son."

They walked across a precisely-edged semicircle of lawn, past a newly-painted brown and white Forest Service sign with neat letters carved into pine board, McCall Smokejumpers. A group of small clapboard buildings were spaced around the lawn and gravel roadways. Green shingles and silver paint, the paint leftover, not chosen. Beyond them, an array of tall poles and towers rigged with rope, blocks, and pulleys. Handmade, hand rigged, care and economy all around.

Thanasis and Charlie were almost as neat and clean. White T-shirts, blue jeans, and Chuck Taylor hightops.

They stepped inside the open door of the smokejumper headquarters building, into a one-room office. They were greeted by a booted man in jeans and tan collared shirt, white undershirt showing beneath the collar, a baseball cap of indeterminate color pulled low on his head. Work clothes, but nearly formal.

"Hi. I'm Valentine Dusek, one of the jumper foremen. Step on that scale while I read out your weight. Then fill out these forms." He handed them government employment forms. The scale, next to his desk, was a large commercial scale, weights swaying to the touch. He slid a small weight left to right along an arm marked off in numbers, stopped and announced "One ninety." Thanasis stepped off the scale. Valentine repeated the process with Charlie.

Someone called out to the smokejumper foreman from an adjoining room. "Valentine, you got to come here and listen to this. Tell him, Dooley." While Thanasis and Charlie dealt with the forms they listened.

"This was last night. I told you about her, didn't I, Valentine. Tell him, Dooley."

A voice associated with someone named Dooley started slowly, seemed to belong to a reluctant storyteller. He had picked up the two of them, mother and daughter, at the Cellar. A couple of drinks and the three of them left the bar and went to the house on the lake where the two women lived.

Someone closed the door between the office and the adjoining room. Thanasis and Charlie completed the forms in silence. When the door opened again, the Dooley-voice said "I'm so sore."

Dooley, having reported the facts of the night, walked out through the one-room office. He wore a large cowboy hat and the same type of logging boot as the foreman. A pack of cigarettes was rolled into the sleeve of his white T-shirt. He nodded at Thanasis and Charlie, said "Howdy." He stopped and leaned toward them. "You know, straight as he is, I think Valentine likes to hear about that kind of stuff." He rolled his eyes toward a forehead lined with comment.

Valentine came back into the office wearing a tired smile. "One ninety," he said. "We told you maximum jump weight was one eighty with your boots on. Training starts tomorrow. First training jump in two weeks. So you have two weeks to lose ten pounds. At one ninety, over on the Challis, you'll come in like a sack of shit. Probably break your legs. See you at calisthenics eight tomorrow morning right after breakfast. Meals are eighty-five cents, deducted from your pay. Go up the hill and find a bunk."

Thanasis struggled through the week, avoiding the kitchen. He ate only oranges, two per meal, began to hate them, began to feel weak. He changed his diet to add pot roast. He felt better and stopped envying the new jumper candidate called Dog Touhey, who came early and stayed late at every meal. Thanasis soon weighed the required "one eighty" in his White logging boots.

Every jumper wore "Whites" and the new jumper candidates did everything wearing the ten-inch logging boot made by Otto White. Calisthenics, three-mile runs, obstacle courses, climbing trees with long-gaffed climbing spurs, jumping from the back of moving pickup trucks to simulate windy parachute landings. Volleyball.

Smokejumper volleyball in logging boots was a contact sport. The new smokejumper class, the "Neddy Newmans" or "Neds," played the veteran jumpers during the first week in camp. It was jungle rules. The net, secured by nylon parachute cord, suffered lunging bodies and thrown elbows. Dog, invoking well-established rules, called a carry on one of the veteran jumper returns. "Carry? How would a Ned know a carry from a cocksucker? Carry this!" The thrown volleyball caromed off Dog's head. Fists flew in a dusty scuffle. The veteran jumpers bought a keg of beer for the first Ned party of the summer.

Leaving the party late that night, Thanasis fell into step with Dog. He wanted to talk about the tune Dog was whistling through a split lip.

"That fella was about twice your size. Your lip OK?"

"Never seen a fat lip wouldn't heal."

"What's that tune you're whistling. I heard it once before."

"You probably heard it lots of times. It's 'Beautiful Dreamer,' an old Stephen Foster melody."

"No. I only heard it once, but kind of over and over. A black man I hitched a ride with was singin' it. But he called it 'Beautiful Streamer'."

Thanasis sang "beautiful streamer open for me, blue skies above me, and no canopy" to the tune he remembered and Dog had whistled.

Dog said "Goddamn," and sang another verse. "Coming in hot, tell that damn spotter I'm missin' the spot."

"Yeh, that's what he was singin'. Over and over."

"Goddamn. You know who your black man was? You met a member of the Triple Nickle."

"What's the Triple Nickle?"

Dog did not hesitate. He had read all winter about the history of the smokejumpers. "They were the 555th Parachute Infantry Battalion of the United States Army. All black GIs. When the white boys went off to defeat Japan durin' World War II the Army put black paratroopers to work puttin' out fires in wilderness throughout the West.

"See, the Japanese were tryin' to burn down the United States by drifting little balloons all the way from Japan into our national forests with fire bombs attached to 'em.

"The fire fighting was secret work so the Japs wouldn't know we were worried about their balloons. There was only one way to get the troopers into the wilderness fast enough to put the fires out. They parachuted them into the mountains out of airplanes. There were no roads, just like today.

"Triple Nickle did over two thousand fire jumps, and some of them died doin' it. There were no Purple Hearts for the 555th. Their deaths and injuries were not caused by the enemy in combat. They were just jumpin' out of airplanes."

Thanasis was impressed by Dog's lecture. How Dog knew these things he had no idea, but he did not doubt a thing Dog told him. "So Biggie Brown was kind of a hero . . . sure couldn't make the weight limit here, though."

They said "Goodnight" at the barracks. Thanasis added "Do me a favor. Eat about a dozen pancakes for me."

CHAPTER EIGHT

The only leftover of the night's conflict and reconciliation between Neds and veteran jumpers was throwing up during morning calisthenics. The squad leader conducting the morning workout, a jumper named Slapper Miller, told them in his best 82nd Airborne D-Day landings voice "You hired out to be tough. Now be tough." Thanasis laughed out loud.

"Give me fifty, Mavros."

Thanasis' headache made the pushups special.

Smokejumper training was structured and dispassionate. It was not focused on getting the trainee through. It was up to the new smokejumper to do that. Like most training, it was boring. Deconstruction of complex acts into parts until they were understood. Repetition of sequential conduct until it was one act.

Boredom edged toward anxiety as training focused on the act of jumping out of an airplane. Splints, tourniquets, burns, and Demerol were a sleepy course of study. Stepping into space to fall into the mountains below was not. It scared them all.

The group of ten Neds stood around a pile of canvas jumpsuits. Slapper Miller directed and explained. "It's a two-piece canvas suit, bib overall pants and waist-length jacket. Stylish. Fits over whatever you're wearin'. Take one of each and put 'em on, jackets first. That easy enough?" The Neds sorted like ragpickers through the different shades of faded canvas, uncertain.

"Don't worry about size and color. This isn't an Easter egg roll. The high collar is to keep tree branches from catchin' you in the throat and poppin' your head off. No, I'm not kidding, Mavros. Your sense of humor is gonna' get you more pushups. Laughin' and cuttin' up is the way to bigger triceps. Give me twenty. Fast now. Don't hold up the rest of these fine Neds or I'll have to put 'em all on the ground helpin' you push the big ball."

Thanasis put out of his mind the image of squad leader Miller's head popping off. He stopped laughing and closed himself to Ned derision, kept calm and finished the pushups.

"Good job, Mavros. You might just be this year's King of Pushups. OK. Listen up. The pants are designed to protect your manhood from the thousands of pine trees growing in Idaho. That strap of webbing in the crotch is not decoration. It starts out as a stirrup under your boot and runs up your crotch and down the other leg to make a stirrup under your other boot. It's your girlfriend's favorite jumpsuit feature."

Dog examined the odd-fitting pants he had pulled on, striding in them, web stirrups and suspenders pulling in opposite directions. He was by far the smallest of the jumper candidates. Nothing seemed to fit. "How do I tell if it fits?"

Slapper waved him over. "I'll check it. OK, face me and spread your legs. Wider. Hands over your head." Dog did as he was told. The D-Day paratrooper took one stride and kicked Dog in the crotch, hard. The squad leader stepped back. Dog still had his hands above his head. He was holding his breath. "It fits, Dog. Breathe. You always that white?"

Thanasis' momentary shock at the assault on Dog gave way to warm confidence that no tree would harm him. He said "What's your point? Dog ain't usin' nothin' down there anyway."

"Not funny, Mavros. I'm funny. You're not. Give me twenty."

Dog leaned over Thanasis doing pushups and whispered "Teach you to pick on little guys. For the record, I think you *are* funnier than Miller. Which ain't much." He stepped on Thanasis' butt as he rejoined the group of Neds.

Slapper did not wait for Thanasis to finish the pushups but lectured on. "One other feature of your pants is the pocket on the outside of your right lower leg. That's for stowin' your hundred-foot nylon letdown rope. The rope has some use when you hang up in a hundred forty-foot yellow pine. Limited use."

Charlie was waving a hand. "No, Mazzarelli, you can't buy a longer rope. Yes, Mazzarelli, that's where you carry your cookies and your Argus C-3 camera. You will also carry two orange eight-foot streamers in that pocket. You'll use them to form letters and figures on the ground to signal the airplane. The letter 'L' means you landed OK. There are signals askin' for Demerol and tellin' the spotter how bad you are hurt. Memorize them in case your jump partner is still unconscious from his landing."

Nervous laughter came from the Neds, huddled together now in front of a silver building marked with the sign Fire Cache. At Miller's direction they began to help each other into harnesses, inch and three-quarter white cotton webbing terminating in a confusion of chiming D-rings, V-rings, snaphooks. The harness and canvas suit—zipped, buttoned, hooked, and strapped—hunched the Ned into a stoop. The posture was good for hanging suspended in mid-air, but made walking a waddle.

"Graceless," Dog said. "Absolutely graceless, Mavros."

Thanasis and the rest of the Neds continued helping each other, with and without nervous gibes. In mutual support they followed the directions of the squad leader for attaching parachute to harness. Folded onto a plywood board and covered with fitted canvas, elastic band stretched around the edge of the board, the existence of the parachute was an inference, a matter of faith. They would not see the "candy-striped" orange and white panels of the chute until it opened a thousand feet above the ground.

"The reserve parachute is the smaller bundle. It attaches to the D-rings on the chest straps of your harness. Unlike the main chute which opens on a fifteen-foot static line fastened to the airplane, you and you alone are responsible for openin' your reserve chute. You do that by pullin' the ripcord handle on the right side of the reserve chute. Take a look now so you know where it is. Don't want you fumbly-dickin' around huntin' for the handle if you have to pull it. And every summer somebody has to pull the ripcord handle and use his reserve."

Charlie was waving his hand. "No, Mazzarelli, it's not a fail-safe system, but no one has had both his main and his reserve chutes fail on the same day. So don't fuck up our statistics." Charlie was awed by the apparent ability of the squad leader to read his mind.

Slapper continued talking about use of the equipment. "When you open the reserve, if you think of it, hold your left hand over the pack to keep the reserve from deploying. Then grab the reserve chute with both hands and throw it out away from you. That'll cut down on the possibility that the reserve will wrap around and get fouled in the failed main chute. If that happens, if the reserve is fouled in the main, be prepared to cut the shroud lines of the main chute. There is, you can see, an eight-inch knife on the top of the reserve chute pack for that purpose." He closed the lecture on the reserve chute, emphatic. "Do not cut the lines of your reserve chute."

The squad leader turned and walked, still talking, toward a group of free-standing telephone poles rigged with block and tackle. "One more thing. If you have to use your reserve and don't bring back the ripcord handle, you owe the year-end party fund ten dollars and you owe me fifty pushups. Leave the chutes in the Fire Cache and join me at the letdown simulator."

The Neds obeyed and waddled to the ropes and pulleys. They were joined there by another smokejumper. He was Webb, the Loft Foreman, in charge of packing and repairing parachutes. His own jump pedigree included 17th Airborne, Battle of the Bulge. He was helping Miller instruct the class on the letdown simulator.

Webb was a master of detail and function. He was patient about both. He began instructing. "You have just missed the jump spot and are hung up in a yellow pine. Fifty feet off the ground. Not a branch between you and the ground. You need to get down and help your jump partner put out the fire. If you don't, he will, in order to return you to your wife or girlfriend, chop your tree down with you in it. There's a way to avoid that. This is how it works. It sounds overdone and Rube Goldberg, but it works. It's time tested. Only smokejumpers do it. If you have questions, ask 'em." The Neds watched the tall, long-faced loft foreman snap himself into a harness. His harness was attached to parachute risers hanging from ropes falling through overhead pulleys.

"Listen up. You take one end of your letdown rope out of your leg pocket. Do not take the whole rope out of the pocket. The last thing you and your jump partner need is for you to drop the rope on the ground with you hanging in the tree.

"Now, run that end of the letdown rope up—I said 'up'—through the D-ring on the chest strap on the right side of your harness." He demonstrated, threading a letdown rope through the D-ring.

Webb completed talking them through the complex letdown procedure.

"You following?" Thanasis and Charlie and Dog nodded along with the rest of the Neds, already uncertain.

He turned to a muscular man pulling on a jumpsuit and harness. "Show them what I just said, Moose."

Moose wore thick glasses, had slightly cauliflower ears. He handed his glasses to a Ned. "Hold these." He was hoisted into the air on the pulleys of the letdown simulator. With a wrestler's quickness Moose threaded the letdown rope through the rings of the harness, tied it off, formed a loop of rope he could stand in, stood in the loop on one leg, pulled the locking pins and released the snaphooks attaching the parachute risers to the harness. He lowered himself to the ground with the letdown rope, the rope buzzing through the harness rings. He took a wrestler's wide, crouched stance, arms outstretched to grapple, and advanced on the silent Neds. He stopped in front of them and said "Go Smokejumpers." The Neds applauded. He reached out blindly. "Give me my glasses."

"Thanks, Moose. Another couple of hours and half of 'em will want to race you." Webb turned back to the Neds. Questions flew. Webb patiently went through the letdown procedure again and again. All the Neds, hanging alone on the telephone poles, slowly mastered it to some degree. Except Charlie. The ritual of the ring sequence was confusing, threatening. He was hanging in the letdown pulleys, bitching. "Fuck your D-rings."

"They aren't my D-rings, Mazzarelli. They're your D-rings. You do what you want with 'em." Webb turned away from the letdown simulator and dismissed the rest of the Neds. "You have half an hour until supper. Stow your gear."

The smokejumper Max walked up. He had been watching from near the volleyball court, eating an apple. "Wayne, no point you missin' supper. I think I see what's goin' on. Why don't you go on up and I'll watch Mazzarelli make friends with his letdown rope."

"If you want him he's yours. He may need some more instruction. He stopped listenin' a while ago." Webb joined the Neds walking to dinner, past Charlie hanging in the air. The Neds were silent, did not look at Charlie. Veteran jumpers on their way to the mess hall took the event they were passing as opportunity for loud discussion of nicknames for Charlie.

"You could call him 'Late'."

"I think I see a 'Tree Toad' sittin' up there, don't you, Barney."

"Name should be 'Letdown'."

"I like 'The Simulator'."

Max was the camp's unofficial clearinghouse for nicknames, and every jumper had one. He cut the hazing off.

"Charlie already has a nickname. He's The Dago, fastest man in camp."

By the time the jumpers had moved on to dinner Max had strapped himself into an adjoining set of ropes and pulleys. He hoisted himself into the air next to Charlie. He explained the threading of the letdown rope and demonstrated the letdown.

When Charlie said he thought he had it, Max lit a cigarette. "Charlie, bet I can beat you down. Smokin' a cigarette. Two out of three."

"How much we bettin'?"

"Loser carries the winner up to the mess hall on his back and buys dinner."

An hour later Charlie carried Max into the mess hall. The few remaining diners were Neds. They had waited. Led by Thanasis and Dog they cheered and stomped their feet. Charlie bowed, grinned, and ate.

CHAPTER NINE

The Neds began and soon completed ground training for the act of jumping out of an airplane—exiting, chute handling, landing.

They practiced exiting the plane by stepping into space through a mockup of the Ford Trimotor door. The mockup door sat atop a homemade thirty-two-foot jump tower. A log boom ran back-to-front across the top of the tower, extending beyond the front of the doorway, a pulley on the end of it. A rope was attached to the Ned's harness as he sat in the doorway. The rope ran through the pulley to a spring fastened to a concrete block set in the ground at the back of the tower. The spring, wrist-thick coils painted silver with leftover paint, had been rescued from a railroad boxcar. When a Ned stepped out the mockup door, he fell from the tower, accelerating at thirty-two feet per second per second. When he reached the end of the rope, he stopped. The boxcar spring did not give a bit. The Ned experienced the opening shock of a deploying parachute.

At the end of the first day on the jump tower, back in the barracks, Thanasis, Charlie, and Dog compared black-and-blue marks at the front of their shoulders. "I guess exit position is more than a concept. Seem to be consequences," Dog said.

Chute handling presented limited training options. There were talking-head lectures. "You can turn 'em. Clockwise or counter-clockwise. You can make them go faster in the direction you are facing. Faster means two or three miles an hour faster. Or you can just hang there watchin' the scenery get closer." It was Webb lecturing, offering generalities and underselling possibilities.

The new jumpers would learn that if Webb was the spotter in the door it was altogether another matter. There he told the jumper how to avoid the river, the sheer canyon wall, the yellow pine snag, and the stacks of down logs near the landing spot, with detailed instruction, full of judgment that three hundred mountain jumps had shaped. Whatever he said, it always worked.

Webb talked about their upcoming first jump. "Some of you have military jump experience. Well, we don't do it that way. We don't put hundreds of men in the sky all at once. Our landing zones are small, steep meadows surrounded by trees and rockfalls. We don't want more than two of you in the sky at the same time maneuvering to get into those small spots. A two-man stick is the most you will see going out of a smokejumper airplane. Often, particularly if the plane is a Travelair or Twin Beech, you will jump one man only on each pass over the jump spot. But the two-man stick is standard. Tomorrow, because it is a graded training jump, you will jump one man at a time out of the Ford."

The night before their first jump the Neds did not sleep. Part of it was anxiety. Part of it was hazing by a small group of veteran jumpers who came to the barracks at two a.m. They cradled a bottle of Wild Turkey they wanted to share with those who, they told the dazed Neds, "will surely die tomorrow."

A jumper named Paperlegs, weaving at their bedsides, warned them of the peril of "crystallized D-rings." At certain frequencies and temperatures, he warned, "the metal in the D-rings will crystallize and just any load will fracture them. Your chute opens and pops the D-rings right off your harness. Goodbye parachute. Nobody around here says anything about it, but government reports are full of it. More jumpers are killed by crystallized D-rings every year than anything else. I'm tired of the damn cover-up." He drank from the bottle of Wild Turkey. He turned to another jumper. "You need to pray over these men."

He was talking to the Ponderosa Pope, an ordained minister who jumped wilderness fires during the summer and spread the word of Jesus Christ throughout the year. He drank whiskey only one night each year and this was it. The Pope, dressed in black cassock with a stole around his neck, read portions of the funeral service from a book of prayer. "From dust thou art, unto dust thou shalt return," he said with a solemn face.

The Neds objected. "Cut the happy horse shit. We need some sleep." The veteran jumpers followed the bottle of Wild Turkey out of the barracks.

In the morning Thanasis and Charlie and Dog, nerves ragged, gathered with the rest of the Neds in front of the Fire Cache. They helped each other into jump gear, then rode the mile to the airport in the back of a pickup truck. Excitement and fear mixed in equal parts, with varying effect. Thanasis became silent. Charlie chattered non-stop. Dog shivered, chewed gum vigorously. Others were sleepy, withdrawn.

The Ford Trimotor sat alone on the dirt runway. Its thick high wings and boxy fuselage made it look muscular. When children draw airplanes they look like the Ford. The pilot walking around the plane, occasionally slapping its corrugated skin like an old dog, was shielding his eyes from the bright clear morning.

Carrying a clipboard, Valentine Dusek came over to the group of Neds. "Time to load up. We're goin' to take you in two loads. I'll read off five names and you go get in the Ford." The first group waddled to the airplane, Thanasis, Charlie, and Dog among them. Valentine checked chutes and harnesses, told them once again how and where to hook the static line inside the plane. The Neds put on their helmets, some white, some brown and black, looking like nothing so much as the second-hand football helmets they were, modified with a wire mesh mask, hinged at the top, covering the face.

As they waited for the plane's engines to start the Neds sat on the floor of the Ford, legs extended. They talked to distract themselves. "Valentine. That's a hell of a nickname. How'd he get that?"

The spotter, a jumper called Barney Bear for reasons of appearance alone, said "It's not a nickname. His mama gave him that name. Valentine is a love child. Long after his brothers left the family farm Mr. and Mrs. Dusek fell to huggin' and kissin' and along came Valentine."

"You're shittin' me."

"Nope. The way Val tells it his brothers, Bud and Babe, left the farm and became professional wrestlers. They were known as the Dirty Duseks when they wrestled back in North Dakota. His mom didn't like her sons being known as the Dirty Duseks. She wanted her sweet boys to be known as sweet boys. So she gave Valentine the name of love. He is as sweet a man as you'll find. But don't fight him. Deep down he is all Dirty Dusek."

The Ford taxied to the dirt runway. The engines roared, it rolled forward, its tail hoicked up, and the "Tin Goose" took off in a couple of hundred feet. Barney kept the Neds' attention, instructing them. He yelled to be heard over the throb and drone of three no-nonsense engines.

"You're goin' to be jumpin' on Big Meadow north of town. No chance to hang up in a tree. So don't worry about it. There'll be a big orange X on the ground. That's the target you're tryin' to hit. You won't, so don't worry about it. You'll be jumpin' from fifteen hundred feet. Webb'll be on the ground today with a bullhorn givin' you instructions about chute handling. Turn right, turn left, plane. Listen to him. Just do what he says over the bullhorn. You're being graded. Do a good Allen Roll when you land. Feet together, flex your knees, turn your hips, butt down, and roll backwards over your head. Just like you practiced. Absorb the energy."

They felt the vibration of the engines through the floor and straight sides of the Ford. The plane banked. The Neds knew it was circling the jump spot. Barney was yelling to be heard.

"When I call your name come to the door and hook your static line to the cable on the wall opposite the door, behind you." He pointed, grabbed the cable. "Then take a kneeling jump position in the door, one leg out the door on the step. I will be busy spottin' the jump so you make sure your static line is hooked." He would check every one.

"When we're over the jump spot I'll slap your leg. That's your signal to jump, to step out of the plane. Souk, in the door."

The Ned named Souk had been in Army Airborne the previous two years. He had a McCall nickname based on the 101st Airborne Screaming Eagles shoulder patch. It was straight forward like most jumper nicknames. "Screamin' Meemies." Or just "Meemies." He was teased from the outset with "What is the poor eagle screaming about?"

Souk went to the door. He hooked up, but did not sit or kneel in the doorway. Barney, lying near the door, slapped the floor and told him to sit in the open doorway, one leg out, foot on the step. Souk continued standing, gripping the doorframe, hands tense inside the fitted soft leather gloves they all wore for chute handling. He looked like he was analyzing the situation. Moments passed. Barney looked up from the floor.

Souk stepped back and said "I'm not doin' it. Not for all the tea in China and sure as hell not for a dollar fifty-six an hour." The Neds sitting on the floor could not hear. Barney stood up, spoke into Souk's helmet.

"Are you drunk?"

"No."

"Are you scared? That's alright, you know."

"Of course I'm scared. Everybody in the damned airplane is scared. This is an unnatural act."

Barney softly slapped Souk's helmet and pointed to the front of the plane. Souk unhooked his static line and walked awkwardly past the seated Neds. He took his helmet off as he went, sat down against the forward bulkhead. The Neds looked at him through their wire face masks. Souk looked at them, shrugged his shoulders, palms up and open. Agnostic, rational, uncompromised, he prepared to return alone.

"Mavros, in the door," Barney yelled, motioning to him. Thanasis immediately understood. The only experienced jumper in their group had looked it over and refused to jump. Barney was not giving them time to think about it. He yelled again at Thanasis. "Mavros." Pointing at the cable opposite the open door he yelled "Hook up."

Thanasis shuffled to the door. He snapped the static line hook to the cable. The fifteen feet of static line, a web strap, was designed to peel off his back when he jumped, pull the cover off the parachute, pull the parachute off the backboard until it was fully extended, and stretch a small cord tying the top of the parachute to the static line until the cord broke.

Barney returned to a prone position on the floor, a slim spotter's parachute pack on his back, his head out the door, left arm extended toward the cockpit, guiding the pilot to the jump spot with hand signals.

The door framed a swath of green, the mid-spring gift to Idaho of melting snow. Meadows and pine trees filled the foreground and ran in mosaic to distant mountains. The mountains offered an irregular, broken reach that supported any argument you wished about the shape of Earth, round or flat. Two-lane blacktop ran to the town and was swallowed among its cottages.

Thanasis knelt in the doorway, his right foot on the step outside and below the doorsill. He had his hands on the sides of the door, his eyes on the horizon, unseeing. He was numb, did not hear the roar of the engines or the rush of air inches from his face. Barney raised up and slapped Thanasis' left leg.

Thanasis stepped out of the plane in trained reflex, arms folded on top of the reserve chute pack. He was in an upright position, feet together, falling. He had no sensation of falling. The Ford engines backfired. He did not hear the loud report, though people fifteen hundred feet below him did. In less than four seconds the opening shock of the parachute hit him. He did not feel it.

Thanasis looked up and saw alternating orange and white panels and shroud lines running to the skirt of the parachute canopy. Everything was exactly where Webb had told them it should be. He yelled in relief, then again in pleasure. As taught, he reached for the control guidelines, nylon cords, one running from each riser to one of two slots in the rear of the chute. Pulling and releasing the control guidelines closed and opened the slots, causing the chute to turn to the right or the left.

He began looking around, a sightseer concerned that he might never pass this way again. He picked out creeks, meadows, cars and cows, looked for the lake. High snowcapped peaks stood out to the northwest, the Seven Devils. He swung his feet, front to back and front again, lost in good feeling.

Something began to press against the good feeling. A voice demanded "Mavros, pay attention!" Thanasis started to look around, realized it was Webb on a bullhorn, instructing him from the ground. Thanasis paid attention, made the maneuvers called for by the loft foreman talking to him in a one-way conversation.

He realized the ground was coming up fast. He tried to call up the movements of the Allen Roll landing. Just as he pulled his feet together he hit the ground. A sharp stinging blow traveled up his legs. He pitched forward on his face mask and helmet. He completed none of the elements of the Allen Roll. He knew it and his legs hurt.

He stood up, dazed and breathless at the abrupt end to the high point of his life.

Dooley Smythe, a second year jumper, came over and asked if he was alright. He began helping Thanasis put his jump gear into a Bemis seamless sack. Thanasis appreciated the help. He felt wrung out, not yet pulled together. Dooley shook his hand. "Way to go, man. You took a soil sample but you're walkin' and talkin'."

Thanasis walked over to one of the squad leaders holding a clipboard. He wanted to see his grades. He looked over the squad leader's shoulder and saw a score card with his name on it. There were letter grades in various categories of jump performance. Under LANDING the squad leader had written PP.

"What does that mean?"

"Piss poor."

Thanasis walked away, disappointed. He began planning tomorrow's landing, visualizing it as he walked back to his pile of jump gear. Walking in the meadow grass he reached into the air, grabbed imaginary risers, flexed his knees, rotated his hips and upper body, sank to the ground, and rolled over backwards.

"Good Allen Roll. A little late," Dog said as Thanasis got up. "Good perseverance."

Thanasis grinned at being caught so deep in earnest planning. "How did you do? I missed your landing."

"Self-centered bastard. You missed the jump of the day. I was just two baby steps away from hitting the X. Captain Marvel couldn't have done it better."

"I'll buy Captain Marvel a beer tonight. Congratulations."

The Neds had not been paid yet. They were low on cash but went to the Yacht Club anyway. They thought someone would buy them a beer. *Hell, we've jumped out of an airplane. Somebody will buy us a beer,* Charlie thought. While they waited on that charity they told each other, once again, how grand it was.

Paperlegs, a Yacht Club regular, listened for a while, then spoke to the bartender. "If they are goin' to tell second-rate jump stories they might as well have a beer in their hands. Set 'em up."

As they talked several of the Neds said they had blacked out from the time they left the plane until their parachute opened. Thanasis knew he had not blacked out but he had no recollection of what he had seen before his chute opened. He listened to the blackout stories.

Paperlegs listened until he could stand it no longer. "You're not blacking out. You're just cowards. You're closing your eyes when you jump. You open them when the parachute tells you it's OK. Gawdamighty." Paperlegs turned to the jumper sitting next to him at the bar. "Dooley, take care of these people. I'm serious. I can't stand to listen to any more." He paid for the round and left the Yacht Club.

Dooley, an onion seed farmer before the summer heat had killed his onions once too often, took Paperlegs at his word. These were his Neds to take care of. He started by pulling out his billfold and counting. "I've got twenty-three dollars. That comes to ninety-two beers . . . provided you don't mind me joinin' you for the evening."

The Neds cheered Dooley "Here's to Dooley, he's first class." Dooley didn't mind that the only rhyming words they knew were "horse's ass." They were smokejumpers. He ordered beer.

No one mentioned Meemies that night.

When they got back to the barracks Charlie asked "Thanasis, do you think we are underpaid?"

"Well, we haven't been paid a damned thing yet. But, no, I would do this for free. Every day. Wouldn't you?"

CHAPTER TEN

Thanasis recalled the winter stories of old stockmen, stories of murder and arson and suicide blamed on feeding livestock in deep snow. He agreed. *Feedin' hay can cause strange behavior*. So he felt justified in his modest plan. He told Andrew McEvoy.

"When the sheep and cows go out on grass I'm goin' to Mexico and then smoke jumpin' again."

"Those are both bad ideas. You'll get the clap, get knife cut, and then break your legs. Only a matter of time. Hope it scares the shit out of you."

Thanasis hitchhiked to Mexico in the spring. He met Dog and Charlie there as they had all agreed at the end of their first smoke-jumper fire season. They loafed in Tijuana, drinking beer and getting warm on their way to McCall.

Charlie had spent the winter at the Chicago Paper Box Mfg. Co., courtesy of someone his mother knew. "Cardboard is made out of trash and hot water. Slush that smells like wet dogs. I was the guy dumped the trash in the big vats. For six months I smelled like a beagle. By March I could lick my nuts. Do you know what they make boxes out of? The macaroni boxes, the Wheaties boxes? Dixie cups and old kotex is what. You know how many girls will go out with a guy smells like a beagle? Nada."

"How about a guy can lick his nuts?" Dog asked.

"You think I didn't try that? They couldn't get by the dog smell."

"Charlie, I think your luck is about to change." Thanasis was staring over Charlie's shoulder at the best looking whore he had seen in Tijuana. She was walking toward their table. Dog agreed. "This one's wearin' fuck-me shoes, doesn't care how you smell. Just pony up."

Charlie turned to see what his friends were talking about. He saw a light-skinned Mexican woman in tight black pants and red knit top. The top was short-sleeved and V-necked. Charlie began talking. Big smile, friendly, snappy.

Nothing registered in the face of the woman. She looked at Charlie and lifted the top, hands crossed to opposite sides, as if she was taking it off over her head. She stopped raising the light material as soon as her breasts were exposed.

"Those are tits could get a girl out of a speedin' ticket. You don't look like a motorcycle cop, Charlie. Whatcha think she's tryin' to say?" Dog asked.

She said nothing, looked at Charlie in silence.

"All right, honey, how much for each item you are sellin'?" Charlie asked.

The woman pulled a pen from nowhere and wrote on her palm. She extended her palm in commerce. Charlie looked at the number. He reached out to take her hand, as if to bring the number into focus. The number was clear and obvious. He sought her hand anyway, held it, perhaps longer than she wanted. She pulled it away hoping to avoid negotiation.

As he considered his counteroffer Charlie saw that her demand sat atop a palimpsest of faded blue numbers, rubbed and washed away. *Lot of traffic.* He mentally reduced his counter, told her to guess the number he was thinking.

Her face remained impassive and again she said nothing.

"Charlie, you can stop talkin'. You are fallin' in love with a deaf-mute."

"Shut up, Dog. You're just tryin' to steal my good-lookin' woman."

"Just tryin' to help. She might be able to read your lips, buddy, but she's got no words. Shit you not."

Charlie was quiet. He shook his head and said "You mean she's handicapped?"

"Not any way that matters to you and me."

"You ever fucked a handicapped woman?"

"No."

"I'll flip ya to see who goes first."

"Sure." Thanasis reached in his jeans for a silver dollar. "You worried you'll catch somethin'? Be a deaf-mute for the rest of your life? Die without sayin' another word?"

Dog added "And by the way, 'first' is only a figure of speech when you're talkin' about a Tijuana whore, specially a good lookin' one."

"Winner uses the other man's money?"

"Sure. Call it."

The dollar arced toward the table top. "Heads," said Charlie.

He grinned as he walked away with the whore and some of Thanasis' money.

In the morning they crossed the border with black-dog hangovers. They congratulated themselves they were not knife-cut or deaf-mute. Squinting into the sun they headed east, to Silver City, New Mexico, on the rumor the "Doug," a DC-3 jump plane, would be returning smokejumpers to their home bases from the early fire season on the Gila National Forest. They made the flight and checked in at McCall. They were in the usual financial condition of returning jumpers, flat broke and a month from the nearest paycheck.

"Where you sending us on project, Valentine?"

"Tell me where you are on the jump list," the foreman said, pointing toward a list posted outside the office door. They stepped outside and found their names on the jump list. They hooted and punched each other on the shoulder.

"Sounds like you are high on the list."

"Top ten, Valentine."

"Top ten stay in camp for fire calls. Everybody else goes to the boonies. I've got plenty of work for you. You start painting the loft exterior tomorrow right after calisthenics."

"Wasn't it painted last year?"

"Yeh, it was. Good job, too. Paint it again."

"What color?" Charlie asked.

"What are you, some kind of nance, Mazzarelli? Do you see any color around here but silver? We won't run out of silver paint until the Second Coming of Christ. See you in the morning. Bright sunshine in the forecast. A hangover would be ill-advised."

"You know we don't have any money, Valentine."

"Yes, I do. Keeps you coming back. Your Government applauds you boys for resisting the sin of property."

They settled into the make-work jobs for on-call jumpers held in base camp. They knew the menu. Digging up stumps, digging sewer line trenches, cutting and peeling poles at Paddy Flats for fence rails and posts. And painting. It was boring on its own terms, but bored them mostly because they were waiting. They waited for the Klaxon horn announcing fire and a jump plane.

They fought boredom in the usual way of camps. They bet on things.

Wary but unbelieving they bet Max he couldn't throw horse shoe nails and stick them, one at a time, in a barn wall. They were unaware Max had practiced doing that throughout the winter. He won about two hundred beers before they believed.

They bet the first man on the jump list he would not eat a horseshit sandwich. With the help of packs of mustard and ketchup, he did. He won eight dollars from a pool of astounded bettors who refused to smell his breath.

They bet on who could eat the most chili peppers riding in the back of the pickup going to Paddy Flats. The loser had to eat only baby food out of small jars for the next two days.

They bet on which of them, shirtless, could attract the most mosquitoes to die in one slap to the back.

They bet on who would dance with the homeliest girl at the Saturday dance in New Meadows. The farm girls who believed the boys' unlikely stories were a small sad pool in which the jumpers gladly swam, waiting for the call of the Klaxon horn.

Dog walked up to Charlie's bunk. "You and Thanasis are painting by yourselves today."

"What you doin'?"

"I have garbage detail. I'm the G-man."

"Oh brother. You are the biggest brown nose in Idaho. I hate to imagine what you did to get this."

Dog deadpanned. "The Forest Service rewards superior work. I paint so much better than you and Thanasis. I'm Picasso compared to you tools."

"So you're not going to breakfast."

"Or lunch."

The G-man did not have to buy breakfast or lunch because the white-haired women of the kitchen fed their garbage-boy-of-the-day cinnamon rolls and milk when he came to pick up the morning garbage. They repeated with treats from the luncheon menu for the afternoon garbage run. The cooks would not hesitate to turn in a jumper who took an orange without writing down a meal charge. The G-man got no-cost love along with the softest job in camp.

"And you're not doin' calisthenics?"

"Nope. G-man has to be prompt about cleanin' up. You boys draw flies. Don't have time for calisthenics, much as I like them."

Dog's solemn lie was interrupted by the Klaxon buzzer on the front of the loft. One long blast to get the attention of on-call firefighters, followed by short blasts, one for each man on the jump list called for the trip to the airport. The just-wakened jumpers listened as they finished pulling on frisco jeans and boots.

"It's eight. It's a Ford-load," Dog said. He was number eight and excited at the summer's first fire. Dog and Thanasis, by their placement on the list, were jump partners. They would jump a two-man stick, seventh and eighth men out of the Ford. It was early in the season for an eight-man fire.

"Let's go, JP," Thanasis said, throwing a big arm around the smaller shoulders. "Fire in the hills." They were grinning as they took off at a trot for the Fire Cache.

The area in front of the Fire Cache was quiet except for the sound of buckles and rings jangling as jumpers bent to fasten themselves into jump gear. Suited up, they climbed into the back of a pickup truck, sat on bench seats along the sides.

With self-conscious camp the eight pulled saffron signal strips from jumpsuit leg pockets and tied them around their throats in extravagant scarves. It would not happen again that summer. Only on the Glory Ride. They shouted at the squad leader driving the pickup. "Glory Ride!" The squad leader acquiesced to the tradition and drove through the middle of town, smokejumpers waving at people in the streets, blowing kisses as if on a parade float, playing heroes passing to glory and honor, scarves flying.

Swank was not part of the smokejumper meter. Except as part of the first ride to the first fire jump each season. The squad leader spoke to the jumper with him in the truck cab. "Where the hell did this half-ass tradition start? It mocks what we do."

Dog answered the question as if it was not rhetorical. "Nobody knows. Mocking traditions are always of unknown origin. This one smacks of *Pirates of Penzance*. You know. Gilbert and Sullivan. Not Forest Service at all." He hummed a tune, then sang in falsetto:

"Go, ye heroes, go to glory,

Ye shall live in song and story."

He hummed the tune again, then sang in baritone, arms outstretched, "ye heroes, go and die!"

The squad leader looked at Dog. "I have no idea how the fuck you got in the smokejumpers." The two rode in silence toward the airport.

All other smokejumper rides to the airport on all other days were on a back road, avoiding town and proceeding directly to the gravel airstrip, Forest Service efficient and without saffron scarves.

The top of the jump list was on the Ford ten minutes after the fire call. Dog was still singing songs from *Pirates of Penzance*. To the jumpers sitting on the floor of the plane, accompanied by the high-pitched whine of the electric starter motor, engines firing and back-firing, he sang:

"Oh, men of dark and dismal fate,

Forego your cruel employ."

The squad leader who had driven them on the Glory Ride was in the plane as spotter. He told Dog to sit down. He wanted to tell him to shut up but airplane engine noise had taken care of that. *Why can't we just hire Mormon boys out of Logan?* ran through his mind once again.

The Ford took off in four hundred feet and pounded toward Hells Canyon on the Snake River at one hundred miles per hour. The pilot addressed the nose-heavy, wallowing response of the plane, frequently turning a trim tab crank, up and behind his head, then synchronizing the three engines by hand. He flew west, the newly-risen sun throwing long black shadows before the planeload of jumpers.

M.I.A.

The POW felt he owed the three men he slept with on the dirt floor, shoulder to shoulder, feet padlocked in wooden stocks, legs numb. They had saved his life with talk. He had nothing to offer in return. Except an escape plan.

Not all of them agreed to the plan, but they went along with his preparation because for them it was passive. His point had been "You've got to pee somewhere. You got no choice. I just want you to pee in a particular place. On the post." To the last dissenter he said "Let's do it this way. Bet I can hold it longer than you can. You win, I'll shut up about where you pee. I win, you pee on the post." The POW won and the plan went forward.

The plan involved removing one of the vertical logs in the wall of the hut. In their emaciated state they could slip through any opening into which the prisoner with the largest hat size could fit his head. They identified the prisoner and the log. A small piece of found metal was fashioned into a pick which worked to open the padlock, freeing them of the stocks at night. The mud they made at the base of the post permitted them to move it from side to side, noiselessly enlarging the posthole diameter a quarter inch. In the dark, they tested their new doorway, removing the log. Everyone's head fit through the opening. They replaced the log.

The Air America pilot came to the POW and congratulated him on the progress of his plan. "The guys will be behind you. But they're worried about the rest of your plan. You're going to have to rally them. Maybe you could do it by telling them one of your smokejumper stories, one about backin' each other, persevering against the odds, without sayin' as much. You know?"

He did know. It made him uncomfortable, leading when he was not sure what would work. The worst part about leading escape from prison, his repayment to them, was risking their lives.

On the other hand, he knew that jumper stories could be fitted to any point. He gave it a try, rehearsing the story to himself, lying on his back in the dark. He imagined whispering *"This is no shit. It's about Dog I've told you about. Little guy, weighed a buck and a quarter. We were jumpin' out of Silver City, down in New Mexico. The occasion is a two-day dance hall fight at the Casa Loma. Smokejumpers versus rodeo cowboys. It started when somebody turned out the lights, Dog dancin' on the bar. . . ."*

He polished the story to make sure it included all the points he wanted to make. A couple of nights later, when he had finished telling his smokejumper story to the pilots, there was puzzled silence. One of the Navy pilots whispered "And your point is . . . ?"

The POW thought for a moment and said "Dance hall fightin' is a metaphor."

"For what?"

"For survival of little guys. In case you haven't looked recently not one of you boys weighs one-twenty. You're not gonna survive unless you escape . . . and you can't escape unless you focus, anticipate your buddies' needs, and persevere. The cardinal virtues. The greatest of these is perseverance. Dog was a virtuous man."

The metaphor was lost on everyone. On the night he chose to escape, the other prisoners helped the POW remove the post in the hut wall but they would not follow him.

He slipped through the opening and stood in pounding rain. Certain that the guards were concerned only with shelter, he walked directly to the barbed wire fence. He stripped his clothes off and crawled through the narrow spaces between the tight, crisscrossed strands and the spirals of concertina at the top and bottom of the fence. He was cut, but he got through the wire without getting hung up. He reached back through the fence and worked his small ball of clothes through the maze of wire. He began pulling shirt and pants on as he walked toward a stream. He waded into the current of the flooding creek. When he was up to his waist, he lay out on the water and began floating downstream toward the west. The other prisoners watched.

"There goes one crazy sonofabitch. Think we'll ever see him again?"

"Yeh, and he'll be in bad shape when we do."

The POW floated for days and the rain never stopped. He left no tracks and saved energy by holding onto logs or bunches of bamboo as he floated. The risk of travel in the creek was the many villages, increasing in number as the stream grew into a river. Enemy patrols moving near the river raised the jeopardy. With increasing frequency he abandoned his makeshift floats and left the river, working his way around villages by walking into the jungle. At times his departures from the river took him into greater danger—minefields, patrols on jungle paths, roads filled with troops and trucks. The roads brought bombing by Lao and American airplanes, the bombs exploding as close to him as to the enemy, blast debris falling on him, the concussions compounding his deafness.

The river and rain kept thirst away, but hunger was part of every hour. He ate every creature he encountered—crickets, lizards, tadpoles. They were never enough. It was twenty days since he had gone through the barbwire and he knew he was even thinner than the man who had threaded himself through the prison fence. He tied pieces of vine through belt loops to keep his pants from falling to the ground.

He knelt by a small pond in the jungle, scooping tadpoles into his mouth, not chewing, not raising his head, just swallowing as they swam in his mouth. He waited for the disturbed pond water to settle again. When it did he saw reflected in the still surface the figure of a man holding a rifle.

He jumped to his feet and ran. He saw other men in front of him and stopped. He heard the sound of wooden signal clackers. The men in front moved to encircle him and he was quickly surrounded by unarmed farmers. He thought about running again, breaking through them, but they were joined by armed soldiers.

The weeks that followed were filled with pain, more than he had known. If it had been torture he would have confessed. It was, however, punishment, and he had no option but to endure. It took the soldiers, most of them guards from the prison camp, two weeks to march him back to the prison. It could have been done in half that. They took their time. He was theirs.

At night they chained him upright to a tree where he was attacked by mosquitoes and terrestrial leeches. His meager diet resulted in boils over most of his body. The boils burst against the tree. The combination of leeches and boils left him streaked with blood each morning. Every wound, bite or break in his skin became infected.

When they reached the prison the soldiers walked him around the compound, outside the wire, several times. They whipped him on his legs with bamboo canes to make him move. The prisoners inside the wire tried to turn away. Guards poked them with bayonets to make them watch.

When the POW passed out, guards dragged him to yet another bamboo cage, out of sight and away from everyone. When he regained consciousness, he was alone. There was no talk, except the taunts of guards.

CHAPTER ELEVEN

The spotter picked his way through the jumpers sitting on the floor of the Ford, hunched to pass through the opening in the cockpit bulkhead, spoke briefly with the pilot, and returned to the cabin filled with jumpers and their gear. He squatted between the two jumpers nearest the cockpit, Thanasis and Dog.

"I'm going to drop the first six on the fire we were called on. Pilot has spotted another fire a few miles farther down Hells Canyon. Dispatcher says to drop you two on that one. It's a single tree. Cut it down and go home. You'll be out tonight. Got lucky again."

Thanasis and Dog relaxed and watched as the other jumpers prepared for their fire jump, pulling on helmets, checking each other's harness and chute packs. The two sought windows as the pilot positioned the plane to scout the fire.

Thanasis looked at the smoke blown about the drainage below them and realized that the wind had been changing its direction, blowing fire throughout the bottom of the canyon. The wind had not settled into any particular run. He saw flames dancing in the brush and consuming small Christmas trees, unusual for this early in the day.

"I think we're gonna have a good fire season, Dog. Hot and dry already."

Dog nodded and grinned. "Big Ernie, the fire god, loves us."

"Big Ernie actually loves girls."

"So he created us."

The spotter chose an open meadow for the jump spot, one that his jumpers could work into regardless of wind direction. He discussed his choice with the pilot and they agreed. The pilot began flying a long oval, one side of the oval passing over the jump spot. He fit the track to the shape of the ground to avoid flying into rising terrain as he made his drop runs. He repeated the oval pattern for each two-man stick, the spotter releasing jumpers at the same point on each pass.

Thanasis caught Charlie's eye as he lined up in the open doorway above the sheer walls of the deepest gorge in the United States. Thanasis gave him a thumbs up. On the spotter's signal, Charlie pushed himself into space. His jump partner, standing behind him, immediately took one step to the doorway and, without pause, stepped out of the plane into the air above the fire.

When the spotter and pilot finished putting the six jumpers on the growing fire, they turned the Ford north to the other, smaller fire.

The two-man fire was still a single tree, but dropping live coals and ash, spreading new fire in the grass and brush surrounding it. The stricken tree stood on a narrow ridge running out into Hells Canyon. The ridge was a thousand feet below the rim of the canyon, a fin jutting out from vertical canyon wall. It fell away on its three remaining sides, cliffs scored by goat paths. It was an island in space, anchored in black basalt above the Snake River.

The spotter called the dispatcher on the radio. Thanasis and Dog listened as best they could to the conversation, some of which was about them.

"Yes, the jump spot is big enough, better than marginal but not much. There's no wind to speak of at this point. They can get in. If they mess up, they'll get hurt, but that's not different. Don't know how the hell they're gonna get off this fire. But they'll figure it out. If they can't figure a way we can pick em' off there with the Bell helo." He paused. "Then there's this. When they cut the tree down there's no guarantee it's just gonna lay there. Ridge is all slope, any way you go from the tree. Could just as easy roll off and fall a thousand feet into the fuel below. And believe me there's plenty of fuel on the bottom. You tell me what you want."

The spotter came over and knelt next to them. "Dispatch is leavin' it up to me. Maybe this isn't your lucky fire. I say you don't jump."

Thanasis was thinking about the jump, the fire, and the packout. He saw mostly problems. He heard the spotter with a mix of relief and disappointment. Then he heard Dog say "I'll jump your fire."

Thanasis hesitated only an instant over the choices—stare daggers at Dog or say "Me too" loud and clear.

"Hell yes. This is para-camping. Drop the drift chute."

The spotter considered his options. Jumpers always wanted the jump. Few spotters in few circumstances would scrub a jump when the jumpers wanted it. High wind was the universal exception. There was no wind.

"Alright, Mavros. Hook up and get in the door. I'm goin' to drop you one at a time. As soon as you open, hold down on one steering line, right or left it doesn't matter. I just want you circling all the way in to the spot."

When Thanasis jumped, the island in the sky looked narrow and easy to miss. He pulled down on his right steering line. The parachute slowly turned clockwise. It circled within the perimeter of the ridge. He came into the ground with no forward speed. Thanasis relaxed as he approached the ground, knowing he would make it, did not notice that his feet were not together. That and the unevenness of the ground put all his weight on one foot. The foot turned under. He felt sharp burning pain in his ankle. He was cursing before he completed his roll.

"Goddamit, goddamit, goddamit." He grabbed his ankle, thinking what to signal the plane. *Don't signal sprains. Only breaks. Workin' the fire will be a bitch.* He pulled the orange streamers out of his leg pocket and spread the L on the ground. *An absolute bitch.* He stood on one leg and watched Dog's circling descent.

Lookin' good. Gonna make it. Aw shit. He watched Dog smash through the branches of a snag, hands above his head on the risers, prepared for landing. The largest branch caught Dog low in the chest, doubling him over before it broke and dropped him face down on the ground.

"You all right?" Thanasis yelled. There was no answer and Dog lay still. Thanasis hobbled through rocks and bunch grass to his jump partner. By the time he reached him Dog was trying to move and breathe.

"Wind knocked out?" He got a nod from Dog.

"Anything else?"

Dog held one hand against his right side and pointed there with his other hand.

"Ribs?"

Dog sat up with a grimace. "You oughta be at the fuckin' Mayo Clinic. Medical genius." Dog was on his knees, struggling to stand. Thanasis held out his hand and Dog waved him off, stood up. "Could use a little help gettin' out of my equipment. Reachin' isn't workin' real well."

For the next twenty-four hours, Thanasis and Dog fought their fire on hands and knees. They built a fire line, crawling one behind the other. They dug a trench to capture and hold the burning tree on the line on which they chose to fall it, building the sides of the trench above ground level with borrowed rocks and dirt and wooden stakes shaped with a Pulaski.

They tackled the tree, working the crosscut slowly across the trunk, awkwardly for both of them, with pain for Dog. They wore their high-collared jump jackets to protect their backs and arms from falling ash and coals. They made progress until, after an hour of effort, the saw began to bind in the resinous pitch of the tree.

"If we had some kerosene we could loosen this right up," Thanasis said, "but we're fresh out."

"You should have thought of that, you goose. Time for a blow anyway. Let's sit and think on this."

"How you feelin'?"

"About the same as the time I got knocked under the sheriff's car in that Fourth of July scuffle. Remember that?"

"Course I do. I remember every time you start a fight. 'Cause it usually results in me gettin' sucker punched by a total stranger. Know what might work here? You still carry canned bacon in your food pack?"

"Sure. You talkin' about the misery whip?"

"Yeh. What we need is lubrication. We can cook the fat out of your bacon, use that to get the saw blade to slide through the pitch."

Bacon grease worked. They spent their second day on the space island dropping the tree in the trench, chopping the fire out of it, covering it with dirt, cold tracking the fire. On the morning of the third day they began planning the packout.

Dog said "I feel like shit."

"Me too. Maybe they will helicopter us off."

"If they don't, which way you want to go? Up or down?"

Before they could address Dog's question the Ford flew over and dropped a message. The message told them big fires had broken out and the Forest Service helicopter was busy on those. They would have to walk out. Were they in good enough shape for that? If so, they should put out an L signal. The message did not offer an alternative if they were not "in good enough shape."

"That's cold," Dog said.

"Let's get the hell off here. You OK?" Thanasis asked.

"I'm fine. All I see you have is a purple rash on a gimpy leg. You'll be cured by the time we get back to McCall."

"Let's leave the gear up here on the ridge and when they get a helicopter freed up they can come pick it up."

"OK. But I'm personally throwin' the crosscut over the cliff," Dog said. He returned to his question. "Up or down?"

Thanasis said "Don't know." He dug in his jeans for a silver dollar. "Heads we go up. Tails we go to the Snake." Snake River won and they went down over the cliffs. They took water canteens, a can of mandarin oranges each, and their letdown ropes.

By the time they left the cliffs for grassy benches broken by bluffs and draws they were out of both water and mandarin oranges. The letdown ropes had been captured forever by the cracks and rock of the cliffs. They were in pain, Thanasis with each step, Dog with each breath. They said nothing to each other. Staying within themselves they reached the pale green water of the Snake after nightfall. They did not stop at the shore but waded into the water and drank from the river. They slept on a river beach next to a driftwood fire, rising to replenish it when the air chilled and woke them. Thousands of stars filled the winding canyon sky that opened above them. They felt chosen.

The next morning they flipped to see if they went up river or down. Up won. They alternately swam or crawled along cliffs. They watched huge fish in the clear green water. They swam with cigarette packs in their teeth. They swam and crawled and walked for two days without food.

"You sure you're not holding out? You don't have a single fig newton or anything?"

"Thanasis, the only place I have to hide anything you don't want to look . . . but if you find anything there, you got to share it."

They lay back on the shore of the Snake, exhausted, but eventually admiring trees and river again.

"How far you think we've come, Thanasis?"

"Never measured swimmin' before. Pure guess is ten miles."

"How much farther to that all-girl fishin' camp?"

"It's right here and only right here. Deep in your dark and dirty mind."

"We're probably headin' toward the fire that Charlie and them jumped on. Think they're still there?"

"Not likely. Probably drinkin' beer in McCall."

They came to an old mining road paralleling the course of the river and followed it.

"God I like walkin' on level ground," Dog said.

"Well don't walk so fast. It all pays the same whether you're sittin' on your ass or walkin' down the road."

They walked in silence until both of them smelled smoke.

"Smells like they lost their fire."

"Yeh. We must be gettin' close. Be glad to get a fire camp meal. Could be steak and potatoes. Even ice cream."

They came to a high ridge that blocked the road and ended in a sheer wall above a waterfall and steep, churning rapids. A tunnel had been cut through the ridge. As the two jumpers approached the tunnel they could not see light indicating the other end. "Must be a long one. Watch your step," Thanasis cautioned as they entered the dark.

The smart pace on the road full of sunshine slowed to a shuffle in the dark. One foot ahead of the other. Short slide, short slide, short slide as if they were on ice. Thanasis thought he heard a sound. It was distinct for a moment, then lost in the sound of sliding boots.

"Stop."

Dog bumped into him. "Do that again and we're dealing with a sodomy charge."

"Listen."

"What?"

"Just listen." Thanasis slid his boot on the tunnel floor. The boot noise was answered with a rattle of linked joints. Unmistakable. "Rattlesnake," he said.

Thanasis slid his boot again. The response was several, rattles to both sides and in front of them. He thought a moment.

"We have a tunnel full of rattlesnakes. Fire drove 'em in. Scared and pissed off. Turn around and walk back out."

They walked back out the tunnel, longer strides, holding their breath, listening. Once more in the sunshine, they breathed large uneven breaths, like spooked horses.

"Jesus H. Christ. Is this a horror movie or what. This boy has taken his last step on this sorry road." Dog sounded and looked frightened. "Yes. I am afraid of snakes. No. I am not goin' back in that tunnel."

"Dog, up over the ridge is the only other way. I really don't think I can make that climb." He unlaced his boot and pulled down his sock to show Dog a swollen purple ankle. "I won't ask you to go. But I have to walk through that tunnel. You can go over the top. But I have to walk through. I have an idea. I'm not asking you. I'm just telling you an idea."

"Well tell me the sonofabitch."

He laced his boot, talking slowly, not looking at Dog. "We pick up as many rocks as we can carry. Make a bag out of our shirts. We walk into the tunnel slowly. Rolling rocks in front of us. Scaring the snakes. Light a match every once in a while, make sure the snakes are moving out of the way." Thanasis stopped talking.

"That's it? Bowling for snakes. Purely stupid."

"OK. Flip to see which way we go? Up or through."

"Shit. Flip it."

The tunnel won and they walked into the dark carrying a shirt full of rocks. No jumper ever argued after a coin flip. The flip was the decision. Dog, hating the plan, was an early and vigorous rock bowler. A few matches showed the plan was working. Dog began chanting in the dark.

"Snake, snake, we don't shake."

When they walked out of the dark they were sweating in spite of the cool air of the tunnel. With their last match they lit cigarettes.

"How's your ribs?"

"Fine. How's your rash?"

At the fire camp they got a ride out of the canyon and another back to McCall.

"That was so bad I don't even know how to brag on it," Dog said as they rode in the back of a Forest Service pickup.

At the smokejumper base they talked as they picked up new jump gear and filled twelve-pound food bags. "Thanasis, you think a coin flip is a fair way to decide things?"

"When you don't have information it's all you got," Thanasis said. He knew Dog was talking about the snakes in the tunnel.

Dog thought for a minute, and said "I think I got it, Thanasis. A coin flip is an allegory. It symbolizes what jumpin' is about. You're either goin' to get hurt or you aren't. Luck of the draw."

"Yeh, you got it."

Dog selected a new Pulaski and shovel. "Think the president of the United States ever uses a coin flip?"

"If he's afraid of snakes, he does."

CHAPTER TWELVE

The black woman at the piano stopped singing when the smokejumpers came in. She looked across the piano at the three that had entered the Yacht Club.

She was known in town as Big Rose. She nodded and said "For the McCall smokejumpers." She began playing again and sang.

"So I smile and say,
When a lovely flame dies,
Smoke gets in your eyes."

Thanasis, Charlie, and Dog lined up facing Big Rose across the piano and did a slow, synchronized doo-wop dance step to her song. As she finished they applauded and Big Rose laughed.

"Oh, Dog, honey, I told you to come to Memphis. You have such style. We would be the most stylish couple on Beale Street. We could get our own mojo at Taters, maybe a little Lucky Hand Root or some Black Cat Bone."

Thanasis removed Dog's baseball cap and pushed him forward. "Lady's talkin' to you. Show respect." Dog bowed from the waist and said "Thanksh." They had been to the Cellar and the Green Lantern before the Yacht Club. They all bowed and slid over to the bar where Froggy the bartender asked "What'll it be?"

"Three Lucky Lagers." It was not clear who spoke.

Froggy bent to get the beers. As he opened bottles he looked immediately beyond the jumpers. He reached under the bar once more.

"Kind of a pussy dance you faggots do." The voice came from behind the jumpers, close, a country drawl. "Guess your nigger girlfriend likes it though."

The jumpers turned toward the voice. It came from a stocky teenager in cowboy boots. He had two companions, muscled, smirking.

Dog spoke immediately, with no hint of slur. "You don't like pussy dance? Then I'll dance on your head. As for the nigger, she is our nigger and you will now apologize to her for your jackleg redneck mouth." Dog grabbed the stocky boy by the throat before he finished the demand for an apology.

"Take it outside! Now!" Froggy was banging the bar with a two-foot sap pulled from under the bar, rasping in a gravelly voice. He was no older than any of the gathering fire-eaters, but he had the authority of huge hands, a square head the size of a basketball, the deep voice of a bullfrog, and a piece of black polished wood.

The combatants, feigning cool, walked out the side door to an alley running toward the lake. The blows, curses, and howls began immediately. The howls came mostly from young cowboys being hit with the sap that Charlie had grabbed from the bar. Froggy was a friend of Big Rose. He shrugged and turned to washing glasses.

Thanasis was whaling a large boy who would not go quietly. The jumper took a couple of hard punches and charged. Using his weight and ranch-hand strength, Thanasis threw his opponent to the ground and put him in a choke hold until he felt him go limp. The large boy came to quickly. Coughing and spitting, he got up and walked dazed from the fight.

Dog was taking punches to his ribs. Having bitten into the stocky boy's neck and seeing that as an advantage, he held on fiercely, regardless of the pain in his side.

Charlie walked over and hit Dog's tormentor in the head with the sap. He told Dog to stop biting and hit the other fighter again with the sap. The stocky boy staggered to his feet and ran to the street, shouting "faggots" and "nigger lovers" as he ran.

"If you have time for a cold beer, Dog, I'm buyin'," Charlie said. "And you should apologize to Big Rose for sayin' she is a nigger."

When the three stumbled back to the barracks at 2:00 a.m. they found a handwritten sign taped to the door. It announced 14-MAN FIRE TEAM—FORD AND TWIN BEECH—NO FIREPACKS—BREAKFAST

AT 4 AM, WHEELS UP AT 5 AM. In other circumstances the note on the door would have brought excitement. The three were not enthusiastic. They wanted sleep, only sleep. They decided to flip a coin to determine what they would do. Thanasis handed over a silver dollar and announced his intention to go in the toilets and throw up.

The flips were complicated by the number of options, real and surreal. It took several minutes. Thanasis was still cleaning up a toilet stall when he was told the result. They would change into boots and work clothes and play poker until breakfast. They could sleep on the plane. Thanasis changed his clothes and accepted a cigar.

There were already twenty jumpers on the Pole Creek Fire. The additional fourteen had been requested by the Fire Boss to act as overhead supervising inexperienced Mexican ground crews being sent to the two thousand-acre fire. The fire had blown over fire lines several times, crossing drainages and threatening to trap fire crews. It was in the mountains an hour drive north of Sun Valley resort.

A newsreel photographer from Movietone News was at the McCall base filming a short subject on smokejumpers for showing in movie theatres before feature films. He chose to ride along on the early morning fire jump. He sat up front in the right-hand seat of the Ford. From there he could lean out the co-pilot window with his movie camera to film jumpers as they came out the side door of the plane, maybe catch the floating chutes working into the jump spot in the mountains below. He was wide awake and full of enthusiasm.

The flight of the Ford across the Idaho Primitive Area to Pole Creek was two hours of pitching, rolling yaw through turbulent air. The Movietone cameraman began sweating. He gradually changed color, until the glistening sweat and gray-green color gave him the appearance of a large catfish somehow taught to operate a camera.

The faster Beech made the trip in half the time. The downside for Thanasis and the jumpers in the smaller aircraft was that they were thrown about even more violently than those in the Ford. The nausea of airsickness grew after the two-engine aircraft arrived at the jump site. Unlike most jumps they did not have to hunt for a landing spot. The Pole Creek meadow was over two miles long and a mile and a half wide, the size of the adjoining fire. Nevertheless cautious, the pilot and spotter scouted the fire and the jump spot, sending the Beech through tight, banked turns. Lateral Gs pushed the smokejumpers and the liquid content of their bodies from side to side.

Thanasis realized he was about to return to his condition in the barracks. He stepped around Charlie and Dog who were scheduled to jump ahead of him, said "sorry" as he passed, and crouched in the open door of the Beech.

He turned to the spotter without looking at him. "Forget the drift chute. If I don't get out now I'll barf in your lap. We got miles of room down there."

The spotter took one look at Thanasis and began hand signals to the pilot, lining up the first jump run. Thanasis pulled his wire mesh face mask down in place, buckled it.

He looked out the door hoping the horizon would steady the vertigo that was seizing him, hold the gorge of breakfast in place. The horizontal stabilizer of the tail structure drew his gaze. The stabilizer looked like it was immediately to his left, within reach and slightly below. He knew jumpers who had jumped upward leaving the Beech to see if they could touch the stabilizer as the plane passed. They never got close, they reported. The illusion of the Beech tail configuration always made him feel disoriented. Now it caused nausea to flood over him.

He unbuckled his face mask, turned to his right and vomited next to the door in which he sat. Charlie looked away, pushed himself a few inches back from the mounded pool at the side of the door. The spotter said "Buckle your mask and hook up. We're coming up on it. Keep 'er into the wind." Thanasis could barely wait for the signal to jump. He leaned forward.

The snap of parachute opening shock, the cool mountain air, and escape from the centrifuge of the turning Beech ended the nausea and cleared his head, as if nothing at all had happened. He landed easily, almost standing up, in the middle of acres of sagebrush. *Jump was cake.* He got up with a sigh. He still wanted to sleep.

As Thanasis chained the shroud lines of his chute for stowing, Charlie walked over and helped. Charlie eyed Thanasis. "I don't mind you took my spot but, Jesus Christ, Thanasis, chew your food. There was whole peaches in there without a tooth mark on 'em."

Thanasis stopped chaining the lines. "I'm sorry about all that in the Beech. Think the spotter will ever talk to me again?"

"In case you didn't notice, the spotter's name is Moose. Has muscles on his muscles? That one? He'll talk to you, but he will be holdin' you down on the ground while he does."

The Ford arrived over the fire as the Beech finished its last drop. The ten jumpers in the Ford had completed their jump preparations and held their static line clips ready for hook up. The spotter, a short volatile jumper named Roselli, went to work, aligning the plane as it approached the big meadow. Given the size of the meadow, he was considering three-man sticks. Head out the door, he adjusted his goggles and dropped the drift chute.

The Movietone cameraman leaned out his window in the front of the plane. He did it in spite of how he felt, which was falling-down sick. *Got to get this.* The plane circled right. He saw Roselli's goggled face turning toward him as the spotter followed the drift chute. He pressed a button to activate the camera, heard the camera motor running. He wanted to say "Great shot!" but his mouth and nose filled with the contents of his stomach. He choked and gagged and sneezed in spasms. Everything rushed from his throat, now raw and scoured. Everything streamed back toward the spotter in the door. A professional, the cameraman held tightly to the camera, tried for the shot of the jumpers. He saw the spotter wipe his goggles and pull his head back inside the plane. He felt bad about that.

Roselli stood in the door of the Ford wiping his receding hair. He tried to wipe his hands on his jacket. Then, carefully, he wiped around his mouth. What he found there caused him to spit and wipe again.

"Fucking asshole and his fucking camera. I'll break 'em both." He started toward the pilot's cabin, pushing the first jumper out of his way. The next jumper in line threw an arm out to stop Roselli and said "Take it easy, Mussolini. It's just puke."

Roselli stopped and looked at his ten jumpers. "Ten-man stick. Everybody hook up and get the hell out of here. Move it."

A jumper on the ridge watching the Ford over the meadow shouted to his buddy. "Brown. Brown. You gotta see this!" The two of them watched in disbelief as ten jumpers poured out the side of the Ford, one after the other.

"Bet the spotter was Airborne, having a Normandy flashback. Just couldn't help himself."

"Or he's drunk and Lloyd will chew his ass. Might chew his ass anyway." Lloyd, the longtime Smokejumper Project Leader, was on the Pole Creek fire because of press coverage flowing from the proximity of Sun Valley. He had witnessed the remarkable jump.

Thanasis was assigned a crew of Mexican firefighters. He led them to the existing fire line. His instructions were to widen it. In spite of language problems he got the crew working. They worked slowly, persistently. They knew from their lives that labor could not be hurried to an end, in fact had no end. Thanasis, in his first role as supervisor, enjoyed instructing, scouting ahead, providing. He taped their names on their hard hats.

CHAPTER THIRTEEN

Thanasis was full of energy by the end of the day. He took his crew to the food tent, a white, gold trimmed and tasseled affair, courtesy of Sun Valley resort. The fire camp food was catered by the Sun Valley commissary. Fewer choices, but the same thing the Lodge guests were eating that night. The Mexican fire crew was dazzled.

After dinner Dog hurried up to Thanasis. "The Sun Valley food guy offered to take us into town in his commissary truck. Says there's a dance in the Holiday Hut at Sun Valley, whatever that is. He's coming back out in the morning at four o'clock. Says if we meet him at the commissary he'll bring us out with the camp breakfast. I asked Lloyd if it was OK. He was suspicious but said OK. He knows this fire is down, not going anywhere. Won't miss us. You coming or you still need your beauty rest?"

"If I don't come you'll just get in trouble and Lloyd will fire you."

The ride in the dark of the food truck gave them time for naps. Some were going to visit a jumper in the SunValley Hospital who had broken his leg in the earlier jump on the ridge above Pole Creek. The rest were going to the dance. Dog had told the Project Leader that all ten of them in the truck were going to visit the jumper in the hospital. Though the Project Leader wondered at the many close friends the hospitalized jumper had made, it was not in his nature to question a perfectly good lie.

Thanasis, Charlie, and Dog washed up—hands, necks, and faces—in a restroom at the SunValley Inn and called it good. They hurried to the dance in the Holiday Hut, a Quonset hut that doubled as Sun Valley employee cafeteria and auditorium. They wore high-collared canvas jump jackets and logging boots, smelled of the fire line. The jumpers stood out and apart from the rest of the dance crowd, a mix of Sun Valley guests, residents, and well-dressed young people in town for the weekend. After a few beers they ended their segregation by doing Allen Rolls off the stage. The orchestra leader identified them for the dancers as firefighters saving Sun Valley. They were applauded.

"You gonna dance? You could get lucky, meet a Mormon girl. Highly promiscuous," Dog said.

Thanasis weighed the possible truth of Dog's statement. *Not likely.* Nodded anyway.

"C'mon." Charlie beckoned to Thanasis. He and Dog were joining a conga line of possible conquests. Three steps, kick. Thanasis was stepping toward the line when he saw the girl he wanted to dance with. He stopped and moved away from the dance floor. He waved at Charlie and Dog, and turned to look at her again.

She stood near the door marked EXIT, highlighted by the aurora of the sign. Blond. Red color at her high cheek bones. Full lips in a wide mouth. Wide-set eyes, oddly dark and almond shaped in the Nordic setting of her face. White peasant blouse showing tanned shoulders. Dark skirt cinched at the waist, fitted at the hip, flaring at mid-calf. He felt like he was recording the images permanently. He did not move, but felt he had to talk to her.

She was holding an unlit cigarette. He walked toward her thinking *I'll offer her a light.* She was watching someone on the dance floor. As he approached she looked at him and smiled. He felt as if he was about to confess all. Whatever was asked he would confess.

He spoke to her and as he did he was in control of himself again. "I hope you're not leaving. Would you like a light?"

"I don't smoke but I'm thinking about starting. So I'm holding a starter cigarette. Maybe you should be the one. To start me. How do you feel about that?"

"I'll do my best. If you have any regrets, I would feel real bad."

He reached inside his jump jacket and dug a sheepherder match out of his shirt pocket. Looking at her mouth he said "Hold it between your index and middle fingers and bring it to your lips."

"Like this?"

She looked practiced as a movie star. He did not move to strike the match. "Yes. You're good at this."

She held the cigarette away from her mouth. "What's next?"

He held the match up, just outside his shoulder. Without taking his eyes off her face he flicked the match head with a thumbnail and it burst into flame.

"That's cool. Will you teach me how to do that?"

"Yes. But only on our second date."

Her eyes were now on his. "We're dating?"

"We've gotten this far. I think it might work out."

She looked at the match. "You had better do something with that match or you're going to lose our fire."

He moved the flame forward, held it between them. She put the cigarette between her lips again and leaned forward. She drew softly.

"A little harder."

Her cheeks drew in and then she pulled away from the match. She opened her mouth slightly. Then, tentatively, she inhaled. She coughed.

"I'm not sure I like this. Probably just not any good at it."

Thanasis wanted to hold her and tell her she was good at everything, the best in the world. "You'll get the hang of it, just like anything else. Take another puff and in a few seconds you'll feel a buzz. You know, like a little dizzy. Then we'll dance. We'll celebrate your addiction."

She laughed and took another puff. She waited, looking at him, waited for the promised feeling. "You're right. I've got a little buzz. So dance me. I'm Maria Echevaria. What's your name?"

"Your name is musical. I'm Thanasis Mavros." He walked with her to the dance floor.

"That's beautiful. Foreign sounding, like mine. Where are you from?"

"The name is Greek. I was born there."

"Does the name Thanasis translate? Does it have a meaning in English?"

"It's a short form of Athanasios and means 'without death.' It's a family story."

"It sounds like a scary one. Will you tell me? On our second date?"

"Yes. It's a long story. May take more than one date."

"If you're not going to die, we have a lot of time."

"Your name sounds Mexican. But you don't look like that."

"We are Chilean. Spanish many generations ago. And a thousand years before that we were Visigoths and blond. Then we invented the mulatto and had to leave the country."

"I believe some of it."

"Someday you might believe it all."

They danced, holding each other carefully as if there might be breaking or tearing. They relaxed and became comfortable with the touch of their bodies. She declined other dance offers, danced only with him.

"Your friends think you are either having a good time or that our buckles got stuck." She nodded toward Charlie and Dog grinning and watching them.

"My buckle is just fine. My friends happen to be morons."

She said nothing, but seemed to dance a little closer, her cheek next to his. The band signaled the last dance. They danced to the slow swing of "In the Still of the Night."

"What are you doing between now and four o'clock? I go back to the fire line then. We could smoke a lot of cigarettes, tell a lot of family stories, rehearse our second date."

"I came with a bunch of girls, friends from Boise and McCall. I need to be with them this evening. That wouldn't always be the case. They don't always come on my dates." She took his arm as the last dance ended.

"Where can I get in touch with you?"

"I live with my parents in McCall. We're in the phone book. I would like it if you called."

She said good night and disappeared into a group of girlfriends. Thanasis felt like he could run all the way to Pole Creek, wake his Mexican crew, tell them. He wanted to tell everybody.

CHAPTER FOURTEEN

Thanasis stood in the semi-dark of the Fire Cache, empty food bag in his hand. He had dumped the cloth bag on the worn wood floor of the cache. He picked up the small cans of beans, tomatoes, sardines, and chocolate milk, put them back in the bins on the wall from which they had come, and looked for cans of food to take their place in the bag.

Jumpers were always changing out the contents of their fire pack—replacing the dying batteries of headlamps, adding socks for the pack-out, a new roll of toilet paper stuck on the handle of the lady shovel.

No one, however, changed out the canned food in their fire pack. It was canned, it would still be good at the end of the summer. There he was, changing out the cans in his food bag. Not replenishing, but exchanging them. He had done all the other things a jumper does to maintain his fire pack. He was extending the task into eccentric territory.

He knew why, though he would never admit it to anyone. Working on his fire pack, prolonging the task, left him alone. To think uninterrupted about her. To fantasize another evening with her, on the lake, or an afternoon picnic together. The fantasy picnic was on his mind as he selected the food for his fire pack. *What would Maria like?* He moved, food bag in hand, in the step-close-step of an imagined dance toward the bins of canned food. She was next to him, moving on the dance floor, as he sang to himself, for her.

In the still of the night

I held you, held you tight.

He added "doo wop doo wah" aloud as he turned.

"Thanasis, what the hell you doin' in here?" Charlie had thrown open the double doors of the Fire Cache. Sunlight streamed in. "You been in here for two hours. I figured you was knittin' a fire pack. Now

I see you're practicin' for a dance contest. What's up, bud. You been actin' weird ever since Sun Valley. Word goin' around is you're pussy whipped. I tend to agree."

"You wouldn't know pussy from parsley, Charlie." Two strides carried him across and outside the Fire Cache. "I'll whip any man says I'm pussy whipped." He caught Charlie on the lawn outside the loft and doubled him over, knees to nose, cradled in a wrestling hold. Charlie was giggling more than resisting.

"She smells better than you, Charlie. She feels better than you. She dances better than you. And by god I think she rassles better 'n you. Bottom line, I think she's neat." He released Charlie and stood up. "Better work on your escape, Dago."

"That the way you feel I'll just put my suitcase in the hall." Charlie pushed his lower lip into a pout. He waited a few counts and said "She's fine lookin'. Do your damnedest."

"Thanks, I guess. Probably won't see her again, what with the fire season hot and her busy datin'."

"Well, you comin' tonight? To the Big Flip. Keg in the lecture room. Five dollars to enter. Lose a flip and you're out. Last man standin' takes the whole pot. No second place. Unless you count the beer you drink."

"Maybe. Thought I'd ask her out though. Know anybody would loan me a car for an evening?"

"Reid might. Unless he's still courtin' that girl down at Council. Don't know when the man sleeps."

"How about Johnny?"

"C'mon. Nobody but Johnny will ever drive that Cadillac. Besides, you drive up in that fine car it's just like tellin' the girl a lie. Get off on the wrong foot. Wish I could help you." Charlie started to walk away. He stopped. "Thanasis, you get to rasslin' tonight, I doubt she'll like that hold you put on me just now." Thanasis faked a lunge and Charlie danced out of reach.

Thanasis called the Echevaria residence from the pay phone at the drug store. Pulled a soda fountain chair over to the phone, sat on the back of the chair, feet on the seat. He wanted to sound casual, look casual. Instead, he felt like a salesman with a bad product. The Echevaria telephone rang.

"Hello. This is Maria."

At the sound of her voice he straightened up. The quick movement sent the chair over backward, bentwood clattering on the linoleum, Thanasis to the floor. The public phone flew out of his hand and rebounded on its metal jacketed cord into the wall. Thanasis scrambled to his feet and grabbed the swinging phone.

"Maria. You still there?"

"Thanasis? I'm glad you called. Did you drop the phone?"

"Something like that." He hurried on. "I hope you're free tonight. I'd like to see you."

She was available and, without a car, they agreed to a walk by the lake, maybe drinking a beer with their feet in the water. "Then when the moon comes up we can work on your smokin'."

They sat on a dock in front of an unlighted house on the lake. "They live in Boise. Friends of my family. They come up on weekends, so we're alright sitting out here." Their talk quieted.

"Beer's gone. Moon's up. Cold yet?"

"No. But I'll pretend I am and you can put your arm around me to keep me warm."

He pulled her to him, kissed her on the mouth. They stepped through the last small distance of you and me and made out, folded in an embrace that moonlight fled, left them alone. He ran his hands over her, stopped in the middle of some heavy breathing.

"Pretending?"

"Never was."

"Neither am I."

"I can tell. So I'm going to make a decision. It's time for a moonlight swim and a walk home. Rules are no looking until complete immersion, no touching until I'm on my doorstep."

"For your sake this water better be cold."

"I'm counting on it. Now turn, look over at the Shore Lodge."

He stood and looked away at the soft lights. "I'll follow right behind so you don't grow an icicle on your nose. Those no-looking rules of yours run both ways?"

"Yes."

"Liar." He heard her slip off the dock. He kicked his jeans off and dove, came up blowing. He saw the silhouette of her head, the moon bright on the water. He swam slowly toward her.

"Talk to me before I freeze. Tell me a smokejumper story."

He did not feel the cold, but ached. Smokejumper stories were the last thing on his mind. He dutifully began one.

"Just so you know, all smokejumper stories begin the same way. First you say 'This is no shit.' Got it?"

"Yes. This is no shit! Please go on while I towel off. Are you cold?"

"No." He feigned a storyteller's pause and stole a look as she climbed onto the dock, the white of her back becoming the shadowed round of her ass, strong legs raising her from the water. He knew the picture of her wet in the moonlight would never leave him.

He looked away and began. "This is no shit. We were on a fire on the Boise, big enough and close enough they could bring in bulldozers to make fire line. They brought in several. One of the cat skinners was a fella shows up on a lot of fires. Mostly because he is so skilled. Mexican skinner by the name of Wahoo Ibarra. Carries a thirty-ought-six clipped on his cat. Says he needs it because you never know when a cougar might jump out of a fire. Anyway, on this fire I'm talkin' about another operator got his dozer hung up, too far out over the edge of a steep fall, couldn't back off. Wahoo was called over to take a look. He climbed up and waved the other boy off."

He was chilled and talking faster. "You ready yet?"

"Just about. Then what happened?" She was fully clothed, in her sweater, seated on the dock and watching him, hugging her knees. *Slay the dragon, honey.*

"Wahoo dropped the blade and that carried the bulldozer over the edge. He threw it in reverse and did a back flip out of the driver's seat. Dozer ran out to the bottom and they were able to drive it out of the ravine. End of story. Comin' out ready or not." He looked over to where she was sitting, grinning. He roared and splashed lake water at her. He swam to the dock as she ran to the shore.

He dried off, got into his clothes, and walked up the dock shaking his head. "Don't know what I'm gettin' into do I."

"Thanasis, honey, you were so pretty. I couldn't stop looking at you. And you were so into your story. I wanted to hear it all. Wahoo! Women like that in a man. Put your arms around me, man." She kissed him warmly. They did some more kissing on her doorstep, until her mother flicked the front porch light several times.

"Do you like rodeos?"

"Yes. Can we go?"

"There's one in Council next week. If I'm in town let's go."

As he walked to the base his head was full of Maria drying herself in the moonlight. Maria in his poetry.

At the barracks he found a flashlight and wrote in the darkness, for her.

CHAPTER FIFTEEN

The orange and black high-wing Curtis Travelair was 1920s. Its single engine was uncowled and all its surfaces fabric covered. It carried the pilot, a spotter, and two jumpers, Thanasis and Charlie. The Travelair was made for delivering jumpers to the favorite smokejumper fire, a two-manner in the wilderness.

Charlie sat in the open door of the aircraft, both feet outside resting on a step, hands on each side of the doorway. He was thinking about how close he had come to winning it all the night before at The Big Flip, then losing on the final flip. Always uncomfortable at disappointment, Charlie turned to thinking about what he would yell as he jumped. "Geronimo" was too old hat, not clever. Maybe he would try "God save the Queen" again. He liked that it usually caused everybody in the plane to yell "Fuck the Queen."

Thanasis had not jumped with Charlie this summer and, when he saw they were together on the jump list, he had begun looking forward to being in the wilderness with his buddy. Thanasis knew his jump partner, whoever he was, would take care of him. When he thought why that was he could tick off what seemed reasons—the working, eating, and partying together. Mostly, though, it was they were hooked on the same drug, stepping out the open door of an airplane and all that followed. The fact his jump partner was Charlie made it all the better.

Today, however, he was not thinking about his jump partner and why they would take care of each other in the wilderness. He was thinking about Maria, how her blouse would sometimes etch the outline of her nipples. He was not paying attention to jump preparation.

"Hey, Mavros. Put your hat on. We're doing final on your partner. Be ready."

Thanasis pulled on his helmet, buckled the face mask. He moved closer to the door to watch his jump partner.

Charlie's plan today was to exit the plane in a spread-eagle dive to the rear, showy and unapproved, and then to slip his parachute, making it spill air and fall faster into the landing area by climbing the lines in the front of the chute, scary and unapproved. He hailed the Queen and pushed himself into a broad spread eagle.

The parachute opened and immediately malfunctioned, one shroud line crossing over the top of the chute, dividing the canopy into two smaller compartments. The result was loss of air and rapid descent combined with loss of control.

The spotter and Thanasis shouted "Mae West!" in unison. Though few smokejumpers had ever seen the actress, her name was accepted shorthand for the two compressed bulges straining against silk and the loss of function that followed. Both the spotter and Thanasis knew what Charlie had to do. They hoped he remembered.

"Climb it!" They were unheard cheerleaders, but Charlie remembered. He climbed a handful of lines, pulling a section of the skirt of the chute down, hoping to slip the problem shroud line off the canopy. It was not working. The uncontrolled descent hurried him toward an open ridge. Thanasis could feel the hard landing coming. *Good roll and he'll be alright.*

Charlie did not get a chance to roll. He was blown into a snag thirty feet above the ground. The chute draped over the short grey limbs of the dead tree, canopy tearing on the hard projections, lines fouling and holding on the remains of dead branches. He hung there.

"Good. He's not breaking out," the spotter said. "We'll watch him get his letdown started."

The plane circled the figure hanging on the side of the snag. Thanasis sat in the open door, static line hooked up, watching below. "I don't see him moving."

"Wind knocked out. Maybe just plain knocked out. He came in pretty hard." The spotter signaled the pilot to take the plane in lower, past the snag, rearranged himself on the floor for a closer look.

They saw that the jumper in the snag had moved. He had raised his arms and now held the tree in an embrace. His legs hung below him, not moving. Nothing suggested he was trying to use his letdown rope. The lines of the parachute blew in the wind, without tension, unweighted. They looked for a signal from the jumper. There was none.

The spotter sat up. "Thanasis, I'm gonna put you in there soon as we get altitude." He was signaling the pilot to take the plane up. "I don't know what the hell is goin' on. I'm gonna drop a radio same time I drop you. Keep your eye on it and get over to the snag with it. Tell me what's goin' on. He may need help. I'll drop you a pair of climbing spurs. Watch for 'em."

The plane leveled off quickly and made a sharp turn into its jump run. "I'm gonna drop you about eight hundred feet. You'll be on the ground fast. Hold 'er into the wind."

Events seemed to move double-time. Thanasis was aware of nothing but his jump partner hanging on the snag. In seconds, it seemed, he was on the ground, completing his roll and sliding in the bear grass. He shed his jumpsuit and located the radio. He ran toward the snag, checking the radio as he went. He hooted.

There was no response. He yelled "Dago. Talk to me." There was only wind and silence on the mountain.

Thanasis stood at the base of the snag looking up at his jump partner. The hard grey trunk in front of him reminded him of the climbing spurs. He looked around in time to see the Travelair making its cargo drop, marked the spot where he saw the spurs go in.

He went back to yelling to his jump partner. "Charlie! Can you hear me? Are you OK?" He saw the hanging figure's head move, still helmeted, face mask in place, arms holding the dead tree as if to keep it in place. Then he heard his partner's voice, faint and straining as if the speaker did not want his sound to cause movement. Thanasis could not pick out words, only sound, ending in a short convulsive breath.

"Can you do a letdown?"

The white helmet moved slowly. A brief negative.

"Can you move?"

The helmet moved again. Negative.

"Are you in pain?"

This time the head was motionless. The answering voice was small, but clear. "Yes. Need your help."

"I'm comin' up for you, buddy. Hold on." Thanasis looked down at the ground, tried to focus on next steps. He saw a blood spattered rock at the base of the snag. He did not connect it to Charlie hanging on the snag until more red splashed on the rock, splattering his boots. *Jesus.* His thoughts made him grimace.

"One more question, buddy. Got to know. Where's the blood comin' from?"

The voice was strained with effort, but the words clear. "Stob . . . dead branch . . . came through my jumpsuit." The sentence ended in a gasp again. Thanasis was about to tell him not to talk when the voice continued. "Through leg . . . up groin."

Thanasis doubled over, imagining. "Have you out of there in no time." He keyed the radio microphone and hurried to pick up the climbing spurs, talking to the spotter as he went. "He's impaled on a broken branch. Through the leg, into the abdomen. Pinned to the tree. He's bleeding. He's got big pain. Drop the Demerol. I'm gonna tie him to the tree, cut the stob at its base, then lower him to the ground with a letdown rope. When you drop the Demerol drop me a saw, somethin' small I can use to cut the branch off. I can't use the crosscut. Give me somethin' small. Maybe a hacksaw out of the airplane tool kit."

There was static on the radio, then the spotter's voice. "Not sure about you takin' him out of the snag by yourself. What if you drop him on his head? And cuttin' the stob sounds risky. Too much like surgery. You might be causin' more injury. I'll call for a rescue jump and a Stokes litter. We'll have a dozen guys up here in a couple hours to help you."

Thanasis wanted to scream. He kept hearing Charlie's voice, imagined his buddy's full weight on the stob, the thick broken branch, splintered and knotted, slipping past gut, seeking bone and muscle. He put the microphone on his hip and looked again at his jump partner hanging on the side of the dead tree. *There isn't a goddamn spotter even knows what state he's flyin' in. Bring on the goddamn Stokes litter. We'll need it to take a dead man out, you dumb sonofabitch.*

He took a deep breath and keyed the microphone. "A rescue jump is a good idea, but you know they won't be on site and doin' good in time. Hell, Larry, he'll bleed to death in half the time a crew gets here.

His heart is just pumpin' it on the ground. I've got to get him down. It's exactly what the guys would do on the rescue jump, but it'd be too late. Drop the Demerol and a saw and then call for a rescue jump. We'll need the Stokes and a crew however this turns out."

Thanasis turned the radio off and strapped on the spurs. He cut a piece of letdown rope and looped it around himself and the trunk of the snag as a climbing rope, to lean into and use his arms in climbing. He climbed the snag, and when he reached Charlie he removed one end of the impaled jumper's letdown rope from the jumpsuit leg pocket.

He climbed up to the level of Charlie's chest. He put the sound of what he thought was calm and competence into his voice. It was more like brusque, scared. "You awake, buddy?"

The man behind the face mask looked at Thanasis through the mesh, eyes exhausted with pain. "Yeh."

"Good. You fall asleep, they'll dock your pay."

Charlie smiled. "Only hurts when I laugh, asshole."

"OK. Listen. I may need you to move. Just a little bit. Gonna tie you off. Through your D-rings. Gonna remove your reserve chute first. Lean out just a skosh."

Thanasis stuck his butt out in the air, as far from the trunk of the snag as he could, leaned into his climbing rope, and prayed that the gaffs of his climbing spurs would continue to hold in the weathered wood. With one hand he gripped Charlie's harness while, with the other, he released the clips holding the reserve chute to the chest. He pushed the chute pack out from between Charlie and the snag, heard it fall to the ground. Charlie groaned but did not move.

Thanasis threaded the end of his jump partner's letdown rope through the two D-rings on the front of the helpless man's harness. He gingerly let go of the harness and used both hands to tie the rope to the rings. Sweat was running into his eyes as he finished the knot. He heard Charlie breathing rapidly through gritted teeth, the breathing interrupted every few seconds by a grunted "Unh."

"Hold on, buddy. We're nearly through tyin' you off. You don't have to move again." He thought about telling him to hold tight to the tree.

Thought better of it and tried to show optimism. "Hold that tree any way you want." He knew only the stob was holding Charlie in place.

Thanasis climbed a few feet above Charlie's head and passed the letdown rope over a thick branch and fastened it to the rope lead coming up from Charlie's harness, using a half hitch. He let the remaining rope uncoil to the ground and climbed back down to his jump partner.

"OK. You're tied off now."

"I can tell, 'cause I'm so fuckin' comfortable."

"I'm goin' down now to get the saw. I'll be back in a minute and cut it off."

"Cut what off?"

"Your dick, silly. Gonna auction it off to the women of McCall. You'll be a wealthy man."

"No, I'm serious. You're gonna cut the stob?" Charlie was quiet for a moment, his breathing sounding like short punches. "You know what you're doin?"

Thanasis hesitated, knew his buddy was worried, knew he could not kid the worry away. "It has to be done this way." He did not explain.

He found the saw and the Demerol in a first aid pack tied to a cargo chute. Thanasis was glad to see it was a hacksaw. *Thin enough to get between Charlie and the tree.* He checked the Demerol syringe. It looked ready to go, to the extent he could recall the first aid lectures and demonstration. *I hope the fucker works.*

He climbed back up the snag. He showed Charlie the saw and the Demerol. "We got tradin' goods. You're gonna like both of 'em. The Demerol will be your favorite. So you're gonna get it first. I'm gonna put it in your butt, just like they show us. I'll cut a slit in your jumpsuit so the canvas won't bend the needle. Then I'll just shove it through your jeans. Ready?"

"Just give it to me. I'm fadin' fast, Dr. Asshole." Thanasis saw a faint smile, then tired lines again. Within minutes after pushing the syringe plunger Thanasis saw a much bigger smile, a sloppy smile, on Charlie's face.

"I'm gonna cut the stob now. Right up against the trunk of the tree. I'm gonna slide the saw between you and the tree. If I hurt you with my sawin' let me know by yellin' out. Hear?" He looked at the grinning Charlie. *You're not goin' to feel shit are you, buddy.*

The tiny teeth of the hacksaw cut through the hard branch quickly. Thanasis glanced at the silent Charlie once or twice. The branch was two inches thick at the base and covered with blood. Little of the limb was visible. With the last cut of the hacksaw blade through the stob Charlie dropped several inches down the trunk of the snag, taking up slack in the material of the letdown rope. He groaned with the movement. Thanasis' heart raced at the unexpected drop and tensioning of the rope. Everything held and he blew out air, took in more.

Thanasis positioned himself to climb down. He held the loop of climbing rope, arms stretched out in front of him, and saw his hands covered with blood. *Hope I didn't fuck you up. Don't bleed out on me Charlie. Please don't goddamn bleed out.*

When he reached the ground he grabbed the letdown rope trailing from the branch above Charlie. He checked the jumper's position on the other end of the rope, braced himself and slowly pulled, releasing the half hitch. Charlie dropped again, this time taking up slack from the released knot.

Thanasis took his jump partner's weight in his arms until they were fully extended, then wrapped his legs around the trunk of the snag to anchor himself. He lowered Charlie to the ground, hand over hand. Charlie came to rest on his back, arms at his side, nearly unconscious. The crotch of his jump suit was dark with blood. Thanasis removed the injured man's helmet and pillowed his head on a jump jacket. He cut away a section of the jumpsuit pants to examine the wound, check the extent of bleeding. He was relieved to see that the stob seemed to be stopping flow of blood from the jagged wound. He hoped it was doing the same thing inside Charlie's belly.

Thanasis moved his jump partner onto one of their sleeping bags, covered him with the other. He called the still circling Travelair and reported. "He's pretty uncomfortable. Pulse feels OK, about like mine, a little faster. Not much bleeding now he's on the ground. What's the story on the rescue jump?"

"The Ford's in the air. Ten jumpers and a litter. They'll be here in an hour. Because of the kind of injury there's a medical doctor gonna jump with them. You should go out with 'em. We'll jump another crew on the fire. We don't have much fuel left so we're leavin' ya." The spotter paused and continued. "Thanasis, I seen what you did. Good job. And the doc says leavin' the stob in him was the right thing. See you in McCall."

Within half an hour of the rescue jump the doctor had examined Charlie and pronounced him ready for travel. "Won't know the internal injuries until we get him into a hospital and do the necessary surgery. But it doesn't look like it hit any arteries and there's not much bleeding. Good blood pressure and pulse. You young fellas are healthy. And lucky." He asked the patient "Ready to go?"

Charlie said "Yes, but you haven't said how you liked your first jump?"

The doctor hesitated, then said "Just like takin' a shit." He grinned sheepishly, added "A smokejumper told me to say that." The nearest jumper slapped the doctor on the back, dislodging his hard hat. The rescue crew lifted Charlie onto the Stokes litter and lined up for the trip out, one man on each side at the middle of the litter, one man on each end in a shoulder harness. The rest of the crew prepared to lead the way, clearing trail with saws and axes.

The lead man on the trail crew walked over to Charlie with a two-man saw in his hands. "Before I leave, you want to help me to cut that snag down? We'll catch up with 'em."

Charlie seemed to think about it. "Naw. No hard feelings. I would like it, though, if somebody carved my name on it."

Thanasis took out his pocket knife. "I'll take care of that." He picked up the climbing spurs and looked up at the snag. "I know just where it goes. How do you want it?"

"How 'bout 'The Dago was here.' All caps. Can you do italics?"

CHAPTER SIXTEEN

"Norris, did we screw this up?"

Norris Wright and his CIA boss, Major Casey, were having lunch in the Senate Cafeteria, seated away from everyone, trying not to look like CIA agents dealing with a potential embarrassment. They looked like congressional staff catching a bite to eat. Norris knew that "we" referred to him and no one else.

"No."

"Then why do we have a security breach?"

"Could be you have a funny definition of security breach."

The two CIA agents had a long history. It permitted them an easy familiarity and, on matters of substance, caustic argument regardless of their reporting relationship. Norris reported to Casey, who had recruited him into the CIA from a smokejumper base following brief service together in OSS during what Norris called 'War Two.' He and Casey expected 'War Three.' They thought their country was already in it, and had behaved accordingly throughout their careers.

Their own theatre of undeclared war was Southeast Asia, increasingly so since the fall of the French. Support of Tibetans in their struggle against the Chinese also had their attention. Most of their relationship was structured around air support of foreign surrogates fighting U.S. wars against the threat of communism.

"There isn't a security breach," Norris continued. "The Company hired the Project Leader of the McCall smokejumper unit to run our airborne infiltration and resupply operation. The fellow we hired to do that told the Payette Forest supervisor, his boss, he was quitting to go to work for us. That's all he did. Neither of 'em know how or where we're going to use smokejumpers. Just that we plan to. At some undisclosed time and place. Maybe. Nothing was disclosed about capacity or plans or operations."

Norris stopped, then hurried on before he could be interrupted. "The whole world knows our government trains smokejumpers. Everybody knows smokejumpers drop things out of airplanes to people waiting down below. Thousands of people saw that Hollywood deal, *Red Skies of Montana,* popcorn and everything. Filmed right on the Missoula smokejumper base. Hell, the Forest Service jumped four guys on the Ellipse, between the White House and the Washington Monument, so President Truman and anyone wanted to look could see what they do." Norris was leaning hard across the table, his tie trailing in his Senate bean soup. He was pointing a finger at Casey, emphasizing. Casey was laughing and pointing back.

Folding a napkin around his dripping tie Norris worked to control what had become a colorful bloat of broth and silk.

"Any other points, Norris?"

"Sorry, Major. I got a little expansive. I'll just say this and it's probably all I should have said. I don't think we should have withdrawn the offer. Now the guy doesn't have a job in either place."

Casey responded. "Too bad. The point is we have a requirement, for good reason, that nobody knows who works for us. He ignored the requirement. Breached it."

"These are people as close-mouthed and patriotic as you can be. But they have their own code. They don't eat their own." Norris hesitated over his next thought. *Not sure that's true of the Company.* He let it go. "The jumper boss told the man he worked for he was quitting and why and that's all he did."

Casey sat back. "OK. Let's say I'm persuaded. You win. Know what you win?"

"Kinda depends on what win means."

"You think the smokejumpers are special? Then you're going to run 'em. You make sure they get trained, have what they need, know and keep the rules. When they are asked about us or what they do, they know nothing. Period. What they are getting into is going to become visible and controversial . . . and non-attributable. They can't be visible or controversial. They don't exist. We're coming to hard places. You're going to push them out the door. Make sure they're ready. Without 'em there's no Third Option." He stopped again and continued. "And you can't love them," each word emphasized.

Lunch ended with somber small talk. They left Capitol Hill, traveling separately.

The sunken tie had been his favorite. Norris dropped it in a trash can and hailed a taxi for National Airport. He was headed for Saigon on routine Company business. In the taxi, away from Casey, his mood was elevated. He was imagining his new assignment. It put him in the middle of War Three. A black world of aircraft without tail numbers. Aerial resupply of exotic, stubborn people waiting in ambush for Communist armies. Training remnants of the Middle Ages in the generation-skipping technology of modern war. Clan-driven, inborn war, barefoot and on muleback. Non-nuclear and deniable. What covert ops intellectuals called the Third Option, counterinsurgency by surrogate.

As he flew west he began to organize what he needed to do. He identified the "hard places." The names fell out of the communiqués and doctrines of what he realized, once again with pleasure, had become his profession. *Tibet. Laos. Cuba. Congo.*

He compiled a short list of training bases, security essential. The names came again, like a familiar language. *Saipan naval facility. Black site in the Philippines. Camp Hale in Colorado. The Farm.*

He defined potential operations sites through a matrix of aircraft range, base security, and access to fuel and maintenance. *Kadena on Okinawa. The old Japanese base in Thailand, what's the name, yeh, Takhli. Kurmitola in East Pakistan. Guatemala or Panama?* He thought about aircraft, knew he would have to find out more. *C-118s and B-17s from Civil Air Transport and Western Enterprises. Range issues. Short-takeoff-and-landing issues, what are the new STOL aircraft. Got to find out what the Air Force is working on.*

Then he thought about his smokejumpers. They were his. Casey had said as much. *Didn't he say that? What did he say? No Third Option without 'em?* Thinking about smokejumpers he felt stymied. The problem was recruiting. He knew they would all come. All he had to do was ask. All three hundred of them. He could empty every Forest Service jumper base if he wanted. What he needed, however, was a handful, selected in a closed book process. He was having difficulty imagining a hidden, selective, exclusionary process. How would he pull a few out of what was a tight group and keep it secret? What standards could he use they would not all meet? How would he exclude buddies when they were all about their buddies?

Norris left his scheduled flight at a west coast stop. He had decided to talk to a smokejumper about his recruiting problem. He knew from his smokejumper days before joining the CIA where he could find a good one. He rented a car and drove toward Missoula, Montana. After two days of drinking beer with Big Andy, his first jump partner on the Lolo National Forest, he broached the subject and made the offer.

"You'd be my first hire. Whadaya say?"

"You know you didn't have to drink beer with me for two days to get me to say yes. Guess you just like me."

"Man told me not to love anybody I hire for this job. So the beer was a bribe."

"Consider me bribed. What's to say no to. I'm makin' two bucks an hour and your bunch is gonna pay me eight hundred a month plus eight hundred for each flight I kick cargo. And it's seasonal? Work Asia in the winter and go back to smoke jumpin' in the summer? Perfect. Count me in. How many you hirin'?"

"Here's where I need your advice, Andy. Yeh, you got to earn your beer. I want about ten smokejumpers. For now. Maybe more later. I don't want to hire everybody out of one base. These are small bases in small towns. Ten and then more? That's gonna get noticed. This thing can't be noticed. It is secret. I'm talkin' national security secret. I'm not shitting you, Andy. Even the Chairman of the Senate Foreign Relations Committee doesn't know about this operation. I want to pick one or two guys out of each of the jumper bases. But I can't show up at every jumper base in the West. By the time I got to the fifth base I'd be leading a hundred car caravan. Here comes the man with the money!"

"Second thing is, how am I gonna find the ones I want. I can't have 'em fill out personnel forms and line up in the parking lot of a Salt Lake

City motel for interviews. How do I get the skinny on these guys? I gotta have some insight on 'em."

"Finally—and this one gives me the willies—how am I gonna keep a bunch of hard-drinking, story-telling, lover boys from sharing with everybody in every bar and whorehouse in the West that they are having the time of their lives. The first time one of 'em says 'Takhli' out loud all hell is gonna break loose. I'm not talkin' about somebody gettin' fired. I'm talkin' about nuclear war. The reason our wars are secret and deniable is so Russia and China won't drop the big one on us. It's that simple and that real."

Big Andy was cracking shells off peanuts, popping nuts into his mouth while he listened, staring at his beer bottle. He looked up when Norris stopped talking, swept peanut shells from the table with an oversized hand.

"Norris, you're workin' this much too hard. Keep it simple. Let the smokejumpers drive the recruitin' bus. You hire me and a couple of others I can vouch for. Then we make recommendations to you. Do we know everybody? No, we don't. But we know the ones you want to know. Not just from Missoula. You remember Silver City, New Mex? It's staffed two months a year with jumpers from bases all around the country. Only the big boys go there, before they go back to their home bases for the summer fire season. They do a lot of things in Old Mexico they don't talk about. I know 'em all. Let Silver City be where you recruit. You never have to show up, you'll get the right ones, just a few spread out over each of the different bases, and they'll lie to everybody but you."

"Sounds like a blackball operation run by Big Andy. Nothin' personal, Andy, but I don't think the Company would let me sublease the operation to you."

"Hell, I wouldn't be runnin' nothin'. By the time you have three smokejumpers selected the rest of the hires would be consensus between you and those already on board. Flip a coin on the tough decisions. Yeh, it would be a blackball, but one run by the group you're recruitin'. If they're gonna be back-to-back in some weird place I think you would want that. I know they would. We're not talkin' about how you run your operation. Just recruitment, and you have the final say who goes to work for you. How about a cold one? I'm fresh out of ideas and beer."

As they drank their next round Norris warmed to the idea of recruiting in the remoteness of the Gila National Forest. "OK. Say we do it that way. Who's your first recommendation?"

M.I.A.

The POW stood at attention in front of the uniformed interrogator. It was part of a ritual now, every session beginning the same way.

The Vietnamese officer sat in the only chair in the room, legs crossed, smoking a cigarette. He ignored the POW, appeared to be lost in thought. They faced each other in silence, the POW forbidden to look at the interrogator. When he finished the cigarette, the officer began asking questions.

"What did you do at the secret CIA base?"

"Now I have to ask. Which one you talkin' about? They have a bunch."

"I will remind you later that there is a 'bunch.' For now, I want you to tell me about the one at Marana, Arizona. What did you do there?"

"Well, we dated the girls at the local colleges in Tucson and hung out at a bar in the desert. The bar offered free beer any day the sun didn't shine. Never got a free beer."

The Vietnamese officer looked at the POW without expression, until the prisoner knew that he had probably made a mistake.

"Very amusing . . . I do not have to tell you that I will not accept any form of ridicule or evasion from you. If you do that again, the conversation will once again become . . . less comfortable. What did you do at Marana?"

"What we did there was invent things for the CIA."

"Who is 'we'?"

"Me and the other smokejumpers."

"What did you invent?"

"There was a bunch of things."

"Name them."

"The best one was the GPU."

"What is the GPU?"

"It's the Ground Proximity Unit. Mac was really the inventor."

"Tell me about Mac and the Ground Proximity Unit."

"Mac was a regular CIA case officer, not a smokejumper, but he was assigned to Air Branch. He didn't know about parachutes but he knew all about gettin' shot up makin' low level air drops. Ground fire in Laos was takin' a lot of our guys down, and Mac came up with this idea. The smokejumpers developed it, tested it, and manufactured thousands of 'cm."

"What idea did Mac have?"

"Ground impact system."

"What is that?"

"That was my exact question to Mac."

The interrogator stared at him in a way that made the POW hurry on.

"What Mac described is this. You drop a parachute cargo load to your troops from higher than where the commie 12.7 and other guns can reach the airplane. The parachute is reefed—that is, it is tied closed at the bottom so that it won't open. Like when you reef a sail on a boat, ya know, tie the sail closed to a boom."

"I know what reef means. Go on."

The POW noted the irritation in the interrogator's voice and focused his account. "A weight is attached to the parachute and it hangs below the chute on the end of a 180-foot nylon cord. The weight on the cord holds open an electrical switch mounted on the parachute."

The Vietnamese officer had taken out a pen and small notebook, was taking notes. "Say that again, just the part about the open switch."

The POW repeated the part about the switch and continued. "When the weight hits the ground, that takes the weight off the cord. Taking the weight off the cord allows the electrical switch to close. That completes a battery-powered electrical circuit. The electrical charge fires a cutting device that cuts the reef line and the parachute opens 150 feet above the ground."

"Did it work?" the interrogator asked.

"Fuckin' A. I personally dropped about a hundred GPUs every day out of Long Tieng. Supplied Meo positions we couldn't otherwise hold. Kicked ass."

The Vietnamese officer seemed hesitant, edgy when he asked his next question. "Has the GPU been used in the American War in Vietnam?"

"Oh yeh. The smokejumpers manufactured about six thousand GPUs a month in the Marana parachute loft when things were hot in Laos and Nam. U.S. Army and Marines were resupplied in Nam—at A Shau Valley, at Khe Sanh—with the GPU."

The POW and the interrogator stared at each other in silence until the Vietnamese officer said "We had them surrounded you know."

"I know."

"We won both battles," the Vietnamese said.

"Not by our body count." *And we didn't even count all the bodies you dragged away.* The POW kept the last thought to himself. He was knocked to the floor anyway.

The interrogator stood over him and said "We did not leave the field of battle. Either time."

"A lot of you did. In bags." The POW saw the kick to his face coming, wished the officer's English was not quite so good.

CHAPTER SEVENTEEN

CIA recruitment of smokejumpers for covert operations began at Silver City, New Mexico, soon after Norris' meeting with Big Andy. Those chosen were flown to Washington, D.C., tickets purchased with more cash than they were used to outside of a craps game. Each jumper was given an intelligence test, a polygraph test, an assumed name, a bank account in that name, immunization shots, a cover story, and a briefing on why the CIA was about to begin night-time air drops of agents, arms, and gold to Tibetan resistance deep within that country's borders.

Questions were permitted.

Not everyone understood the geopolitical briefing on Tibet or the significance of the Dalai Lama or the problems with India that required use of an obscure World War II airstrip in East Pakistan and avoidance of Indian radar. "Don't the Indians hate the Chinese, wanna help us? What do you mean neutral?"

Not everyone understood the tax ramifications of covert income. "Now you've told me some of my income is gonna be cash under the table. You say the CIA will do the income tax returns for that piece of it. Does that get credited to my Social Security?"

Not everyone understood the necessity of a cyanide ampoule strapped to a cargo-kicker's arm. "Hell, if I can walk out of the Middle Fork of the Salmon without a map or gun I can walk out of Tibet. You *are* givin' me a map and a gun?" The question was an assertion. The response was that there were no maps of Tibet and "of course you will be provided a weapon."

Within months the first half-dozen smokejumpers hired by Norris were in Okinawa, staging in and out of Kurmitola, East Pakistan, by the phases of the winter moon. Winter because navigation and aerial resupply ended with beginning of the monsoon season in May. The moon because CIA pilots could navigate at night from the three thousand-foot Kurmitola runway out over the Tibetan plateau and return only by its full light. The snow-covered Himalayas flaring in white silhouette beneath the moon gave the night-long flights the look of silent spectacle.

The discomfort of flights in the C-118 drop plane offset the beauty of the Tibetan night. The underpowered four-engine plane was far from ideal for dropping cargo. Paperlegs sat in a bar on the Kokusai strip in Naha, Okinawa, and counted off the shortcomings of the CIA-owned aircraft for three smokejumpers, Charlie, Dog and Dooley, newly recruited to the CIA.

"Basically it's an old DC-6 made for carryin' passengers on commercial flights. That means you can't open the airplane's doors in flight. So you take a door off if you want to drop cargo. Know what the temperature is at twenty thousand feet in winter time in Tibet? Freeze the balls off a brass monkey. After seven hours flyin' to the drop zone with an open door you're the brass monkey. And the door is on the side of the plane, so you're rasselin' five thousand- pound pallets the length of the airplane on rollers so you can push 'em out the side. And you're doin' the rasselin' with an oxygen bottle hangin' around your neck. Then the pallet straps hang up on steel ribbing inside the fuselage. You have to cut it free so you can push the damn thing some more. Then you worry you've cut the static line that's supposed to open the cargo chute."

"Ever do that, Paper? Cut the static line?" Dog asked.

"Never did."

"What you think of the Tibetans?"

"They're all legs and lungs. Hard workin', walk forever, fearless about heights and knife fightin'. Only had to throw one of 'em out the door of the airplane."

"You didn't!"

"Did."

The audience waited. Paper continued without being asked "Why would you do that?"

"When we drop an agent with cargo at night we tie the pallet and the jumper together with a three hundred-foot line so they don't lose each other in the dark. One night we push the pallet out the door and the Tibetan guy tied to it decides he is not goin' to jump. He's standin' there shakin' his head and the three hundred-foot line is peeling off his chest. For some reason he's forgotten he's tied to a five thousand-pound cargo pallet which is now fallin' through the dark. He doesn't realize that the moment he and the cargo pallet are three hundred feet apart it is goin' to pull him through the door frame or some other part of the fuselage. If he breaks my airplane I am goin' to end up in a Chinese prison, at best, and the CIA is gonna say they never heard of me. So I threw him out the door. Saved his life. Unless the Chinese were waitin' for him. Sometimes they are."

Paperlegs paid his bar bill and prepared to leave. "Where's your buddy, Thanasis? Thought he'd be with you."

"He's in love. Otherwise he'd be here. We're gonna have our picture taken with some of these Japanese bar girls sittin' on our laps. Show him what he's missin' out on."

"Shouldn't have any trouble arrangin' that. C'mon, Dooley." Paperlegs walked toward the door with Dooley.

"Hey, Paper. Any truth to the story going around you were involved in gettin' the Dalai Lama out of Tibet last spring?"

"Never met the man, Charlie."

"Not what I asked."

When they were alone, looking over the bar girls, Dog said "Thanks for sharing Thanasis' letter. Sounds like he and Maria are getting pretty tight. Think we'll ever see him in this business?"

"Not likely, the way he goes on about her. Only thing would bring him into the CIA is I'd have to hang myself up in a snag by my nuts again. Not doin' that. Not givin' him another chance doin' surgery on me. Least not in Tibet. Think those girls would like to see my scar?"

"They already seen it." Dog nodded toward the door through which Paperlegs and Dooley had left, and continued talking. "Dooley sure ain't Thanasis. Shit, I don't mind Dooley hangin' out with us but he doesn't know *how* to hang. I'm gonna write a letter to Thanasis and tell him to get his ass out here. Maybe I'll write Maria. Hell, she finds out how much we're makin' she'll *send* his ass out here."

By Norris' calculation and generally accepted Cold War standards, the CIA Air Branch operation in Tibet was a success. The Peoples Republic of China committed 150,000 troops to chasing and fighting the guerillas of Tibet for three years. By the beginning of 1960 there were a dozen smokejumpers on Okinawa dropping people and arms into the fight. The C-118 had been replaced by an unmarked C-130 Hercules, the newest Air Force cargo plane, and Kurmitola had been traded in for the more modern and commodious Takhli, Thailand base. His smokejumpers had their own safe house at Takhli.

In the spring of 1960, however, those things pretty much went to hell. An American spy plane was shot down over Russia. The pilot was prisoner of an enemy nation armed with nuclear weapons. The president ordered the end of foreign overflights, including the CIA supply operation in Tibet.

Norris and Casey met within the week. The subject was the shootdown and unused smokejumpers. Norris had a plan but he needed approval. He thought he knew how the wind was blowing for Air Branch but he could only be sure if he heard it from Washington.

The two men sat at the bar in the Zebra Room on Wisconsin Avenue in Northwest Washington, D.C. It was a neighborhood watering hole for two groups that otherwise seldom met. It was geographically convenient for bootless bureaucrats and American University students. The CIA agents arrived at the bar separately. They felt comfortable posing as members of the former group, bumping into each other from the neighborhood.

"You look like a juicer to me," Casey said.

"And you look like you might run a tab here." Norris raised his glass to Casey. He looked around the dark room. "If I were sensitive I would call the Zebra Room cozy. I'm not sensitive and it doesn't look like any other patron is either. Why meet here?"

"People who don't want to be bothered go to this bar. The Company has a safe house around the corner. They use the Zebra Room for meeting people they're keeping in the safe house. Whether the guest is sensitive or not."

They drank in silence in the manner of people who don't want to be bothered. After a while Norris raised the subject of their meeting.

"Speaking of tabs and juicers, I have a dozen smokejumpers on the Company payroll hanging out in the Far East and threatening to exhaust the world supply of Singha and San Miguel before this stand-down is over. I'll summarize what I want to do with them. I want to relocate them, put them through full CIA paramilitary training, and use them, when they aren't in the field, to develop and test new techniques and materials for air supply. These guys are very inventive and don't mind getting their ass in a crack. I don't need more people in that role than I have now. To fill the need for kickers in the future—and I assume there is a future—I would change the hiring from direct hire by the Company to contract hiring by Air America and Intermountain Aviation. Kickers with smokejumper background wouldn't need further training for most air delivery operations."

"That it?"

"Yes. But before I propose any of this I would like to get your views on this U-2 shootdown. Right now I'm sitting on my hands. Am I still in business?"

"You're in business. The president still thinks Laos is the next domino and he will make sure his successor understands that. Tibet will never go away. You haven't dealt with your last yak butter. Bet on it. Biggest thing coming down the road is Cuba. It's still under study but the Company and your smokejumpers will be in it if it goes. Where are you thinking about relocating your jumpers?"

"Marana, Arizona."

CHAPTER EIGHTEEN

A French priest traveling to Meo villages reported to his superiors that the Meo are "allergic to all kind of authority. They are stubborn, capable of great eruptive anger, cruel, do not like to lose, give no quarter, reject assimilation into any civilized group." Many held that view of the Meo.

Norris read the notes and reports of the cleric as he flew, stop after stop, across the Pacific, along with hundreds of other pages collected within the Agency about the people he was to meet in their mountains, to assess, to recruit. He did not feel hope or enthusiasm.

This was, after all, about defending Laos. The Meo were not an obvious choice. True to their character, they had not integrated into the new Lao homeland, though they had more than a century to do so and a receptive host. They were different than the Lao in every respect—ethnically, culturally, religiously, linguistically. They were unrelated to and cared little for the lowland Lao who lived to the south, along the Mekong River, and who governed Laos through a royal family. He fumed about the likely failure. *Why does anyone in the Company think the Meo would risk everything to defend a separate, different other?* Norris did not think it would work and was in a funk about his assignment.

Washington wanted to try. They had no other option. Demographics and geography drove the choice. Half the population of three million were lowland Lao, most of them subsistence farmers. Jack, an old smokejumper and CIA asset who had been in the country to assist U.S. Special Forces training the Royal Lao Army, put it strongly to Norris. "Lowland Lao soldiers? Worthless as tits on a boar."

Another third of the population were Lao Theung. Original inhabitants of Indochina, their devolution over the centuries led them to be called *kha*, slave. The dark-skinned, wide-cheekboned Lao Theung had joined Lao military units in response to many calls to arms. With few exceptions their service was unremarkable. Their officers drank too much.

That left the mountain people, mostly the Meo. Nearly half the thirteen hundred-mile Laos-Vietnam border, tracking up the Annamite chain of mountains, passed through the territory of the Meo.

Norris, nearing Udorn, Thailand, on his flight from Saigon, thought about the briefing by the Saigon station. The Meo borderland, defined by jungle and mountains, would have significance in the coming Vietnam conflict. The intelligence shared with him in Saigon said that Hanoi had lost patience with the pace of reunification of North and South Vietnam. The North Vietnam Politburo and Central Committee had signaled its South Vietnam agents to achieve reunification "by all appropriate means other than peaceful."

Hanoi asserted control over the Viet Cong insurgency. It began construction of the Ho Chi Minh Trail through the Meo borderland. The Trail was nothing to the Meo. It was, with other events more specific to Laos, of great moment to those in Washington seeking to define the U.S. response in Laos.

The events specific to Laos, trigger to a rock fall of larger events, were small and quiet. It was only a minor military coup in the administrative capitol, Vientiane.

The Pathet Lao and their North Vietnamese ally rushed to the side of those in the coup. They seized the Plain of Jars and Sam Neua and Xieng Khouang provinces, the heartland of the Meo. They were immediately supported by the Soviet Union, Ilyushin IL 14 and Lisunov Li 2 military cargo aircraft landing daily, unloading AK-47s and the larger stuff of war.

The response of President Kennedy was secret, known only to a few within the nation. He ordered covert war in Laos by the Central Intelligence Agency. Without expectation as to what it would achieve, he secretly sent U.S. Special Forces troops to South Vietnam. The task, in the language of bureaucracy carrying out secret instructions, was the conduct of "denied area missions," unconventional operations in Laos and North Vietnam. The president wanted lethal but totally deniable resistance while he sought agreement with Russia on a neutral Laos. The final stand was not to come in landlocked Laos, but neither would Laos be the first domino.

The secret orders came with cash, and Norris was carrying part of it to Udorn and beyond in C-ration boxes. The boxes were the subject of his meeting with the Udorn CIA station chief.

The station chief reached across his desk and shook Norris' hand. "How you like that Helio Courier? Take off and land on a Thai hooker's belly. You got cash for me? What we're doin' only works on cash."

Norris and a Thai aide lifted several C-ration boxes across the desk.

"How much?"

"Nobody told me," Norris replied. "Just said three boxes to Udorn and one across the river, upcountry to my Meo contact."

"Good."

Norris wasn't sure the station chief meant it. He was trying to think why that was when another man entered the room. He was bespectacled, serious, dressed in pressed short-sleeved white shirt and creased trousers. He looked like a neat, self-possessed, claims adjuster.

"Norris, meet Bill. He's with the Company. Been in Thailand ten years trainin' the Thai Police Aerial Reinforcement Unit, the PARU, in unconventional warfare in case the Chinese invade. Gone native, married a Thai woman. Well connected in Thailand." Turning to Bill the Chief said "Norris is goin' across the river to meet the Meo you got together. Vang Pao and some of his, that right?"

Norris thought he saw Bill flinch at the reference to his marriage, wondered if that was his real name and background. The two men, introduced, nodded to each other, shook hands.

"Yes," Bill said. "Norris will be flown in an Air America H-34 to Padong, a mountaintop site about seventeen kilometers south of the Plain of Jars. It was chosen by Vang Pao as the site for this meeting. He wants to show it off. It's where he plans to train his men. It would be the central point for parachute resupply of the Meo. Both the troops and their families." There was no flair, just facts, brevity, competence.

This was the first Norris had heard of Meo families.

"What's contemplated by our government is guerilla operations," Norris said. He thought *What we want is death and destruction on all sides for as long as it takes.* He did not say that. "I can't imagine the Meo *maquis* taking their families on ambush or cratering roads while stationed with children on some mountaintop. What in hell's the deal with families at an operational site?"

Bill responded without hesitation. "The deal is opium. If we take the Meo men to fight they can't grow or sell opium. It's their cash crop. Without it the Meo can't survive. They grow most of the opium traded in Asian markets. The French colonial administration used to buy it all. Now the Lao government, mostly the military kingpins, along with a few Corsicans and Chinese merchants, buy the Meo opium. What we are proposing to do is going to screw all that up in ways we haven't even thought about. The only thing for sure is we are going to be in the business of feeding every Meo family that sends a man to shoot Communists. Aerial resupply in spades. Your game."

This was unexpected news. Norris expressed no surprise, just said "Yes." He was doubling, tripling numbers in his head, wanted to make notes.

"Norris, you'll be working closely with Bill. Your job is going to be marryin' the Meo and the Thai PARU. They are going to be training the Meo in unconventional war. The PARU are good at it, thanks to Bill. He's been trainin' them at Hua Hin on the Gulf of Siam. We're buildin' a new base for 'em at Phitsanulok, north of Takhli. They've worked for us in riggin' and packin' cargo for our Tibet operation. The marriage is gonna' be interestin'. The PARU are the best physical specimens on earth and skilled in the best unconventional warfare on the same planet. The Meo are a bunch of skinny rednecks in black pajamas who have never seen a wheel."

The station chief was looking at Norris, waiting for some reaction.

"What weapons are we supplying them?" Norris asked.

"Project Momentum is what DOD is callin' this show. They are funding it through the CIA." He patted the C-ration boxes. "The weapons to be supplied are M1 rifle, .30-caliber BAR, 60-millimeter mortar, 3.5-inch rocket launcher. Basic stuff left over from World War II and Korea."

Next morning Norris and his Thai military aide climbed into the H-34. The president of the United States had ridden in the Marine Corps version many times, waving to small crowds on each occasion. The affection of the Marine crews for the last piston-engine military helicopter had been part of Kennedy's decision mix in transferring sixteen of them to Air America for the Laos war that was not a war. Norris, still concerned about what he had heard with respect to the Meo, was nevertheless excited about flight on a war machine, even if it was civilian VIP flight. The metallic taste in his mouth was familiar.

They landed on a mountaintop, some of it recently cleared with chain saws. A few small square buildings had been put up at the edge of the clearing. Norris saw split bamboo walls and thatch roofs, houses built directly on the ground, without windows. *Built to be dismantled, carried,* he thought.

Taking his cue from Bill, he wore clean, pressed shirt and pants. He stood in the tall aircraft, straightened his clothes. He moved toward the door that had been opened by an Air America crewman and walked down the steps from the helicopter, the aircraft still in Marine Corps green but without markings.

Ten paces in front of him was a short round-faced man dressed in khaki fatigues and a bush hat. Standing at attention, the man saluted him. Norris returned the salute. Then, at the suggestion of Bill, he gave a *wai*, the traditional Lao/Thai greeting. Palms together, hands raised upward, fingertips below his nose, he gave a small bow. A gesture of respect for the Meo military leader, Vang Pao.

The two men went immediately to one of the bamboo houses and began a discussion in English. They sat at a table and two chairs positioned on the stamped earth floor so that they looked out at a distant mountain through an open door. There was a fire pit and a bamboo platform in the living area. Vang Pao talked about two things, Meo killing Vietnamese and American contribution to the killing.

"Forever. That is how long the Vietnamese have lusted for Laos. The lust of empty bellies for rice. A hundred years ago, when the Meo were new here, the king in Luang Prabang asked us to fight a Vietnamese invasion. We defeated them then. We are ready again."

Norris tested the younger man across the table. "They have better weapons now. They will come in thousands. In Soviet tanks."

"You will give us even better weapons. Their numbers do not matter. The tanks do not matter." The small man grinned. He pointed toward the parked helicopter. "There are no roads."

Norris continued his argument. "Even the Chinese no longer fight the Vietnamese. Too tough."

Vang Pao responded "Meo have killed many more Chinese than the Vietnamese have."

Norris countered "This time the Vietnamese do not want Laos. It is something more important. They want their country back. For a united Vietnam they will make every effort, spend everything. They will build roads. To the base of this mountain. To any mountain in Meo territory. When you see the roads you must leave that mountain or die. The Meo have not seen such war and you must not think you can fight the tanks and cannon. They will understand that they must crush you, like the *fackee* at Dien Bien Phu, and they will spend every one of their young men to do it."

Vang Pao shook his head. "The Americans cannot afford to lose Laos. They have given more military assistance to this country than any in the world. They will make an even greater effort than the Vietnamese. They will give us airplanes."

The small man's confidence in the Meo and their resolve to fight for their mountains—and his belief in Americans—told Norris that Washington had lucked out. They had chosen the right people to fight the surrogate war, the Third Option.

The same things also worried him. *He doesn't get it. The Meo will lose if the Vietnamese push. Whatever we do. For us the whole operation is deniable, reversible, and he doesn't know that. Can't conceive that.*

For the first time it came to Norris. Maybe he had to tell him. At least say it. So the blood was not on his hands.

"As soon as we start to drop guns and food to you this mountain will be nothing but a target. Why do you choose this mountain? The Vietnamese will come here in force."

Vang Pao smiled again, patiently, as if explaining to a child. "There are no roads. It will take them three days to get here. Three days after the Americans parachute arms and food to us. In three days the Meo will be trained. First day, how to use rifles. Second day, how to use mortars and howitzers. Third day, training in ambush, trip wires."

Norris could not believe his ears. The brief, overnight, rudimentary training Vang Pao was describing could not possibly create an army that would match up with the Peoples Army of Vietnam. The PAVN was the best army in Southeast Asia, well led, well equipped with the most modern Soviet and Chinese weapons, highly motivated, tested and proven by their war with the French. He looked at the Thai colonel, his aide, standing several feet away from them. The colonel, a member of the PARU, made a small nod, affirmed that creating the Meo army would be done as Vang Pao had said.

Norris looked away, out the front door. The open area in which the helicopter had landed had filled with Meo. Men, women, and children. All were barefoot. All were dressed in black, the women's dark dresses adorned with bright needlework, green and fuscia, and old French silver coins. Mothers carried children on their backs in colorful slings. The men carried crossbows and homemade muzzle-loading flintlock rifles without stocks. Some held nothing but machetes.

Norris made up his mind. He motioned to the Thai colonel to join them. "I want you to repeat what I say. In his language. I want to make sure he understands."

He looked at Vang Pao and spoke slowly, with pauses for translation. "From the day you start—on this mountain or wherever you choose to fight—you will have Americans with you. And arms and money. More than you have ever seen." He paused, leaned forward toward Vang Pao. "There will also be a day when the Americans leave. You will be alone. Without arms or money. Get ready for it. If the Vietnamese are still here, they will try to destroy the Meo for what you have cost them and because they know they cannot govern the Meo. The Meo must be prepared to leave. On foot through the mountains of Sayaboury province, across the Mekong into Thailand. The Vietnamese will not be able to follow you." He paused again. "You must have a plan. Sayaboury or a better one."

Vang Pao was frowning. He pursed his lips, nodded, not at Norris, but into a shapeless space.

Within a month, at Vang Pao's urging, most of the Meo clans had agreed to war in support of the king and the Americans. Within days of the Meo pledge smokejumpers were in the back of Air America airplanes kicking food and arms—"rice and hard rice"—to ten thousand Meo gathered on Padong.

CHAPTER NINETEEN

Tidewater Virginia is rich in history. Colonial Williamsburg, the Yorktown defeat of the British, the skeletons of Cold Harbor, antebellum plantations and slave quarters. All open to historians. On a peninsula between the James and York rivers, concealed by native oak and pine and the assumed name Camp Peary, is a rumored CIA facility. Most of those called to it name it "The Farm." It is without history and not open in any sense.

A dozen smokejumpers were sent to The Farm for CIA paramilitary training. They came secretly and in disguise. Their first trip there was in a bus, owned by the Company, from Washington, D.C. to Richmond, Virginia, a city on the James upstream from The Farm. The talk behind blackened bus windows was about what in the world could take six months of training.

"I mean, Dog, we did the whole smokejumper training in *three weeks*."

"Charlie, did anybody in McCall ever teach you how to kill a Chinaman with your bare hands? That's got to take a month all by itself. Did Moose or Barney teach you any secret codes? They don't even know any secret codes. Anybody in all of Idaho ever show you how to set a Ojibwa bird snare or poison a secret agent you're fuckin'? Wake up, man. This is a whole 'nother level."

"But six months?"

"Company is signin' checks the whole time."

"OK. Life is good." Charlie changed the subject. "Speakin' of the good life, what you think Thanasis and Maria are doin'?"

"What you think, fool?"

"He's sure dropped out. Think they're gonna get married?"

"I suppose. You wanna help 'em pick out furniture?"

"Stop cuttin' me, Dog. I wish the Black Man was along on this." The nickname was a loose translation of his Greek surname, Mavros.

"Sorry. Me, too."

The jumpers got off the bus in Richmond as members of a college wrestling team, athletes and coaches. Most wore athletic warm-up jackets and carried duffel bags marked in school colors saying COUGARS. They checked into a cheap hotel fit for low-budget collegians. Over the next forty-eight hours they checked out, in twos and threes, and disappeared as instructed into cars heading by various routes to Camp Peary. Dog called their final transportation "bank robber cars. You're gonna rob a bank you steal an old oxidized blue car nobody can remember or describe. That's your getaway car. Now this clunker we're ridin' in fits the bill. CIA has bank robbers on its payroll."

Inside the high chain-link fences of The Farm they passed old buildings. Some looked like the World War II Seabee barracks they were. Others looked like the abandoned homes of relocated black families. As soon as they arrived at the base headquarters the jumpers were assigned to a single barracks without other occupants. When all the jumpers had checked in they met with Norris in what looked like a classroom.

"Welcome to The Farm," he said. He knew each of the jumpers he was addressing, had personally selected them. "While you're here you are going to be participating in the CIA paramilitary training that every agent goes through. Not all of it will take place at The Farm. Some of it will be at a new training base in North Carolina. That's our bomb school. Some of it will be at Fort Sherman, Panama. Escape and survival. You'll eat snakes and run out of water, most likely get captured. There will be other places. Your Morse Code training will be on Okinawa. Some of you have already been there. Any questions so far?"

"Will there be any jump training?"

"Don't you know everything about jumping yet, Charlie?" Laughter, but over quickly. Many had the same question.

"I mean specialty stuff."

"Yes. I know you all are interested in the wild side. There will be some free falls and there will be night jumps. Many of you have no experience with that. On the other hand you all know stuff that CIA jump instructors don't. You will be called upon to contribute your experience. Anything else?"

"Do we have to do calisthenics?"

"Yes, Dog. Many of the guys who will be goin' through the program with you will not be as fit as you. For example, there are a number of downtown lawyers goin' through the same training. You may not need it, but you have to do the same PT as everybody else. Calisthenics, without hangovers."

There were boos and rank comments about the CIA.

"While we're on that subject. There is no prohibition on drinking while you are in the program. But drunkenness is not going to be accepted. It's a basis for throwing you out. Instructors will be looking for reasons to throw a few of you out. Just for the sake of control. Understand? Any objections?"

There was silence.

"Hearing none I assume you are on board. One other thing. You all seem to get in fist fights wherever you go. If it happens here, that nonsense will get you thrown out of the Company. Period. Whether it is among yourselves or with others. Whether you stay or go is up to you. Any questions?"

Again there was silence.

"Now, I'm going to say something about the others, the other CIA trainees in this program. What I say stays in this room." Norris paused, wondered again how his comments would be taken. "They're different than you. Some come from the learned professions. Doctors and lawyers and engineers. Many have gone to Ivy League schools. Some come from wealth and know the leaders of the country personally." Norris coughed, pretended to shuffle some papers. "Most of you on the other hand are rough stock. You think so and so do I. Some of you never went to college. Some haven't been off the ranch, your lives all cows and catch twine. Some went to smoke jumping because you didn't have a dollar to your name. And some don't know who the hell the Secretary of State is or what he's paid to do." He heard a few chairs moving.

"You know I don't care about any of that. Those things don't mean the others are better than you or that you're better than them. It doesn't mean they are smarter than you. It doesn't mean they aren't. They won't be able to do things that are second nature to you. And vice versa. Any questions before I go on?"

A boy from a Montana ranch asked "We got girl singers here?"

"I'm not sure what that means. But it probably relates to what I want to say. You and they are different in ways that will cause you to hold them in disdain and cause them to hold you in disdain. I can't tell you or them not to. But in order for this service to function, you have to let it pass, look the other way. Accept them and get accepted. Do that and just get your job done. If you can't, you're out of here."

There was silence among the jumpers, but affirmative nodding of heads and some thumbs up. Then they were all looking at the Montana ranch hand, joining in a chorus of "What the hell is a girl singer?"

"It's them Ivy Leaguers. You seen it. A guy does a lot of posturin'. To impress you and women. You know 'em when you see 'em. I ain't met him, but the Secretary of State probably is a girl singer."

Within days the jumpers were in a classroom with doctors and lawyers and engineers studying the use of tides, submarines, and zodiac boats. Difficult, until they were in the field. There, the rest was sport. They were used to swimming in White logging boots, not losing fire packs and tools in rapids fed by snow pack. The lazy York River in wet suits and fins, with a knife strapped below a knee and a pistol in a waterproof bag, was a hoot.

They were often surprised. Lecturers came to The Farm from outside the intelligence community, persons certified as renowned in their subject by both the Ivy League graduates and Dog. They listened without note-taking to oddly compelling talks colored by personal tales. They recognized the form as being from the same stock as smokejumper stories. The syllabus included "History of Communism", "Psychological and Security Underpinnings of Need to Know", "Covert Action Theory and Options", "Intelligence: Penetration vs. Machines—A New World."

Dog shared his opinion that it was better than anything at Columbia, "or any of your Ivy League schools." He was not challenged.

After a month two jumpers had been thrown out of the program for fighting, two American Indians accused of trying to scalp each other. One had called the other a "blanket-ass Indian." The response had been "the only blankets you know anything about is when you're tryin' to fuck your sister." All bad enough without alcohol. There had been alcohol. They left the program and drove back to the Blackfoot Reservation together.

The jumpers moved on. They traveled to another peninsula, ninety miles south of Camp Peary. It too had a military cover, Harvey Point Defense Testing Activity, and a classified status barring public access. Harvey Point, North Carolina, a spit of land on Albemarle Sound run by the United States Navy, housed the CIA training center for demolition, anti-personnel mines, trip wires, sensors, making shaped charges, acetylene cutting of steel, and other tools and skills of clandestine war. It had a four thousand-foot asphalt runway that did not appear on any aviation map.

The CIA trainees dressed in military camouflage fatigues and trained in small squads, moving from one site and subject to another at "The Point." Charlie and Dog spent their first day in a squad learning about the Army's M18 Claymore mine. A large instructor was holding a small rectangular jungle-green plastic case in front of him, lecturing. His hands threatened to cover the entire subject of his lecture.

"It weighs three and a half pounds. You could put a half dozen of 'em in a lawyer's briefcase and he'd never know the difference. It is loaded with a pound and a half of C-4 explosive."

The instructor bobbled the Claymore mine in his large hands and it fell to the hard ground of the gunnery range. He yelled "Oh Jesus!"

He grinned as he watched jumpers and lawyers dive to the ground, some on top of each other. He always enjoyed this part of his lecture.

"If you will get out of your pile I will explain that the Claymore mine does not explode on contact. I will show you how to hook up an electric charge to detonate this mine." He waited until they were standing and brushing themselves off.

"The C-4 explosive is important but that is not what does the damage. The Claymore is a big plastic shotgun. When detonated it drives seven hundred steel balls a hundred yards in one fan-shaped direction. It is a modern version of the grapeshot of Civil War cannon fired into advancing troops. It is intended to take out ten percent of an attacking force at one hundred yards. At half that distance kill rate will improve to thirty percent. The steel balls are similar in size and shape to .22 rifle projectiles. Each ball arrives at the target with fifty-eight foot-pounds of kinetic energy. That amount of kinetic energy is what is necessary to cause a lethal injury. You don't have to do the math. Some professor has already done that. All you have to do is point the Claymore."

He moved his large hands so that they covered only the sides of the green case. He extended his arms toward the training squad until they were able to see embossed lettering on the curved surface of the plastic case facing them. The letters said

FRONT
TOWARD ENEMY

"If you have any trouble aimin' the sonofabitch you should talk to your career counselor. You may be in the wrong line of work." Everyone was laughing. This was his favorite part of the lecture.

"We are now gonna have you fellas deploy this mine in its usual applications. Trail ambush. Anti-infiltration of your perimeter. Pursuit deterrent. Don't feel you are limited in your use of the Claymore directional mine by that short list. Remember, it is a big friggin' shotgun. You just can't hold it while you shoot it."

CHAPTER TWENTY

Three months into the CIA paramilitary training program the agent trainees flew to Fort Sherman. Located on the Atlantic side of Panama and the western bank of the canal, across Limon Bay from the city of Colon, Fort Sherman was a small collection of barracks and classrooms housing the U.S. Army's Jungle Operations Training Battalion on twenty-three thousand acres of tropical jungle. The jumpers never left the barracks and classrooms except for the jungle. The object in both venues was to train the candidates in escape, evasion, and survival.

The young Army officer in charge of their training was crew-cut, dressed in jungle camouflage uniform, trousers and boots bloused in the manner of airborne troops. He spoke to them casually.

"There won't be a written exam. But you damn well better listen to me. One hundred percent of the time. The final exam is this. We are going to dump you in the jungle without food or water. Then two hundred members of the Training Battalion are going to hunt you and chase you until you puke and give up. When you give up you will be sent back to your daddy's law office or to an Idaho brushfire with a letter thanking you for your time. You will have failed the final exam.

"The Training Battalion will be assisted by Choco Indian trackers. They are tribals who live in the Panama jungle. They can track an ant in the dark. The only advantage you will have is that one of the Chocos will teach you how to survive, to find food and water in the jungle. You will earn the right to continue in this program only if you return through the jungle to the Fort Sherman check-in station, your starting point, without being captured by members of the Training Battalion. Or the club-wielding Chocos." He stopped talking and glanced toward a doorway at the side of the classroom. "Just kidding about the clubs. But the rest of it is dead on. So listen up." He was pointing at the doorway.

"Anselmo, here, and I are going to give you a day's orientation starting now." A copper-colored man with straight black hair cut in a bob entered the room and faced them in silence. He was five feet tall, muscular and ageless. He stood before them naked except for a G-string, a glass bead necklace, and canvas boots. "Anselmo is the only Choco you will ever see. He will be in the jungle to help you, but only if you are in distress. We don't deal in body bags. The rest of the Chocos will be there, but you will not see them, even when they steal your hat."

Through an interpreter, Anselmo talked to them with a recurring smile, almost shy.

He described cutting arm-thick liana and other jungle vines to get water the vines carry. "It will run in your mouth until you can drink no more."

He described food from the Chagres River. "Fish, caiman, turtle, anaconda." He spoke of jungle animals that could be trapped and skinned and cooked. "Tapir, iguana, monkey. I will show you." He described the plants they could eat. "Coronza tree leaf. Palmetto. Yucca. Taro root. I will show you." Those things they could not eat, all the rest, were too numerous to name.

After half an hour of talk Anselmo left to prepare his survival demonstrations. The Army officer continued the orientation. "The escape and evasion trial is time driven. Even if you evade capture you fail the course if you do not get out of the jungle and back to Fort Sherman within twenty-four hours.

"We will take you into the jungle in the back of a truck. You will be off-loaded at the Chagres River, put on LCM landing barges and taken ten miles upriver. You will unload into the jungle. We will give you a compass heading for Sherman, because you won't know where the hell you are. Then you will wave goodbye to me and Anselmo.

"Time will be a problem. Jungle reduces visibility and makes movement slow and noisy. You can't afford noise. Gets you captured. Silent travel in the jungle will be about three hundred meters per hour, about the length of three football fields. You will need to cover eight hundred meters per hour, half a mile, in order to return to Sherman within twenty-four. No can do? Tango Sierra." He paused, continued. "NATO phonetic alphabet for you non-military boys. TS stands for tough shit. Figure your rate of travel as you go."

The worried trainees grinned. The trainer went on, emphasizing points at a blackboard.

"*Travel* is the key to survival."

"Move in the direction of your compass heading. *Don't* move in a *straight* line."

"*Work* your way to avoid noise. That means turning your shoulders, bending, moving your hips to the side to avoid contact with vegetation."

"Travel only in the *daytime*. You can't avoid noise in the dark. You can't avoid accidents in the dark. Either will kill you."

"Stop and listen every fifteen minutes. The bad guys will."

"Use no insect repellant or soap. The Chocos will be able to smell you. Hell, I'll be able to smell you."

"Avoid trails and lines of drift in the topography. Training Battalion—and real bad guys—will expect you there."

"Begin drinking water immediately. Four quarts while you are out there."

"Learn Anselmo's lessons."

Following a week of survival lessons they were loaded into a canvas-topped Army truck and driven away from the Fort Sherman classrooms. After nearly an hour on a potholed, root-beleaguered jungle road the trainees had no idea where they were. The truck stopped and they were quickly boarded on a waiting LCM landing barge. Only the smell of salt air, if they had noticed it, would have told them it was the river mouth. The six-foot steel sides of the landing barge denied them sight of where they were. Diesel engine smell and noise drowned other sensations that might have oriented them. The leathery wall of jungle, storied above them, discouraged imagination, anticipation.

Sequestered, they followed Anselmo's example, covering exposed skin with the juice of the jagua berry to keep mosquitoes away. The clear juice of the yellow-brown fruit turned the skin black. Anselmo assured them the artless tattoo would go away in a couple of weeks.

"I'd like a cold beer. Here's my plan." Dog was speaking to several jumpers, hiding his voice in the sound of the pounding twin engines of the barge.

"Oh, shut the fuck up, Dog. Only way we get a beer is give up. Then we're out of the best payin' job I ever had."

"You can't tell a man to shut up just because he's thirsty. If you got a plan speak up. If not, listen up."

Silence gave Dog the floor again. "They only sell beer on or about roads. You want a beer you got to find a road."

"You got any more than that, Dog? 'Cause it's gonna take more."

"Sure I got more. I got a road."

The jumpers looked at him. Someone said "You're full of shit. We're in the jungle."

Dog leaned toward the speaker. "When we were flyin' into Fort Sherman you were asleep. Not old Dog. Intellectually curious by nature, I wanted to have a look at the Panama Canal and, of course, Gatun Lake from which they fill the locks of the canal. Gatun Lake was made, of course, by damming the Chagres River."

A lawyer who had joined them said "We're *on* the Chagres River."

"Mind like a steel trap. I'm gonna buy you a cold beer soon as we get on the road."

"What's this about a road?"

"Listen up. When we flew into Fort Sherman we landed from out over the ocean. Landed goin' south. But before we landed we circled some and here's what I saw because I was lookin' out the window. Across the jungle and southwest of Sherman, the Chagres River flowin' out of Gatun Lake and runnin' northwest. On the north side of the river, on the Sherman side, across a short stretch of jungle, an improved road leading north up Limon Bay from Gatun Lake right to Fort Sherman."

Dog held up a piece of paper on which he had drawn an equilateral triangle. He pointed to the apex. "Sherman."

He pointed to the bottom side. "Chagres River."

He pointed to the right side. "The road to Sherman. About a six-hour walk on a clear night."

The lawyer asked "Where did you get that?"

Dog looked at the lawyer. "I drew it from memory. You're not listening." Without waiting for a response he addressed the group of jumpers. "We can't walk out of here fast enough to beat twenty-four hours unless it's on a road. We get off the boat, walk into the jungle until the trainers can't see us, then tear up the hill at right angles to the Sherman heading they give us and we come to a road. We take a left and go get a cold beer."

No one said anything.

Dog shrugged. "We can flip a coin between that and swimmin' out on the river. There will be patrols on the river. And anacondas swimmin' in it. One or two could make it that way, but not the whole bunch of us. Besides there's no beer on the river."

The jumpers chose Dog's road.

The lawyer started to move away. Dog stood. "By the way, you're goin' with us. Can't risk you talkin' out loud about our plan, to say nothin' of them Chocos turnin' you," Dog teased. Two more jumpers stood, one on each side of the lawyer.

The lawyer said "OK" and sat down.

They left the LCM, walking off the unloading ramp directly into the jungle. Within a hundred yards they turned right and walked away from the Fort Sherman heading, the jungle covering them in gray and green. When they reached the road they hid in dense re-growth until the sun set. Dark night joined them instantly and stayed throughout their walk on the road.

They combined their rucksacks so that some were carrying empty canvas. Taking turns, one was sent ahead, unburdened, a point man beyond their sight. If a Training Battalion patrol was on the road only one would be captured, the others warned.

By dawn they were sitting on a beach near Fort Sherman, the empty rucksacks now full of beer from a roadside store. When they finished the beer they entered Sherman and walked to an empty check-in booth in fresh camouflage fatigues. It was the twenty-fourth hour and concerned Training Battalion officers had left the check-in point to organize Choco Indians in a search for the lost evasion trainees.

From the jungle, Anselmo watched the six well-groomed trainees, as he had all night.

CHAPTER TWENTY-ONE

When they had completed CIA paramilitary training the smokejumpers received new assignments. Those sent to solve the riddle of supplying the Meo in a strange Southeast Asian war traveled by way of Tokyo, in the first-class cabin of a Pan American World Airways 707.

The smokejumpers were not concerned about the extravagant first-class fare. Company was paying. In return, it told them how to dress and act. "No White logging boots. Wear sport jackets. Look like everybody else. Act like you've been there before, and don't expect a parade when you come back. Parades in covert wars are secret."

They did look like everyone else, but younger. Acting like they had been there before required more effort. They tried the champagne, did not like it and went back to Schlitz. They smoked and read and ignored their buddies. Dog read medical school admission materials. He had figured it out. Another year with the CIA and he would be able to afford medical school. Charlie, disguised in a Notre Dame sweater, talked to everyone in the lounge that ever had an opinion about college athletics. Having just finished sports pages from across the country the "student" was full of opinions.

"Yes, I know Daryle Lamonica. Roomed with him. He's gonna make you forget Hornung. An even better guy, though, was Magic Mike Dugan out of Omaha. But you're never gonna see him. We broke both his legs in the first scrimmage."

On the plane he fell asleep reading the *Wall Street Journal*. He awoke to the movie *Spartacus* and memorized Kirk Douglas lines, worked on an impression. Dog punched him on the shoulder when, for the third time, Charlie jutted his jaw and exhorted rebelling slaves "Tomorrow—we march on Rome!"

When the jumpers landed in Tokyo they called a telephone number they had been given. They followed terse instructions from the telephone voice and made their way to Yokota Air Base, thirty miles northwest of Tokyo. Guided by an Air Force captain, they changed into U.S. Air Force jumpsuits and boarded a military flight to Taipei. From there, still dressed as military personnel, they took Mandarin Airlines' scheduled service to Saigon. "Mandarin Airlines" was just a name. The airline was actually Civil Air Transport doing a long-term CIA favor for an ally, Nationalist China, connecting it in the flashy *ao dai* silk pantaloons and slit tunics of Vietnam, to capitals throughout Asia. The smokejumpers flirted with the stewardesses and then dispersed into the city by commercial bus and taxi.

Charlie and Dog met the next morning on the veranda of the Continental Palace Hotel. They were to have breakfast with the Saigon Station Chief to hear about their assignments. They expected to be assigned up north, kicking cargo in Laos. Dooley had already left for Hua Hin, Thailand to train Thai PARU in timber jumping.

Charlie tried to capture his mood. "We've got it made in the shade, Dog. We go everywhere first cabin. We get top-dollar pay. And it's low risk. Right? Nobody's gonna shoot at airplanes droppin' rice to Chinamen happen to be down on their luck."

"Charlie, they aren't Chinamen. They are Meo. Properly called Hmong. Four thousand year-old culture. They aren't down on their luck. They have chosen to go to war for Uncle Sam. Because of that choice there may, indeed, be a Chinaman shootin' triple-A at you and your bag of rice."

"Been readin' again, Dog?"

From the hotel veranda they looked out on a wide boulevard, Tu Do Street, skirted by plane trees and coconut palm. As Dog was about to accept that they did indeed have it made in the shade a man in a cream-colored suit and narrow tie approached their table.

"Good morning. I would guess you're Mazzarelli and Touhey. I'm Andrew Campos. Chief can't make it for breakfast. Maxwell Taylor's comin' into Tan Son Nhut this morning, unannounced, doing fact-finding for POTUS. Chief needs to be there to make sure he finds the right facts."

Dog was cautious, but direct. "You CIA?"

"When you're in-country you call it CAS. That's an acronym for controlled American source. That's code for Central Intelligence Agency. Don't use the other term."

"How long you been *in-country*, Andrew?"

"Eighteen months."

"Charlie, man's a pro. Learned a new language since he been here."

Charlie saw Dog turning Irish donkey, refractory and stubborn. He moved to cut it off. "Andy, how about some breakfast and you can fill us in on Saigon and our assignments."

"Sure. Sorry about the language stuff. Depending on who's talking and who you're talking to there's about four ways to say anything in Saigon." Campos sensed Dog's antagonism, but did not have a clue as to what was causing it. He would be careful what he said to these rough characters, as some case officers described them, leave bringing them into line to the chief. "I'll have a scotch and soda," he said to no one in particular.

"Me too," Charlie said, solely to show support for Campos. He had never drunk anything other than beer. He signaled the waiter to the table and they placed their drink and breakfast orders. Dog did not ask for a drink. Charlie thought that was a good sign and relaxed. Over the next hour he realized he liked scotch and soda very much. He thought it fit his new image as a CIA agent engaged in clandestine service. He and Dog were now part of Special Operations Division, Southeast Asia, home based in Saipan. He had not been there, was not sure where it was. Charlie was comfortable with that. *Need to know,* he told himself. *Probably good I don't.*

In the course of a three-scotch-and-soda-breakfast "need to know" pretty much ended up on the tiled floor of the veranda. Campos gave good gossip.

"The Nung are probably the best fighters in Southeast Asia. Chinese hill people. Just not enough of them to make up an army. So they are everybody's favorite security guys. Including CAS. You can spot secret Company real estate by the presence of Nung guards out front dressed in spiffy camouflage uniforms. Get the picture? USAID office in Vientiane, cover for case officers and their secretary, two uniformed Nung guards out front at parade rest. Some cover." Campos snorted, took another drink. "And they only fight if you provide them whores and beer. You can imagine the security problem. We have to fly in whores from the Philippines for the Nung just so they don't have a common language!"

Campos stopped talking, afraid that he may have stepped over the line. Talking about agency security problems did not bother him. The line that gave him concern lay in an imagined minefield somewhere between him and his breakfast companions. They had spent the morning questioning him about local women and beer, and *here I am badmouthing people that fight only for whores and beer.* Their conversation had led to an invitation that he join them in a visit to the nightclubs of Tu Do Street. He had declined but given them all the information necessary to get there. That was the right thing to do, he thought. Friendly and helpful, but stay clear of them. He did not need Tu Do Street. *I have my dark-haired girl.* The passing thought brought the images that came more and more often when he thought of her—kneeling beside the bamboo pipe, needle in her hands, tar ball of opium on the end of a needle cooking over a flame, the small smoking ball held for him over the pipe bowl, inhaling through the jade pipe mouth, reverie, euphoria. He considered having another scotch and soda.

The mention by Campos of Vientiane reminded Dog they had heard nothing about their assignments and had better ask. The questions brought Campos out of his daydream, relieved at the change of subject. *Maybe now I can stop talking to this pair about their low ambitions.*

"As you've been told we have started dropping military hardware and food to the Meo on a mountain about a hundred miles north of Vientiane. We've been doing that out of Okinawa using some of your smokejumpers. The logistics of that are bad and we want to move the supply operation into Laos. We're going to start with Vientiane. Most of you will be going there as cargo kickers. You will operate out of Wattay Airport, it's part Lao military and part commercial airport for the town. You will be run by the CAS Chief of Base at Udorn, Thailand. You'll be kicking cargo out of Air America C-46 Curtiss Commandos and

C-47 Dakotas. You're probably familiar with them. If not you'll pick that up at Wattay."

"You said most of us. Who's going somewhere else?" Dog asked.

"One of you two is going to stay down here. We have an operation at Long Thanh that requires training Vietnamese in jungle parachuting."

"What's Long Thanh and what's the operation?"

"Plantation de Long Thanh was a French rubber plantation. About thirty klicks from here. The South Vietnamese government operates the plantation now. We've borrowed a piece of it for working up operations that require such a facility. It has a small dirt runway. There are several barracks. We went to the Forest Service and secured a copy of drawings for the letdown and jump towers at McCall and Missoula. The Long Thanh training area should seem quite familiar to you."

Dog looked at Campos in silence. Campos started talking again.

"Yes, the operation. Project Tiger. On the recommendation of General Lansdale and the Saigon station chief, the president has directed that covert intelligence operations be undertaken inside North Vietnam by South Vietnamese agents under the direction of CAS." There was local pride in the way Campos identified the provenance of the White House-approved project.

"Part of that operation will involve parachuting seven-man civilian and commando teams into North Vietnam with instructions to penetrate various elements of North Vietnam's military and industrial organizations, including intelligence. Our job is to train the South Vietnamese infiltration teams in parachuting into mountain jungles and providing the jump planes. Smokejumpers are, of course, a natural choice as trainers. Because many of the trainees do not speak English, we will be assisted by Lieutenant Phan of the ARVN First Observation Group. That's a special forces type of group in the South Vietnamese army with the task, among others, of conducting intelligence operations in enemy areas. Even now they have some operations underway in North Vietnam. Lieutenant Phan has himself participated in some of those and knows North Vietnam well."

"Which one of us is going to Long Thanh?"

"You can make that selection yourselves."

"We'll flip a coin. Let you know first thing tomorrow."

"Good. I'll pick you up here in the morning. We have some administrative matters to take care of, including getting you personal weapons." Campos pointed an index finger at them like a cocked pistol, brought his thumb down, and winked. "Can't have you running around a war zone unarmed."

Shitfaced, Dog thought.

Late that night Charlie and Dog flipped a coin. Charlie got Long Thanh. After a night on Tu Do Street he thought being that close to Saigon was a definite win. "Can you believe it, Dog. A steam bath, a massage, and a blowjob for one dollar."

"Life is good, Charlie."

Dog was not sure that was true. He had spent two months packing parachutes in a CIA depot in San Antonio for an operation in Cuba. He had waited on the day of the Bay of Pigs landings while four C-130s, loaded with military supplies strapped to cargo chutes he personally had rigged, were canceled, one after the other. He still felt shamed by what happened. The Company looked bad, careers had ended. Now the young president was edging up to another fight. He saw that the war had already started. Chicken wire hung in front of Saigon restaurants to keep VC on passing motor scooters from rolling grenades into the nightlife told him so. He was glad to be getting a weapon.

"Betcha in five years this place will be crawlin' with Army grunts and your girlfriend will charge you ten dollars just to buy her a Saigon Tea." Dog immediately regretted being a wet blanket. "Meanwhile you've died and gone to heaven. See you in the mornin'. We'll go get armed and put an end to this nonsense."

In the morning Campos took them to an area in the basement of the United States Embassy marked RESTRICTED. There were Marine guards with automatic rifles. One of them checked CIA identification against a list. Another escorted them to a steel door at the end of a series of crossing corridors. It looked like it had been part of a bank vault. Their Marine escort spun a dial, entered a combination. He turned a wheel that unlatched the door, pulled it open, and stood aside.

"Mr. Campos, as you know, ammunition for the weapons in this room is kept in a separate locked area. Once you have selected your weapons I will personally check them out. You may then take them with you or I will have them delivered today to CAS headquarters, Saigon, your attention. In all events the appropriate ammunition will be delivered to your attention at CAS headquarters. Take whatever time you need." Though he was not, the Marine guard appeared to be standing at attention as he spoke.

Campos led Charlie and Dog into a brightly lit room filled with rack after rack of guns, personal weapons, in dazzling variety. M-16, Uzzi, Swedish K, AK-47, Schmeisser machine pistol, Thompson submachine gun, British Sten, Colt .45, Browning 9-pmm.

"The P-35, the Browning 9 millimeter pistol, is made in the white specifically for CAS. In the white," he explained, "means no manufacturing number or other identification. It has a thirteen-shot clip." Campos handled a P-35 as he talked.

The two smokejumpers became little boys again, engaged in the familiar fantasies of war. Charlie and Dog each selected a P-35 pistol. Impressed by the folding stock and thirty-six-round banana clip of the Swedish K, Charlie picked one up and said "I'll need one of these, too."

Campos nodded. "When you have a little free time today, we'll put together some survival gear over at CAS headquarters. Maybe a lightweight pistol, a .22 Bearcat. A mirror, flares, fish hooks. We'll look at what the Air Force is doing for their pilots."

The necessity for survival gear, taught from their earliest CIA orientation, caused a mix of excitement and apprehension in the two smokejumpers. The next day Charlie and Dog said goodbye.

Dog said "Let's go to war and not tell anybody." Charlie said "I wouldn't do this without you. You're my hero. A little underweight for that, but that's who you are. Stay cool." Dog flew to Vientiane in an Air America C-123. Charlie took a taxi to look for a woman named Anh on Tu Do Street.

CHAPTER TWENTY-TWO

Recruiting by the Army of the Republic of Vietnam was straightforward. An ARVN unit of appropriate size surrounded two city blocks and took every male above the age of fifteen. When Project Tiger needed candidates for infiltration training the Army looked to their usual recruiting method. They captured the necessary number of people in the city of Saigon and trucked them to Long Thanh.

Charlie had been on the job at Long Thanh for two months before he blew his top. He confronted Lieutenant Phan. "Phan, what in the goddamn hell is going on? Where are you getting these miserable sonsabitches? They steal everything that isn't tied down or locked up. And that doesn't stop 'em. I come in yesterday morning and they'd stripped every foot of nylon cord, tape, and rope off the goddamn letdown tower and the goddamn jump tower. Did Ho Chi Minh send you these worthless bastards? I think they're all gomers, total screwups. I come in today and some particularly incompetent dink has tried to force my locker open. Tryin' to get my guns so he can kill me in my sleep. Well, let me tell you what the next breakin' and enterin' slope is facin'. I have U.S. Army standard issue fragmentation grenades and I'm gonna run some U.S. Army standard issue trip wire and blow them straight to hell. You have twenty-four hours to get these people under control before I start killin' 'em. I want you to post warnings and I want you to sweat these boys. How we goin' to infiltrate these dumb bastards into Hanoi?"

Charlie was yelling at the top of his voice as he made his last point. Then he stopped yelling at Lieutenant Phan. He had simultaneously run out of breath and become slightly reflective. He added "I don't mean you're a dumb bastard, Phan."

Lieutenant Phan did not appear to have taken offense. "Charlie, I appreciate your concern. I will bring the problems you have identified to the attention of Captain Do Van Tien. He is the deputy responsible for Project Tiger recruiting. He reports directly to the CIA Saigon station chief. Without doubt he will focus on identifying better educated and more patriotic volunteers."

Charlie had seen many recruits come to Long Thanh with cuts and bruises on their faces. "Maybe Cap'n Tien should stop knockin' the shit out of the volunteers before he sends 'em here. Kind of affects their attitude." Charlie walked away from Lieutenant Phan, toward a group of trainees. The lieutenant followed.

The trainees had been gathered for their graduation exercise, a night jump into a cleared area several miles deeper into the plantation. Charlie was going to jump with them to make sure they were trained and qualified. He was worried that something was not getting through to the Vietnamese. Theft was not the only problem behind his outburst. He was questioning himself, his competence. CIA Saigon had lost contact with every member of the first two infiltration teams dropped into the jungle at separate sites near the Chinese border. Fourteen men put into the jungle north of Hanoi and not one signal.

The silence chewed on him through the week. He excused himself. *That's over my pay scale. I'm just the jump instructor. General Lansdale's boys gonna have to figure this one out.* But it continued to bother him, losing every jumper he had brought through training. He had to make sure he had not screwed it up. Check the parachutes. Check the hookup and exits. Check the landings. Jump with the new squad.

Through Lieutenant Phan, Charlie called them to attention. In his own pidgin-Vietnamese Charlie asked "*Bao nhieu* bitches?" Literally, how many bitches. Lieutenant Phan translated Charlie's intended "any bitches, moans, complaints." The trainees understood the pidgin without translation because Charlie began every address to them with his homemade show of concern. They grinned and were silent as always.

The jump that night went off without a hitch. The Vietnamese drifted too much in the U.S. Army T-10 parachutes, designed for the weight of bigger men. Some were dragged across the landing zone.

But nothing all that unusual happened. *Happens all the time in New Mex.* Charlie was clear he had not screwed it up. It was something for General Lansdale to figure out. *Whoever he is,* Charlie thought. He let the Project Tiger leaders in Saigon know there was a new seven-man team ready for infiltration.

The new team was given an insertion target the following week, further south, away from the Chinese radar. The operating assumption in Saigon was that the previous insertions had somehow been detected and the first two groups of infiltrators captured or killed. They did not know how. Maybe the first two jump planes had been picked up on the sensitive Chinese border radar and the North Vietnamese tipped off by the Chinese. So move south a little.

Saigon had another idea they shared with Charlie.

As the third infiltration team was boarding the C-46 jump plane Charlie approached one of the men. "Hey, Kim, step over here." Charlie called all the short trainees Kim. This one knew English.

"Kim, I want you to do something. Don't tell anybody else you're doin' it. Don't tell anybody you and me talked about it. Understand?"

The Vietnamese nodded and waited on the unlit dirt runway for Charlie's instructions.

"As soon as you're on the ground get your radio out and dial in this freak." He handed the young spy a small piece of paper with a coded frequency number handwritten on it. "Eat the paper. Freak's a special hookup to a fella' in Saigon. Tell him your situation in less than thirty seconds. If you're in the clear just say that and get off. If you're in trouble, tell what it is and get off. Don't expect help. Thirty seconds. Saigon ARVN needs to know what's happening chop-chop."

Charlie did not tell him his voice would be scrambled or that the special hookup was not with or for ARVN, that it was for Andrew Campos. CIA Saigon suspected there was a sapper inside Project Tiger tipping off the North Vietnamese with coordinates of the insertion drop zones. The presence of NVA troops at separate remote jungle drop sites at the very time of the jump—twice—might have been coincidence, bad luck. Three times would be way outside bad luck. If there was an ambush at the third infiltration jump site the "chop-chop" message from Kim would give CIA Saigon certain knowledge that Project Tiger had in turn been infiltrated.

As they had arranged, Charlie met with Campos at Long Thanh the morning following the jump. Charlie was on edge. Unable to sleep, he had been up most of the night. Campos plunged right in, without emotion.

"They were under attack from the outset. When the radio message came through our guy had already been hit. They resisted but were too lightly armed, outnumbered by NVA. The circuit was only open about ten seconds. We have to assume all were killed or captured. Hanoi is silent. They're not going to acknowledge our infil attempts. They'll keep up the game until they can turn one of our teams, double them. We'll play that."

Charlie's resignation at the bad news slowly turned to disbelief. "What you mean we'll play that? Unless you know who the Hanoi agent is this game is over. Project Tiger is rat fucked. There isn't a green drop zone in all of North Vietnam."

"We don't know who he is, Charlie. In order to find out we need to continue infiltration jumps. That way we can do disinformation on drop zone locations or exclude people from the information loop and see what happens. By a process of inclusion and exclusion we can identify our man."

Disbelief turned to anger. Charlie controlled himself and spoke slowly. "You're dinky dau. Crazier 'n a buckwheat fart. You're tellin' me you want me to intentionally kill the next seven trainees in order to catch a spy. And then maybe kill the next seven if it doesn't work the first time. And then the next bunch. And you expect me to just keep trainin' these poor bastards to jump out the door? Andrew, what in hell is wrong with you?"

Campos looked intently at Charlie, then down at the narrow briefcase lying across his knees. "Chief of station is a smart guy. He thought this might happen with you." Campos wanted to say "All you tough guys aren't so tough after all." He was afraid of where that might lead so he did not. He stayed on message.

"We are switching the Project Tiger infiltration jump training to the Army White Star teams, the military advisory people in Laos. You are being transferred to Vientiane. You'll be a PDO up there, a Parachute Dispatch Officer, a cargo kicker supporting Vang Pao's hillbillies. Chief says you know how to do that."

"You think an Army White Star NCO won't jump out of his skin at the chicken shit you're plannin'? There just ain't no days like that, Andrew."

Charlie shook his head, stood up and walked to the door. He turned once more to Campos. "So you're demotin' me to Laos to work with Dog. Out-fucking-standing. You don't mind if I take the rest of the day off to celebrate do you? Need me I'll be on Tu Do Street."

Charlie went from the CIA Saigon safe house to Vientiane by way of Bangkok. It took a week and involved spending all his money. He arrived in Vientiane with only the clothes he wore and a non-specific urethritis. He was very down on the Company and wanted Dog's conversation.

The two of them sat in the vinyl covered chairs of the Tropicana Bar. They had eaten their fill of crispy noodles at a noodle shop and were settling into a beery reunion.

"I don't suppose the beer's gonna improve your delicate condition, Charlie." Dog raised his chin as if asking whether they should continue.

"I can hack it. Clap's the clap. Another round of Dead Man Beer, please." San Miguel beer was served to white men throughout Asia with, as standard condiment, the story of an industrial accident. After fishing the drowned worker out of their brew vat, the Philippine brewery supposedly bottled and sold the affected product. It tasted fine to expats and locals alike.

Charlie, after singing the praises of the inexpensive women of Saigon and Bangkok, complained to Dog about their employer in Saigon.

"Dog, we are supposed to be the good guys and the smart guys. Holding the line against communism. Keeping American blood off the floor. Supporting the little guys in the fight. Dog, there is nothin' redeeming about what we are doin'. Not what I saw at Long Thanh. We walked those guys off a cliff."

"Charlie, it's a war. Just because it's messy doesn't make it wrong. Don't try to make it noble. It isn't. The bones of the guys who died at Waterloo were dug up and sold to farmers for fertilizer."

They listened to the jukebox, Patsy Cline singing "Crazy," drinking beer in silence. Charlie broke the silence again.

"Dog, I want to be a stand-up guy. But I'm startin' to feel shit that isn't stand-up. Ya know? I'm shook. I'm ashamed. I'm not sure I can do it. I don't trust the Company to do the right thing."

"All you're feelin' is fear, humiliation, anxiety, distrust. The basics. Congratulations, Charlie. You've cut through the myth."

Charlie looked like he did not understand and said so. "I'm sure you'll explain, Doctor Touhey. I'll have another beer while you do."

"OK. Let me ask you. What's the first book you read—outside of school?"

Charlie thought a minute. "Hardy Boys. *Secret of the Old Mill.* I read every one of 'em." He grinned at the thought, remembering his small boy's pleasure. "So?"

"I read Lucky Terrell flying stories. That make-believe sonofagun killed most of the Japs and Germans in the world without gettin' a scratch. Read the whole series. Took almost as long as World War II. So there you have it. The shit in your head and my head and the head of most every male in the country is the myth of boys' adventure stories. The myth gets cranked into adult decisions to go to war. No more complicated than that. The problem is the myth leaves out the basics you've just been rollin' around in. You and I have outgrown the comic books we read when we were ten. Finally. So I say congratulations to you, Charlie."

"That's it? It's all OK as long as I'm clearheaded about it?"

"Kinda. I been readin' again, Charlie. I know that's a shame but it's true. Read some the other day when I didn't feel like goin' to a whorehouse. It was theology about war. The guy talks about good war, says that's OK to do. He says the choice is not between moral and immoral, but between the immoral and the less immoral." Charlie was looking hard at him, trying to hear and understand above the bar noise.

"Don't get all tied up in your underwear, Charlie. You been runnin' on Tu Do Street so long you probably can't tell immoral from less immoral."

"Fuck you, Dog. I was trained in moral theology at Mount Carmel High School. I understand everything you said. I'm thinkin' we're in a good war. Fightin' communism, helpin' the little guys. Whadayou think?"

"I'm gonna help the little guys long as I can. I feel OK about that. But here's the thing that'll keep you awake nights. What if you come to think there's no purpose to the war? That the only thing holy about it is there's good boys in White loggin' boots died in it? The first dead man justifyin' the next one. Keep your eye on that one."

They kept falling into silence and it came again. Charlie did not like silence at the best of times. He asked a question.

"Do you trust the Company to do the right thing?"

Dog did not answer right away, seemed to be balancing double-entry columns.

"They want to. They're smart. If they don't it'll just be SNAFU. We have a good case officer runnin' the kickers here. He keeps us up to date on everything that's goin' down. The case officers are hands on, they're not pogues, sittin' around a table in a non-combat job. We had a bunch of good ones on Padong. Fosmire and Poe and Landry and Lawrence. Back to back with the Meo. They were just kickin' hell out of the Pathet Lao. It took a whole brigade of NVA regulars to drive the Meo off Padong. This war is gonna be between the Meo and the NVA. The Pathet Lao in their Donald Duck hats can't hack it. But you know all that stuff."

"I don't, buddy. Tell me where we are. Big picture."

Dog summarized the job in Vientiane. "We're supposed to be in a stand-down while talks go on in Geneva. Kennedy is tryin' to get the Russians to agree to a neutral Laos. NVA don't know the word for stand-down, so the fightin' in the jungle goes on. They drive the little guys off Padong. The little guys go twelve klicks away to the village of Pha Khao and start their trainin' all over. Because of the peace talks we're supposed to stop droppin' guns to the Meo. So all we're droppin' right now is rice. One flight a day, fourteen thousand pounds on Pha Khao. That's my job. It'll be your job, too. I go kickin' tomorrow with a couple of other PDOs. You'll get a day or so familiarization before you start. I'll introduce you around."

He pushed away from the table. "I'm up and on the tarmac at O-dark-hundred. Got to turn in. You comin'?"

They left the Tropicana and walked through the streets of Vientiane to the apartment Dog had invited Charlie to share near the Mekong waterfront. The streets, mostly unpaved, were lined with acacia and jacaranda trees, the trunks whitewashed waist high. Concrete sidewalks were edged with shops in two-story cream-colored buildings. Their apartment was in a similar small building, its red-tiled roof framed by the purple flowers of the jacaranda.

By the time the sun lighted Wattay airfield Dog was inside an unmarked C-46 with two other smokejumpers. They were checking the loading of pallets of rice bags. The pallets, loaded with sixteen bags each, were positioned on conveyor roller tracks mounted in the floor of the C-46. They were secured in position on the tracks with two-by-four chocks until ready for dropping. Chocks released, the pallets would be pushed out the door by the kickers.

They flew within the hour. The short flight to Pha Khao—forty roadless kilometers from Vientiane—took only minutes. Dog watched sharp peaks of karst, eroded limestone rising out of the jungle, pass below. The scene was familiar now and he thought about other things as he watched. Today he thought about silk. His plan for the afternoon was to shop for the material, a gift for his girlfriend, sister of one of the smokejumper PDOs in the plane with him.

They arrived over Pha Khao and began descending, watching small figures gathering near the clearing below. Dog talked to the pilot about the number of passes necessary to empty the plane of its cargo and the direction of the drop. They knew it by heart but talked it through anyway. The rice was free-dropped in sacks that were less than full, turning them into airfoils that flew to the ground and did not burst as a full sack would. They prepared to move seven tons of rice out the side door as the reliable workhorse flew back and forth over the clearing, low enough the kickers could smell the jungle vegetation.

The plane was straight and level on its first approach. The pilot activated a bell that signaled commencement of the drop.

Crouched near the door, ready, Dog straightened up as soon as he heard the engine noise drop by half. He knew immediately they were flying on one engine.

He heard the pilot yelling over the intercom. "Get the shit out of here." The experienced Air America pilot meant the rice. He meant, frantically, he could not lift the fully-loaded plane on one engine. The kickers thought he meant they should jump. The absurdity made them laugh. They wore no chutes.

The confusion in meanings was irrelevant. Within seconds the left wing of the sinking C-46 caught a limestone karst. The wing failed and sheared off. The kickers and rice were thrown forward against the bulkhead, then centrifuged against the side of the cartwheeling airplane. Dog was conscious, grinning at the ironies passing through his head, until the plane hit the jungle floor and burst into flame. He died in minutes, neck broken, unaware of fire consuming the rice in which he was buried. He was twenty-two years old.

CHAPTER TWENTY-THREE

The cat was out of the bag. Word of the smokejumper deaths in Laos drifted through the firefighter community.

The McCall Project Leader told Norris he would no longer be involved in clearing availability of jumpers or deal with seasonal job conflicts. "They can do whatever they want. I don't want to know." The deaths touched him more than he would have expected, had he anticipated them. He had not.

"What are we doin' over there?" The question was asked throughout the smokejumper base in McCall. No opinions were offered, none were held, even in the parachute loft, the source of jumper gravitas and wisdom. No one had known their friends were in Laos, or why.

Thin cover stories were recalled—mining in Colorado, Coast and Geodetic Survey in Alaska, graduate degree in sociology—and heads shaken. "I can't believe those bullshitters never talked about bein' CIA. Never. You believe that?"

"There were some tells if you paid attention," a barracks poker player said. "Some of 'em always had money. They didn't win it from me and they wasn't savers. Girlfriends gettin' mail from Marana, Arizona. That kind of stuff. What the hell smokejumpers doin' in Marana."

"You're right about that. But Max and Pete and them never told much truth at the poker table. Hard to tell."

"What are we doin' over there? Near as I can tell it's landlocked jungle. Guys dyin' for that shit?"

There were no widows to inform with regret. None of the three dead men were married, a rule imposed on his recruiting process by Norris. He had expected harm, and thought there would be more. He replaced the three, transferring smokejumpers from Marana to Laos immediately.

For Thanasis the death of his friend Dog caused its own disturbing response. A telephone call from Charlie brought the news.

"No, they weren't shot down. An engine failed when they were comin' in on a food drop."

"A fuckin' mechanical?"

"It happens," Charlie said. "We are in a stand-down. Not even fightin'."

"A waste. A total waste. Over goddamn nothin'. Is anybody in touch with Dog's parents?"

"Norris is takin' care of that."

"How about his girlfriend?"

"Norris is doin' that too."

"I'm gonna call her," Thanasis said.

"That's good. But, Thanasis, keep it cool. Don't get wrapped around the axle. We are just doin' a job here."

"What the fuck are you doin' there? Why did we waste Dog? And then you next? Get out of there."

"I'm doin' it for the right reasons. I know why I'm here." There was a pause. "My buddies are here, Thanasis."

"Are you drunk?"

"Course I am." There was another pause. "Thanasis, I'm not sayin' you should be here. You stay the hell out of here."

Thanasis heard Charlie sob. "You stay the hell away, you hear," Charlie said and hung up the phone.

The night Thanasis received the telephone call from a drunk Charlie telling him Dog was dead the nightmare of his father's murder returned to Thanasis after a decade's absence. It stayed, and so did the feeling of failure and shame that had always accompanied it. Thanasis alternated between depression and anxiety attacks. He got drunk as often as he could, picked violent fights in small town bars, easy enough to do.

He became sexually unresponsive, the passionate intimacy with Maria withering in long silences. Her efforts to understand the source of his destructive slide were turned away.

He was distracted at work, ran a sewing machine needle through his index finger as he repaired torn parachutes, made errors in packing chutes. Squad leaders took him aside, asked what was going on. His cold response ended efforts at intervention. He was removed from work in the rigging loft.

The tiny McCall police department made clear to the smokejumper project leader that Thanasis' behavior had reached a level they too would not tolerate. He had been refused service after vomiting into the well of the bar as he sat on a barstool, staring. He left and returned with a Pulaski. He was splintering the shiny bar top with the axe and adze when the police arrived. He was released the next day into the custody of the project leader on the understanding he would pay the bar owner for the damage and be transferred out of McCall.

"I can't look the other way on this one, Thanasis. How do you want to handle it?"

Thanasis apologized for embarrassing the jumper base in the community. "I'd rather resign than you fire me. But that's up to you." He paused, eyes closed, waiting for a space in the hangover that would permit speech through a shrunken bear-head filled with bright light. "I'd ask one favor, though," his voice a nasal vibration. "I'd be in your debt if you'd recommend me to the CIA guy that Dog and the rest have been workin' for. I want to go to Laos."

"What you want to do that for?" The project leader frowned and shook his head as if any answer would be the wrong one.

Thanasis shrugged. Pressed by silence and headache, staring at the floor, he finally said "I can't let it pass again."

"What do you mean 'pass again'?"

Thanasis shrugged once more, hands stuck in his jeans pockets. "It's all I know to do. No other way to go. Can you help me with the CIA?"

"I've already told Norris Wright I'm not gonna be involved in recruiting for his CIA projects. I did my war. I'm not interested in doin' another one by proxy." The Project Leader hesitated before continuing. "I don't know why you're so miserable. I know you and Dog were tight. But it doesn't help matters to go burn your own house down." He waited, hoping Thanasis would accept counsel, tell him he would forget about Laos. He looked at the silent man in front of him and gave up. "You quit the boozin', I'll call Norris."

Thanasis walked with Maria in the quiet of the lake shoreline. It was dark early and cold, fall come to the mountains. He was anxious to repair damage and share his new plans. He had no trouble beginning. He apologized for his drunkenness and withdrawal. He said the words he hoped would recognize and mend what she had been through—neglect, abashment, humiliation. He was right on all counts.

She said words of forgiveness and held him close. She wanted to ask questions, wanted to know what black, rooted thing she had missed. She held back, head against his chest. *Later. He'll talk it out. There's not a secret in him.* She pushed herself up and kissed him.

He said "I want to marry you. I want us to do it now."

She was surprised and briefly excited. In moments those feelings passed and she felt disappointment. The proposal seemed to come from nowhere, without source. The past was missing. In the months since Dog's death their relationship had broken, slowly, like twisted bone. It was pieces and pain. That had to be talked out or it would not heal. She tried to give a kind name to the reservation weighing on her. The words would not come through her growing sadness.

He saw her reservation quickly and then misread it just as quickly. She was stunned by what he said next.

"I know you're thinking the CIA doesn't hire married jumpers for the Laos pipeline. But we don't have to tell them. It's not a real rule anyway. There's lots of married agents. They won't enforce it. And I hear they're thinking about changing it for the jumpers. I'll be able to get you over to Vientiane or Savannakhet in a couple of months."

She was angry before he finished, so angry she thought she would hit him. She pushed him away and began rating him loudly. "Thanasis, sweetheart, you are dumber than cat shit. You have by some deluded process decided to get in a *pipeline* with your beer-drinking friends so you can all go die in a war you don't know anything about and that doesn't have anything to do with any of you. And you don't even talk to me about it. In the same breath you ask me to marry you. That's just brilliant. Not only will you get killed in a dumb-ass war nobody else knows about, but I get to be a widow! Am I pregnant, too? In your fantasy?"

She stopped, red-faced and furious. In the next instant she was crying, her face wet and distorted, hidden in her hands. He reached to hold her. She struck his arms, spun away and walked from the lakeside, stumbling, legs feeling disjointed.

Within the week he left for Marana without seeing her again.

He drove from Idaho to Tucson, Arizona, stopping only for gas and sodas, depressed and numb with loss. As he crossed the Mogollon Rim he tried to cheer himself with recollections of fire jumps out of Silver City. The memories were worse than the numbness. They made him feel sorry for himself, until he became disgusted. *Why don't you just pull over and sit on a pity-potty, suck-calf.* Self-awareness did not make him feel better, but embarrassment made him want to get himself together. He started by focusing on what he had to do in Tucson.

In Tucson he found a payphone and dialed the number Norris had given him. A man answered and Thanasis identified himself. The man gave Thanasis the address of a motel near the airport and told him to show up for a polygraph test the following morning. "Ask for Mr. Smith's room and do not discuss what you are doing with anyone."

The next morning Thanasis knocked on the door to Mr. Smith's motel room. He was greeted by a balding man in a rumpled suit. A small piece of toilet paper was stuck to a shaving cut near his ear. Thanasis shook the man's hand. It was sweaty. He told Thanasis to relax and take a seat. He pointed to a chair next to a table holding a small machine with several styluses resting on graph paper wound through the machine, creating a surface on which they could mark.

"That's the polygraph and I am the polygraph operator. Do you have any questions about the machine or what we are doing this morning?"

"No. I assume this is routine for CIA jobs."

"Let me tell you how the process works. I will pre-interview you before hooking you up to the polygraph. That is intended to let you know in advance what the questions are that the exam will focus on. It is also intended to get certain things out of the way. If you are a Communist or a homosexual you can just tell me that upfront in the interview. The polygraph test will tell me that anyway. It is highly accurate in detecting lying."

"I hate Communists and I don't fuck men."

"We'll see."

"If those are bad answers you just tell me now."

"There are no bad answers, just lies." Mr. Smith explained how the polygraph machine detects lies. He considered explaining galvanic skin response but thought it would be wasted on somebody in logging boots.

Thanasis was not sure he believed Mr. Smith's claims for the lie detector. The sweaty palms and toilet paper were affecting his view of the man's credibility.

They completed the pre-interview, which did ask about sex and communism, and the polygraph operator attached sensors to Thanasis' arms, fastened a band around his chest. The process of asking control and actual questions seeking yes and no answers took no more than ten minutes. Thanasis thought a lot of the questions were not relevant to loyalty or any other employment issue.

On reflection, as he drove away from the motel, he thought he had probably lied when he answered "No" to whether he had ever destroyed government property. *There's the time I set the fire on Forest Service land. But nobody would say sagebrush counts as property. And the two-man chain saw we threw into the fire on Cache Creek really shouldn't count. It was obsolete the minute it was invented.*

The property destruction and the mental reservations had not occurred to him when the question was asked. That or the distraction of the toilet paper band-aid had kept his autonomic nervous system from registering a lie with the sensors. The sensors apparently did register some other things that Mr. Smith conveyed to Norris Wright when he telephoned him shortly after Thanasis left the motel room.

"He's good to go if you want him. Kind of aggressive like the rest of 'em I've done for you. He's a little wound up on a couple of things. He says he doesn't have a sexual relationship but the machine says he sure misses the one he had. He doesn't like Communists, but the polygraph says he has rats in his head on that one. He will like killin' the bastards. If that's what you're having them do."

Norris sighed. The polygrapher was well-regarded, but he frequently was bored. His reports were often embellished, crediting his machine with insights that were personal to Mr. Smith.

"Smitty, the issue is did he lie on the relevant questions. Your untrained psychiatric stabs in the dark are not useful to me and I am going to assume you are not going to include them in your written report. Did he or didn't he?"

"He told no lies, at least none he is aware of. He will love Marana."

CHAPTER TWENTY-FOUR

Marana Air Park lies parched in the desert northwest of Tucson. Norris had penciled in the World War II Army airfield, with its three long runways, large apron and hangars, O-club and swimming pool, as the clandestine headquarters of CIA Air Branch operations. He leased it through a front, Bob, owner of an airborne fire retardant operation. Bob asked no questions and never did operate a fire retardant tanker out of Marana.

The work of those employed behind the chain-link fence of the airfield was to provide CIA with all the aircraft it wanted, any time, any place. T-28s and B-26s for bombing and strafing. DC-3s for insertions in enemy states or R&R on the Gulf of Thailand. Volpar Twin Beeches to move embassy couriers and foreign VIPs.

Reflecting the Company's frequent resort to short, abandoned, and makeshift runways, Air Branch became the leading buyer of short-take-off-and-landing airplanes, STOL aircraft in aviation vernacular, principally the Helio Courier. The plane could make a thirty-mile-an-hour turn in the radius of its boxy wingspan. They were sometimes seen at Marana. More often they were unseen, flown in and out at night, serviced and on their way. Air Branch was a buyer of Helio Couriers until it acquired— the original Kansas manufacturer said "stole" in official non-public complaints—the design and manufacturing plans for the aircraft and had it made solely for CIA consumption by Air Asia Company Limited, a CIA-owned aircraft maintenance facility in Taiwan.

There were hundreds of CIA aircraft at Marana at all times. If someone curious or spying stood on the Southern Pacific railroad tracks, he could see the planes to the west, silhouetted against the Silver Bell Mountains, seeming to pulsate in the heat rising from the tarmac.

The cover for the burst of activity at the desert airport was Intermountain Aviation, a charter operator, licensed by the FAA and holding authority from the Civil Aeronautics Board. Neither agency had knowledge of Intermountain's ownership or intelligence missions.

Within the larger culture of CIA secrecy and plausible deniability, Marana, in spite of its size and visibility, was more secret and deniable. It was compartmentalized, with few questions asked of those in other compartments.

Within the compartments of Marana, Thanasis buried himself in work, losing memories, good ones and bad ones. Thanasis sought deployment to Laos, but Norris kept him occupied at Marana. Something in the request of the smokejumper project leader made him suspect Thanasis' motives for joining the CIA jumper crew. He kept him close, watched him. All he saw was hard work and devotion to what the Company was doing. He began to relax about Thanasis, began to see him as another can-do cowboy.

Norris held his cowboys separate from the rest of Marana, with limited opportunity to fraternize. The jumpers referred to Norris' arrangement for them as "the fattening pen." They were held there until, periodically, some or all of them would disappear. Mostly they disappeared on temporary duty as kickers, riggers, jump trainers or jack-of-all-trades air operations officers somewhere in Southeast Asia. When they returned Norris put them to routine work packing military personnel chutes and using large amounts of acetone and toluene to remove identification numbers overnight from aircraft landed in the dark and parked away from other aircraft.

The jumpers kicked cargo for ongoing Tibetan training operations at Camp Hale, Colorado, part of a secret CIA mission into Mustang, Nepal. Smokejumper empathy was engaged when they learned from case officers that the Tibetans, sequestered in the abandoned 10th Mountain Division training site for nearly a year, were homesick, bored, and frustrated.

It sounded to Thanasis like painting and re-painting government buildings in a poor fire season. He knew what to do. The jumpers rented a bus and took two dozen Tibetan guerillas to a night of beer drinking in Leadville, Colorado. Tourists present in Leadville that night later dined out on stories of tall, exotic looking Khampa men, knives in hand, toasting the Dalai Lama and *Chushi Gangdruk,* the name of their army and the mountain geography of their home. No one believed the tourists' claim of eavesdropping on a CIA operation in Mustang with smokejumper cargo kickers. "I'm telling you," they insisted, "Kennedy approved it."

Their isolation within Marana caused the jumpers to request their own "club" at the Air Park. CIA did not think it essential to hire a bartender and food service personnel with security clearances to cater to a separate small group of employees. They turned down the request on grounds of security. The jumpers reopened the negotiation by offering that they would take turns being their own bartender, did not need barfood, and would give up drinking beer on the roof of the Yum Yum Bar, a square roadside building sitting by itself in the desert. That, and the opportunity recognized by CIA to install listening devices in a smokejumper recreation area, carried the day for the jumpers.

Spying on your own is accepted practice within the intelligence community, a control against both systemic enemy penetration and individual bad habits. Norris was confident that his jumpers would not raise a security concern in their eavesdropped conversations. His confidence was rewarded when the surveillance tapes revealed only after-hours exploration of the frontiers of para-cargo technology and an interest in women who frequented rodeos. Their discussions encouraged Norris to give them more responsibility for solving the problems of supplying guerrilla forces and inserting agents in remote roadless areas.

Charlie was rotated back to the Marana fattening pen. Thanasis, on seeing him, pounded him on the back until Charlie asked him to stop. He saw that Thanasis had teared up.

"It's alright, Black Man. Dog was doin' what he thought we should be doin'. He was happy and didn't feel a thing when he went."

Thanasis wiped his eyes. "Not just about Dog, man. About you bein' alive and here."

They celebrated their reunion at the Marana jumper bar. Late in the evening they agreed they would volunteer for Norris' latest project.

Norris wanted eight volunteers to come up with their own individual approaches for jumping, without protective shielding, out of the belly of a B-26 bomber flying at 125 miles per hour. Each would try his personally-devised method in an experimental jump over the Sonoran desert, observed and filmed by an accompanying aircraft.

"Thanasis, you know that is twice as fast as any jump we ever made out of the Beech. You think those chutes won't tear apart?"

"That part will be OK. Chutes will be slow-openers and by the time we pull the rip cord we will be movin' much slower than the airplane. In fact, we can make ourselves slow as an old *Ford. Word from barnstormers doin' county fair freefalls is that a man can turn his body into an* airfoil, damn near fly."

"That part will be OK," Charlie said in sing-song parody. "So what part is it won't be OK?"

"Don't know. That's what we're gonna find out."

What they found was an assortment of injuries associated with some experimental high-speed exit positions. A dislocated shoulder. An ear torn off by shroud lines. There were no deaths. The best exit position was a counter-intuitive forward facing feet-first exit. It converted the secret agent's body into a sailplane that flew through the desert air. The group of eight experimental jumpers had T-shirts made that said 'Tall Buildings In A Single Bound.'

By the middle of the year following Dog's death the United States, Russia, China, North Vietnam, and Laos, after negotiations in Geneva, signed the "Declaration and Protocol on the Neutrality of Laos." The treaty required withdrawal from Laos of all foreign military forces. It was regarded by many in government as a "triumph of statecraft."

All U.S. Army advisors to the Royal Lao Army were withdrawn. CIA withdrew all but two case officers. The many thousands of the North Vietnamese Army never left Laos.

The two CIA case officers remained behind to oversee construction of a secret base at Long Tieng, near the Plain of Jars. What had been a small Lao Theung village in a mountain valley a hundred miles north of Vientiane became a CIA-Meo military camp with a forty-six hundred-foot asphalt runway, an air operations building, parachute packing tables and tower, cargo forklifts, Vang Pao's concrete headquarters, and tin and cardboard shacks on muddy "streets" housing thousands of Meo women and children, along with Vang Pao's guerillas.

Meo guerillas and their families, at Long Tieng and other mountain sites in Laos, were supplied daily by Air America flights operated out of Takhli, Thailand. The two case officers left behind toasted the success of their efforts. "A generation of Iron Age people will grow up thinking rice comes from the sky."

Russia and China embraced the fiction of North Vietnamese-United States compliance with the Geneva agreement on Laos. Thanks to statecraft, the hidden war to prevent the fall of Asian dominoes was now well-organized and on a solid footing, protected from nuclear escalation.

CIA continued to hire smokejumpers, most of them as employees of Company proprietaries Intermountain Aviation and Air America. The smokejumpers were deployed as kickers, based in Okinawa and Thailand, supplying food to Meo guerillas and refugees in the smoldering stand-down with the North Vietnamese regular army.

Jumpers who remained at Marana were engaged as part of the Intermountain Aviation cover as commercial charter operator. To fend off rumors of CIA ownership of a large fleet of aircraft, Agency-owned air carriers began competing with U.S private aviation for charter operations, the more public the better. They were, the carriers said, just like all the other Supplemental Air Carriers authorized by the Civil Aeronautics Board, maybe a little more efficient, but certainly not owned by an agency of the U.S. government. To prove it they had their smokejumpers fly twenty thousand pounds of horsemeat to France, fifteen thousand live chickens to 'Papa Doc' Duvalier in Haiti, and every ton of musical and audio equipment for the Rolling Stones concert tour—from Santa Monica to New York and all the stops in between. Charlie reported that he had "not seen that much dope smokin' since Vientiane."

CHAPTER TWENTY-FIVE

"You must be doing something right, Norris. You fly more airplanes than Eastern Air Lines. You run more smokejumpers than a Forest Service fire camp. And some Company agents think you'll have a hard time finding pallbearers."

"Thank you, Major."

"You're welcome. How are you?"

It was a real question. Casey was concerned about Norris' work load and irascibility. One was about to increase, the other likely to follow. He thought he had the right man but he wanted to make sure. He had arranged to spend a couple of days at Marana to talk through what Norris would be doing.

"I'm fine. I hope you're OK taking in a rodeo tonight instead of doing an all-nighter. The rodeo is work related."

"OK. Tell me. How *do* rodeos relate to aerial delivery by an intelligence agency? Do we have a bull rider gap with Russia?"

"It's about my democratic management style. Our smokejumpers entertain themselves by riding the rodeo in Tucson and around. I told them I thought it was too dangerous, we had an investment in them, and they should find another way to chase women. They told me I'm wrong, it's perfectly safe, I should come and see for myself. So we're goin' to the rodeo."

"I don't know anything about riding horses or chasing women. Sounds dangerous. I look forward to it. Schadenfreude is rampant in the CIA."

That evening they talked no business. They relaxed in the cool night air, taking in the spectacle of cowboys fitting themselves to pernicious broncs and girls in tight-fitting jeans watching riders handle luck of the draw. The CIA overhead enjoyed themselves enough that they stayed through the last of the smokejumpers to ride.

Buckle was the last. He came out of the chute in the final saddle bronc go-round on a thick dun horse full of violence. In two bucks the horse separated Buckle from his hat. With a third spinning leap and a stiff-legged vault the horse removed Buckle from the saddle. Venting malice and irritation it continued bucking in an effort to rid itself of the saddle and flank strap. A great show.

Then both the horse and the CIA bosses were horrified. Buckle was hung up in a stirrup and being dragged by one leg, thumping and twisting across the arena floor. The spectacular peril made the crowd gasp and the dun-colored horse buck harder and kick at the monster writhing in the dirt behind him.

By the time the pick-up man caught the horse and released him from the terror of dragging the smokejumper, Buckle lay without movement. He was taken out of the arena's loamy dust in an ambulance, still unconscious.

As the public address system encouraged the crowd to "give a hand to that young cowboy," Norris and Casey ran to find where their smokejumper was being taken. When they caught up with Buckle in a nearby hospital bed, he was awake, bruised and grinning. The hospital was keeping him overnight for observation.

Other smokejumpers were in his room telling him about the ride. He could not recall it. "You gotta be kiddin', Buckle. Hell no you didn't make the buzzer."

Norris interrupted the several talkers telling the story and asked Buckle how he was doing. In the language of rodeo cowboys he answered "Just right." He tucked the sheet under his chin.

Norris told him to get a good night's rest. He told Buckle's visitors he wanted to see them in his office first thing in the morning. He asked Casey to give him a half hour alone with the Marana jumpers before they met next day.

The jumpers gathered next morning in a conference room off Norris' office. They were apprehensive. Since the Bay of Pigs, Norris had gained a reputation as someone easily provoked, a man with a temper. They were relieved when the meeting was brief and their boss under control.

"You can be in the rodeo or you can be in the CIA. You can't be in both. If you choose to rodeo give me a written resignation by noon." Norris waited several beats as he looked around the room. "You should know for career planning purposes that there are no rodeos in Laos and that's where you are going to be full time startin' this week."

When his audience started slapping each other on the back he added "I thought so."

Casey had given Norris a heads up on a renewed commitment in Laos. He filled in when they met later that morning.

"Laos borders every country the Communists want in Southeast Asia. That means they are trying to control Laos even though it doesn't have any intrinsic value to them. For over a year now Lao neutrality has been the White House answer. Our president, God bless him, got a treaty with the lyin' bastards where they agreed 'Yeh, it's neutral.' But it isn't working. There's been over a hundred violations of the Geneva accord on Laos by the NVA, and the Polish member of the International Control Commission stops any enforcement or sanction against them."

Casey pulled out a cigarette, lit it with intensity. "If this sounds like an angry speech, it is. Because of the neutrality baloney we've lost a year in training Meo and supplying them with arms. Our best option to defend Laos is getting chased all over its own country and killed. They are near quit." He paused and blew out smoke.

"Well, let me tell you that bullshit is over. Kennedy and his State Department are ready to go to war in Laos. Some of the hawks remember their World War II days ambushing Japs with Lao mountain tribes. They want to kill Vietnamese Communists the same way. Kennedy loves anything his Green Berets do with mountain people. Hell, you'd think these Laos hill people voted in West Virginia."

Norris asked "Last time around, before the stand-down and the treaty, the Laos counterinsurgency was on the QT. Who gets to know about it this time?"

"Nobody except the people we are killing."

"What's the cover story? Just in case somebody from the newspaper asks?"

"We're installing USAID equipment at the request of the Royal Lao Government."

"How long is that supposed to take?"

Casey shrugged, palms turned up in a 'who knows' gesture. "I don't know. Because we have the treaty there are no U.S., Chinese or Russian troops involved. Everybody else can fight like hell, as long as nobody admits it. The National Security Council has accepted the position that the United States will appear to comply with the Geneva agreement but *aggressively* train and support a Meo counterinsurgency through the CIA. When I say aggressive I mean belligerent. We are to create a Meo military that will keep the North Vietnamese Army out of Laos. This is no longer about dropping rice and rifles in Meo training camps. This is full-scale battleground supply of whatever weapons a Meo army needs and wherever in the battle it needs them. It's your people that are going to do this, Norris, and they are going to be under fire from some of the best shooters in Asia. Are they ready to go to war? This isn't a rodeo."

Norris took the grim heckle without a smile. "The Air America pilots are as good as any in the world. The smokejumpers are can-do guys. They may be civilians and ride for their own brand, but they see themselves as American soldiers. Gunsmoke won't bother them."

"And how about you, Norris? Your plate is already full."

"Like Buckle said last night, I feel just right. My guys are ready and I'm ready. Who will I be reporting to?"

"Not me, though I want to be informed by you on all aspects of what you do. The president has put the ambassador to Laos in charge of this war. He has a letter from the president authorizing him to direct you and all your people. The ambassador—name is Bill Sullivan—is your chain of command."

"OK, he's got a name. How'd he do on the lie detector?"

"I hear he's a clever one, if that is what you're asking."

"I meant to ask is he diplomatic corps or just some well-heeled politician?"

"Sullivan is a Foreign Service career officer. He is his own man, and on Laos he is connected all the way to the top. He and Averell Harriman have been the point men on negotiations with Russia over Laos. Putting Sullivan in charge tells us that Kennedy is determined to keep this war secret, in the hands of the CIA, the military excluded."

"Is Sullivan a fighter we can go to war with?"

"With all the micks in the White House, I think that's a safe bet. But we won't know until it happens."

"Let's get a map down here and talk about it."

They worked through the night. Norris made notes as the discussion moved across the secret war zone. He marked a map with letter-number designations, the letter "L"—Lima in international alphabet code—identifying CIA airfields and short-takeoff-and-landing sites, some already scraped into hillsides, others only imagined. He wrote:

> *Long Tieng—Vang Pao's home base--Lima site 20A // provides logistic support for Meo // manned by case officers and jumper riggers, kickers—make sure Vang Pao loves you and you return the favor*
>
> *Savannakhet—Ho Chi Minh Trail watch--Lima site 39 // need jumper Air Ops here to support Trail watch and Royal Lao Air Force bombing—look to Saigon for U.S. military Trail needs*
>
> *Luang Prabang—Lao King Savang Vatthana's palace--Lima site 54 // home of Lao coalition government // protect king as directed and otherwise stay out of this*

Arizona morning sun ended their meeting. Norris slipped the map and notes into a briefcase and said goodbye to Casey. He began deployment of his people to Laos. The deployment would be long, the process of beginning it was short, a matter of brief individual phone calls.

Within forty-eight hours Norris was standing on the tarmac in Da Nang, South Vietnam, addressing the jumpers he had collected out of Marana. He talked them through their assignments in Laos and Thailand, and sent them on to Udorn, Thailand in a waiting C-47 for an overnight briefing on the renewed secret war. He kept two of the jumpers with him in Da Nang.

"Thanasis, Charlie, let's go meet the Army's Special Forces B-Teams you're goin' to be trainin' how to jump into the woods."

While they waited in a conference room Norris gave them their assignment. "We used to run an insertion operation out of Saigon. You know about that, Charlie. That has been taken over by MAC-SOG, Military Assistance Command, Vietnam-Studies and Observation Group. It's a covert warfare operation established and directed by the Joint Chiefs of Staff. It's outside General Westmoreland's authority because it's mostly done in North Vietnam. Intelligence, taking prisoners, psych-ops, destroying discrete targets. All in the North. CIA will have a representative in the Group and contribute some personnel from time to time. You're this week's contribution."

Charlie spoke up. "You're the boss. But I didn't care for this business last time I was doin' it. I was trainin' dead men." He shook his head. "The Company is dirty on this. We just can't keep killin' our own dinks in hopes we'll catch the other guy's dinks. Why aren't we smart on this? Thanasis, you're with me on this?"

Thanasis assured him. "I know what you're sayin', Charlie. Sure I am."

"I know that, Charlie, Thanasis. The operation has been changed. MAC-SOG is goin' to do short-term reconnaissance insertions in North Vietnam, not the long-term stuff you were trainin' on Charlie. They figure there's less chance of detection. They'll be doing insertions both by air and over the beach. Your job is to train U.S. Special Forces B-Teams in tree jumping. They are the support team for training Vietnamese reconnaissance teams. So you'll be training the trainers. It's temporary. Two weeks. The B-Teams will be freestanding after that, won't need us. Think that will work?"

Both jumpers nodded.

"Charlie, we haven't been able to find a mole in the earlier operation. But by moving it out of Saigon and making it a Special Forces operation out of Da Nang, the Army hopes they've cut out the mole. They don't have control over recruitment of the Vietnamese recon teams. That's ARVN responsibility and ARVN swears they're clean and under control. That's where we are."

Norris saw that Thanasis was frowning.

"What're you thinking about, Thanasis? Need more time for training? Problem with control over recruitment?"

"Two weeks is enough. Don't have an answer on recruiting."

"But?"

"If Special Forces does their insertions well enough North Vietnam is going to be pissed off. They'll do something about it. These MAC-SOG chickens are gonna come home to roost. If we train Special Forces to do war and they do it, isn't Ho Chi Minh going to respond? Who in Washington is in charge of this? Do they want it that way?"

Norris had taken to chewing on Cuban cigars. He was quiet for a moment, then said around the cigar in his mouth "Washington wants it that way, and it's the only war Special Forces has. We give Army a hand now and maybe they'll return CIA a favor down the road. For you and me, it's that simple. Help Special Forces out, expect somethin' back. Then you're goin' on to Long Tieng in two weeks to fight your own war, one that only the president knows about."

Norris followed his own advice and began doing favors for Special Forces NCOs.

CHAPTER TWENTY-SIX

Thanasis and Charlie, finished with the Special Forces project in Da Nang, flew into Long Tieng. As they approached the growing CIA base they could see through the trees below, single file on footpath trails, refugee Meo. Some were alone, some in strings of family.

The Air America pilot maneuvered the Pilatus Porter for landing, keeping up a chatter about the long-nosed, square-tailed airplane he was flying. "Fully loaded with three thousand pounds of whatever, this homely girl will take off in about ten percent of the runway you're lookin' at. See them two karsts at the end of the runway. Call 'em Titty Karsts. Most planes can't clear 'em. Means everybody has to land from the east and take off to the east. Except my homely Porter here. She'd fly right over them karsts. Hell, I could take off goin' crossways on that strip and not use it all."

The Porter settled onto the asphalt and began a long, slow taxi. The pilot continued his talk as he taxied. "See how the rise in the runway makes it look like the karsts are right there in the middle of the runway. Some pilots comin' in here for the first time think the karsts are half the distance that they really are. Think they're comin' in too hot and they're gonna hit 'em. So they pull their landing gear up for a quick belly-crash-stop." The pilot laughed as if he had never heard or told the story before.

As soon as the taxi ended Thanasis and Charlie thanked the pilot, checked in at the CIA office, and began a familiarization tour. They were to take over the rigging loft, run airborne logistic support of the Meo guerillas, and assist the CIA case officer in charge of training Meo fighters on parachuting into jungle.

The job seemed straightforward. They would, their tour escort told them, begin each day receiving and unloading three C-130 Hercules or C-123 Provider cargo planes arriving from Udorn or Takhli at fifteen-minute intervals.

"That's twenty-three tons on the C-130 and twelve tons on the C-123 when it's outfitted with jet pods. We call it Thunder Pig then. That means *unloading* twelve to twenty-three tons every fifteen minutes. You could be dealin' with as much as sixty-five tons a day." They were guided on their tour by the Montana jumper they were replacing. He was being transferred to Na Khang, Lima 36, a forward support base north of the Plain of Jars.

They were introduced to their work force, Lao and Meo enlisted men, all under the command of General Vang Pao. The short laborers in over-large U.S. military fatigues would unload the large military cargo aircraft and reload it all on smaller aircraft—Helio Couriers, Pilatus Porters, de Havilland Caribou, de Havilland Otters, H-34 helicopters—for redelivery each day to other Lima sites or battles in progress. Redelivery to the small sites was by parachute, STOL landing strip, or helicopter sling.

The Montana jumper finished their orientation tour and gave them his final piece of advice before leaving for Na Khang. "This place is part of a war zone. Carry a weapon. You'll get used to it. You work Long Tieng three weeks twenty-four seven, get shot at occasionally, get R&R three days in Vientiane, then you come back to Long Tieng and repeat. The whorehouses in Vientiane are Rendezvous des Amis, better known as Lulu's, and The White Rose. Lulu's specializes in blowjobs. They'll lick you down like a new born calf. Names I remember are Jojo, Sandy, and Son Boum." He paused, reflecting. "They look like a platoon of hummingbirds they hit the end of that thing."

Norris showed up about a week into Thanasis' and Charlie's assignment at Long Tieng. He had inspected the Air America maintenance facilities at Udorn and Vientiane, followed by meetings in Vientiane with the ambassador and his aides. He had been given direction that he now communicated to Thanasis and Charlie.

The thinking in the embassy was that they had to do more than set ambushes and inflict small unit casualties on the Pathet Lao and NVA.

That was not going to keep the Vietnamese out of Laos. They had to clear the invaders out of areas important to the running of the country, make it look like this is an independent country and not just a rice paddy the "neighbors can shit in whenever they want."

Thanasis and Charlie laughed.

"I'm not playing this for laughs," Norris said. "The ambassador only talks that way when he's mad."

The Embassy plan was to clear and hold the road connecting Luang Prabang and Vientiane, the country's royal and administrative capitols. The 150-mile road was the only meaningful north-south ground connector in northern Laos. The problem as the Embassy saw it was that, with the exception of a few well-led units, the Royal Lao Army was not good at fighting and was not likely to drive the North Vietnamese anywhere. The good fighters, the Meo guerillas, on the other hand, were unlikely to hold any objective once they had cleared it. That was not how they lived or fought. The proposed solution was to combine the two military groups for the operation. The Army attaché named the Embassy initiative "Operation Triangle."

Norris described the CIA/Meo role in the operation. "The Meo will parachute in behind the NVA and Pathet Lao and drive them toward the Royal Lao Army positioned around Luang Prabang. Hammer and anvil."

"Let me ask about the Meo," Thanasis said. "Do they have any parachute training?"

"Like the French commander said about replacements at Dien Bien Phu 'If they can step off a streetcar they can jump out of an airplane'."

"That's fine, boss, but these guys have never seen a streetcar."

"Well you and Charlie are gonna build a streetcar. We are sending seven hundred Meo down to Hua Hin for training by PARU in maneuver tactics necessary for this operation. Your friend Dooley will be down there with 'em providing basic ground training for jumping. They'll get familiar with the gear, how to hook up, how to do a letdown, and so on. When Dooley and the Meo come back up to Long Tieng you three are going to put 'em through final jump training, including a night jump on the Plain of Jars."

"We've got your six, boss," Charlie said, telling Norris in Air Force argot they would cover his back. "Where you gonna be while all this is going on?"

"Thanks. Makes me count my blessings, Charlie. I plan to be in Vientiane and Udorn coordinating the air ops side of this operation, as well as buildup of the logistics operations at Long Tieng and Savannakhet. You guys are talkin' sixty-five tons a day like that's a big deal. Better start thinkin' what you'll do with five hundred tons a day."

Charlie whistled and rolled his eyes. Thanasis said "You're talkin' twenty-five flights a day comin' in here fully loaded?" He stopped to think about the rest of it. "And several hundred STOL flights takin' it out again all day long?"

"That's right. Bet on it. But right now I have a small problem you could help me with. I've rented myself . . . ." He stopped because he had started to say "an old colonial villa in Vientiane" but thought better about what he should say of his quarters. He finished with "a couple of rooms in Vientiane. I will be flying around a lot and need someone to take care of it. A housekeeper. Got any ideas?"

Thanasis swung his arm in a wide arc. "Take your pick. Take two, they're small. We got lots of 'em. You'll need boo-coo kip, of course. Cost about ten thousand a month for a live-in maid." He saw Norris was calculating, based on what he understood of the local exchange rate. "That's fifteen bucks a month U.S. Maybe Vang Pao can arrange a discount for the head of Air Branch."

"There's rules, though," Charlie said. "Rule one is you can't fuck your own maid. Rule two is you can fuck anybody else's maid."

"Thank you for your sensitive advice. I've got fifteen dollars and a dirty kitchen. I think I'll walk around."

Norris walked to the street of thatch-roofed hutches paralleling the runway. The square shanties were framed out of boards from abandoned cargo pallets and poles cut in the jungle. They were sided with flattened blue and red fifty-five gallon aviation petrol drums and old rice sacks. An open air market was filled with stalls selling lettuce, cucumbers, tomatoes, onions, eggs, and opium. There were no sewers, only open latrines filled with human waste. Following military practice the latrines were shoveled out by hand into barrels in which the sewage was burned.

The rough dirt street was filled with Meo women, children, old men, and the sound of many conversations. As he went, Norris too sought conversation, about the labor market. He attempted English, French, and Lao. He knew little Meo. He found some of the older Meo were fluent in French.

As he turned from a halting conversation with an old man, a young woman passed. Like most Meo women she wore an ankle-length black dress bloused above a bright sash at her hip and a short black jacket embroidered with colorful yarns. Norris was struck by her appearance—more fair-skinned than those about her, little or no epicanthic fold beneath her eyelids, dark eyes, an oval face with full lips and long straight nose, nostrils slightly flared. He imagined her European, then Asian, then—he really did not know. He thought her exotic, alien. He followed her, watching her quick barefoot steps in the dust of Long Tieng.

He walked faster and caught up with her. He spoke to her in French. She stopped, looked at him and averted her eyes, said in Meo that she did not understand. She appeared shy and did not seem to understand what he said, whatever language he said it in.

Norris hurried back to the nearest old man with whom he had spoken and led him quickly to the young woman, who was walking down the street again. He told the old man he needed an interpreter.

"Tell her I want to hire her. To keep my house clean and prepare a few meals. I'll pay her thirty dollars a month."

The old man looked at him. He said "Thirty?"

"Yes. Go ahead. And ask her name."

"Where is your house?"

"Vientiane."

"I know her. Her name is May Ly. She will not go to Vientiane. She must stay with her dead husband's family, work for them. She has refused to marry her husband's brother as required and cannot repay the bride price."

"Tell her."

The old man and May spoke in Meo. She looked at the ground and he turned to Norris. "It is as I told you."

Norris took in the facts of Meo marriage customs. He understood it, but felt it only as rejection of personal, urgent need. What minutes ago was mere household administration had waxed into a full moon of desire. He no longer saw the young Meo woman as slim housekeeper.

The following day Norris attended a luncheon at Vang Pao's home. The two-story block house was offices on the first floor and Vang Pao's family residence on the second. The luncheon was held in the residencc. It was not a private lunch but a regular event with the general's senior officers, American advisors, and Meo clan leaders present as they could or wished to be. Even though the Americans referred to the luncheon fare prepared by Vang Pao's six wives as "grits, grass, and gristle," they were frequently in attendance rather than suffer their own food preparation.

Today the food was better than usual because Norris was the guest of honor. The steamed rice and boiled vegetables in a communal basket spiced with chilies and unidentifiable herbs, bitter and astringent, was accompanied by chicken. As guest of honor Norris was given the head of the chicken. He understood that he was expected to suck out the brain and he did that. He swallowed and asked for lao-lao. He was toasted by Vang Pao in the Meo moonshine that smokejumpers said tasted like tequila and kerosene. In Vang Pao's wish of success and good health Norris was called "Uncle," a term of respect.

When the meal ended, Norris asked to meet privately with Vang Pao. They did that in the offices on the first floor. Vang Pao understood the Embassy purpose in Operation Triangle and was pleased the Americans wanted him to fight in this modern way. Vang Pao understood as well that the CIA man seated beside him in an office chair was not there to talk about Operation Triangle. The luncheon had been for that. This was a personal matter and he was pleased, again. He would be asked a favor by an important American, which he would grant. One would be given to him in turn.

Their conversation was discrete, indirect. They talked about May Ly. When Norris sought history about the young woman he was told of her marriage to Thua Ly and the rumored circumstances of the headman's death. When the discussion turned to housekeeping in Vientiane, inducements were identified and exchanged between the two men. They had an agreement.

The next morning Norris drove a jeep to a waiting Helio Courier. It was early, barely light. Waiting at the edge of the tarmac, one hand entwined in the straps of a red, green. and blue cloth bag, was May Ly. She was smiling, still shy. In English she said "Good morning, Uncle." He reached for the bag but she picked it up and walked to the airplane.

New voices greeted him. "Good morning, Uncle." He shook his head and turned to face Thanasis and Charlie.

"I suppose you're busy, up this early. So don't wait on me. I'm headed for Vientiane. Need to get my housekeeper and my office set up. My present plan is to tell the ambassador good things about you. Don't give me cause to rethink that. G'bye, you two."

As Norris walked to the plane, Charlie called after him. "Did you get a discount?"

Norris thought *Not if you count the ten-pound silver bar*, but said nothing. May was already in the plane and he pulled himself up into the seat beside the pilot. Through the short flight to Vientiane and some days thereafter he thought how he would do what he had undertaken.

As for May, what worked was universal. It was powerful circumstance that she was desired. Feminine narcissus, the wish to be the object of erotic admiration, gave rise to her own desire. It came in the form of a fantasy of being wanted so much by the tall warrior who directed her daily tasks that the warrior would risk overpowering her, would take her. The fantasy created an intimacy and connection with him that affected her body in the ways she remembered from her marriage. Sometimes she remembered with the sadness of loss. Her longing, unstated, but expressed in familiarity and kindness, fed his hunger until one evening, ignoring the meal she had prepared and served, Norris took her hand and led her to his bedroom. They became lovers, unsurprised and without a plan that looked beyond the event.

The new life of intimacy and cheer from the man ended May's quiet sadness. When Norris sought to confirm pieces of her history she would rest her arms around his neck and speak a flood of Meo and English, words recapturing all the good and ill of her life, making it all his and he took it as a gift. He listened for her feelings and what she intended when she spoke of those responsible for Thua Ly's death. There was pain and venom when she spoke of the Pathet Lao and the Corsican at Phong Savan.

Norris, professionally committed to the war in Laos, began to see it in personal terms and in light of special opportunities it provided. There was, of course, the wealth of the drug trade. The Air America planes he controlled could be part of that, as could his old relationships with the Corsicans. With May in mind he made his move. It was a quiet campaign of favors, sought and given, within Air America, within the ranks of Special Forces B-Team trainers, within the Corsican drug trade.

What Norris pursued was not wealth, but information about the Corsican at Phong Savan and the feasibility of individual covert acts done with Company assets.

Late that year, at the beginning of dry season, the elements of his campaign on May's behalf coalesced in a small action in the jungle of Laos. A Special Forces sergeant returned a favor to Norris. Dressed in ghillie suit and sniper's slouch hat the Special Forces sniper sat cross-legged in jungle scrub at the edge of a large clearing. He faced the several stone buildings that made up Phong Savan, the nearest, the one he understood to be an inn, was eight hundred yards away.

Long, but doable.

He again sighted through the scope of the Russian sniper rifle, a new Dragunov, supplied by his CIA friend Norris. He had fired it only twice before. He pointed the rifle at the door of the inn, continued his quiet breathing.

Easy with pretty Snayperskaya.

He glanced over his shoulder at the dense jungle behind him, made sure his exit route was still clear.

He noticed movement at the door of the inn. He quickly looked through the scope, acquired the man's image. *Yes.* It was the man whose photograph he had been shown. Dark curly hair, swarthy but obviously a European, not a local. The sniper had been told by Norris the man was a Pathet Lao supporter, reason enough for a CIA kill. It was all the sniper needed to know.

He had been told the man's name was Alain Vecchio. Vechio was standing in the entry portico, dressed casually in a white suit, hands on hips, looking at the jungle in which the sergeant sat. The sniper hesitated.

Kiss your ass if he's PL.

The sniper, breathing even more slowly than before, squeezed the trigger. He heard nothing, but knew from what he saw—curly-headed figure in white punched backward and falling to the flagstone of the ambulatory in front of the inn—that there had been an explosion, inches from his own head, spinning a Russian sniper bullet through the length of the chromium-lined rifle barrel and a half-mile beyond. He turned and slowly crawled on his belly into the dark wall of green behind him.

The sniper boarded an unmarked helicopter two miles from Phong Savan. It lifted off immediately and flew southeast. He patted the rifle lying next to him. "Sure would like to keep this mofo. Make a hell of a deer rifle."

The pilot looked across the small cockpit at the sniper. "No can do, sergeant. When we cross the Trail we toss it out. Right where you might expect to find an abandoned Russian rifle. Right in the middle of a bunch of cut-and-run Commies. Got it?"

CHAPTER TWENTY-SEVEN

"You're gettin' kinda tomato-faced about this, Thanasis," Dooley said. Jump training of the Meo was raising temperatures among the Long Tieng smokejumpers.

"Do the Meo need to be taught how to roll when they hit the ground? That's all I'm askin' you, Dooley. No point you tryin' to fight me about it. I'm askin'. Not disagreein'."

"Godamighty, look at 'em, Thanasis. They don't weigh a hundred and twenty. They'll be standin' up when they land. If they come down at all. I didn't teach Allen roll or any of that down at Hua Hin."

"OK. You think so, that's the way we'll go."

"I think that's right," Charlie put in. "The ARVN at Long Thanh never did a roll. Didn't have to. They were all standup landings. Little guys."

"Then there's no point throwin' seven hundred guys out the back of a movin' truck to teach 'em how to roll is there. Let's get the chutes on 'em and run 'em out the back of a C-130. They know how to do that?"

"Goddamit, Thanasis. I told you they been through all the ground trainin' a man can do. I know you're in charge here. But I was runnin' Hua Hin. So let's just put 'em in an airplane and I won't have to call you out."

The sweatwork of loading hundreds of tons of military supply every day and then pushing it out the door of small aircraft taking massed fire in low-level parachute drops was beginning to stress the three smoke-jumpers at Long Tieng. The added burden of training seven hundred Meo guerillas in airborne jumps was threatening to wear friendship beyond thin.

Thanasis ignored Dooley's pique and tried harder to focus on what they had to do. "Gotcha bro'. We'll run a jump on the Plain of Jars day after tomorrow. I've got two C-130s out of Takhli for the day. That'll be two planes droppin' 140 every hour. Charlie and I are gonna jump with 'em, make sure they are checked out in the air and organized when they hit the ground. I need somebody to get the little guys on the planes out of Long Tieng. In unit order, on schedule. Can you run that piece of it?"

"You got it. Just let me know when you want 'em in the air."

The practice jump of Meo on the Plain of Jars went off without a hitch. Because of the size of the "little guys" Air Force advisers had assured CIA that the C-130 could jump 10 percent more Meo troopers than U.S. Army paratroopers. Seventy men per plane.

The following week, in full monsoon, a jump load of Meo troopers was standing at attention in pounding rain. It was dark and cold and everyone was wet through to the skin. They were about to board the plane. Thanasis was doing a last minute check of the unit, walking down the lines of Meo in camouflage uniforms darkened to a single shade of green by the rain, their faces shadowed by dripping helmets. He was counting.

At the end of the last rank he turned to the Lao lieutenant. "You got seventy-seven people about to board this airplane, sir. Two things are wrong with that. It means seven of these people don't know how to jump. They are not part of your unit and have not been trained. Can you identify those people for me?"

The Lao officer shook his head without embarrassment or concern.

Thanasis, tired of Lao passivity and rain, could feel his anger building. In ten days, the Meo troopers were to do a night combat jump as part of the opening assault in Operation Triangle. The over-limit screwup was threatening the first and only night training exercise for the Meo troopers. *I won't be able to reschedule the goddamn airplanes.*

"They're probably support staff on a lark, tryin' to piss me off! Right?" Thanasis hoped the Lao officer would realize the Meo were making a mistake and that he was playing with fire. He thought he saw the officer shrug in the dark. *OK. You just don't give a shit. Well, think about this.*

"This aircraft is only cleared for seventy troopers. It is overweight and out of spec if we go with seven men over full load."

The lieutenant had seen the huge aircraft unload jeeps, howitzers, and tons of rice. Seven more five-foot Meo did not suggest a problem to him. "No problem," he said.

The added load did not bother Thanasis either. The C-130 Hercules was capable of carrying most of the relatives of the airborne unit as well. But if something went wrong on the training flight—anything, related to the load or not—*It's my ass,* Thanasis thought. He turned away from the lieutenant because he wanted to punch the man. He saw Dooley, standing expressionless, arms folded across his chest.

Thanasis felt the blood pounding in his ears, felt himself becoming explosive, and then it came. "Goddamit, Dooley. You knew they were over-limit. You and the lieutenant. Either that or I can't trust you to do the simplest fuckin' thing—like countin'." He was walking up to Dooley, fast, face darkening in a rush of blood.

Dooley's arms came off his chest, fists clenched. "Gettin' the troopers lined out and on the plane is my job and you got to stick your nose in. Big man has to take over. You give me a job you stay the hell out of the way, big shot."

Without more both men were throwing punches, grunting with effort. In moments blood and snot was flowing on both faces.

Charlie walked up to the Lao lieutenant. "This is gonna take some time. Put 'em on board and let's go airborne. I'm your jump master." The Meo troopers boarded and the C-130 took off headed for a wet night jump on the rolling Plain of Jars. The fistfight was still underway as the aircraft cleared the valley.

When the fight at the muddy edge of the Long Tieng tarmac stopped, both men, leaning against each other exhausted and covered with red mud, had no idea what they were fighting about, but felt better about whatever it was.

The CIA chief of base at Long Tieng reported to Norris by telephone that night. "Sorry to call you so late. They really busted each other up. They'll need a little medical attention and you might consider rotating them out of here for awhile. It isn't them. It's the job. It's chewed 'em up. I think it'll blow over. But you know 'em better than I do." He also reported on a successful night training jump by, apparently, a reinforced Meo airborne unit.

Norris had all three of his Long Tieng smokejumpers sent down to Vientiane on the first helicopter out the next morning. He transferred three others into Long Tieng on a temporary basis from Savannakhet and Saigon. Norris interviewed Charlie and decided that three days R and R in Vientiane was all that was needed.

"What did you tell him, Charlie?"

"I told him, Thanasis, that you both had shell shock from snoggling homely girls while dead sober. Also told him neither of you could throw a punch."

"What did Norris say?"

"Though I argued against it he said what we needed was intercourse and intoxication. Based on Christian values I was able to impart, he compromised. He said you could each have one blow job at Lulu's, but then you had to go back to Long Tieng and kick cargo. Said you both look like homemade horseshit, don't know squat, whores won't have you, and that I'm to hold all your money while we're in Vientiane. Hand it over."

The three slept until late in the afternoon the following day. After a water buffalo steak in the booths of the wood-paneled Concorde restaurant they went to the Purple Porpoise on the Mekong waterfront for cold beers. The breeze from the river and rest and removal from Long Tieng put them in the mood to run the table.

They hit Vieng Ratray, renamed by them The Green Latrine for the bar in McCall. Tequila boilermakers led them to the Lucky Bar. They drank a few bom-de-bom—Ba Muoi Ba beer—at the Lucky Bar before moving on to The Spot, the hottest nightclub in Vientiane. It was run by the Corsican mob. Charlie's efforts to prove Corsicans were Italian, not French, earned them an invitation to leave. It was more the noise of it than the proof in his argument. Charlie objected to leaving. The guns in the Corsican waistbands came out and the jumpers left.

They hired samlors, three-wheeled bikes with drivers, and for "boo-coo" cash raced them to Lulu's, yelling "To the boom-boom house, my man." They berated and lavishly tipped the losing cyclist.

Lulu's was a one-time private residence surrounded by masonry walls and overhanging trees. There was a stone walk from the gateway on the street to the porch. The parlor just off the entry had a small wooden bar with two rattan stools at which waiting customers could purchase Singha or Budweiser. The floor was covered with linoleum and lighted by a large light bulb hanging from the ceiling. At Lulu's there were no separate rooms for sex. Off the parlor in a noisy illusion of privacy, there were cubicles separated from each other by bamboo partitions.

Lulu was French, five feet tall, blonde, dumpy, sixty-something, and dressed at all times in a muumuu. The girls working there were short, slim, good looking Asian women with multiple identities and a highly communicative pidgin mix of languages.

When the three grinning jumpers entered Lulu's parlor the place was empty of customers. The girls flew to them topless in spike heels and thongs. A Ray Charles recording was on the record player, filling the house with the beat of "What'd I Say."

"Hey mama, don't you treat me wrong

Come and love your daddy all night long

Unh(oh) unh(oh) unh(oh) unh(oh) unh(oh) unh(hey)"

"Hey slant-eyed brown sugar ho. No GI take you home to meet his mama? What's this world comin' to. Well, long as you still sportin' you come put that lip lock on me."

"You hab rubber? Me hab number one pussy."

"You're not listenin'. We are talkin' about BJ. And blow is just a figure a speech."

Thanasis drifted in and out of articulate. He took out a handful of money and pushed it at the young woman like a drunk man in a whorehouse can do, without looking, counting, or caring. He did know that money was the key to unlocking something simple, something that he once knew complete but was now slipping beyond comprehension.

Ray Charles was followed by Edith Piaf singing "Non, je ne regrette rien" in the uncrowded house of love. Lulu liked sad street singers.

A brown-skinned girl took Thanasis by the hand, the one filled with money, and led him to a bamboo cubicle. The girl waited, one hand on her slightly cocked hip, as he stood swaying, unfocused, beside the narrow bed. She finally giggled and undressed him where he stood. She reached behind her and dropped her thong on a chair, without looking, in sure knowledge that it was there.

She placed her hands on his hips, looked below his waist, then up to his face. She smiled, again with sure knowledge, and spoke to him seductively, adding a gasp to nail it. "I don't believe it. Me too little."

Gathering himself from beery distraction he was able to say, slowly, "You'll believe it when you feel it. Bet you're tight as a mouse's ear and clean, too. But tonight is blow job night. My back's a little sore." He touched an index finger to her cheek, and rotated it back and forth.

She smiled and said "I know blow job," nodding as if to assure him. He sat, then lay back slowly on the cot.

"Nose hurt?" she asked.

"See what other parts you can identify."

They went through a couple more Piaf songs before money and bodily fluids were exchanged.

He raised himself on an elbow, leaned there a while, and then sat up on the cot. He looked at the soft, rounded figure of the young woman, black hair falling to her shoulders. She was standing across the small harsh space of the cubicle. He motioned her to come to him.

"Want to hug you," he said, words spaced unevenly.

She stepped toward him and swung a leg across, straddling him and the cot, sitting on his lap. "You want pussy boom-boom now, hot-shot smoky jump man? I give you free."

"Just want to hug, like *tealoch*. Be like lovers." They hugged for a few minutes, his face between her breasts. He was remembering Idaho, another almond-eyed woman. The prostitute pushed him down on the cot, inserted his penis in practiced motion, and slowly rocked her pelvis. She made a kissing motion with pouted lips, the low sound of doves in her throat. The whorehouse fantasy *à deux* played out against the background of more Piaf. When she felt him ejaculate she rose and left.

Thanasis lay still for a few minutes, until he heard Ray Charles again, Charlie doing a sing-along. He pulled on his clothes and walked barefoot out of the cubicle. He saw Charlie chinning himself on the outside of another cubicle, trying to sing in accompaniment to "What'd I Say." He walked over and joined Charlie hanging from the bamboo partition. They were looking down on Dooley keeping time with Ray Charles, the whore Son Boum looking up at them, cheerfully. Charlie and Son Boum were singing the antiphonal refrain from the song on the record player.

"Unh(oh) unh(oh) unh(oh) unh(oh)"

Son Boum was giggling. So was Charlie. Dooley, breathless, said "I don't come, I ain't payin'."

That news brought Son Boum's full attention to the customer. She said salacious things that made Dooley come. Charlie and Son Boum accompanied Ray Charles again. "Ah! Make me feel so good," the three of them sang.

Norris met with his hungover, relaxed smokejumpers the next morning. "I want you three back up at Long Tieng and in the planes for the Meo airborne drop. It's their first time in the barrel. They'll be more gung ho if their trainers are a hands-on part of the operation. And I'll feel better if you're runnin' the follow-on resupply. Your heads on straight?"

They nodded and said "Yes, Uncle."

"There's a surprise sittin' on the airstrip. As the air ops guys you'll be supporting their presence at Long Tieng."

They were helicoptered from Wattay to Long Tieng. The surprise on the airstrip was six T-28 combat fighter-bomber aircraft. They were air support for the coming operation.

Vang Pao had lobbied for his own tactical air force and the training and use of Meo pilots. The ambassador to Laos had long resisted. He came around only when it was agreed that the success of his personally conceived operation might depend on air control of the only supply and reinforcement road leading from North Vietnam to the road between Vientiane and Luang Prabang. The crossroads was the intended battleground. The ambassador yielded on the condition that he retain control over use of the aircraft. As a practical matter that meant CIA control.

The T-28s were once Navy trainers. The rebuilt attack version, brought into being for use by the CIA in cooperation with brand new air forces of low-tech countries from Laos to Congo, was formidable. A two-seat aircraft with a 1,425 horsepower engine and two .50 caliber machine guns flush mounted in its wings, the T-28 could carry 3,500 pounds of bombs.

Operation Triangle turned out to be a walkover. Though the monsoon rains limited use of the T-28s, their sporadic sorties over the two roads at issue was new and threatening enough to assure that Vang Pao's crossroads offensive met little resistance. The ambassador, full of victory smiles, was committed to air warfare in Laos.

The Long Tieng smokejumpers, familiar with the effect of monsoon rain on the red laterite roads of Laos, thought that mud may have accounted equally for the victory.

"And Meo fallin' from the sky. Gotta scare hell out of Communists," Charlie said.

CHAPTER TWENTY-EIGHT

The cagey ambassador to Laos used success in securing the road to Luang Prabang as leverage in assembling a secret air force. There were impediments. He had few airplanes, few pilots, no flight trainers, no aircraft maintenance, no airfields. He addressed each need outside U.S. Air Force doctrine and command structure. He started with airfields.

Secure places on which airplanes can take off and land had an easy solution. It was the rightist Lao generals. Smuggling opium and gold gave the generals an appetite for clandestine air transportation. Because airfields were a necessary adjunct to their outside interests, the generals controlled the airfields in Laos.

The ambassador found the generals amenable to providing him secure airfields to support his air force. He did not seek a broader partnership in the generals' interests, nor did he seek to police them. All they had in common was a need for secure airfields.

The ambassador set up air operations centers at five airfields in Laos. Norris, working with the CIA officer assigned to the ambassador, stationed smokejumpers at each facility as Air Operations Officers. They coordinated with CIA and military personnel in Udorn who were directing Meo guerilla operations. The use of smokejumpers as air ops officers reflected no particular expertise. They were just good at problem solving and perseverance, strong virtues for war in sleepy, passive Laos. It reflected, too, the ambassador's fastidious effort to use civilians rather than military in Laos, in compliance with treaty obligations and presidential direction.

Lack of airplanes also had a simple solution, though it was accompanied by bureaucratic complexity. The ambassador asked Norris to buy sixty T-28s and two C-47s for his air force. Norris simply used a CIA Air Branch black account for the purchase.

The bureaucratic complexity was General Momyer, Commander of 7th Air Force. It drove the general wild that the State Department was authorized to operate a separate air force within the Southeast Asia theatre, his theatre, over which he had no control. The mere thought of it made him jump up from his chair and pound his desk.

It also upset him that aircraft used by the separate air force were slow-moving propeller driven planes, when Air Force doctrine called for an all-jet force in Southeast Asia. The general and his staff considered the attributes of propeller-driven aircraft pre-historic. They did not appreciate that the war in the Laos jungle was also from another time.

It drove the 7th Air Force commander to distraction that U.S. Air Force pilots were not flying the ambassador's airplanes. "How in hell can you have a war and not allow your own military in the country where you're fighting it?" was as articulate as he could get about what was an intensely felt professional humiliation. The ambassador maintained the facade of compliance with the Geneva Accord by using Lao, Thai, and Meo pilots. There was no place for General Momyer's pilots in the Cold War stratagem by which the nuclear powers pretended they were not at war in Laos.

Training pilots and qualifying them in T-28 combat support of Meo guerillas required the ambassador to turn, nevertheless, to the U.S. Air Force. Operating at the highest levels of the Department of Defense and the State Department, the ambassador made an arrangement that did not involve General Momyer. The Joint Chiefs of Staff ordered Tactical Air Command to send a special air warfare unit to Udorn to train pilots for T-28s and provide maintenance for the aircraft. A detachment from 1st Air Commando Wing of Tactical Air Command was sent to Udorn Royal Thai Air Force Base to carry out the training program, code named "Waterpump." They were assigned space next to the Air America ramp and worked for the ambassador to Laos.

The effort to train Meo pilots presented problems that were never completely solved. The Meo do not have a written language. They were generally illiterate and could not read a pre-flight check list in any language. They had no familiarity with Arabic numbers, which made cockpit instruments a mystery. They had never seen a compass rose and had difficulty with the concept it presented—navigation was as opaque as witchcraft. Few knew English, the language of the Waterpump trainers, and flight trainers could not speak the monosyllabic, multitonal language of the Meo. Few of the trainees had seen a radio and none had ever considered use of one to clear an aircraft for takeoff or landing.

The Waterpump air commandoes nevertheless trained Meo pilots. A commando trainer would sit on one wing, a Lao or Thai interpreter on the other, the pilot candidate between them, the cockpit canopy open. The young Meo was lectured in the simplest terms on takeoff and landing. The student learned the feel of flight by riding the controls as the trainer, in the rear seat, maneuvered the T-28 through taxi, takeoff, and landing. How they learned to deliver bombs and .50 caliber gunfire on target was and remained a mystery to the instructors. Maybe it was the long Meo tradition of hunting with handmade flintlock rifles and crossbows. Perhaps it was nothing but fatalism and inadequate knowledge of their limits.

The ambassador got his air force just in time. The nature of the war in Laos was changing. It had become two wars. One was the old war to protect the Royal Lao government domino from falling to the Communists. The new war, fought simultaneously with the first, was an air war against the men and supplies moving through Laos to South Vietnam on the Ho Chi Minh Trail. The additional Laos war was driven solely by events in South Vietnam.

The Army of the Republic of Vietnam, though assisted by sixteen thousand United States "military advisors," was proving no match for the Viet Cong. President Diem's measure of competence and loyalty in military officers was whether their units incurred casualties. Casualties meant that he was politically unpopular and resisted by his own people. It was career suicide for an ARVN officer to risk casualties by giving battle. It was not a view the officers held because of cowardice. It was just a fact. The ARVN officers accepted the fact and the Viet Cong won at will.

The CIA advised President Kennedy that the military situation in Vietnam was deteriorating and that there could be no success for the South Vietnam army with Diem running the country—and probably none without introduction of U.S. combat troops. Within months both Diem and Kennedy were dead, and the Vietnam situation continued its slide from bad to worse.

The failing public war in Vietnam slowly entwined the secret war in Laos. Then the Vietnam war became an American war.

Norris had no question about the plan of the U.S. commander in Vietnam. U.S. combat troops ranging through Vietnam in helicopters killing NVA faster than they could be replaced undoubtedly would work.

He had begun to have doubts, however, about the war in Laos. Operation Triangle was beginning to look like an aberration.

NVA had introduced an additional division into Laos and driven Vang Pao's Meo from the five hundred square miles of the Plain of Jars. NVA soon held the entire Meo heartland.

Norris addressed the complexities the new war introduced. He sent a team of jumpers to Phitsanulok, Thailand to train Thai airborne in jungle parachuting. The number of Thai PARU in Laos was being increased to stiffen defensive forces and augment road watch teams.

He increased air operations staff at Savannakhet, Laos, to support the stepped-up level of road watch activity and the ambassador's bombing of the Ho Chi Minh Trail. He transferred Thanasis to Savannakhet.

Norris kept Charlie at Long Tieng to run air resupply of Meo guerillas.

Norris was slipping into comfort in his role as wartime air boss. He took a day off. To stay sharp, he told himself. That was not the whole of it. His usual self-awareness did not extend to the quiet presence of May Ly. He was blind to the fact he simply wanted, for the day, to be alone with the young woman.

A man unaware, he walked hand in hand with her to the banks of the Mekong. They hired a dugout canoe and were paddled on the river by the canoe's owner. They drifted without destination through the shifting green patterns of jungle and tobacco farms along both sides of the river. Norris finally directed the boatman to Nong Khai, a Thai border town across the river from Vientiane. This part of the outing was one of her favorite things. It came with Coke in a bottle. Coca-Cola could be had for pennies anywhere in Vientiane, but only in a plastic bag. In Thailand the cold drink came in a bottle made in the traditional Coke-bottle shape. The pleasure the montagnard girl took in drinking from the translucent green bottle made Norris grin with his own pleasure.

They sat with their soft drinks in an open air restaurant. It was part of a small hotel with a tropical garden. They watched gibbons climbing in the nearby trees and vines. They ate hot roasted cashews with a spoon, sitting in the garden.

May was happy and thought it was time she spoke of her happiness.

Throughout Southeast Asia that year and in years to come Vietnamese and Lao women would tell American men they were pregnant and, with relief or sadness, take the proffered money. That ending never occurred to the Meo girl. She would have her child. The more usual course occurred to Norris, but passed out of his life like a smooth stone skipping, touching him barely at all.

The news from May focused him for the first time in his life on the need for personal security. He talked to Casey the next day and told him that he wanted a transfer to Marana, that he could carry out his air boss functions in Laos from most anywhere, the moon included. He asked no one's permission when he took the Meo girl with him to Arizona.

M.I.A.

The interrogating officer had asked only one question. "What is the Fulton Skyhook?"

The POW began his response with a request for paper and pencil. "You need a picture." He lectured about Skyhook without interruption or additional questioning. "All you need to know is in the final scene of the James Bond movie *Thunderball*. Get the movie and I'll talk you through it. The Skyhook and the B-17 used in the movie to rescue Bond was owned by CIA. The CIA smokejumpers were the crew that operated the Skyhook in the movie."

In most of his interrogations the POW had cooperated, but he never volunteered. He had to be led. That was not so about Skyhook. It was the high point of many smokejumper CIA careers. He was excited and ready to talk to any audience.

He explained without prompting that the smokejumpers had worked at Marana for months with Robert Fulton, the inventor of the Skyhook, developing drop procedures and CIA expertise in using the airborne retrieval system. The Agency had in mind rescue of agents, prisoners in foreign lands. The POW drew a picture of the Skyhook retrieval system and responded to the interrogator's questions about his drawing.

"The equipment includes a harness attached to a five hundred-foot braided nylon rope, a bottle of helium, and a dirigible-shaped balloon. The balloon pulls the rope up into the air. The aircraft, outfitted with thirty-foot steel arms attached to the nose of the plane, flies into the rope. The rope is guided by the steel arms to a spring-operated anchor on the plane that holds the rope. The balloon is cut free and the rope is snatched by the smokejumper crew with a 'Little Bo Peep' crook and attached to a power winch that pulls the rope and the man in the harness into the airplane." He explained who Bo Peep was.

He rattled off Skyhook facts with illustrative waving of hands and arms punctuated with "See."

"Does it work? Other than in the movies?"

"Damn straight."

"Has the CIA ever used the Skyhook in its operations?"

"Oh yeh. Ever heard of Operation Coldfeet?"

"Tell me about it."

The excited POW could hardly wait. "When our boss got a phone call in '62 asking if the Intermountain Aviation B-17 was available to drop two investigators on an abandoned Soviet ice station—it was breaking up—and recover them using the Skyhook system, he said we were ready.

"Our unmarked plane was flown to Point Barrow, Alaska, with a half-ton of retrieval equipment and four smokejumpers on board.

"Two military investigators, specialists in polar meteorology and sonar, were parachuted onto the Russian drift ice through the 'Joe hole,' the hole in the floor of the B-17 where the belly gunner used to fight. After three days they collected 150 pounds of Russian notebooks and equipment. They were ready to be picked up, so we went and got em'. We did the Skyhook retrieval three times. Once for each of the investigators we had dropped and once for their cargo. Norris gave the guys we retrieved a 'pick-me-up' from his flask of scotch." The POW smiled at his telling of the joke, and said "Skyhook works."

"Are there times it does not work?"

The POW recalled times they did not yet believe in Skyhook. "There was the time we did the demonstration of Skyhook for the U-2 pilots. It was windy and we came in too low to get the dummy off the ground and it bounced along for about three hundred yards in front of a bunch of spy pilots and CIA officials. We offered to do it again." The POW was struggling not to laugh. "But the U-2 pilots walked away saying 'If it's all the same to you, we'd just as soon be captured.'" The prisoner burst out laughing at the joke.

The interrogating officer misinterpreted the laughter as something directed at him, and knocked the POW to the floor. There was always that risk in prison laughter.

CHAPTER TWENTY-NINE

General Vang Pao's jeep skidded to a stop inches from Charlie's leg. The driver, Cork Nose, a Vang Pao bodyguard, looked at Charlie over the hood of the jeep. The bodyguard was a battler. His nose was shot away in a jungle firefight. He dealt with the hole in his face by sticking a cork in it.

Vang Pao got out of the jeep, its engine still running. Cork Nose, continuing to look at Charlie, popped the clutch. The jeep jumped forward and struck Charlie's leg, hard. His boot slid backwards in the gravel, stretching but saving ligaments. "It felt like DiMaggio hittin' me with a friggin' bat," Charlie said each time he told the story in Poppa Chu's Long Tieng mess hall.

Charlie wanted to grab his knee and fall to the ground, but Vang Pao was standing where he wanted to fall. The general, hands on hips, glaring, was yelling at him.

"Charlie, you killed one hundred of my best men this week. That is on top of the hundred you killed last week. If this war is lost it will be traced to one man. You."

The pain in his knee was making it hard to follow the general. At first he thought Vang Pao was talking about the Lao colonel Air America had dropped through the floor of a Pilatus Porter. The colonel had been sitting on a cargo bale positioned over the trap door in the belly of the Porter. The pilot made his drop, opening the trap door without looking back into the cargo bay. The colonel landed on a Meo howitzer from eight hundred feet. The Meo in the gun pit heard the colonel's scream somewhere above them, unaware he was falling toward the gun. Convinced the spirit of the gun had cried out and then split the colonel's head, they never fired it again.

Charlie, dizzy with pain, finally figured out it was not about the colonel. He knew what it was about.

"I'd never do that, general. It didn't happen. What're you saying?"

"What do you think happens, Charlie, when my men get no ammunition because you don't put it on airplanes and deliver it when they are attacked? Look at it stacked up over there. What do you think happens to my men when you do not send them any one-oh-five howitzer shells? They die because Communists with lots of bullets walk up and kill them! You must work harder and get your job done. Stop sitting on your ass or we will lose the war."

Charlie knew the resupply operation was not working. He did not think it was his fault. He was working twenty-hour days. He needed to explain the problem, but Vang Pao was already back in the jeep, being driven away.

He limped over to the office attached to the rigging shed to explain, again, to the Lao lieutenant commanding the men who worked under Charlie in the resupply depot. He was embarrassed and angry about the Vang Pao accusation. He walked into the lieutenant's office without knocking.

"Lieutenant Syborravong. . . ." He stopped as soon as he had begun. There was no point. Charlie left and went to the office of the chief of the Long Tieng CIA unit. The chief was a secretive man, so much so that everyone said his baptismal name was just a cover. They called him "Joe" instead. It seemed to irritate him, so they continued. Like other CIA at Long Tieng, Joe dressed in mismatched civilian and military clothing, carried a 9-mm Browning pistol in a holster on his hip.

Charlie said "Hi, Joe," and explained the status of resupply operations and the problem he was having. He told the chief about Vang Pao's visit and the ass-chewing he got.

"He's tellin' me I'm losin' the friggin' war. Well bullshit, Joe. He's in charge of the Lao at Long Tieng."

The chief of the CIA unit knew where his world ended and Vang Pao's began. Joe said "I can't do anything for ya. But it's got to be fixed and now. You've got to go tell Vang Pao."

Charlie limped from the CIA compound across the hot black runway to Vang Pao's concrete house with antiaircraft guns on the roof. He said he wanted a meeting with Vang Pao and was quickly brought into the general's office by a Meo orderly.

He stood at attention in his white T-shirt and work pants, shuffled his feet, then asked Vang Pao to get rid of Lieutenant Syborravong. Vang Pao said nothing. Charlie hesitated, ran a nervous hand through his crew cut hair, tried to return the cold look of the general. He rushed to complete his explanation before he was thrown out.

"From the minute he shows up at the rigging shed, if he shows up at all, he's so full of opium he can't keep his head off his desk. He's supposed to get me the grunts I need for humpin' and riggin' cargo. He doesn't get me squat because he's in la-la land. Those boys don't show up voluntarily. Nobody shows up except my Thai interpreter and he's useless because there's nobody for me to talk to. It's all me and only me." *If you lose the war, it'll be because of the tarheads you keep around,* he said to himself, closing his report. He brought himself to attention once more.

Vang Pao sat with his chin resting on his fist, jaw muscles clenching and unclenching, pursed his lips and gave a small nod. "I will take care of it."

There was no suggestion of an apology, but Charlie thought he would ask for one more thing. "Sir, would you please not say to people that I've killed your men."

Charlie left Vang Pao and moved slowly to the infirmary. The knee was iced and wrapped, and pain killers provided. He was advised to stay off the fork lift and out of the rigging shed while taking the pain killers. He did not return to work for two days.

The day he went back to work there were one hundred Lao and Meo enlisted men standing among the pallets of rice, rifles, artillery shells, and parachutes. More men than he could use, they waited for his directions. He organized them into work teams to prepare drop loads for the guerilla groups that were identified for him that morning by the CIA operations center in Udorn. He prepared flight manifests for a full day of C-123 and Pilatus Porter drops, identifying cargo and people on each flight. Charlie and Long Tieng resupply were humming.

When he came to a break in the flow of work Charlie walked over to Joe's office. "What happened? When I say shit, these boys ask how much."

"Vang Pao shot the lieutenant."

"No he didn't. Stop jacking around. I'm busy out there."

"He did. He shot him. Vang Pao and his deputy, Colonel Paledimonevong, drove up in a jeep. Vang Pao was pullin' a .45 before he even got to the door of the office. Shot the lieutenant sittin' at his desk, without sayin' hi, yes, or shit. You're pretty persuasive, Charlie."

The suggestion that he had persuaded Vang Pao to kill one of his own men bothered Charlie. "I didn't persuade anybody to do anything. I just reported the facts. Don't you be tellin' anything else. You do and we'll go outside to deal with it."

Joe looked at Charlie in silence. Then he said "You did right."

Charlie remained unconvinced Vang Pao had shot the lieutenant. "I been in there. I didn't see any blood."

"That's the thing, Charlie. It was like a mob hit. Vang Pao walked out and two guys with sponges and a bucket of water walked in. It was like he knew somebody in New Jersey, just made a call. In a half hour they had the lieutenant's office spic and span. I think Vang Pao is gonna put you in the office."

"Not gonna happen, Joe."

Charlie stole the line about the mob hit for retelling in the mess hall. He changed New Jersey to Chicago.

Through the following year Charlie and Long Tieng resupply worked at full capacity. They supplied the Meo guerillas daily in more than nine hundred ground battles with the NVA and Pathet Lao. When the Communists attacked during the dry season—October through May—the Meo engaged in daily ambushes. Charlie and other kickers flew on night helicopter missions in Air America H-34s and Hueys, helping move Meo ambush teams into position. Contrary to standing orders that CIA personnel not fire weapons except in defensive combat, they manned machine guns in the helo doors if the pilot thought the landing zone might be hot. Kickers fired thousands of .50 caliber machine gun rounds in cautionary "self-defense."

When the monsoons came—June through September—the Meo went on the offensive, repeatedly attacking NVA withdrawing to Vietnam for rest and re-outfitting. Air America, working with Charlie and his short laborers, answered every call from Vang Pao for food and ammunition, whatever the weather or battle conditions. In addition they supplied two hundred Lima sites, remote mountain bases, often nothing more than a circle of zigzag trenches, where the Meo guerillas regrouped after attacking the invaders.

None of the conditions of the Long Tieng operation could be controlled—not the weather, not the NVA reaction, not Vang Pao, not the feuding Meo clans living there.

Charlie was never happier.

He celebrated with the Meo. For the Meo New Year, in November when the rice harvest was completed, he bought two water buffalo and had them transported in helicopter slings, bug-eyed and bellowing, to troops in forward positions for the New Year meal in which the celebration culminated.

He entertained them. He ordered bull bells, spurs, and rodeo rigging through Marana and staged a rodeo. He and another jumper took turns riding a bull they named Giap. The Meo laughed and applauded when Giap threw both riders in the dirt of the bull pen.

He played the teasing jokes of the Meo. When a Meo officer continued to park his bicycle in the middle of the resupply work area in spite of requests that he not, Charlie put the bicycle on the roof of one of the CIA buildings with a fork lift. The Meo were delighted at the officer begging Charlie for return of his bike. A terrific Meo joke.

When bickering of the Meo clans forced to live together in Long Tieng threatened the resupply operation Charlie stepped in and arbitrated disputes of place and precedence. The Meo regarded Charlie as fair and impartial, largely because he had no stake in the outcomes. They started bringing their disputes, new and ancient, to Charlie for resolution. He always decided quickly, mostly without grasping the arguments. His guiding principles were never to decide in favor of a particular clan more than once and never to decide in favor of the clan of a girl he was sleeping with. He kept a notebook record of relationships and decisions.

The girls came to him because he had become a favorite of Vang Pao. They were a gift. They liked him well enough, but they were clearly delivering another man's favor. Charlie did not mind.

The clear, cool nights of the dry season were ending at Long Tieng, and the heat had begun to build. Particularly happy after a night with a young Meo woman who thought he was important, Charlie was singing in the shower, planning his day. The shower was gravity flow from a 55-gallon rooftop barrel. Like many things at Long Tieng it was make-shift, but the immersion heater made the shower a long hot luxury. He decided he would fill in as a kicker in a C-47 going north that morning on a cargo drop.

Clean and full of himself he had breakfast at Poppa Chu's. Poppa Chu was a Lao chef with skills that made him worth stealing. The CIA had stolen him from air commandoes in Udorn, using money the commandoes could not match, and set him up as their chef at Long Tieng.

After a breakfast of steak and eggs and many cups of coffee, Charlie bicycled to the ramp where the C-47 was being loaded. He relieved one of the two smokejumper kickers who had been assigned the morning flight.

"You go on down to Vientiane and check out the girls in The White Rose. I'll cover today and tomorrow."

"Why's that?"

"They need someone to change the sheets. Get to keep your pay from both jobs."

"Sounds right. See you in forty-eight hours."

Charlie checked out the load, making sure it was properly tied down, would not shift in flight. He then walked to his room, past two bears in a cage near the karst. The bears had been captured as cubs by Meo children and bartered to the Ravens, a group of U.S. Air Force forward air controllers stationed at Long Tieng. The controllers had been decommissioned to civilian status and were operating in the black, marking targets from Piper Super Cubs for Lao T-28s and, increasingly, U.S. Air Force fighter bombers. The bears were named Floyd, a fat male who drank beer, and Mama Bear. Charlie bought Floyd a beer from the nearby Air America bar.

In his quarters he armed himself with a 9-mm pistol and donned a B-7 emergency parachute. Happy with life, he was becoming a careful, orderly man. He returned to the plane and boarded, the engines turning over and belching dark gray smoke.

He stood in the cargo doorway as the plane taxied from apron to runway. He leaned forward, bracing himself with both arms, watching Long Tieng passing. With the end of the rainy season the fields beyond the runway asphalt were full of yellow daisies and red and white poppies. It was already warm and the slipstream at the door felt good, cooling. He watched communications antennae disappear below him as the plane banked toward the northeast.

No flight in Laos lasted long. Charlie got busy with the kicker's job. As he began he laughed to himself at the kickers' formal job title. *Only CIA could come up with PDO, Parachute Dispatch Officer.*

The floor of the C-47 was laid out with roller tracks that curved to exit at the cargo door Charlie had been standing in. He gave them a once over, looking for obvious damage that would impede movement of the pallets down the tracks. The flight crew had already done a closer inspection. Pilots did not like to land on short mountain runways with a pallet of high explosive on board just because it could not be pushed down a bent roller track.

Charlie inspected the cargo pallets. They were held in place by chains bolted to the floor and fuselage and fastened over the pallet loads. He released the chains on all except the pallet nearest the door for quick response in making the drop.

He completed his preparations by attaching the parachute static line on each pallet to the overhead cable running down the center of the cargo bay. He checked with the pilot on time to the drop site.

"We're goin' east of Ban Ban with the first half of our load. Then into Na Khang with the artillery shells. We're about fifteen minutes out on the first."

Charlie returned to the cargo bay to await the drop signal. He released chains on the pallet nearest the door after placing wheel chocks between it and the doorway. He and the other kicker stood by to knock the chocks away and begin pushing pallets down the roller track.

Charlie was full of good cheer and the small puffs of cloud outside the cargo door seemed to match his mood. The only irritant was that the pilot was doing an awful lot of flying, climbing then slipping the plane back down, changing speeds, banking.

Charlie understood when he saw that the small puffs of cloud were flak explosions just below them. His mood fell with the arc of 23-mm cannon fire, missing as it reached toward the plane, dropping below it. He yelled at the other kicker and pulled at his own parachute harness to indicate. "Find a chute and get it on!" The kicker ran forward, searching.

The C-47 was an easy target for antiaircraft guns. The Chinese gunners had waited until the plane settled into its drop run, positioning for the release of cargo. The gunfire was heavy. That the gunners missed at all was surprising. The gunfire from the ground destroyed both engines and began chewing away the control surfaces.

Charlie could barely hear over the explosions pounding the airplane. The pilot was screaming for them to jump. He grabbed the edge of the door opening and pulled himself out of the disintegrating airplane as it began to roll over, his feet going out from under him. Separated from the plane he pulled the ripcord in reflex. When his chute opened he looked around for the other parachutes. There were none, not at any point on the compass. He felt his feet lift, as if to avoid the jungle below. He felt the legs of his jeans grow warm, then wet and cold against his skin.

CHAPTER THIRTY

The Thai pilots at Savannakhet, CIA site Lima 39, had muscles, tattoos, wide-set dark eyes, and behaved like they flew fighter planes. There were women around at all hours, cold beer, and manful hangar flying.

Thanasis decided after two weeks at Lima 39 that they were the ones he would go to. He addressed the possibility of their indifference like any run-of-the-mill smokejumper problem. He bought two cases of cold Singha, put one on each shoulder, and walked into the air-conditioned Quonset hut that served as the Thai analogue of Bachelor Officers Quarters.

He was greeted by loud American music from a boom box. He was thinking Thai and it did not register. Then it did. *Jim Dandy to the rescue! LaVern Baker? Are you guys for real?* Thanasis tried hard not to grin. He put the beer down on a table, pulled a sweating bottle from the cardboard, opened it and drank, head up, looking only at the ceiling. He did not say hello.

A Thai captain, dressed in equal portions of Royal Lao Air Force uniform and sarong, rose from the cot on which he sat. He had been playing poker with three other flyers. Without taking his eyes off Thanasis he motioned to the flyer nearest the boom box to turn it down. His square brown face registered nothing as he stepped toward Thanasis at the BOQ table.

"Can I help?" The English was American college casual.

"I sure hope so. You can start by helpin' me drink this beer. I'm tired carryin' it around."

Thanasis was soon surrounded by the U.S. Ambassador's RLAF Thai pilots, shooting a load of bullshit and drinking beer. *Came to the right boys.* He finished a second beer and asked for the favor he sought. He addressed the captain.

"Cap'n Channarong, you probably know that I work for the Company and that I'm the new air ops officer for the five thousand feet of concrete outside your bedroom here. You need anything you just ask. I have tradin' goods." The Thai pilots, "volunteers," were hired and directed by the CIA. Thanasis hoped that invoking the combination of employer, airbase authority, and patronage would get him what he needed. He opened another beer and offered it to the captain. The captain took the beer and said nothing, waited for Thanasis to continue.

"I know your men have been flyin' Barrel Roll missions." His reference was to the air campaign to close the Ho Chi Minh trail. It was run by Ambassador Sullivan's air force, and everything was homey, seat of the pants, and unregulated.

Norris had told him that was about to change. The U.S. military, Generals Westmoreland and Momyer, wanted control of the Trail bombing. It was part of their "extended battle field," even if it was in another country and subject to international agreement excluding their presence. They were not sure President Johnson would let them play those cards. It turned out he insisted on it. The bombing would be done by fast movers, jets, operating out of airbases in South Vietnam and from U.S. carriers in the South China Sea. "Steel Tiger," as the U.S. commanders called their Trail bombing plan, would not be disclosed to the American people, any more than the bombing in Laos by the ambassador's propeller driven air force was.

"Tighten up your operation," Norris had told him. "You'll have to coordinate trail watch activities with U.S. military bombing schedules and airplanes we no longer control. There'll be dozens of B-52 sorties every day, not two or three T-28s every week. Most of it'll be at choke points, the mountain passes into Laos. But you should assume there's a three-hundred mile free fire zone, as long and wide as the Laos panhandle, from passes in the north to Cambodia. One other thing, Thanasis. Do me some bomb damage assessments on the QT. Figure it out."

Thanasis continued with Channarong and told him what he needed. "I want you to show me what you guys did up at Mu Gia pass last week.

I need a lesson in bomb damage assessment." The mountain pass leading from North Vietnam into Laos, a starting point on the Trail, had been an on-again, off-again RLAF bombing and strafing mission. Some days the Lao government was concerned the ambassador was baiting the North Vietnamese into destroying the RLAF and pressured him not to risk "their" air force in the heavily defended passes.

Captain Channarong smiled like a movie star on a red carpet. "Sure thing, Mavros. Just show up at first light tomorrow in a flight suit. I'll show you some hellacious craters. Get ready to take some Gs and maybe some twenty mikemike." Channarong was referring to the likelihood of facing 20-mm cannon fire. He laughed out loud and slapped the new air ops officer on the shoulder. Thanasis grew certain he was going to be tested before he got his bomb damage assessment lessons from the captain.

Further into the Singha, he and Captain Channarong agreed to several flights north and south of Savannakhet, a survey of the Trail. With detailed flight maps on his lap Thanasis intended to learn his territory like a route salesman.

As he prepared to leave his new friends Thanasis asked "What's the Z on your nametag stand for? Z Channarong?"

"In Thailand everyone has a nickname. Z is my nickname. You know, like Zorro the Fox. Zorro is the squadron call sign."

The next morning Channarong greeted Thanasis with a broad smile. "Ready to shoot a truck, air boss?"

"I can't be a combatant, except to defend my life or avoid capture."

"We can put you in that position. Either one." The captain seemed silly happy.

They took off in the two-seat T-28 just as the sun sent horizontal rays of light through palm trees at the side of the runway. Sitting in the back Thanasis watched the airstrip fall away as they headed north. They were still climbing above the long tongue of concrete when Channarong executed a barrel roll, a combination of loop and roll creating a horizontal corkscrew flight path.

Thanasis was startled by the unannounced revolutions of earth and sky. He mostly enjoyed the sensations produced by eye and ear gathering unfamiliar information, reading the rotations, sending conflicting messages to and getting straightened out by an uncertain brain. There was enough discomfort that he knew he would be glad when the maneuver stopped.

Channarong's voice in his earphones cut through the alternating float and press of gravity. "That's Zorro squadron's signature aerobatic. Barrel roll."

"Got it, Z."

"You got it. Now what is it you want to see?"

Thanasis imagined the Thai pilot grinning in the front seat of the plane. He asked him to fly over the Trail along several vectors and at different altitudes and speeds.

Whatever Channarong did with the plane, it was impossible to detect anything in the jungle below. No roads, paths, people, vehicles, or depots. Occasionally a dirt road snaked out of dark layers of green and disappeared with only an intimation of its course.

"How do you find it or anything on it?"

"Easy enough. We try to make them shoot at us. Then we kill the shooters. They don't do that for long. Everybody learns to control the urge to shoot us down." The captain paused. "Even when we do provoke them into shooting and locate a segment, it's not there next time . . . you have to get the notion of *it,* a path through the jungle, out of your head. *It's* not singular. It's a web, spreads miles wide. Lots of crisscrossing roads and paths that wander all over the border area. We wouldn't know shit without the trail watch teams on the ground." The captain had acquired a laconic voice for radio communication, probably from U.S. Air Force trainers. His Trail lecture took a long soothing time.

"Help if they'd get rid of some of that jungle down there," Thanasis said.

"Sure. How does that happen?"

Thanasis thought about B-52s and carpet bombing.

"What next, Mavros?"

"Let's go see Mu Gia."

They flew further north, gaining altitude. After a while Channarong, maintaining speed and rolling the plane into a turn, jabbed a finger at the ground below. "Just off the wingtip. You can see the road winding through the pass."

Thanasis saw the road clearly. At their altitude the Trail through Mu Gia pass was a thin line. He could see craters on either side, but there was not a mark on the road. They could see trucks moving west into Laos over it.

There was silence from the front seat of the cockpit. A caustic thought wandered into Thanasis' head. He decided to share it, in some form.

"Captain, you promised me craters. I don't think they count if they aren't on the road. Can you take me through the pass low and slow so I can count the craters in the road?"

The silence from the front seat continued. Finally Channarong spoke. "We'll go low but we won't go slow. About the craters—they aren't there anymore. I wasn't lying to you. Three days ago they were there. Counted them. Four of them. Made one myself. The North Vietnamese 559th transportation battalion puts these roads back together overnight. They use some Lao conscripts, but it's mostly Vietnamese peasants. The bulldozers are hidden underground on the Vietnam side of the pass. We get that from the road watch teams."

Thanasis had heard the reports on NVA road repair. Many of the road watch teams were Thai PARU. He was not surprised that the PARU talked directly to the Thai pilots.

"We'll blow up the road again. Next week, right here in the choke point. Day after that, five-five-nine will bring on the bulldozers. Waterpump can't train enough pilots to keep the Trail closed. We lost two this month. The B-52s will do a better job but they won't work either. Guess how many SAM sites they're buildin' down there right now. Just this one mountain pass." Channarong waited.

Thanasis, without information, said "Two." He forgot to ask how Channarong knew about the B-52s.

"Six. Now if it's OK with you I'm going to go down and shoot up a construction crew on one of the sites. There will be real bullets flying in both directions so think about it."

"Do it. I'm an observer." As he felt the nose of the plane drop over he thought for a second, without resolution, about who he really was, and silently ended the thought with *deniable*.

The plane dove from east of the pass, above North Vietnam, as it had in the past. It did not, as it had in past attacks, shoot up any of the small villages that accompanied the road on its course toward Laos. The plane leveled out and rushed toward the tree- and moss-covered cleft in the skyline at three hundred knots.

Most of the limestone cordillera stood above them. Thanasis saw it as a gray-green wall they would crash into. Over Channarong's shoulder, he saw broken earth, the jungle pushed aside by heavy equipment, red balls lazing toward them, some streaking by. He knew when he heard the thudding of their own .50 caliber guns that they were shooting, being shot at, and maybe being hit. Unaware of his movements, he tensed and lifted one shoulder against a strap, thrust his hip at the side of the plane, like a player at a pinball machine, urging the balls away.

Channarong made no effort to change the plane's attitude, no effort to evade the red balls. To him the plane was its call sign, Zorro, swordsman—stable, aimed, thrusting at the target. He moved away only when it was, at last, necessary to climb above the gray-green wall. Ground fire followed them out of the pass.

The captain checked his instruments. "They didn't hit anything we can't live without. But I'm heading back to thirty-nine. Decided I don't want to explain your death or capture to your government. At least until I know you better."

Thanasis knew he could tease the Thai captain into more flight time. He said only "Roger that."

As they approached Savannakhet, Channarong's voice came over the earphones again. He sounded resigned, maybe tired. "Didn't mean to go dead on you. Just thinkin' about the Trail. You can see yourself Barrel Roll won't close it up. Not nearly enough fire and brimstone. Hell, Mavros, that work crew I shot up back there won't even take the afternoon off. Serious little bastards." He paused. "My whole Zorro squadron will be dead in a year. Fly 'til they die." The Thai pilot was silent a few seconds. Then he added "You come party with us. Meanwhile, don't be flyin' around the Trail in the daytime."

Channarong talked until he finished taxiing the plane. "I mean it. Come party. We'll find you a regular woman. None of that scruffy mountain stuff."

The Laos town of Savannakhet had been a French colonial settlement. The ochre-colored two-story shophouses on the town square, the grid of surrounding streets with villas of long gone French officials, declared the town French colonial. Its site on the Mekong River, between Vietnam and Thailand, had made it a merchant and trading village as well as provincial capital attracting, with French encouragement, Vietnamese and Chinese immigrants.

Thanasis was living alone in nineteen rooms. Like many Company people, he lived in an old French mansion on one of the streets off the town square. It was pink stucco on masonry, a little run down but better than the outlying Lao houses on stilts. There were two baths, Lao guards hired by the Company, and two Lao maids, sisters. He socialized with employees of USAID, USIS, the Company, military air attaches from the Savannakhet airbase, and Polish staff of the International Control Commission. In many cases the employees had families, and wives were included in the social circle. Those circumstances made him feel lonely. He accepted Channarong's invitation to party.

Later that week the Thai pilots rented a riverside restaurant for the evening. Thanasis was invited. He was introduced to a "regular" but beautiful Thai woman. She was dressed in a traditional Thai *pha sin,* a full-length tube skirt, one intended for a fashionable event, silk, multicolored, a suggestion of Indian glitter. One shoulder was bare, the other covered by a *sabai,* a light-colored shoulder cloth. Her English was that of an educated person, one on holiday and enjoying herself. Her hair was black, long but swept up in a formal style leaving her neck bare. Her name was Dao. Thanasis felt taken in tow by her attention. He thought it was purposeful but could not imagine why. He enjoyed himself and was far from lonely.

After a drink together she excused herself and left the room. Thanasis took the opportunity to speak to Channarong.

“I remembered something I wanted to ask you. How’d you know about the B-52s?”

“I could tell you it was just logic. But I heard it from a Thai working in the CIA office here. Thanasis, your intelligence service is a sieve. Maybe not all of it, but, my god, the paramilitary guys never heard a secret they thought worth keeping. It probably doesn’t matter. The B-52s will make a big enough noise that everyone will know.” Channarong paused. “Keep in mind what I said. There’s a large Vietnamese community here. Most of them have been here for generations and think of themselves as Lao. But some are newcomers. We can’t tell about them. And Lao Communist sympathizers are not in short supply. The Communists got rid of the French and that has won them much support.”

Thanasis looked around, feeling the relaxation of the evening slipping away, displaced by tension that had become the background noise of his Lao life.

Channarong noticed. “Don’t worry. Dao is not Vietnamese, though she is a little bit lefty after Berkeley.”

“You know everything here?”

“I know nothing. She’s my sister.”

Thanasis smiled. “She’s lovely. Thanks for the introduction. That’s two favors I owe you. I’d like one more.”

“I don’t have a car.”

“Not what I had in mind. Thanks though. What I have in mind is that you speak to the leader of the PARU road watch teams for me. I think I should go out with them on a road watch trip, make sure I know their circumstances. Because the Company is running the teams and I’m running their helicopters I can make it happen. But I don’t want to force it. I want the PARU road watch leader to accept me, see my presence as useful to him. He has to want me to get smart.”

Channarong promised to speak to his PARU counterpart, said he knew what Thanasis wanted. He nodded toward Dao, who had returned to the room. “Happens all the time. Whenever I introduce her to some guy, he goes off and tries to get himself killed. Don’t know about that woman.”

Thanasis, relaxed again, returned to animated conversation with Dao. As the party got louder the two of them moved away from it to the restaurant veranda overlooking the river. The citrus jasmine smell of plumeria filled the night air.

"National flower of Laos. How do the Thai feel about it?"

"Thai say that it is the flower that brings unhappiness. It shelters demons and ghosts. In some places in the world its name is Dead Man's Fingers." She was smiling.

"How do educated women feel about the flower?"

Dao reached into the nearby plumeria tree, picked a blossom, and put it behind one ear. "To educated women plumeria worn behind one ear means 'I am taken'." She paused, still smiling. "Worn behind the other ear it means 'I seek a relationship'." She was patting the blossom into place.

Thanasis put a blossom behind his ear, on the same side, and leaned down and kissed her. She opened her mouth against his. They walked to the street, flagged a *tuk-tuk*, and rode the motorized samlor to his nineteen-room rundown mansion, kissing, breathing in each other's air.

They stood in his room and she said "I like to be undressed." His hands moved over her in discovery, searching, removing. As she stepped out of the dress pooled at her feet she asked him to wait a moment. He lay on the bed and she knelt beside him. He watched her take delicately carved jade pins from her hair, loosening but holding it in place until it all was free. She slowly let her black hair fall as she bent over him, hiding both of them. Thanasis cupped the silky hair in his hands as if it were a long-awaited gift, and buried his face in its fragrance.

CHAPTER THIRTY-ONE

Sweat blinded Charlie's eyes and fear stiffened his fingers. It did not matter. Sightless and cramping, he ran the letdown rope through his hands and the harness rings with practiced ease. It was like brushing his teeth . He felt brilliant about carrying the 250-foot nylon tape in a chest pack, his own makeshift. He would need it all, he thought. *Tree's biggest in goddamn Laos.*

He lowered himself, burning his bare hands belaying the rope. He thought *thank you Max thank you Max* over and over as he lowered himself toward the floor of the jungle. The mantra of grace calmed him a little, let him think. He stopped his descent every twenty or thirty feet to listen, straining to hear if there were sounds other than those of air moving through trees, straining to know whether there was someone below him.

He never saw the jungle floor until he felt the sensation of standing and, looking down, saw that is where he was. He lay down and tried to control his breathing. He knew he had to remain calm, the first rule of Survival School. What was the rest? It would come if he was cool. He had to concentrate on his situation. See it clearly. That is what the instructors told them. And drink water, four quarts.

Charlie ran his hand down to the canteen on his hip, missed it, quietly redirected his hand. He felt nothing. His skin prickled with alarm when he realized he had forgotten water. Now he was thirsty and angry at himself for forgetting, a thing a kid might do, and he struck the ground with his fist.

The people at Long Tieng would already know they had a plane down. Air America would launch a search and rescue immediately. The thought allowed him to calm himself and focus. He would not have to do anything, just wait for the chopper.

He began to anticipate the rescue. He realized that he had to move, get to an open area. Search And Rescue would never see him beneath the towering trees and dense undergrowth of the Laos jungle. He stood up. Which way to go? Standard SAR was move away from the plane wreck and drink water. *God knows I'm away from the plane wreck. Friggin' water.*

He decided he needed to move toward water. He was appalled by the noise he made with every step but he kept moving. He tried to plan as he shifted and bent and turned his way through the undergrowth. When he got to a river he would float out, all the way to the Mekong. He was beginning to visualize his careful, silent float through the Pathet Lao to safety when the image of a map filled his head. He knew this map. East of Ban Ban the pilot had said. And there was Ban Ban on the map. How far east? The question made him stop moving. Not because he could not calculate how far but because "east" on the map was showing him a reality that did not fit his plan. East of Ban Ban the rivers did not flow to the Mekong. They flowed into Vietnam and the Gulf of Tonkin.

Charlie sat down. He expected anger but he began laughing. *I knew that. They say you lose half your IQ when you jump out of an airplane. I guess so. More if the sucker is on fire.* Laughing seemed to take the fear and anger away. He stood up again. *I was makin' a floatin' movie when what I needed was a walkin' movie. Can't bend the map.*

They had flown from the west, from Long Tieng. SAR would fly the same route, find the crash site. Then they would search west of the crash for people who might have gotten out. *This'll be easy if I just break it down.*

He had started moving west, seeking higher ground, maybe a clearing created by Meo burning, when he heard voices. He crouched and listened. The sounds made him imagine commands and responses as men spread out. The voices were coming toward him.

He looked around for a hiding place. There was dense clumped shrubbery a few feet away. He could not tell how far it ran, how deep. On hands and knees he pushed his way into the bushes. He struggled, boots pushing hard against the ground, tearing it up. He broke branches with his hands. His hands were bleeding but he felt nothing. Once inside the clumps of brush he sat facing the sound of the voices.

Charlie removed the 9-mm from its holster and chambered a round, pulling the slide toward him and slowing its return to avoid the loud blue clack of colliding gunmetal. He had never fired the gun.

The voices, now immediately in front of him, stopped. A grunt from someone beyond the brush was followed by pain in the front of his shoulder. The force of it nearly knocked him over backwards. It happened quickly, and he barely had time to see the sharpened bamboo pole jerked back through the thicket in front of him. There were cries—"Ai!"—and the bamboo probe shot back into his hiding place. This time it missed him and was jerked away even more quickly.

Charlie pointed the pistol into the brush in front of him and fired as the bamboo disappeared. He lunged, firing wildly as the branches caught at his arms and threatened to take the pistol from his hands. He broke out of the shrubbery, continuing to fire. He saw men in black pajamas ducking for cover. They were armed with automatic rifles and firing high, as wildly as Charlie. Turning to run, he stumbled and fell over a man lying on the ground holding a bamboo pole, his face a large red wound.

Bullets ripped up foliage above Charlie. He was torn between staying on his belly on top of the dead man or getting up and running. He rolled over on his back and fired his pistol blindly between his legs outstretched toward the automatic weapons fire. He heard a scream, rolled again, got up and ran in the direction opposite the scream. In his mind he yelled *Adios motherfuckers!* No sound came from his mouth. He was full of terror, rage, exhilaration.

He was sure he could outrun his short pursuers. He sprinted to get beyond their guns, thrashing through the undergrowth head down, legs pumping as if in a short-yardage play. He turned an ankle on a root, felt the deep burning pain that makes grown men reach down to cradle the injury. He did not know whether he cried out or not. The long cross-country stride became one-legged. His breathing was ragged, searing.

He needed water, knew he was done long before they ran him down. That was the hardest time, when he knew he could not escape, and accepted failure.

They caught him just as everyone heard a helicopter overhead, above the canopy of trees. He dropped his empty pistol, raised his hands, open and in the air above his head. A black-clad figure stepped in and struck him in the mouth with the butt of a rifle. Even before he ran his tongue over his teeth he knew they were broken off or hanging in swelling gum. He tasted blood, knew he had been here before, in a bar in Salmon, Idaho, maybe. He threw a punch and was swarmed by wiry men, taken to the ground, and beaten until he was still. He was glad, finally, just to lie there, half conscious, listening to the receding sound of a helicopter. *Air America H-34,* he thought slowly.

When the only sound he could hear was breathing, Charlie said "Water."

The response of the men in black was to pull him to his feet and poke him with AK-47s until, stumbling, he walked in the direction they wanted.

His shoulder hurt but no longer bled. The turned ankle was worse than any he had known in a lifetime of pick-up basketball. It had stiffened and now registered sharp pain at each step. The broken front of his mouth throbbed a dull background for other things that hurt. His puffy, bruised face did not hurt so much as it felt misaligned, like a mask that had slipped, down and to the side.

For all that, thirst was the only thing that bothered him. He dropped to his knees on what had become a trail, and again said "Water." One of the guards—he was clearly their prisoner so he thought of them as guards—hit him in the side of the head with a club and he fell forward unconscious on the hard packed trail. He woke choking on water.

They demanded he walk and he did. He had no idea how far or in what direction. They came at nightfall to an armed camp. Fires had been started. Charlie could see in the little remaining light more black-clad men as well as others in olive drab military uniforms without insignia. *Pathet Lao with NVA stiffeners*, he thought. The fact that they never put their weapons down encouraged him. *They're worried about somethin'.*

There might be some little guys around. He imagined the woods full of Meo, their hair grown long during months of patrol and ambush, tracking his captors.

Charlie saw other men sitting on the ground, bound like he was, hands tied behind, rope continuing up and looped around their necks in a leash. An armed guard stood near them. Some of the other prisoners were bearded. Charlie thought they might be Caucasian. He could not see anything suggesting a uniform on any of the bedraggled group. They were gaunt, sat with heads down in silence. There was no signal from them acknowledging his presence or status. He was kept separate from them.

His guard made him sit, bound his feet together, and then untied his hands so he could eat. Charlie ate the few small balls of rice in seconds. Nothing but sticky rice, it tasted like whatever delicacy made its way into his mind, his appetite finally settling on the mix of frankfurter, mustard and bun at Comiskey Park. He held out the banana leaf plate, signaling and saying "more." The guard slapped the leaf out of his hands and retied Charlie roughly.

He lay down and began to think about escape. *Better do it now before I get like those poor bastards.* He could see the other prisoners sitting in flickering fire light, heads down, their guard standing by.

He checked his own guard. *When these two are asleep I'll go. They'll sleep. I just have to stay awake.*

In the moonless dark he could not see either guard, guessed they could not see him either. He worked patiently to free a hand and finally did. He untied his feet, tried to flex his swollen ankle. There was no flex, just a message in the swelling that said leave it alone. He listened to the breathing of his guard. When its rhythm was that of sleep Charlie decided to go. He would just have to take a chance on the other guard. He remembered how the path entered the camp and tried to move in that direction. It was difficult walking on the sprained ankle. He tried to think of black-and-blue jokes or an ankle joke, anything to distract him from the pain and tension of the slow sightless walk through the armed captors. He gave that up and started a fantasy, referring to himself as *Ankles Aardvark, first man in the phone book. Girls couldn't miss him.*

The walk-ins were fabulous. Between the fantasy and the dark night he was fearless. He left the camp undetected.

He walked for an hour on the path, stopping frequently to listen for pickets or patrols guarding against the Meo. Then he began to worry about Meo. Always quiet and lying in ambush, they would just shoot a figure on a path, no questions asked, unconcerned with another death. Next it was the Lao jungle animals. Tigers and leopards he could not see but could see him and spring unheard while he shuffled on one leg. He finally gave up trying to find threats in the night.

Another hour and he could detect lightening of the sky. That and used-up weariness made him choose hiding over distance. He walked off the path and counted a dozen steps. Then he doubled the number of steps. Still unable to make out what cover he had except by feel, he lay down and went immediately to sleep.

He was asleep when Pathet Lao from the camp found him in the grey light of a mist-filled morning. The search party was led by a man in NVA uniform, an officer even in the absence of insignia. When the Pathet Lao pulled Charlie to his feet they started to beat him. The NVA officer stopped the beating. He said something to the search party, smiling as he did. Charlie did not understand what was said. The members of the team that recaptured him were suddenly nodding their heads. They marched Charlie back onto the path and toward the camp.

When they reached camp Charlie was placed with the other prisoners, in a line. There were seven of them, Charlie at one end. An equal number of guards faced them, rifles ready as if they were a firing squad.

The NVA officer called out and two Pathet Lao trotted forward with a spool of wire between them. They carried it on a short bamboo pole running through the center of the spool, one man on each end of the pole. Charlie recognized the wire. It was one-eighth inch diameter and stiff. *Goddamn. Number nine wire. Hung it for telephones between Big Creek ranger station and Yellow Pine. Probably runnin' the same stuff for commo on the Trail. Small friggin' world.*

Two black-clad men stood on either side of the prisoner farthest from Charlie on the line. At a command from the NVA officer the prisoner was forced to the ground, face down. An easy task given his condition. His arms were stretched out on the ground, beyond his head, palms down. The two men with the spool of wire knelt beside his outstretched hands, chose one, and forced the stiff wire through the hand, back to front. The prisoner yelled a curse and blood ran from his hand into the ground.

Charlie turned away. *Oh my god.* A guard slapped him, grabbed his shoulders and turned him back to face the line of prisoners.

The wire was pulled through the hand of the first prisoner until the guards had a sufficient length for the work of punching the wire through the hand of the next man in line. The serial impalement was repeated on each, the wire pushed and pulled through a hand. In a short time six prisoners had been transfixed on the stiff length of wire, connected by one bleeding hand each, standing three or four feet apart. Some were silent. Others moaned or cursed. Some cradled the puncture wound. No one had tried to escape. Each had screamed or made a guttural noise of animal submission as the wire was forced through his hand.

The prisoners impaled on the wire stood facing Charlie. Some blamed him, made note of his features for a future time. Most were too disoriented by humiliation and pain to see that the guards with the spool of wire had come to the last prisoner, Charlie, or to take note of who he was. Charlie held his head off the ground and watched, a small boy in a dark theatre, as the wire was pushed through his hand. He strained and held his breath to avoid crying out. He was mostly successful, gasping and hissing instead.

As soon as the guards had finished twisting the end of the wire into a large stiff knot that prevented its withdrawal, Charlie stood up. He stepped toward the nearest prisoner and offered a high-five with his free hand. The man did not respond. He stepped to the next man in line, again offering a high-five, speaking this time.

"I'm bustin' out of here whether you're comin' or not." He held up the wire running through his own bleeding hand. "Looks like you might be comin'." The broken teeth gave him a slight lisp. He thrust his chin out and grinned at the prisoner in front of him. Charlie said "We gotta talk." The man did not respond, but looked away.

Before Charlie could move on, a prisoner down the line spoke. “Rudy Dvorak, Prineville, Oregon, professional firefighter, part-time Raven, shot down near Tchepone markin’ targets with Willy Pete. Been walkin’ me north two weeks since, quiet ‘til you got here. Seen those boots before, know you for a smokey, got your six, buddy.” The elision of words had rushed out, as if all were part of a single sentence. Dvorak knew what was coming.

He and Charlie were knocked to the ground and bayonets held to their throats. The NVA officer screamed at them. They were never to speak to each other. None of them. If one of them spoke they would be shot. All of them.

Charlie began planning, making a movie in his head, as he called it. If asked, he would have agreed that every man is a hero in his own movie. If pressed, he would have admitted that can be good or it can be bad.

CHAPTER THIRTY-TWO

"Roongsak is your PARU contact." It was Channarong on the telephone, first thing in the morning. There were not a thousand telephones in the whole country of Laos but the Company arranged installation of a telephone in every employee's housing, "so they can send you to hell and gone at four a.m.," Thanasis had told Dao the night before.

Thanasis said "just a minute" into the phone and put his hand over the mouthpiece. "It's your brother. On business. What should I say if he asks about you?"

"Tell him I love his parties and that I am too busy to talk to him today." She put her thumb to her nose and fanned her hand.

"Channarong, that's great. Where can I reach him?"

"He's pulling double duty. When he's workin' trail watch he's around the airbase and will come in to see you. Otherwise he's at Lima 235, the Keng Ka Bong training site outside Savannakhet. Your CIA boys are there puttin' together a Thai Special Guerilla Unit to make up for casualties Meo SGUs are takin'. He's a specialist in guerilla stuff. Your people trained him at Hua Hin and Phitsanulok. He knows what you want and is happy to have you along on a trail watch whenever you can work it in." There was a pause. "You don't happen to know where my sister is, do you?"

"Nope. But she plans to come by this morning so I can get her on the Air America milk run to Bangkok. Should I have her call?"

There was a short worried-brother silence on the phone, then "Hmm . . . no. Tell her that I think she's in good hands and that I'll see her in Bangkok in a month or so."

Thanasis hung up the phone and threw an arm and a leg over the small woman next to him in the sun-washed room. He ran a hand through her black hair once more and remembered a night of gifts.

"You're not a Communist, are you?" he asked.

"You don't see a beard on me, do you?" Dao asked.

They made love and she caught the noon flight out of Lima 39.

Before her scent had left the room, he received another call. Norris was on the phone. There was no small talk. "I have some bad news and related matters to cover. We've lost a plane out of Long Tieng. A couple of our kickers were on board. Charlie was one of 'em. Air America SAR could not recover bodies. Secondary explosions from artillery shells on board destroyed everything, precluded a search of the crash site. We have reason to believe Charlie bailed out, survived, and was captured by Pathet Lao. Meo guerillas found a B-7 parachute in big timber near the site. Village informants saw a lone Caucasian prisoner, white T-shirt, black crew cut, a little chipped up, with armed PL marchin' him on a nearby trail the same day. We're going to get all the intel possible on where they take him. We'll try to put a Bright Light team in to help on a rescue. Everybody worth talkin' to thinks we need to get him out. Charlie's the first Company asset captured in Laos."

The news shocked Thanasis. He felt the pain of Charlie's capture as if standing in the middle of events, there but unable to change anything. Thanasis knew there was little chance to survive guerilla capture. Prisoners are nothing but risk for guerillas. They are killed immediately after interrogation in the field. He felt the reality of Charlie slipping away from him and he reached as if to stop the slide. "Tell them you're CIA. It's the only thing gives us value in their eyes. They can trade you if you're alive. Stay alive, buddy." In spite of the exhortation, he held no hope and felt only loss.

Until Norris' call, Thanasis had had a day of intimacy and promise. He reacted to the loss of Charlie with a familiar darkening of feeling. He knew the feeling from the black time following Dog's death. No thought of Dao lingered. The past twenty-four hours seemed unreal, fogged. He clenched his free hand into a fist as if to hold on to where he was, not slip further. He began pacing, opened a night stand and pulled an unloaded pistol from the drawer. Cocking his head to trap the phone against his hunched shoulder he slapped a full magazine clip into the butt of the grip and chambered a round with a noisy pull and release. He was breathing rapidly, hyperventilating, anxiety building. He lost track of who was on the phone. He lost track of himself, did not know that until he walked past a mirror and did not recognize the figure he saw. Whoever he was, the person needed to hang up and leave the room, get into the jungle, get to Charlie and Dog.

The voice on the phone was irritating Thanasis. "Yeh, yeh, yeh," he said to whoever it belonged to. "Look, why don't you call me back. I've got something to do."

The dissociation, the strange affect on the phone, startled Norris. He yelled into the telephone "Thanasis, what the hell is going on?"

Thanasis recognized the shouting voice and was startled that he was still talking to Norris. He was confused, but said "Sorry, Norris. I'm afraid I was running ahead. I can't just sit here. I've got to help Charlie. You know how it is." Even if Thanasis had understood he would not have told Norris that losing Charlie was threatening to overwhelm him, like it had with Dog, that it had already pushed him close to an armed jungle fugue.

"Thanasis, you are going to help Charlie. But you're going to do it by following CIA lead and cooperating with the SAR people runnin' this rescue operation. There's no room for John Wayne in this."

Thanasis had opened a bottle of Crown Royal and was drinking from it while he talked to Norris. It was just enough depressant to quell the anxiety attack and let him focus on Norris' directions. The John Wayne sally made him laugh at himself. He paid attention. He was to fly to Udorn the next day and give SAR and Bright Light rescue teams whatever they needed to know about Charlie, how he was likely to react to capture and to death of the crew that had flown with him, what could be expected from him in the noise and confusion of a rescue assault, how he might be responding to torture.

"I'll be on the plane to Udorn, boss. But, ya know, I'm not a psychiatrist. I'm just Charlie's buddy. I know what he'll do in a bar or in an airplane or in a whorehouse. God only knows what he'll do in a prison camp."

"Give it your best shot. Then go back to work on trail watch. Let somebody else worry about Charlie for a change."

When he and Norris ended their phone conversation, Thanasis recalled some of it immediately. *How he'll react to torture? Jesus Christ! Just spill your guts, Charlie. We don't know anything anyway, man.* He took another drink from the Crown Royal bottle and went out for cigarettes.

At the PX, Thanasis stood behind two French airmen trying to buy up all of the cigarettes available at the check-out counter. Thanasis was not drunk but he could not remember how he got there. His mind was locked in a jungle prison fantasy far from Savannakhet. He stepped out of the fantasy long enough to tell the Frenchmen to quit hassling the Lao girl at the register. She was refusing to permit the purchase. When they told Thanasis he could French kiss their asses "and who is first for you" he threw several roundhouse punches, like his arms were somebody else's, knocked both airmen out as they stood, surprised, at the counter. He bought his cigarettes, asked the girl if she was OK, and got a nervous smile. He could not believe how good he felt.

"We won't quit on you, Charlie. Swear," he said aloud as he walked out of the PX.

There were no nightmares. There was no memory of Greece or his father's death. There was no need, because he was somebody else. A nice enough man, but somebody else.

When he got back from Udorn, Thanasis jeeped over to Lima 235 and found Roongsak. Thanasis was still talking about his meeting with Bright Light, optimistic. Roongsak was not.

"Don't be too optimistic. They are good, but he's in Indian country. Full of Pathet Lao, and there's thousands of NVA operating just on the Trail, never mind the rest of the country. Your guy will more likely do it on his own than get rescued. Be patient. Where do you want to go on the Trail?"

Thanasis pushed his disappointment away, trying hard to focus, stay out of the Charlie rescue. "Can you get us near Tchepone? Just north of there, maybe, before the Trail crosses over the border to Khe San. Show me what you do so I don't get you killed."

"Sure thing. We'll 'copter in, across the paddies, and walk east in the dark. We'll have the A-26 Nimrods out of the Thai airbase at Nakhon Phanom bomb them in front of us, just enough to keep their heads down, like it's routine Trail bombing. Can't recon at night in the jungle, so we'll position ourselves for a daytime recon and road watch. Leave the second night. Standard stuff. We know we're comin'. They know we're comin'. Just like Irish terrorists."

Thanasis grinned at the brown man's analogy. "Roongsak, I'm sure you've never met an Irishman. What could you possibly know about Irish terrorists?"

"Let me tell you. We train them at Hua Hin, with the CIA. They come up through Australia, as if that's who they are. Irish terrorists are like a rugby league. They only kill each other, and only on weekends. There's no general terrorism like what the PL and the CIA do." Roongsak too was grinning.

Thanasis wondered if all Asians liked to jerk Americans around. "Don't believe you, Captain Roongsak."

The PARU captain asked Thanasis to show up an hour earlier than the rest of the trail watch team. "Want to check you out. Ever had combat training?"

Thanasis said he had not and Roongsak said "Maybe hour and a half. OK?"

When he walked up to the H-34 helicopter late the next day to be checked out by Roongsak, the team leader handed Thanasis an M-16 rifle.

Thanasis patted his holster. "I have a weapon."

"No you don't. If we get in a firefight, the louder the better. The psychology of trying to kill each other is simple—the louder the better. We'll need an intimidation edge. There's only gonna be six of us. Rifle is better than shotgun is better than pistol is better than throwin' rocks. We want lots of noise and lots of bullets when the shooting starts. So put your M-16 on rock and roll and shoot as fast as possible. Spray and pray. We'll be close to 'em if it happens. The jungle is going to reduce the range of our weapons. Any problem with what I'm sayin'?"

"None at all, Captain. But tell me straight up, how likely is it, really, we're goin' to get in a firefight? I'm not hearin' that about our trail watch teams." Thanasis ran a crew of thirty-eight Thai and Lao riggers, resupplying Special Guerilla Units and trail watch teams. He was supporting a lot of violence in many forms but he had not yet heard of an attack on a trail watch team.

"If I'm any good, it'll never happen. This is low profile recon patrol. We are information guys, not looking for a fight. Our orders are not to engage, to break contact as soon as possible. But if it happens, I want to know your head is on straight, and I want you to know what to expect. You can't go in there thinking this is not dangerous. Just give me my hour and a half. OK?"

"You've got it, Captain."

"Listen up to a little more about sneakin' around the woods. I want you in what we call Condition Yellow at all times. I want you ready. Think dogs. Dogs are always in Condition Yellow. They are ready for anything—fuck, fight or run. Ready means sittin' with your back to the wall. Do not ever relax. Do not fantasize about your girlfriend. Do not play imaginary hands of poker.

"You'll be afraid. That is OK. You may shit your pants. That is OK. I'm used to the smell and it just means the parasympathetic nervous system has shut down. You may shed tears. That is OK. Are you OK so far?"

Thanasis answered that he was and Roongsak continued to lecture and demonstrate until other members of the team began to show up.

"I'll say a couple more things about firefights and then we'll quit. First, you may get hit. If you do you will not be abandoned. If you need help you will be helped. Even if you are dead. I will determine whether you are dead by pokin' you in the eye—if you're alive, your face will scrunch up and we will act accordingly.

"Second, if you are struck by a bullet you may not feel it. You will probably feel the blood before you feel the pain. Don't panic. You can lose thirty percent, half a gallon, before it's a problem.

"A couple of facts about blood and fear. Then I'll really quit. Fear produces cortisol, a coagulant. That's a good thing for a man about to bleed. Fear causes vasoconstriction. That's a good thing if the bad guys are makin' big holes in you. What I'm telling you is that you are going to survive, so never quit fightin'. Buddha will provide.

"Now, put that extra bandolier on and you're good to go. Combat school is over."

Thanasis joined the Thai trail watch team in the darkened helicopter. They were four look-alikes—six feet tall, tattooed with pictures of animal spirits and concentric circles of Buddhist verse to protect them from bullets, wearing camouflage slouch hats, camouflage uniforms, green unit scarves, and smelling of garlic. If the mission was dangerous you could not tell it from the relaxed Thai chatter of the men being carried toward the Trail. When the helicopter began to settle toward a rice paddy that only the pilot, wearing night vision goggles, could see, all conversation ended.

When the team left the area of flooded paddies it moved east, several miles north of Tchepone, at first into elephant grass and then into jungle. They had walked for an hour and were about to stop for the night when they ran into an NVA truck maintenance facility. It was large and spread throughout a stand of hardwood trees. Like everything about the Trail it was camouflaged against observation from the sky. Part of the camouflage was removable trees, roots balled or potted and fitted for relocation by front-end loaders or tractors with power tree spades.

As they worked their way around the truck maintenance compound the team stumbled across an eight-inch fuel pipeline. Literally, one of them tripped over the pipe and fell to the ground. The team followed the pipeline in both directions and found that it crossed beneath streams and was camouflaged where it traveled above the surface of the ground. They located pumps on the pipeline used for moving truck fuel on to the next pump or an ultimate destination. They decided to take a section of the plastic pipe for analysis as to its source and most recent contents. They cut it with hand saws.

The pipeline was empty when they made the cuts, but fuel suddenly began to flow under pressure and splash onto the ground. Pumps were running somewhere upstream. People monitoring fuel flow downstream noted the discrepancy between pump operation and pipeline output. NVA transportation division troops were sent to investigate.

Roongsak moved his team west as fast as possible. It wasn't fast or far enough. The Trail area around Tchepone was full of patrolling

Pathet Lao, and the withdrawing road watch team was, through happenstance, blocked by a ten-man PL patrol engaging in armed reconnaissance, looking for Meo. Both sides were surprised and a disorganized firefight began.

Within ten minutes Thanasis was into his second bandolier and coughing on gun smoke enveloping all of the fighters, seeping among them in the still night air. At first the noise of the fight seemed huge and on top of him. There seemed no distance between him and explosive clatter of AK-47s and M-16s. Gunshots, screams, buzz and smack of bullets, whine of ricochet, all mixed with sound and vibration from larger explosions.

Then his ears began to shut out the sound of gunfire even as he continued to hear metallic cycling of his rifle on automatic. Everything began to happen in slow motion. His vision seemed to clarify and he began to feel he could see in the dark, pick out individual figures moving near the paddy dikes, and the far threat of other men came close, without closing at all. With tunnel vision he aimed, squeezed the trigger, and the black figures flopped and thrashed in flooded rice paddies.

Whatever was directing him was not good at multi-tasking and it elected to have him kneel and shoot his rifle and do nothing else. Roongsak pulled him to the ground. "You're doing great, Mavros. Those shitheads have figured out they can't handle us so they're gonna wait for the NVA shitheads following us from the Trail and coming up on the other side. I have a feeling it will be the transportation gooks following us, after they find the cut in the pipeline, not NVA regulars. So I'm going to send two of our team back to ambush the transportation gooks. They won't know what hit 'em. If I'm wrong and it's NVA combat regulars the ambush will hold them about as long as it takes to drink a beer. Still glad you came along?"

"Yeh, but I've got a better place in mind for drinkin' beer. I know you have other things to think about, but I'm not going to be able to keep up heavy fire much longer. Ammunition will be gone."

"Yeh, you've certainly made a racket. Save two full clips. We're going to follow up on the ambush by breaking off here and attacking back toward the east against the transportation gooks. I've asked Lima 39 to send in a helo to take us out. I've told them I will give them two flares on the ground, one on the west for a Spooky to shoot up and hold these shitheads in place and one on the east to mark the helo pick up site."

Roongsak's maneuver worked. A C-47 Spooky came in and shot up the PL patrol to the west of the road watch team. The ancient plane, called "Puff the Magic Dragon" by troops in Vietnam, had three 7.62-mm General Electric miniguns mounted in the door and windows on the pilot's side of the plane. Flying in slow circles three thousand feet above the battlefield the pilot could push a button and fire all three guns at a five thousand-square-yard area at up to one hundred rounds per second. One slow circle was enough to put a high-speed bullet thick as a pencil into every square yard.

The Spooky killed every soldier that remained of the PL patrol. Everyone involved thought it was overkill, but Roongsak had made sure that the Air Force air commando unit in Thailand understood there was a CIA agent with him whose death or capture would be an embarrassment far beyond Laos.

The two-man PARU ambush, initiated with a Claymore mine, shocked the NVA transportation group into overestimating what they faced. They ran toward the Trail until they saw the helicopter land behind them, then they walked back to the pipeline. Thanasis did not need to use the M-16 clips he had saved. Once airborne, he fired both of them out the door of the H-34 in the direction of the transportation unit retreat.

CHAPTER THIRTY-THREE

Dao's father asked her hard questions. Some were straight forward, like "How do you feel about being beautiful?" The father accepted no fluff, only her real feelings. Most of his questions, however, were riddles or their answer involved choices hard to explain or justify. She did not always understand their father-daughter dance. It was only when she was away at school in California, remembering him in her occasional loneliness, that she began to understand. What he wanted, she thought, was that she know life was about making choices and choices involve enigma. Where would the choice take you?

She was thinking about the new choice in her life. Not surprisingly, it involved a man. A beautiful daughter of an influential family, she attracted men. They all required she make choices, many at blind intersections.

This one was dark and mysterious. His friends called him Black Man. He was obviously rough and adventurous, a risk taker. But when she had practically jumped into his bed only hours after meeting him, he had been gentle and romantic, whispering poetry across the pillow they shared. She remembered it now. She knew the poem from school as Yeats and it had surprised her that he knew it, told her even more about the man she had come to love.

"I will find out," he had whispered, "where she has gone, And kiss her lips and take her hands; And walk among long dappled grass."

That he knew it made him mysterious as the riddling choices in her father's questions. She chose, without any idea where her choice would lead. She would come to him whenever he asked.

Again, she was surprised, this time at herself. But that was an easy riddle to solve. The rough, unschooled man who quoted poetry had come as a gift from Zorro. Her brother would never lead her to harm. She telephoned him at the Savannakhet airfield, nothing special, just her monthly call to the brother she worried about.

"Thank you, Z," she said in greeting.

"Hey, Dao." His greeting was always a hug. "You're welcome. What for?"

"For the introduction to Thanasis. You have hunky friends."

"Sister, are you being good?"

"To get this kind of man you gotta be good."

He knew it was just word games but he was always surprised when she chose to be even slightly risqué.

Rolling his eyes like their father undertaking to lecture them, Zorro said "Oh dear Dao, once again you are reaching beyond your powers of orderly comprehension." The arch phrase of the parent was the signal, accepted between them, that he was going to take the lead as older brother, that for the next few moments he would assume to teach or defend her. It was a usual part of their relationship but one she always pushed back against, seeking independence and her own adventures. As he continued it was familiar stuff.

"You know," he said, "when you get emotionally involved everything becomes bewilderment."

"Pshaw! You should try a little emotional involvement. Who graduated *cum laude*? I am never bewildered."

"OK, girl. Just tell me. Did he put you on the CIA milk run flight? Did he get you safely home?"

"He did."

"And did he treat you right?"

"All . . . ." She had started to say "all night long" and stopped. She loved Zorro and did not want to give him second thoughts about her private life. "Always kind, always respectful." That was true and all Zorro needed to know.

"Good. He's my friend, but if he gets out of line, I want you to tell me."

"You will be the first one I come to with bad news."

He knew he needed to lighten up the conversation. "All I'm saying is I don't want *you* to hurt *him*. I regret I ever taught you kick-boxing."

They finished the conversation with gossip about their parents and the war Zorro was fighting. "Be careful," she said. "We love you and want you back soon."

His absence sometimes made her melancholy. That had been the case since he had, years before, rescued her from drowning in the *klong* in front of their house. He had nearly drowned in the effort. The bond between them was strong and strongly felt by both.

She added "Keep Thanasis safe. And, oh sure, tell him I still respect him."

CHAPTER THIRTY-FOUR

Thanasis got off the train at Hua Lamphong station with Ilias' red and black worry beads in his hand, thumbing them one by one through his palm. It was a habit of connection and comfort, not necessarily indicating worry, and it got him teased in every barracks in which he had lived. This time, however, he was worried. He was worried about Charlie in a jungle prison and the effort to find and rescue him. He worried about the Meo, chased, brutalized, and dying, and about whether he could do what was necessary to support them. He continued to suffer the grief of Dog's death. He was unbalanced by the loss of his family—father, mother, Ilias—and now anyone that relied on him. He moved the beads faster as he recalled the sound of a Meo laborer walking into the tail rotor of a helicopter. The man had worked for him. He felt control slipping away, tried to stop himself.

Unseeing, he walked into a woman and child. Unaware, he continued walking.

Only the sound of a child's voice calling out in sing-song "*farang, farang, farang,*" identifying him as foreigner, brought him back to the reality of the crowded railroad station and the woman picking up her bundles. Thanasis apologized in the awkward Thai phrases of a tourist and helped gather her belongings. He laughed at the child's observation and said "Yep, that's me, buddy."

He put the carved beads in a pants pocket and focused on his surroundings. Absorbing details of the station architecture kept the images of loss out of his head. Gold-colored glass in two-toned Art Deco patterns, vaulted ceilings common to the Baths of Diocletian and Beaux-Arts railroad stations from Bangkok to Chicago, triumphal arches at the ceremonial building front, rotating electric departure board, all lent their striking images to checking the other.

By the time he reached the street Thanasis was in control of himself and looking forward to time away from the war. Dao had invited him to spend the weekend with her in Bangkok. He followed her instructions and took a taxi to a pier on the Chao Phraya River near the temple Wat Pho. She had advised that "it houses the famous reclining Buddha, but don't stop there. I will take care of all the reclining this weekend." He was smiling by the end of the short ride to the river, and looked around for her as he paid the fare.

He did not see her, but noticed a figure wearing a coolie hat, dark tunic and fisherman's pants waving at him. He walked over to the person who was now motioning him to come to the edge of the pier. They were close enough to talk without being overheard before the short person in baggy clothes bowed and removed the hat. The stranger straightened and it was Dao, grinning and holding her arms out to him.

"I am practicing CIA disguises. I want you to feel at home. You didn't know me did you. I didn't even have to use the mustache." She held an index finger at horizontal under her nose and giggled.

He bent to kiss her and she said "Wait until we are at home. No public displays of affection in Bangkok." She turned away from the crowded street and curved gold and orange roofs of the royal neighborhood. Faced toward the river, she added "But you may place your hand beneath my tunic, as if you are catching your balance, as we get into the sampan. Try not to linger." She stepped into a small flat-bottomed skiff, still grinning, and motioned Thanasis to the center of the shallow boat as she sat down in the rear next to an outboard motor. She started the motor and asked "Are you ready?"

He felt like a race horse being led to the starting gate. "I'm a-prancin' and a-dancin'."

She pulled away from the pier, turning upstream into the current of the wide river. He watched her navigate through the flotsam and heedless boat traffic. She was expert. Steering into the current she shaped a course more or less directly across the Chao Phraya. When they reached the opposite shore, the Thonburi side, she proceeded upstream a short distance and steered the sampan into a wide canal.

"This is the *klong* Bangkok Noi," she said. "My home is on the canal. We will go slowly. I want to show you."

She shut the engine off as another sampan approached. The sole occupant, an old woman in a peasant hat, was paddling her small market to them. It was apparent Dao had been a customer before. There was familiarity in their greeting.

"She has cold beer for sale if you would like something while we tour the canal."

Thanasis bought a beer for himself, a soda and flowers for Dao. She restarted the engine and eased away from the old woman and her floating variety store. She drove the sampan slowly through the canal, minimizing her wake. Houses entered the water on both sides, pushed there by crowding orchids, trees, and naked children. There were few sounds, even from the glistening children playing in the canal waters. Thanasis picked out only the chugging of the small outboard and the rhythmic chirp of cricket song.

By the time she turned the boat and doubled back along the canal he was transported from the war. He wanted to hear her talk about herself. Anything would do. He started by asking about her boat skills.

She told him "My family's first house, where Zorro and I grew up, is here on the water. It is where I live now, where we are going. We always had sampans, because it was the easiest way to get around Bangkok, and the prettiest. My brother taught me everything I know about boating. Even boat engines. He always knew that kind of thing. It's why he is in the Royal Air Force."

"He must think you're pretty special."

"He may, but no. He was the special one. He shared everything with me. Stood up for me. Even to my parents. If he had not stood by me, argued for me, I would never have been permitted to go to school abroad, to the U.S. If he had something, anytime, anywhere, he insisted that I have as much. When we were children, he even played "Doctor" with me, in spite of his friends laughing at him."

"So he got to examine you?"

"Oh, no. I was the doctor. I examined him. Took his pants right off. But you must never tell him I told."

"My point exactly. He thinks you're special. So do I."

"You must be right. He gave me you to worry about, just like he does." Dao splashed water at Thanasis and turned the sampan toward a small pier in front of a typical Thai stilt house.

The house sat on wooden pilings, eight feet above the canal. It was made of unpainted wood. The ridge of its steep, tiled roof curved upward at the top of both gables. The gables displayed an odd extension at each end of the house—fascia ran from the roof eaves to the curved ridge line and then beyond to form a small but easily seen X above each gable. Dao told him the architectural detail, repeated on many houses, was a centuries old signal to rural bandits that the house had already been robbed, there was nothing left to take.

She tied the boat to a piling and led him up stairs, across a wooden deck, to a small terrace open to the sky, filled with flowers and a single tree that had grown there for many years. The terrace was surrounded by the individual rooms of the house. Furnishings were simple, some teak, some rattan wicker, multicolored *mon khwan* pillows on the floor, three-sided to provide support for sitting. Thanasis sank into the spare domesticity, separating further from the war, sensing that what he wanted from the Thai woman lay beyond the coming night. He focused on the night before him.

He kissed her and ran his hand over her tunic, palm and trailing fingers crossing belly and breasts. Slowly, deliberately he removed the pins that had held her hair up beneath the coolie hat, loosing her hair but holding it in place until he had finished. He let her dark hair fall into his hands, held it to his face. It had become their ritual.

They woke long after midnight. The crickets' notes of love had not ceased or varied since afternoon.

In the dark she said "You are not a likely candidate for a Thai wedding."

"Why is that?"

"Because virginity is very important in Thai weddings. You would have to elope."

"How would anyone know? You're not the kind to kiss and tell."

"Right after the wedding luncheon the newly married couple is sent off to the bed chamber. Some don't come out for three days. The chambermaid will tell all."

"What if the girl is already pregnant?"

"Again, you would have to elope. Also, you would have to apologize to the bride's family." She added "The people of Thailand can count you know."

"Are you pregnant?"

"No."

"Why are we having a conversation about weddings?"

"Because I am taking you to a Thai wedding tomorrow. A girlfriend who says she is a virgin wants me there. I want you to be informed and look like you have been there before. Not just some handsome Greek I picked up on Patpong Road. Is that a plan or are you too tired?"

"That's a plan and I'm not tired. You sure know the way to a Greek boy's heart."

"No, I don't know."

"Make love to them and feed 'em lamb."

"Sorry, I was short on lamb."

The following morning Dao laid out their clothes for the wedding. "Zorro's tuxedo will be fine. I've hugged both of you enough to know." It was a little snug, but she was right. They took a taxi to the Oriental Hotel.

On the way she talked more of the day. "My girlfriend is beautiful and comes from a wealthy family. Unlike the U.S. there is no dowry from the bride's family. On the contrary, the groom must pay the parents of the bride. He paid a large bride price. Fortunately, the groom has lots of money. He is an army officer and sells opium and guns. While that is against the law, no one questions it. It is the war. Everyone except our king is involved. Oh, and Zorro. He sells nothing."

Thanasis thought he should say something. "I agree. Zorro sells nothing. He's pretty far over on Communists, far as I can tell. Makes him serious about the war, a patriot I guess."

"How about you, Thanasis?"

"I hate Communists."

"How about opium and guns? Some Americans buy and sell those things."

"Yes. Some do. I don't." He thought about pilots and kickers that did. He did not want thoughts of them in his time with Dao.

They entered the hotel and immediately found the wedding party. "That dress is lovely," Dao said. The bride's dress was a clinging light pink silk. Thanasis offered no response, but did ask how long the wedding celebration would last.

"It will be very fast. There are no vows or religious ceremonies, just an exchange of rings and gifts. One of the monks will bless the couple."

Thanasis had counted nine monks in saffron robes. He asked "Why so many?"

Dao said "The bridal couple decides how many to invite. Nine is a Thai lucky number. Lunch will be served by the hotel. The monks will eat first, before anyone else. Even the bride and groom."

The marriage ceremony went as quickly as she said. The couple bowed to Buddha, recited a brief prayer, exchanged rings, and lighted incense sticks. One of the waiting monks blessed the two by marking their foreheads with a dot of paste. He did not touch the young woman with his hands in giving the blessing, using a candle for the blessing touch.

Thanasis and Dao enjoyed a leisurely lunch, chatting with Dao's friends, holding hands.

When later that night Thanasis and Dao finished making love under the mosquito net they were tired and did not talk for a while. Dao broke the silence. "When I was helping you dress this morning I ran across a bracelet of red and black beads in your jeans. I never see you wear them. What are they?"

He explained they were worry beads that had belonged to his mother's brother. He did not stop. He poured out the story of his father's murder, his mother's death in war, the separation from Ilias, the death of Dog, the capture of Charlie, the dying Meo. When he finished, Dao saw the unshed tears brimming in his eyes, saw how he was moved by the accumulation of loss.

She left the bed and returned quickly. She had the worry beads in her hand. She lay down and pulled the worry bead bracelet over her foot and up, over her calf.

"Buddhists are good at prayer. Let me do the worrying for us. With your worry beads I will pray for the safety of the people I love, you and Zorro. Make love to me Thanasis and I will put your worry beads to use."

Thanasis rolled between her legs. She wrapped them around him, the worry beads rocking and clicking, the only sound they heard.

CHAPTER THIRTY-FIVE

In the turnabouts of capture, escape, and recapture the Pathet Lao had forgotten to take Charlie's boots. It was standard procedure for controlling prisoners. While they had him on the ground with a bayonet at his throat, they remembered the boots and took them. They twisted his sprained ankle when they remembered that.

His feet bled through the next two days of walking. They stopped bleeding but remained tender, every step sore.

Dvorak whispered support. "You can do it. I knew a Raven ran barefoot in the jungle three miles a day to toughen his feet in case he got captured and they took his boots. He was a jumper too. You don't want to end up second place in the jumper Olympics."

The Pathet Lao guards knocked Dvorak to the ground for talking to another prisoner.

Charlie said "Thanks, Rudy." The guards, busy beating Dvorak, did not hear Charlie. Neither did Rudy.

Charlie had been trying to find a way to think about the long thick wire that stuck out both sides of his left hand. The pain of other injuries was private. He could avoid most of it with tricks in his head or a change of posture. The wire was different. It made him part of a society, the members of which caused each other quick, unpredictable pain every day. Each stumble by a prisoner jerked the wire through someone else's hand.

After Rudy's beating caused the usual chain reaction of falling prisoners and pulled several inches of wire through the hole in his hand Charlie tried controlling the shock with his free hand as he walked, braking the travel of the steel by holding tight. When guards saw him protecting the wounded hand they clubbed his free hand away from the wire with their rifles.

The prisoners were marched northeast each day by their Pathet Lao captors. When Air America search planes and helicopters flew over, the prisoners were shoved into jungle brush close by their path, forced to the ground at gunpoint. Charlie knew they were invisible to the searchers. He focused on escape.

By asking permission of fellow prisoners and, where that was not successful, pushing and shoving, Charlie managed to lie one night next to Dvorak. He whispered "Rudy, that you?"

"Naw, it's Ho Chi Minh. Whasup?"

"This is the worst packout I've ever been on. I'm leavin'. You comin'? I'm goin' to invite everybody." There was no response from Rudy. Charlie continued. "They're marchin' us to North Vietnam. Search and rescue will never find us. We'll just rot in prison until war's over. You know that isn't gonna be soon."

"I'm goin' with you. But half these guys won't go. Too broken. The other half will make a break just so they have a chance at killin' you, Charlie. They blame you for the wire." There was a brief silence. "I don't side with that."

"I'm goin' tomorrow night."

"How we gettin' off the wire?"

"You bend it enough times it'll break. You did it with balin' wire when you were a kid. Back and forth and it'll break. Take a while but no big deal. We should start right after beddin' down tomorrow night. Tell the guys behind you. I'll get the rest."

Charlie and Dvorak could recruit none of the prisoners to join them. The man next to Charlie on the wire wished him well and added "You'll be dead or back here in twenty-four hours. They know you're CIA, and they've been sending assassins to kill Ravens like Dvorak. They aren't goin' to let you two go. Ever. They'll beat you near to death just to slow you down for the next time. But they won't let you go. I don't blame you for runnin'."

Charlie thought his fellow prisoner probably had it right. In moonless dark Charlie and Dvorak crawled through elephant grass for a hundred yards. Then they stood and ran. It really was not running. Charlie's ankle hurt, slowed him. Dvorak stopped and waited for him. Charlie told the Raven to go on, not wait on him. Dvorak said "Let's go."

They walked through the night, most of it in a steep ravine heavy with brush. They knew they had to go down to find water. They also knew they had to go up, find a clearing where they could be spotted by search and rescue aircraft. Tired and thirsty, they went down, obsessed with water.

They found a small stream on a narrow valley bottom. The stream ran through a string of villages, no more than two or three bamboo huts in each. They weighed the risks and drank from the stream. The risks were detection and dysentery. They were not detected.

After hiding and climbing all day, they stood bent over in a small clearing, hands on their knees. They listened but heard no airplanes. They straightened up and looked at the sky, blue hazed with humidity. There was nothing else.

"I wish it was the monsoon season. I could just suck my shirt sleeve. But it ain't. So we're gonna have to make like the Meo." Charlie faced down the mountain. "Walk down at night for the water and walk up another mountain in the mornin'. I tell you, Rudy, it's like fightin' fire on the breaks of the Salmon and the spotter forgets where he put you out."

"Tain't funny, McGee. Let's go."

They returned to the water, choosing a point further down stream. They took turns sleeping and staying awake. Charlie felt better in the morning, optimistic and hungry. They were near a village, close enough they could hear voices and smell food cooking on a fire.

They argued about whether and how they should approach the villagers. They agreed they had to get food. They finally agreed that only one of them should go into the clearing where the huts sat. The villagers might feel threatened if there were more than one.

Charlie said he would go. Rudy said he wasn't going to rely on a one-legged man for breakfast.

"In the jumpers we'd flip a coin to decide this. I'm fresh out of coin. What you boys in Prineville do for a game of chance?"

Rudy appeared to think about it, then grinned. "We played 'getting the upper hand.' You've done it. We all did. It's how you choose up sides. The two best players toss a bat, one to the other. Where it's caught is where you start grippin' the bat, hand over hand, takin' turns. Last hand on the end of the bat is winner. Winner gets first choice of a player for his side. Fair as life itself."

Charlie knew the playground process. "That'll work."

"That piece of bamboo next to you will do. I'll toss it, you catch it one-handed. No chicken claws. Loser goes and begs for food in a strange language."

Facing each other, the bamboo tossed and caught, they gripped the stick, starting with Charlie, then alternating, one man's hand immediately above the other's until there was no room for another hand on the bamboo. Charlie's was the last full hand.

"So you win. You wait right here, out of sight. This'll only take a minute. Did you say over easy?" Rudy turned and walked down a path into the clearing where villagers were eating.

Rudy called out a greeting in Lao. The small group was startled. They were mostly women and children, only two older men among them. One man, legs muddied from farming, naked above the waist, picked up a machete and walked toward Rudy. Without warning or sound he swung. Rudy did not move and his head, unjointed at the neck, fell to the ground. The headless body stood for a moment, blood spurting from the dark red opening at the top of a dirty T-shirt. It then collapsed on the ground, near the head.

Charlie blinked his eyes to make the scene change. When it did not, he looked away. His senses would not let it go. They held clear evidence and it was permanent. He stopped denying what he had seen. He looked again at the dark figure on the ground, everyone around it now moving in slow motion, and accepted what he had seen. He did not experience fear, anger, loss, or anything he would have recognized as emotion. There was no disorientation or confusion. He thought he would probably die, too, but that did not give him concern. He felt only a nonspecific need to act. He turned and left the valley, searching for a mountain clearing where he could be seen by the people on his side.

When Pathet Lao pursuers found him next day he was standing in knee-high grass in just such a clearing. He was bent over, his bowels cramping without interruption. Diarrhea had turned his pants to foul abrasives. He felt too weak to do anything but submit. He accepted the reality of the automatic weapons.

The guards shouted a command. Charlie raised his hands over his head. "You boys got here just in time. This gone on much longer I was gonna have to tie my asshole to my leg. Got any kaopectate?"

They bound Charlie as usual, tied at the elbows behind his back, rope looped around his neck in the manner of a leash.

When the search party rejoined the main group with their prisoner, there were more prisoners. No one was any longer attached to the wire. All were quiet, watching him. They were in a prison camp called Ban Na Kay Neua Village Prison. It was in Sam Neua province near the NorthVietnam border.

Charlie was shoved into an open area surrounded by huts. The huts were camouflaged against aerial observation. Two men were digging a narrow rectangular hole in the middle of the open area. A wooden box of the same shape sat near the hole. It looked dirty and used. When the depth of the hole had reached the diggers' waists, the open box was dropped into it. Charlie was walked to the edge of the hole.

He thought he should run, a quick death in a fusillade of AK-47 bullets preferable to what they were obviously planning. As if the guards had read his mind he was grabbed and thrown into the box. He tried to climb out, panic mounting as imagined suffocation sucked at his lungs. He thrashed wildly, throwing punches and gasping for air as he was clubbed to the bottom of the hole.

He pushed against the boards of the lid as it was forced down on the box. It was an awkward contest for his captors in the tight space of the hole and Charlie, eyes wide and gathering precious light, thought for a moment he could actually prevent the closing of the lid, could resist any weight, no matter how much. The weight of one more man closed the box. Charlie tested the loss of light by forcing his eyes even wider. He screamed as he heard nails being pounded into the lid, felt the finality of hammer thumps.

In the darkness, he breathed cautiously, not knowing how much air there would be. The box was made for a smaller man. With his knees flexed to the lid, the top of his head and soles of his feet touched the ends. His shoulders rested against the sides, not solid contact but lightly, confinement always there. He smelled his own stink and that of others who had preceded him in the box. The darkness ceased to terrify him, became indistinct from sleep.

The lives of the saints came rushing back from another time and Carmelite Brothers. The stories were specific to his circumstances. Thomas à Kempis, exhumed as part of beatification, denied sainthood because the skeleton in the coffin, dressed in vestments of a priest, hands full of his own hair, suggested a man mistakenly buried alive and dying in despair.

Charlie was able to fend off despair. He knew the Pathet Lao wanted him alive. He worried, however, about the others, the small diggers that gnawed at his box. The rats were relentless, never stopped gnawing and scratching. The hardwood of the box was slowing them. He knew it would not stop them. He screamed, not at the men he imagined standing above him on the ground, but at the rats, hoping his scream would frighten them away. The rats never slowed their effort to reach him.

He wondered where on him they would begin gorging. His lips he thought. Maybe his eyes, wet and squinted shut against them. He squirmed as he imagined the small intimate mouths seeking out favored parts of his stinking body. He was sinking deeper into fear-choked fantasy when he realized madness would be waiting around one of the corners his mind was turning. He had to think about something else and end the fantasy of the rats, not hear their sound.

He tried thinking about women. As always their bodies came smooth against him and he ran his hand over their downy bellies. Only this time, by some limbic kink, his hand came to rest on small sharp teeth hiding within the dark fur of a favored fantasy. He screamed, then laughed. He stopped, afraid the laughing was a sign of dreaded madness.

He tried again. No more women, but it had to be just as intense. He did not select. Rather, it just came, in the way Thanasis told him poems sometimes came. It was about smoke jumping with Thanasis. It was a jump story. He grinned. He could not tell whether it was a fantasy or something remembered. In the sightless time in the box he found he could bring the stories to mind simply by willing them, effortlessly, and he was able to lose himself.

When the Pathet Lao dug him up two days later everything seemed loud, not painful but irritating and jarring. That was alright, any sound was, as long as it was not the sound of small animals digging. The bright light was painful. He was helped out of the hole. He closed his eyes against the light and fell to the ground, unable to maintain his balance.

A voice issued commands. He recognized the language as Vietnamese, but the voice was different than that of the NVA officer that had strung them on the wire. Hands grabbed him by each arm and raised him to his feet. The Pathet Lao on either side of him began to walk him forward. Still unable to stand upright, he fell. The guards did not let go of his arms and continued walking, dragging him toward their destination, face down, legs stretched out behind him. The stony soil removed the skin from the top of his feet, tore out toenails.

They pulled him to his feet beside a shallow creek and indicated that he was to take his clothes off and wash them and himself. He took his clothes off and sat down in the creek. As he sat bathing, his balance, sight and hearing slowly returned. He prolonged his time in the creek by rubbing his filthy jeans on rocks worn smooth by water. The guards, on a different schedule, deemed him clean enough, waded into the creek, stood him up, and pulled him across the compound naked.

They walked him away from the other prisoners, to a bamboo cage. It was five feet high in front and sloped to half that at the rear. The guards indicated that he was to enter the cage.

Charlie wanted to speak to the other prisoners, tell them what had happened to Rudy. He stepped away from the guards to yell across the compound. The guards threw him to the ground, and kicked him until he crawled into the cage on hands and knees.

Charlie's cage was fifty yards from the rest of the prisoners. He could not see them and they could not see him because of stands of bamboo and elephant grass that grew between them. He could hear no conversation from the direction of the prisoner compound, doubted if any was permitted. He was in solitary confinement.

The cage was made of bamboo poles tied together with quarter-inch rope. It was slightly longer than Charlie and four feet wide. The roof was covered with a thatch of leaves. Its corner posts were tied to stakes driven deep in the ground. The floor was dirt with small rocks imbedded in it. The entrance door was also bamboo, tied in place to secure the entrance opening. It was invisible from above, its shape obscured by overhanging bamboo.

A rope was tied around Charlie's neck. The other end was tied to a stake in the ground outside the cage.

He did not know how many days he had been buried in the compound. His hunger and weakness said it was a long time. He was brought a bowl of soup and, ignoring the worms floating in it, swallowed it at once. Over the next few days hunger made him relish the few rats, snakes and leaches he caught in his cage and ate. He captured beetles he had seen Meo eat. He missed the point that they did not eat the brittle carapace. He thumbed the second beetle from its shell and popped it in his mouth. *Much better,* he thought.

At night his hands and feet were bound to discourage escape attempts. The rope remained around his neck. After a few days of digging small sharp rocks out of the ground he found he could sleep through the night, even when the ropes were tied too tight.

His stool told him that his diet had brought him worms and parasites. The only medical attention he received was an all-purpose salve that treated the ringworm in his feet and puncture wounds in his hands. Lack of protein in the little food he was given caused his vision to dim over time.

When they felt he was strong enough they brought him to a hut for questioning. They tried to persuade him that he should make a radio broadcast statement against the war, otherwise no one would know that he was alive.

"My old man hopes I'm not alive and the women I been fuckin' aren't the kind that give a shit." Charlie hoped the latter was not the case. He refused to cooperate and was beaten with bamboo canes. He sensed in the interrogators a mixture of awe and hatred for the CIA. They knew he was CIA, no question about that. They even knew about Marana.

"How could a dink in a bamboo hut know about Marana?" Charlie wondered out loud. There was no one near him to respond. He returned to the jumper story that had been interrupted by his most recent interrogation. Between stories he worked on the ropes that lashed the bamboo of the cage together.

CHAPTER THIRTY-SIX

The Director of Central Intelligence, the Secretary of Defense, and the Secretary of State listened to the president's response to what they had said in the Oval Office minutes before.

"I know what the Geneva Accord of 1962 provides. But I'll be goddamned if I'll be the first president of this country to lose a war. We need to improve the effectiveness of U.S. bombing in North Vietnam. For you country boys that means we need to bomb the shit out of them, night and day, rain or shine.

"I know that the monsoon blows rain, fog and clouds into North Vietnam and that our planes can't bomb in those conditions without a ground-directed radar system. I know for the radar to see all the way to Hanoi you have to put it on a mountaintop, and I know North Vietnam is not gonna make a mountaintop available to us so we can bomb the shit out of them." The summary of his recently acquired knowledge was delivered in a mocking Texas school teacher twang.

"You don't need to tell me this a whole bunch of times. I know it. So listen to me." The President paused and continued. "I am ordering you, in what's left of this year 19 and 67, to find the highest mountaintop in Laos within pissin' distance of North Vietnam, install a radar bombing system on it, staff it with the best Air Force radar technicians you have, sheep dip those boys in a civilian defense contractor and put 'em in Hawaiian shirts so that the Geneva Accord does not apply. Then bomb the shit out of North Vietnam. This year, all year. Any questions?"

The CIA director cleared his throat and said "Based on our site survey we've chosen Phou Pha Thi, a mountain in Sam Neua province, Laos. It has a line of sight to aircraft sorties against the Hanoi area. We think the North Vietnamese will move to destroy the radar site within six months because the radar-directed bombing will hurt them. We cannot predict the outcome of such an NVA effort at this time."

"I want it to hurt," the president said. "Protect the site for long as you can."

The Air Force pulsed the personnel files of radar technicians, identifying candidates from whom it could seek volunteers for insertion onto an indefensible mountaintop near the border of North Vietnam. The airmen chosen were formally discharged from the Air Force and the same day became employees of Lockheed Aircraft Service Corporation. The story if anyone asked was that the radar belonged to the government of Laos and was being installed and run by American civilians for use by the RLAF in its war in Laos. In the world of self-restraint that governed troop deployment in the secret war in Laos any pretense would do. Only the American public remained unaware of what went on at the top of Phou Pha Thi.

The mountain, sacred to the Lao, is a narrow north-south ridge fifty-six hundred feet high, 120 miles from Hanoi. It has sheer cliffs on three sides. Much of the ridge is no wider than a Meo foot path. Near its midpoint, at its greatest height, the ridge widens to a treeless 70 by 130-foot table of limestone large enough to hold the base and pedestal for the radar dish of a TSQ-81 Radar Bombing Control System.

The sheep-dipped Air Force construction crew dynamited part of the plateau in order to create an infinitely level surface for the radar dish and an assured line of sight toward Hanoi. Screw jacks under steel beams assured a 'dead nuts level' surface.

The dynamite blasting, like earthmoving everywhere, brought all kinds of locals to the top of the mountain for a look, including Pathet Lao dressed in saffron robes of Buddhist monks. There was no security. Hanoi knew the purpose of the operation code-named Heavy Green from the outset.

There was a preexisting helicopter landing zone, left over from the French Indochina war, southeast of the radar site, on the same ridge top but several hundred feet lower than the radar and its crew. The landing zone and radar were connected by a footpath. Like all Meo footpaths it was without switchbacks and went straight up the hill. Helicopter was the only transport to the sacred mountain, now designated Lima 85.

Site construction was completed just as opaque rains came to Vietnam. Radar control began operating and made the sky transparent. Bombing of Hanoi became daily, round the clock, and effective.

Like every U.S. asset in Laos the radar facility was owned by the U.S. ambassador and had an on-site CIA presence. Norris put Thanasis and another smokejumper on Lima 85. They lived in a wooden shack next to the LZ, and were armed with M-16s, 12 gauge sawed-off shotguns, M-40 grenade launchers, and 9-mm pistols. The Air Force radar crew was unarmed and untrained in any weapons. Along with two hundred Meo and forty Thai PARU encamped near the LZ, the two CIA agents were defenders of the only way out of Phou Pha Thi.

Norris talked to his two men by secure telephone before they were flown to the mountain. "You'll be six weeks on and ten days off. You'll be bored stiff, but you have to stay focused. I want you to do two things. Check security all around the mountain and tell the officer in charge of the Thai what you find and what you recommend. After that you're the canary in the coal mine. When you think the site is about to go down and the Air Force boys have to come off the mountain, you tell Udorn so they can inform the Ambassador."

There were small Meo villages on the steep sides of Phou Pha Thi. The lives of the villagers seemed unaffected by the military operations on and around their mountain. They had planted opium poppies in all the open ground next to the long helicopter landing area. They tended the plants as if there was nothing in the presence of the soldiers and technicians that had meaning for their villages.

During their first week on the mountain the two smokejumpers did a reconnaissance of the site defenses and security. With a Meo lieutenant they visited bunkers on slopes near the bottom of the mountain guarding Meo villages and potential access points to the mountaintop. There were seven hundred Meo soldiers in the bunkers and otherwise deployed around the lower part of Lima 85. Asked how many Pathet Lao and NVA were in the area, the Meo lieutenant told them "many, many." The smokejumpers did not understand that "many, many" meant entire NVA battalions, three thousand infantryman and supporting artillery.

The CIA team assumed from their reconnaissance that the Meo defenders were outnumbered and surrounded. That did not particularly concern them. The Meo were there to warn of the inevitable, not hold. In addition they had been told in a pre-deployment intelligence briefing by the Air Force that the mountain was its own defense. "No military force can attack those cliffs in sufficient strength. They are three thousand feet high. In addition, any attack will be met with overwhelming air power directed by the radar site on the mountain."

On a cool morning the two jumpers decided to check out the intel briefing about the mountain cliffs. Neither was trained in rock climbing. With care and many stops they were surprised to find they could scale the western cliff above which the radar sat. Small trees in the vertical cliff face provided handholds that made their lack of technical rock climbing skill irrelevant.

Still sweating from their effort, they reported their finding to the Thai lieutenant in charge of the PARU. Thanasis recommended that the lieutenant mine the lower western slope and obvious climbing routes on the western cliff face, and suggested he create a bunker at the top of the cliff to be manned at night. The recommendations were received with a smiling "Thank you," and ignored.

The smokejumpers reported their findings and recommendations to Udorn CIA. After a twenty-four-hour delay they were told to relax, Air Force had assured CIA once more that no attacking force could scale the cliff in the face of air attack. It made sense and the smokejumpers relaxed.

The following month was quiet, pure paramilitary boredom that not even the Communist buildup below the mountain relieved. Thanasis, time on his hands, spent hours of every day trying to imagine Charlie's prison routine. He spoke frequently with Norris about the status of the search for Charlie, the planning for prison raids. There was never information about Charlie, nothing to plan. He was at a loss how to change that. The feeling of impotence ate at him. He was frustrated and anxious, decided he would ask to be taken off the Lima 85 assignment and volunteer for a search and rescue mission. Norris told him he was needed at the radar site. "Hang in there. The best in the world are looking for Charlie. You can't do anything until we find him."

The radar on Phou Pha Thi was used increasingly to kill NVA gathering around the mountain. Half the radar-directed bombing was focused on Hanoi and half on the enemy forces probing defenses around the radar itself.

Thanasis kept Udorn CIA informed of the growing pressure on the radar site. He and Norris discussed the relative merits of unarmed technicians staying on the mountain much longer.

"State Department is aware of the intensity of the envelopment of Phou Pha Thi," Norris told him. "The Secretary of State has been advised by us and State's own intelligence people to expect a ground assault within two weeks."

"It's growin' faster than that. They're comin' in a couple days, not weeks," Thanasis said. "As soon as their artillery gets within range of the helicopter landing zone it will be near impossible to fly those Air Force radar guys off here."

The ambassador to Laos, reconsidering his earlier decision to underscore the civilian status of the airmen by keeping them unarmed, had authorized issuance of M-16 rifles to the Air Force radar technicians. The action struck Thanasis as boneheaded. "If NVA gets through Air Force bombers and the Meo and Thai PARU," he told Norris, "good luck with those rifles."

After a night of heavy fighting on lower parts of the mountain left Thai and Meo commanders hedging about their prospects, Thanasis advised Udorn CIA it was time to take the technicians off the mountain and blow up the classified radar gear. Udorn advised the ambassador and the ambassador advised the Air Force. Thanasis found the response of the Air Force—"Leave the airmen in place a while longer. Bombing targets are lucrative."—chilling and he was still angry when the NVA artillery shelling of the top of Phou Pha Thi began.

The smokejumpers went to a rock bunker near the LZ. The concussion of a near hit deafened Thanasis' jumper buddy and shrapnel struck the man's forehead, knocking him unconscious. PARU medics treated him with first aid, assured he would be all right, just "not good for fighting."

The shelling continued for an hour and a half and stopped. Thanasis heard by radio from outposts on the lower slopes that NVA infantry were attacking in battalion force. The shelling started again.

The airmen in the radar building were busy directing A-26s and F-4 Phantoms attacking NVA around the lower slopes of the mountain. The Meo, protecting their villages against traditional enemies, were putting up a stiffer defense than anyone had anticipated. The combination of angry Meo and radar-directed bombing was generating hope in Udorn and Vientiane.

Hunkered down and sightless, no one heard or saw the thirty-three members of the *Dac Cong* unit, NVA special forces commandos, who had scaled the western cliffs during the night's artillery barrages. Thanasis became aware of them only when the NVA commandoes began killing Air Force radar technicians on top of the mountain sometime after midnight. He heard the fire of AK-47s and explosion of grenades. There was little M-16 fire. The fight did not last long. It was a slaughter of surprised and dutiful radar technicians.

The NVA commandos dug in around the captured site, their task now to hold against counterattack. They commandeered the bunkers, throwing bodies of dead airmen over the western cliff.

CHAPTER THIRTY-SEVEN

One message from the dark silence on Phou Pha Thi was that the airmen, surprised as they worked, had been unable to detonate the thermite and destroy the radar and its documentation. The evidence of secret war in Laos was as public as North Vietnam chose to make it.

At first Udorn did not believe Thanasis. The idea that a military site created at urgent presidential direction and protected by planes of the United States Air Force and Navy could be overrun in an hour by a few dozen men climbing three-thousand-foot cliffs in the dark had no credibility anywhere in the CIA or Defense Department. When the ambassador was awakened in Vientiane to be told that Phou Pha Thi had fallen he believed it at once and told Udorn to get the two CIA smokejumpers and any wounded off the mountain as soon as there was enough light to carry out helicopter rescue flights.

Aware that classified material and equipment at the radar site probably had not been destroyed, the ambassador told the CIA to have their people on Lima 85 do what reconnaissance they could to establish the extent to which the facility was still in existence. He called the Air Force to ask that they stand by to bomb the site once he confirmed that Air Force and CIA people were off the mountain.

At first light, Thanasis led eight Meo guerillas up the path toward the top of the mountain. He carried a sawed-off shotgun. They moved slowly in single file, not knowing what they would face, nervous, slipping in the stony soil of the path. They paused frequently to listen. After twenty minutes Thanasis was far enough up the path that he could, by lifting only his head, see most of the site without exposing himself. The squad of Meo stopped while Thanasis, lying on his belly, looked out over the flat surface. He saw neither NVA nor airmen. Only squat, pre-fabricated buildings. All of the buildings were standing though some showed damage. The communications area had received a direct hit from either a mortar or a rocket-propelled grenade. The crew quarters building was full of shrapnel holes. The radar dish and its related electronics looked like they were ready to continue the mission.

"Let's look around some corners," Thanasis whispered to the Meo next to him. "If there's wounded airmen they don't want to be here when their buddies show up with napalm."

Thanasis stood and walked out onto the surface of the radar site, crouching, shotgun held ready. He had taken only a few steps when a uniformed Vietnamese rose up in a bunker. The NVA soldier aimed a rifle and shot the Meo, the bullet tearing through the calf of one leg. Thanasis turned toward the bunker and shot the NVA soldier in the chest.

As Thanasis later said in CIA debriefings, "All hell broke loose, NVA jumpin' out of buildings firing automatic rifles on the run. The only reason any of us lived is they were surprised, probably searchin' the site for classified. When they killed the airmen at the site they thought they had everybody, most of the Meo and Thai havin' fled the mountaintop."

Thanasis grabbed the wounded Meo guerilla, who was still on his feet, and helped him back down the path to the LZ. He wrapped the leg wound and reported to Udorn by radio. Thanasis was told evacuation helicopters, Air America and Air Force, were in the air and would begin showing up at the Lima 85 helipad at eight a.m. and "lift off throughout the hour—have everybody ready. Mavros, get your classified docs boxed and in the helo."

When an Air America Huey assigned to the evacuation landed on the LZ, Thanasis helped load his wounded smokejumper buddy and wounded Meo and Thai soldiers on board. As the helicopter lifted off the mountain, he returned to the CIA shack and threw anything that looked like it might be classified into boxes.

A half hour after the first wounded had been lifted off, an Air Force "Jolly Green Giant" landed on the helipad near other wounded that had been collected beside the LZ. The helicopter was rushed by Thai and Meo troops trying to catch what might be the last flight off the mountain. A Meo officer threatened able-bodied soldiers with a pistol and turned them into litter bearers. As soon as the Jolly Green lifted off with its load of wounded most of the remaining soldiers began walking into the jungle.

When the Chief of Base at Udorn learned that Thanasis was still on Phou Pha Thi he ordered another Air America helicopter in the area to "do whatever is necessary to get him off the mountain." Thanasis was looking around for some gasoline to burn his documents in case there were no more flights when the Air America helicopter, another Huey, landed about a hundred yards away. He picked up one of his boxes of documents and hurried to the side of the helicopter, its rotors spinning for a quick lift off. By the time he got there several Thai soldiers had gotten on board. He asked them to help him get the other boxes. They looked away without response. There were other potential passengers milling around. Thanasis made five more trips for the boxes and finally sat down in the last seat on the Air America rescue helicopter. The aircraft raised off the LZ and proceeded to the Meo base at Na Khang.

The last rescue was completed at ten o'clock in the morning. That afternoon U.S. Air Force and Royal Lao Air Force planes destroyed the radar site with bombs and napalm. The bodies of the dead, American, Meo, Thai, and Vietnamese, disappeared in fire and pulverized limestone.

Thanasis flew from Na Khang to Vientiane where he found Dooley. They went to The White Rose. The name of the whorehouse was spelled out with white rope above an arched doorway, Lao script on the left, English on the right. The specialty of the house was Asian girls smoking cigarettes with their pussy.

"Billy took one of those girls home with him. Married her. You believe that, Thanasis? Smoked about a pack a day."

"I don't believe anything, Dooley. And I believe everything."

The smokejumpers drank one beer apiece, did not bother with the girls, and turned in early. It felt like the end of August in a long fire season, buddies gone and the point of the whole deal receding toward early winter. Thanasis dreamt of Charlie lost in a winter storm.

Twenty days later President Johnson ordered a halt in the bombing of Hanoi. He also announced that he would not run for reelection. The loss of the radar site at Lima 85 was not mentioned by anyone in Washington when they discussed those subsequent events.

CHAPTER THIRTY-EIGHT

Zorro and his wingman were patrolling the Trail in their T-28s, looking for targets of opportunity. They were not very good at the search business. They had too much speed to get a good look at anything in the jungle. Today, like every other day, they would rely on the Ravens, Forward Air Controllers flying low and slow in small fabric airplanes, to find targets in the jungle.

They got a call from a Raven they all knew as 'Magnet Ass,' a name his flight mechanic had given him. That was because the Raven's single engine Cessna got shot a lot. On returning to base he always reported the condition of his plane as "1," no damage. His mechanic usually marked it "3," not flightworthy, and substituted another plane for the FAC's use the following day.

The Raven was patrolling near the Trail in his high-wing airplane, looking for targets at eighty miles per hour. He found one and, with no trace of his excitement, called for any T-28s operating in the area. Zorro flight responded.

"Zorro One, I've got you a whole forest full of people dressed in green and none of them is elves. I don't have any idea what they're doin'." He was disguising his elation, slowing his Texas drawl to tar level. "They didn't bother to shoot at me. Must be a goddamn maypole dance. You won't be able to see 'em at all, but there's more than a company of 'em. I'll put my smoke in the middle. Just box the smoke front, back and sideways and you'll get 'em all."

The T-28s circled off to the west, away from the Trail, keeping an eye on the tiny Cessna 0-1 Bird Dog moving slowly above the jungle. When they saw the Willy Pete smoke rockets the RLAF fighter planes broke off and dove toward the target, even before they heard the Raven say "Zorro, you're cleared in hot. Box my smoke a hundred yards on each side."

Channarong flew at the area the FAC had indicated, slightly nose down, tapping his rudder pedals, yawing the plane and its guns side to side without banking. He and his wingman covered everything in the imaginary box, right to left and back, with .50 caliber. They shot up everything they carried in two heavy passes, waggled their wings at the lingering Cessna, and returned to Savannakhet.

A few days later several Buddhist monks walked into Lima 39 and asked to see "the commander of the pilots." They told Channarong they had been near the air attack, that they had walked through the area afterward. The two Zorro pilots had, in their brief assault, killed four hundred NVA infantry, a group in training, part of the twenty-five thousand NVA troops now defending the Trail. Channarong said to the monks "Buddha will provide."

He celebrated with Thanasis over beers, describing the grand attack. "They never even knew we were in the same sky." After a few beers he commented, as if surprised, how impersonal it was, that he had no remorse about the people he never saw and killed.

Thanasis thought he could get away with a joke about the insensitivity of back shooters, but did not try.

The conversation seemed to veer, Channarong saying "You shouldn't be pointing the sole of your boot at me, Mavros. To a Buddhist the foot is unclean. That is a great insult."

"Sorry, man. Didn't think you were religious." He had one leg cocked, resting on the other, the bottom of his foot facing Channarong. He uncrossed his legs.

"I'm not." Channarong drank from his beer, thought how he would say what he was thinking about.

"Mavros, I've heard your CIA buddies kidding you about 'going bamboo.' I think I know what that means. Are they talking about my sister or is it some other Asian? It is derisive isn't it?"

Thanasis sat up and leaned across the table. "Channarong, you've spent time in the U.S. hangin' with American buddies. You know kidding doesn't mean a thing. If I was sneakin' it with the Queen of

England those bullshitters would be sayin' I was goin' native. I've gone to Bangkok a couple times to see Dao. So the chatter is about me and her, but it's not derision. It's envy."

He waited for a reaction from Channarong and got none. "Are you OK with that or do we have a problem? Shit hot pilot like you can't be havin' that kind of stuff on his mind." He thought about pointing out it was Channarong had introduced him to Dao, but let it go.

"I'm OK if Dao is. Does she know she's bamboo?"

"I'll let her know the buzz when I see her this week. That kind of stuff really doesn't faze her. But you know that."

"Good. I'm turning in." Channarong stood up to leave. "Have a Trail patrol tomorrow. Need some sleep." He looked tired.

"Why don't you give the Trail a rest. It'll be there next week. Hell, next year. Let the BUFFS take care of it." He was using the fighter pilot acronym for B-52s, Big Ugly Fat Fuckers. "Go fly cover for the Meo up north after you get rested up." He thought *It's safer than Trail work,* but knew saying that would just keep Channarong over the Trail. "The little guys need it more."

"Mavros, pay attention. The Meo are ignorant mountain trash. My men are not going to waste their lives on people who don't bathe above their knees and believe that rocks and trees have spirits that can get angry and punish you."

Thanasis was aware of the Thai attitude. PARU consistently treated the Meo badly. He had not seen it in Channarong. He was surprised.

"Have a good night, Channarong." *Man is tighter than a bull's ass in fly time.*

The next morning a flight of four Zorro T-28s, Channarong as lead, were working the Trail. A Lao Theung road watch team had spotted trucks. As was often the case the location description from the Lao Theung was not very good.

Though he knew the NVA monitored his radio frequency Zorro called Savannakhet. The four planes in the flight were just burning aviation gasoline without more information. He made his contact short and obscure in an effort to keep the gunners along the Trail guessing what and where the Zorro flight was targeting.

"Hey Lima 39, we need the twenty on four-bys and big motherfuckers go tsss, tsss. No joy on Lao Theung report. Repeat, no joy." 'Twenty' was military 10-code for 'location.' The rest was about the fact they could see no trucks.

Savannakhet responded. It was one of the smokejumper Air America dispatchers Channarong knew. "Ten-four, Zorro. Hold one while I ask."

Channarong led his flight in a couple more circles before Savannakhet got back to him. "We have no clarification. How about we send you a Raven. It'll take forty minutes out of Nakhon Phanom."

"Bring him on. We have the fuel."

The Raven 'Magnet Ass' responded out of the Royal Thai airbase at Nakhon Phanom, immediately across the border from Laos, and went to work. He told Zorro flight that he would not mark with smoke but would waggle his wings, "so watch me close." Marking with a flight maneuver was not usual but the antiaircraft fire over the Trail had gotten so thick FACs were reluctant to forewarn targets and guncrews with smoke markers.

The T-28 pilots watched the Cessna working the Trail. Channarong had about concluded it was a wasted day when he saw the small observation plane rolling from side to side, waggling its wings.

"Tallyho, Raven. We're on it."

One after the other the planes in Zorro flight dove on the stretch of jungle canopy indicated by the forward air controller. Even before they had completed their bombing and strafing run they began to get secondary explosions. The Raven had found a truck depot and fuel storage facility. Vehicles and gasoline were exploding and spreading fire throughout the large facility and into the surrounding jungle.

As the T-28s began their climb-out the jungle erupted with 23-mm fire from quad-barrel NVA guns. Thick gunfire chased the planes, trying to get in front of them, overcome the surprise of unannounced arrival. The NVA added 37-mm antiaircraft guns, filling the sky above Zorro flight with an umbrella of black explosions they would have to fly through in order to escape the rapid fire 23s.

Channarong, climbing steeply, felt a thump and, looking right and left, saw a piece of wing fly off. The plane yawed back and forth as one wing and then its shortened partner tried to assert their function as airfoil. The two of them, unable to achieve flight, flipped the plane over on its back. With no more solution than beetle, crab, or turtle, the T-28 tumbled end over end. Channarong fought his disorientation, lurching and whipping within the cockpit. He sought the control stick that had popped out of his hand and, finding it, felt only wild oscillation without aircraft response. He could not, in the end, hold the stick. His feet were thrown off the rudder pedals by violent piston movement, floor to full top, generated by god-knows-what force on the tail rudder. Recognizing it was no longer an airplane he was trained to fly, he punched the ejection button and blew through the cockpit roof.

He floated toward jungle in pain. He felt it as a specific thing, but he could not tell where the "thing" was. He gave up trying to locate his pain and thought of other problems. The last thing he thought was statistical, an abstraction from intel briefings, that only five percent of pilots shot down in Laos survive. *Was it meant to make me fight harder?* he asked just before he passed out.

When he came to he saw that he was being carried in a sling tied to a bamboo pole. The bamboo rested on the shoulder of a Meo at each end. The clan of the two bearers backed the Lao Communists. The pace of movement on the rough trail was fast and uncomfortable.

Channarong had been trained in escape and evasion. He tried to recall principles, organize them into a plan. With the next bolt of pain he laughed out loud, causing the Meo bearers to come to a halt. He stopped laughing. He had started and stopped laughing for the same reason. He knew he was too badly hurt to plan escape, to carry out a plan. Escape was laughable and he gave it up. That felt OK. Imprisonment was something he could accept. *Buddha will provide.*

CHAPTER THIRTY-NINE

The war changed for the Meo as well. They were no longer defending homeland. That part was gone. The CIA, at the direction of the National Security Council, had changed the mission. The mountain farmers were now fighting to support somebody else's war in a place none of them called home. They were no longer guerillas, choosing targets by the seat of their pants, harassing and ambushing enemy, stealing away into their own mountains. Their battles were now meant to protect American soldiers across the border in Vietnam. The Meo were to tie down as many North Vietnamese Army divisions as possible and make it costly for the North to supply their Vietnam war through the heavily defended Ho Chi Minh Trail.

For the North Vietnamese, the goals of the secret war had also changed. Complete destruction of the Meo became the end of military action in Laos.

The barefoot Meo were fighting more conventional battles, facing increasingly destructive concentrations of mortars, artillery, and tanks supplied by the great nations. Personal heroism with machetes at close quarters became irrelevant in the face of technology. The depersonalized killing had taken one in ten of the Meo population, a literal decimation. Thousands of others were returned by helicopter to remote villages, unable to walk or see their way.

The numbers introduced a separate terror. To recruit enough new fighters Vang Pao resorted to lies, threats, and, in the end, acceptance of the only thing Meo families had left to offer. Their children. The brown-faced boys, ten- and twelve-year-olds in baggy rolled-up uniforms, were shorter than their rifles, half the age of the Sky men who flew them to the battlegrounds.

The changed war was septic. Struggling against anonymous death in a combat where both sides sought only attrition, the Meo hero's heart ran amok in mutilation and atrocity. Battle corpses were decapitated, chests cut open and hearts ripped out, prisoners nailed to trees.

Meo were a people who could not lie. They had no gene or culture for it. Their lives were local, without myths that reached beyond their mountains. Without a sustaining myth the decade-long war against communism became spoliation without higher purpose, done to themselves for a distant other people.

Awareness of this among some of the Meo led to resistance to Vang Pao's commitment to war. One of his own men shot the general in the elbow and neck on a visit to Na Khang.

Na Khang, Lima 36, northeast of the Plain of Jars, was a forward staging area for the CIA and Meo, a search and rescue base, and a critical link in resupplying Meo operating to the north. Physically it was a knoll, the highest point in an area of rolling hills with few trees, most of which formed a tree line on two sides of the knoll. The other sides were open and covered with elephant grass taller than a man. Though fortified with trenches and wire and air support, it had been successfully attacked several times and then retaken. Its perimeters were probed nightly by Pathet Lao. It became 'The Alamo' to the smokejumpers who defended and worried about it.

Following evacuation from Phou Pha Thi, Thanasis was reassigned to Na Khang. He was the only CIA officer at Lima 36. Norris had tried to sell Thanasis on the assignment.

"NVA is moving the same divisions they had at Phou Pha Thi west to Na Khang. They're settin' up to attack Na Khang again. I need somebody there who's been through this before."

Thanasis laughed. "I lost the last mountain you gave me. You're just punishing me aren't you. Well I think I'll avoid all the aggravation and just turn this one over to 'em before anybody gets shot."

"I sometimes forget. Thank you for the handsome defense of the last mountain. I think the president would have called you but the White House was busy with Vietnam. Are we friends again?"

"Whatever you say, boss. But you owe me ten days in Bangkok."

"You've got it as soon as your replacement gets off his ten. Are you OK with the situation at Na Khang? You know the NVA doesn't like this place. We usually beat 'em back with close air support and napalm each time. There's no reason to think that won't work again. You'll have all the A-1 Sandies you want."

Thanasis felt comfortable with the defense of Na Khang. There were four thousand Meo in trenches behind concertina wire and Claymore mines facing the tree lines. The Sandies would make it no contest. The World War II plane was a dump truck of ordnance and guns. It carried twice as much as any jet fighter. It carried two canisters of antipersonnel cluster bombs, two pods of rockets, two white phosphorus bombs, and four 20-mm guns with two hundred rounds each—eight thousand pounds altogether. It was noisy, short, and driven by a four-bladed fourteen-foot propeller attached to an eighteen-cylinder engine. Dozens of them were available for the defense of Na Khang.

One thing Thanasis did not like about Na Khang was that it was a pest hole. The only buildings at Lima 36 were two small corrugated metal sheds off to the side of the runway. One shed housed radio communications equipment. The other contained his bed. Both were sandbagged, reflecting the frequent presence of Pathet Lao snipers.

Mosquito netting hung around his bed. There were no mosquitoes. It was there to prevent rats from having access to his head. They would come each night and nibble on his hair, waking him. Thanasis hung the net and requisitioned a pump .22 rifle with a silencer. He used it to shoot rats in his bedroom. He shot them every night.

Na Khang was not the worst Lima site, but it would make anyone's top ten. Thanasis was grateful when his buddies visited him as they passed through Na Khang, a busy air transportation center, on their way to a new assignment or R&R. The previous month it had been Paperlegs returning to Marana. Last week it was one of the Johnson brothers, Buckle, on his way to train PARU at Phitsanulok, Thailand. Today it was Dooley, on his way to Bangkok R&R by way of Udorn.

On their arrival at Na Khang, Thanasis pressed each smokejumper for word of Charlie. There was never any information. Raids had been made on Pathet Lao jungle prisons based on rumors. None of the raids turned up anything about Charlie or anyone else. The prisons were there, just as rumored, but they had been recently abandoned. The news of failure depressed Thanasis, sometimes for days. He became paranoid about possible security breaches forewarning the Pathet Lao and frustrating the raids.

Thanasis tried to rally before the departure of each friend, for their sake as well as his, and made his visitors sign the corrugated shed he lived in by shooting a hole in the door, drawing a bull's-eye around the hole, and initialing and dating the damage. He and his visitors at Na Khang always carried M-16s. They never put the black guns down.

He gossiped with Dooley before the shooting-of-the-door ritual. "Yeh, Vang Pao was shot right over there." Thanasis pointed. "Thought it was a sniper at first, but he was told it was one of his own men. So he took care of it the Meo way."

"Shot him?"

"Nope. He made every Meo on Na Khang drink "special water." He told them the spirits of the water would kill anyone who did not have a true heart."

"Did it work?"

"They're still here, dug in, and haven't shot him since."

There was wood smoke in the air, farmers slashing and burning the hills. The smell of wood smoke brought Thanasis a memory, sharp and complete. He was smoke jumping, taking a break on the fireline, smoking a cigarette, the taste of tobacco leaf and burning pine mixed in sweet formula. Sore-backed but feeling good. In the Primitive Area of Idaho, just him and his jump partner, Charlie, laughing about a good time, an old time.

"Gimme one of those, buddy." The request for a cigarette brought him out of the Primitive Area, back to Na Khang.

The mountain air moved and told him he had not showered in a couple weeks. Maybe more. He held a pack of cigarettes out toward Dooley, shook it upright in the air until a cigarette jumped up.

"Fifteen cents in the PX. They're cheap enough even you can afford them, Dooley. And you only call me buddy when you're moochin' cigarettes or tryin' to get close enough you can slobber on my girlfriend."

"You ain't got a girlfriend, 'less you countin' your hand."

They stopped talking and listened, watched down the mountain toward the tree line.

"Thought I heard the little guys talkin'."

"You did. Watch. They'll clear the trees in a minute."

They heard more talk, Meo approaching through the trees.

"You don't usually hear that much from 'em. They're excited. They caught somethin'. Maybe a wild boar."

There was no wild boar. Two short men, lithe and dark haired, wearing black shirts and floppy black trousers, stepped from the trees carrying M-1 rifles at the ready. They were followed by a line of slightly taller men, more Asian-looking, hands tied behind their backs. Two more short men in black followed, their rifles pointed at the backs of the prisoners.

They recognized one of the men carrying rifles, a leader of Vang Pao's ambush teams. They greeted him.

"Hey, Longfellow. You gonna fatten those boys up and eat 'em?"

Longfellow grinned. "Yes. With duck egg on top. Whiskey too." He repeated the conversation in Lao for the benefit of the prisoners, laughing as he finished. There was no reaction from the prisoners. Longfellow stepped in and slapped one of them, hard. Then he turned away, disinterested.

Longfellow spoke to the CIA men. "We have prisoners for Sky boss. Do what he say. Now send helo."

Thanasis nodded and spoke to Dooley. "I'll call in the helos. We'll need a couple. You mind pullin' guard duty on the way out?"

"No. That'll be fine. I assume Lima 36 is providin' the beer. Case of Olympia if you don't mind. Why all the prisoners? I count twelve. The little guys usually don't take any. Mean little shits."

"Oly it is. Why so many? I don't know. Maybe they lost count. But you heard Longfellow. Chief of Base in Udorn wants 'em. Probably thinks he needs to squeeze somebody about troop buildup around here or on the Trail. You just know that's where the ambush team got these guys."

"Sure. Looks like they did pretty good. At least half are NVA. Bet chief gets what he wants. Slap me with that pizzle I'd talk all day long."

Dooley was talking about their CIA boss in Udorn. Called Stick behind his back, he carried a leather riding crop made from the penis of a bull. The leather stick was present on all occasions, twenty-four hours a day as far as anyone could tell. He slapped it against his leg. It was impressive in the offices and clubs of the Royal Thai Air Force Base. It brought snickers in the rest of Southeast Asia. Prisoners used to worse from the mountain people would not be impressed.

Before Longfellow departed, Thanasis took him aside and asked him if he had heard anything from any of his people about The Dago or any Sky prisoners. Longfellow shook his head and said "Hear nothing. No The Dago in jungle prisons."

Longfellow and two of his men left Na Khang at the rapid Meo walk, breathless if you were not Meo. One man was left to guard the prisoners, wait for the helos. He did that, making them lie face down in silence. He squatted facing the prone bodies, rifle across his knees, throwing the bolt for effect. So they would not be tempted.

Thanasis got on the radio with Udorn, asking for transportation. Finished quickly, he came out of the radio shack. He looked at the sky, hands on hips.

"Shit."

"Whasup?"

"Plain of Jars is full of NVA. Big fight. Everything committed to Vang Pao. Lima 36 and its prisoners get hind tit. Not a goddamned helo from South China Sea to India you listen to Udorn."

They sure fight a lot over a place full of sunflowers and butterflies, Dooley thought. "What you gonna do?" he asked, as if it was not his problem, but interested in the answer.

"Generous bastards are sending a five-passenger Helio Courier. Narrow gomer butts make it a six. Sending it without a guard, so you and four of them get to ride out. You the guard until you get to Udorn. Only way you're gonna get down to the LBFMs. You owe me."

Little Brown Fucking Machines. Dooley's attention drifted with the thought. He focused again.

"I'm your guard. Appreciate the ride. I'll pay for the first twenty-four hours of your next trip to Vientiane." Dooley added "You smell so bad it won't cost me a dime."

"C'mon, Dooley. I'll help you get started on your case of beer. Refrigerator cold. Fly in the beer and generator gas once a week."

"Hear from Norris?" Dooley asked.

"Only long enough for him to tell me where to go."

"Puts us in here and disappears forever. He oughta be tellin' us where this is goin'. Not as much fun as it used to be." Dooley opened a beer. "Money's good."

"We bought it all. No point bitchin'. I'll try to get him into Saigon. Maybe Tokyo. Get him in for talk in a fancy hotel."

Dooley blew a strange insect off his beer can. He looked at Thanasis. He had another question but hesitated.

"What?"

"Hear from Dao?"

Thanasis seemed to think about what to say. He finally said "Things kinda cooled off after Channarong went down. She is real close to her brother. She pulled back, got real down, quit work. Probably depressed. Not returning my calls. I'd like to see her but she's got to work it out for herself."

Dooley looked away. "Hear anything on Charlie?"

Thanasis did not want to talk anymore, but he did. "Dao's not the only one is depressed. I feel like I'm living in full time shit. Nobody has a word or thought on Charlie. He's disappeared. Sometimes I feel good about that. Like it says they know what they've got, know he's CIA. So they are gonna be real careful about hiding him, so they can embarrass us or trade him or both." Thanasis paused. "Other times I think he's dead. I don't know which is better."

They had drunk a six-pack by the time the Helio Courier landed. The airplane taxied toward the group of prisoners lying face down at the end of the runway.

Thanasis said "Finish your beer. The Meo guard can get 'em on the plane. They won't fuck with him." *They might fuck with you* hung unspoken between them in the smoky air. They watched the prisoners and the airplane from the shade of one of the sand-bagged buildings, half way up the runway.

At a shout from the guard the prisoners stood, clumsy without the use of their hands. Using the barrel of his rifle he prodded them into line, ready to board the plane. He looked up expectantly at the pilot still seated at the controls. Wordlessly the pilot addressed the impossibility. He pointed at the prisoners and shook his head at the Meo guard, mouthing words without sound. He held up four fingers, again pointing at the prisoners. He repeated an indefinite motion with his hand, the four fingers still extended. There was no response from the Meo guard.

The pilot was becoming agitated but remained pilot cool. He pointed at the prisoners and then at the interior of the plane behind him. He held up four fingers again. He paused. He crossed his hands in front of him, palms outward, then separated and crossed them several times, waving the Meo off. He held up four fingers once again.

The Meo guard considered the pilot impassively, then nodded his head. He shouted at the prisoners, motioning them away from the plane with the barrel of his rifle, told them to sit. They sat cross-legged on the ground. The guard walked slowly around the group, looking them over, individually, assessing aspects of them apparent only to him. To some he spoke, asked questions.

"Where are you from?"

"You are from Vietnam?"

"Viet Minh old time?"

"VC?"

"What do you think of Vang Pao?"

"Do you have a wife?"

"How many children?"

He reached down and grabbed the pants leg of a prisoner, dragged him from the group.

It took some time, pulling four prisoners from the group and putting them one at a time into the plane. The pilot remained at the controls, pistol in his hand, watching the prisoners in the plane. He was strapped in, engine running, prepared to leave. The four prisoners were tied down by the Meo guard, faces bent near their knees and marked with blood and bruises. The pilot no longer watched the prisoners sitting in the orange dirt. He was calculating how many flights he would have to make to transport them all to Udorn. He began revving his engine, turning the plane to position it for takeoff, kicking up dust, waiting only for his guard.

The pilot thought the first shot was his engine acting up, backfiring. It worried him, the thought of trouble with his single engine in the mountains. He recognized the second and third shots as gunfire. It was close, easily heard above the sound of his engine. The shots were evenly spaced, but he could not tell from where they were coming. All he could think was he had to get off the mountain before the bullets started finding his plane. When he heard the fourth and fifth shots he knew the bullets did not seek the airplane.

The smokejumpers having a cold beer heard the shots. At the sound of the first they put their beers down and pointed their rifles, searching the tree line. The even spacing of the shots made some trained, unconscious part of them relax. It was not the wild sound of firefight, of AK-47, of surprise attack. They recognized the sound of the Garand, the old M-1 rifle issued to Meo. They remained on guard. The regular, rated firing of the rifle was nothing they had ever heard. Maybe on the range. Never in the field. They did not like the mystery of the rhythm and ran their eyes across the surface of the mountain, scanning, listening, coming in the end to the idling airplane, the Meo guard aiming his rifle.

He aimed at something below his waist, recoiled in cadence with the sound of each measured shot.

The Sky Men screamed and the scream was full of failure and fatigue and anger. They ran toward the Meo guard, screaming in English and Lao and Meo.

The guard would have done whatever they told him but he could not hear them over the sound of the airplane engine.

He shot each seated prisoner in the chest. Except the last, a Vietnamese struggling to get to his feet. He kicked the man, the bottom of his heel knocking the prisoner back to the ground. He circled the struggling figure, jammed the end of the rifle barrel against the top of the man's head and pulled the trigger. The explosion sent a 9.8 gram ball of lead, shaped to a point and jacketed in gilding metal, yawing through the prisoner's brain at twenty-seven hundred feet per second, forcing crushed matter through the apertures of the head, collapsing the roof of the mouth, pushing one eyeball from its socket as the bullet passed.

CHAPTER FORTY

The season *Xuan-Mau Than,* Spring-Year of the Monkey, was a grim time for soldiers in Vietnam as well as those in Laos. The Tet Offensive, presented daily on American television, sent forty-five thousand North Vietnamese soldiers to their death against what American generals called the "meat grinder." The massive coordinated attacks on nearly every South Vietnamese provincial capital, and focused on Saigon, surprised American military commanders. They had not thought the North Vietnamese capable of such an effort. NVA soldiers and Viet Cong supplies, after all, moved only in the dark on jungle paths winding through the mountains of Laos.

U.S. and ARVN forces turned back the NVA and Viet Cong, repelled the spring offensive. Rather than celebrating victory, the media and the American public were shocked. Secretary of Defense Robert S. McNamara resigned. Walter Cronkite began saying on the evening news that the war in Vietnam could not be won. A group of six men, advisors called The Wise Men, told President Johnson the war in Vietnam could not be won. The six said nothing of Laos.

In the fall of the year smokejumper overhead in McCall sat down to review applications for positions for the next fire season.

"Gawdamighty you learn to make coffee in the Army?"

"The very same. I'm popular in an elk camp."

They drank the coffee, adjusted their chairs around the long table, cleared their morning sinuses with rasping and hacking. They turned reluctantly to the folders stacked in front of them. They hardly had begun the review of government forms when one of the reviewers slapped the table.

"What are the goddamn rules this year? Are we only hirin' queers or is there a quota?"

There were grins and silence. The men around the table waited for the Project Leader to take control.

"I know from your behavior around town, Gene, that you're not expressing a personal preference. Refill your cup and let's move on."

"No, I'm serious. You seen the shit we put up with the past couple years. We got jumpers wearin' bandannas around their heads. Their hair is down to their ass. They're playin' guitars and singin' where have all the flowers gone. How can you be a smokejumper with ribbons in your hair. I'd rather fight fire with Jane Fonda than some of those pussies."

"You may get your wish. There's women applyin' for these jobs," one of the squad leaders said, tapping the stack of folders in front of him. "I heard Washington is sayin' it's gonna happen. Get ready."

"Oh great. Now I get to carry two elephant bags when I pack out?"

"But you'll be warmer at night."

"You hear about the woman firefighter got killed in a blowup last year? Went back for her purse."

"Cut the crap. My sister can outwork you."

The Project Leader let the rant go on for a while. It was old and winded and would not last long. No question things were changing. Some of his friends were confused by it.

He left the room for a while, did some paper work, and returned. "Your views of the world haven't changed in a year. So let's go back to work. Let's hire some people before the CIA gets 'em all."

More jumper candidates were hired that year, both in the Forest Service and in the CIA.

CIA headquarters was no longer located in Washington, D.C. Norris and Casey were meeting in the McLean, Virginia, headquarters for the first time. They were having lunch in a private dining room looking out on a Virginia forest of tulip poplar, oak and hickory. Casey was telling a story like older lawyers do, close to the facts but not needlessly so.

"The Agency bought the property in the '50s, construction was completed in the '60s. Within the two hundred acres the CIA wanted to acquire for its new headquarters was a privately owned thirty-five-acre tract on which sat, in bucolic splendor, a white clapboard house. It was the home of Margaret Scattergood and Florence Thorne. The two women had worked as Samuel Gompers' personal secretaries at the old American Federation of Labor.

"When Dwight Eisenhower and Allen Dulles authorized condemnation of the Scattergood-Thorne home and payment of modest eminent domain compensation they learned what most folks inside the Beltway already understood about these ladies. The girls knew where the bodies were buried. All hell broke loose. The two women went to Capitol Hill and lobbied Congress. Congress quickly enacted private legislation giving Margaret and Florence the right to live in their own house in the middle of the CIA's most secure facility for as long as either of them lived.

"To this day they share an address with CIA Headquarters. They may be here long after we're gone. Norris, let's talk about wars that are winnable." Casey raised his glass. The martini at lunch was something new. "Fill me in on Laos."

"The Alamo fell. Two battalions of NVA came out of the elephant grass, opposite what they had ever done. Meo were surprised and ran. It happened so fast USAF close air support couldn't get on site and help. We napalmed them after the fact, killed a bunch. But we're damned near out of northern Laos. Too many Meo kids fightin' too many NVA regulars. About all we got left in the north is Long Tieng. Got some electronic surveillance out of Bouam Long, but that'll go too."

"How did you get our guys out of Na Khang?"

"Air America Huey, guns blazin'. One guy only. Mavros."

"What are CIA casualty figures to date?"

"Same as front line infantry. About one out of ten."

"That true for your smokejumpers?"

"Between me and Air America we've had ninety-two jumpers workin' Laos. We have nine dead. Various wounded. Several MIA. One of those is a smokejumper POW. We have not been able to find out where they are holding him. Soon as we do we'll go in after him."

Casey was silent as he fished an olive out of his martini, concentrating. He popped it in his mouth and said "There're going to be congressional hearings on Laos. They are runnin' for cover. Deny they ever heard of it. For most of them, that's true."

"Who'll testify?"

"The CIA director. Then mostly State Department. State, as you know, is running the Laos war. We're the operations guys carrying out the ambassador's directions."

"We're a pimple on Vietnam's ass right now. Where is that deal goin'?"

"As everybody knows bombing has been stopped in North Vietnam so both sides can sit down in Paris and talk. Nixon told us in the campaign that he has a plan to end the war. He hasn't said a word what that might be. It'll end. Can't tell you when. 'Til then keep your guys sharp, heads up. What are the prospects for holding Long Tieng?"

"We'll need more Thai PARU. The Meo are about done. Can somebody work on that?"

"I'll take care of it."

"We'll need all the air support we can get. It'll be a duel between NVA rockets and USAF bombs."

"No problem. With the bombing halt in Vietnam, there's nothing but excess aircraft and pilots for Laos. You'll have more than you can control. That's a warning."

CHAPTER FORTY-ONE

A subcommittee of the United States Senate Foreign Relations Committee, the Subcommittee on U.S. Security Agreements and Commitments Abroad, began hearings on American involvement in Laos. A much censored transcript of the hearings was released. It carried the testimony of the Deputy Assistant Secretary of State for East Asian and Pacific Affairs that "the United States has no commitment to Laos or to the Meo tribesmen whom we have supported in their fight against communism. We have approached the war in Laos with this overriding rule: In all events, we must position ourselves to be out in eight hours. That may have grown over the past several years to twenty-four hours. But you take my point. Our commitment is no greater than that. The United States is without obligation in Laos."

President Nixon followed up on the congressional hearings with the first public acknowledgement of U.S. involvement in the war in Laos. The "secret war" was no longer secret. It remained, however, obfuscated. The president joined his public disclosure on Laos with the assertion that "no American stationed in Laos has ever been killed in ground combat operations." No mention was made of prisoners of war.

The White House press office revised the statement within forty-eight hours, noting death of twenty-six civilians and one military advisor in Laos. It was explained that the deaths had previously been reported in the category "deaths in Southeast Asia" and "through oversight, not specifically related to the more particular geography of Laos." The White House did not define "civilians."

By the time the president acknowledged American involvement in Laos the NVA controlled the northern half of the country except the

CIA base at Long Tieng and the cities of Luang Prabang and Vientiane, the royal and administrative capitols of Laos.

The air supply operation out of Long Tieng was the key to defense of the surrounded capitol cities. The NVA began their siege of the CIA base. Two divisions of NVA, operating from the Plain of Jars, invested the mountain valley and attacked the defense positions on the surrounding ridges.

It was a two-year battle, day and night, NVA mortars, 130-mm artillery, and 122-mm Katyusha rockets against U.S. and Lao air force bombing. For those surrounded in Long Tieng, the rockets, screaming and indiscriminate, were the worst. They were unguided but when they hit they destroyed reinforced bunkers, trenches, airplanes, and people. During one stretch the defenders of Long Tieng were hit by rockets for 153 straight days. Along with Meo and Thai there were eighteen CIA agents and smokejumpers defending during the seige. Their training and experience included Marine Corps, Army Airborne, CIA paramilitary, and war with North Korea. They came to believe that everything that went before was just preparation for Long Tieng.

At first the radar bombing by the new F-111 night and all-weather fighter kept the NVA infantry at bay around Long Tieng. The long range rockets and artillery of the attackers kept the defenders in their bunkers full of cans, bottles and expended shell casings. The entire war became a cage fight in a small mountain valley, both sides fully committed.

Limits on maneuver of jet aircraft imposed by weather and the surrounding mountains finally gave the NVA infantry assault a foothold. They were able to dislodge Thai defenders from the western half of Skyline Ridge. The ridge paralleled the Long Tieng runway along its northern side. The NVA and Thai fired mortars at each other on the long ridge day after day. The NVA stopped only long enough to turn their mortar fire on the runway below them every time a cargo plane attempted to land. Lao T-28s napalmed the ridge in advance of supply missions.

In spite of the close-quarters mortar shelling, supply operations from Long Tieng seldom deteriorated as the battle crashed on. Air delivery out of Long Tieng ran at three hundred thousand pounds a day, most of it to constantly-moving Meo guerillas engaging the enemy around Long Tieng and the Plain of Jars.

Much of the Long Tieng cargo loading took place under long-range shelling. There were few direct hits on the cargo loading ramp, but it happened. A 122-mm rocket landed on a forklift surrounded by a Meo crew loading a C-123. Thanasis ran to assist his crew at the site of the explosion. His approach chased a feeding dog from the open back of a dead Meo loader. The dog ran with a bright red human kidney in his mouth, trailing parts of the man's viscera. Thanasis worked for the next twenty-four hours without a break, not because his effort was necessary to evacuate the wounded and clear the ramp and continue delivery of ammunition to Meo fighters. He worked to avoid the image of the feeding dog.

Smokejumpers flying out of Vientiane checked on Thanasis and the other jumpers at Long Tieng each time they flew into the base. Mostly they did not see each other, but spent a few minutes on the radio as they circled, landed and left.

"What you doin' Mavros?"

"Duckin'. Don't you dare come down here. Nothing is green. The garlics and the gomers are givin' each other high-angle hell day and night. Either one of 'em could kill you just by bumping their mortar a frog's hair right or left. Go back to Lulu's."

"We got to come down. We got orders. A woman in Bangkok sent you a case of Oly and I can't carry the damn thing around forever. Her scent will wear off it."

The message was greeted with silence.

"Oh relax, Mavros. She don't love you. Just thinks you're an alcoholic."

"Thanks, asshole. I mean it, don't land."

The plane circled in radio silence. It suddenly straightened over the runway and dived. As it pulled out of the dive a small white parachute opened, a case-of-beer sized package suspended beneath.

A smokejumper voice came back on the radio. "You are really cold, Mavros. I had expected you would share this with us. You come out of there soon. Hear? You're startin' to smell again. Funny she don't mind that. Over and out."

NVA sappers blew up the Long Tieng ammunition dump. Their infantry repeatedly assaulted the runway itself, cutting through concertina wire and advancing nearly the length of the base before machine gun positions manned by Meo teenagers turned them back.

Thousands of Meo families were flown out of Long Tieng by Air America. Many thousands more fled on foot into the jungle and the mountains to the west. Some Meo fighters left the defense of the base, following their families to protect them from the surrounding Vietnamese who casually murdered Meo women and children when they found them. Air America flights out of Thailand dropped bags of rice ahead of the fleeing Meo.

The bodies of Meo fighters that stayed and died in the shelling and night attacks were removed to Meo villages for burial by their families. The Meo interpreter working with Thanasis was one of those. He was the educated son of a village headman. He stood outside a bunker watching the fireworks of an F-4 attack on an NVA mortar position that had been shelling them. The 'fast mover' mistakenly attacked its own bunker with CBUs, small antipersonnel cluster bombs. The steel flechettes shredded the boy's throat and chest and nailed him to the bunker wall. The bomblets, some exploding in the air immediately above them, wiped out a Meo platoon hunkered down in nearby trenches.

Thanasis, operating a radio in the bunker, heard the explosions and screams outside and looked out a view port. He took in the bloody tableau and ran to the young Meo. Thanasis and the interpreter had rarely been apart. Language was their first bond. It made possible their second important bond, smoke jumping. In their little time away from battle and air supply Thanasis entertained and rewarded his interpreter with smokejumper stories and the idiom of jumpers. The young Meo regarded the Sky Men as heroes. He made sure he dressed like them and spoke English like them, often in a language far removed from the English of the schools. The boy's lungs filled with blood as he tried a last time to speak "smokejumper" English to Thanasis.

Thanasis accompanied the body of the interpreter when it was taken by helicopter to his Meo village for burial. A white flag, signifying death, was hung at the front of the parents' house and the boy soldier's death announced to the village by three rifle shots, fired slowly, one after the other. The body, washed by the women in the family, was dressed in black pants and jacket. The only departures from his daily wear were the bright-colored embroidery that now trimmed his jacket, and his feet were bare. The body lay on a red cloth stretcher. The father had traded a homemade flintlock rifle for the cloth. Next to the stretcher was a crossbow, a knife, and a pair of White smokejumper boots given him by Thanasis. The dead boy would need these things in crossing to the Otherworld.

Incense filled the one-room house, floating over partition walls, and masked the smell of rapid putrefaction. Wailing and groans came from relatives seated on the floor around the body. Others fanned the air to keep flies away from the object of their sorrow.

Thanasis could feel his own peculiar form of grief stealing toward him as he watched and listened to the sounds of death. He had earlier experienced the dark dream of his father's death and he was thankful he could not remember its details. He had been distracted during the helicopter ride and found himself in clothes he did not remember putting on. It was appropriate dress for the Meo funeral, but the episode had the feeling of finding unfamiliar things in his belongings. He struggled against a slide toward what he knew was not real. He focused hard on the concrete, the things he would say to the family. The narrow focus, kept spare by the fact he had to speak to the family through an interpreter, got him through the funeral.

When he spoke at the funeral Thanasis said to the young man's family and friends "He worked for the Sky Men, but like all warriors he chose what he did, he chose his life. He chose out of love for his people, his family, his buddies. I only know that your son acted out of love, and it was in acts of love that he gave his life. His spirit survives him and will protect those he loves when he has reached the village of his ancestors."

The body was taken through a wall, out the side of the house. The funeral procession traveled downhill and out of the village, avoiding the spirit evil caused by carrying a dead person across a hillside above a house. The procession then turned to the West, the direction of death, to the gravesite. When the body was buried the red cloth stretcher was chopped up and placed on the grave. A crossbow was shot across the grave to frighten evil spirits.

Thanasis went back to the fighting at Long Tieng and the demands that guaranteed his hold on reality. As the helicopter looked for a break in the clouds above Long Tieng he felt a new anxiety, that he might not be able to get back to the violence that made him collect himself. He shook his head and made a distracted mental note. *I better get that fixed.* The only fix he could think of was the bars on Patpong Road in Bangkok. Then he remembered the note with the parachuted case of Oly, and he thought of Dao. He realized that she was reaching out to him, for herself and for him. Her gesture made him think about her loss in the war, her needs. Her attempt to reach him signaled the end of her grief over the loss of her brother. Getting in touch with her became his priority. It was the first time in a decade he thought of getting out.

The nature of the NVA siege began to change. More and more the NVA felt the logistic strain of the daily B-52 bombing of the Plain of Jars, their supply and staging area. Each B-52 carried 100 five-hundred-pound bombs. Each sortie was made up of three of the Cold War bombers. There were dozens of sorties flown each day. The mysterious two thousand-year-old Plain of Jars slowly disappeared. In less than a year the uncontested B-52s, flying at forty thousand feet, had destroyed everything in a hundred-mile square. An ancient caravan route of stone jars had become nothing but craters.

The NVA on Skyline Ridge and around Long Tieng turned from siege force to starved defender. Vang Pao rallied his Meo and drove the NVA off Skyline Ridge. The general demanded that Thanasis move his air delivery rigging operation to the battlefield and join pursuit of fleeing Pathet Lao and Vietnamese. The shelling had reduced the Long Tieng runway to a helicopter sling operation. Thanasis decided they could rig and sling-load helicopters from the moonscape of the cratered Plain of Jars as readily as from cratered Long Tieng. He and his loaders followed the advancing Meo, and rigged in the field.

The T-28s and Meo families returned to Long Tieng. Thanasis and the rest of Sky left their bunkers and moved back to the two-story western-style living quarters. A smokejumper flew in to replace Thanasis.

“Take your time gettin’ to the next one, Thanasis. It all pays the same.”

“Think I’ll go by way of Bangkok, see Dao. She seems recovered from loss of her brother.”

“Good on ya, buddy. Have you heard anything about Charlie?”

“No.”

When Thanasis said nothing more, the fellow jumper knew to drop it.

CHAPTER FORTY-TWO

Norris was in a conference room at Marana, meeting with executives and engineers from Hughes Tool Aircraft Division. The subject was black helicopters and noise.

To open the meeting, Norris chose brusque. "My wife is Meo. Her people have the same problem with your helicopter that the folks in Beverly Hills do. They can hear it coming two miles away. The difference is that in Beverly Hills helicopter noise doesn't get people killed. I understand you're working on it."

The police department of the Los Angeles suburb had sent their two helicopters back to Hughes. Citizen complaints about the noise of police patrols had reached critical mass in Beverly Hills.

The Hughes executive was curious who the people were that might get killed because of helicopter noise. Because he was in a secret CIA facility talking about a potential CIA aircraft buy, he did not ask.

"You're correct about the Beverly Hills situation, Mr. Wright."

"Norris."

"Yes. The response of the Beverly Hills police department to noise associated with rotorcraft flight got our attention. Police work is a significant potential market for helicopter sales. There is also a lot of Department of Defense research money focused on the noise issue. Our engineers got right on the problem."

Norris interrupted. "Are some of the people you brought today engineers? Have one of them tell me what they found and what they can do about helicopter noise."

"Yes. Roger Byrd can do that for you. He has headed up this project in Hughes."

The Hughes engineer asked to show a movie with "actual sound" of the flight and landing of a Hughes 500 light observation helicopter demonstrating the results of his department's work. He talked over the sound of the movie. There was in fact no sound until the aircraft was within what Norris judged to be a hundred yards of the camera position.

The engineer said "We found that the biggest noise-maker was the tail rotor. We took care of that by doubling the number of rotor blades at that position and changing drive gear ratios. That permitted us to cut the speed of the tail rotor in half, reducing noise significantly. We continue to identify and eliminate other noise sources."

Norris was concerned that his years around aircraft had impaired his hearing. May Ly told him as much. Maybe he had missed something on the soundtrack of the film.

"Leave that film and its sound track with me, please. If we detect any effort to doctor any aspect of the presentation, Hughes is out of the aircraft business. Subject to flight demonstration and training of four pilots, I'll take two. Delivery in one month, with instructors and parts, at Cha Shan Air Base, Hualien, Taiwan. We'll put your people up on base at our expense."

Shortly after his meeting with the Hughes people, Norris talked to Thanasis at Long Tieng on a secure phone. "Remember your Locks and Picks course from The Farm?"

"Sure."

"And the wiretap handicraft you learned there?"

Thanasis was not sure what he remembered about wiretaps, but he said "Oh yeh."

"Good. You're going to train eight Lao Theung commandoes how to climb a telephone pole and tap a multiplex telephone line on the Cau River near Vinh, North Vietnam."

There was silence on the phone as if they were negotiators, each waiting for the other to disclose something or make a commitment. Norris spoke first. "I'm sure you have questions. I'll answer the first one. No, you're not going into North Vietnam. You're just going to get the Lao Theung in and out safely with wiretap installed."

It had not occurred to Thanasis that he might go into North Vietnam. CIA agents never intentionally went there. He asked "Can I know what we're looking for?"

"Yes, but Project Whisper is top secret and you cannot share it with the commandoes, the helicopter crews, or anybody else, CIA or not.

"China and the Soviets know North Vietnam has won, that our troop drawdown leaves us with less than ten thousand people in South Vietnam. Most important, they want the confrontation with the West to end. North Vietnam is cut off by land and sea and giving us what we want in Paris. So what's the problem?

"The only thing that gives Kissinger more heartburn than negotiating with Le Duc Tho is negotiating with the South Vietnamese. The ARVN generals keep objecting to any deal, saying that the North Vietnamese won't abide by it, that they're planning to invade South Vietnam the moment the U.S. is gone. The Company can't say they're wrong. Kissinger doesn't have an answer for the South Vietnamese. He wants to know what NVA is planning so he can say to his own side 'here, listen to six months of wiretap—see, they aren't planning to invade'."

"Why is that gonna show up on this telephone line?"

"Part of the multiplex line is the NVA command channel. If anything is going on, it'll show up there. Ready to go?"

"Give me the word, boss. You still owe me ten days in Bangkok."

"Go to Bangkok or wherever for now. In a month or less you'll go to Pa Doung, Thailand. As soon as they unwrap our two Hughes 500 helicopters and fill the tanks, you'll board one and fly to Pakse Site 44, the Lao Theung commando outpost. That's where you'll train your boys.

"The helicopters look like the 500s Air America has, but they're unmarked and like nothing you've ever been on. Hughes calls it "The Quiet One." NVA can't hear 'em coming."

Thanasis, also approaching deafness from exposure to jet engines and explosions, found quiet helicopters hard to believe. "Guess I'll believe it when I see it. Why are we going into Pa Doung? It's a hole."

"Because it's remote and there are no North Vietnamese sympathizers. The Quiet One is new technology, top secret. We can't land the

C-130 the helos are on at Pakse 44. So we need to stage it through a safe site. Safe sites are all rotten places, so have a good time in Bangkok."

Thanasis called Dao and she picked him up in a samlor at the Bangkok airport. He had expected quiet and reserve, a continuing withdrawal in the face of loss. She was anything but. She was flirting and teasing, wearing bright colored pantaloons and halter, a puckish smile, the corners of her mouth turned up as if restraining an even bigger smile. She stood on tiptoe to give him a big public kiss and hurried him off immediately to Hua Lamphong rail station. They caught a train south along the Gulf of Siam. She did not tell him he looked pale and done in. She thought the house at Hua Hin was the right idea.

"We will be by ourselves in an old colonial house on the beach. It belongs to friends of my family. It is next to Klai Kangwon, the grounds of the royal vacation residence. No one will bother us . . . no massage parlors stocked with sturdy farm girls, no bar girls. Is that alright, Black Man?"

"Well, I've always liked farm girls. But I'll get over it."

She flexed the muscles of her bare arms and shoulders in a body builder "crab" pose. "You won't be sorry."

"Can I have a cold beer, too?"

They spent two weeks lying on the beach sand of the Gulf coast, served by a decorous house staff and left alone. Going into the third week and feeling fine Thanasis checked in with Norris. He was told it was time to meet the helicopters at Pa Doung.

Dao delivered another promised massage, rubbing sun screen into his back as he lay on the beach their last morning at Hua Hin. One bare leg rested against his shoulder while she sat next to him and applied lotion to his ears with the tips of her fingers. He drifted toward sleep, the drowsy feeling imprinted with an image of sweat and sand between her brown foot and the thong of her sandal.

When she woke him he stretched and tried to remember a fuzzy dream. He could not, and instead focused on where he was. He grinned and said "Well, so much for farm girls."

It was not until they were on the train to Bangkok that he remembered the dream on the beach. It had been about Channarong. He still could not remember details, only that it was about her brother. The recollection was followed by the thought that Dao had not mentioned him during their entire stay. He wanted to ask if she had heard anything from Zorro, but did not. *If she's not talking about him, guess it's bad. I'll ask our intel guys.*

The transition from tropical sunlight to full dark seemed, as usual, to last only moments. They kissed in the train station and said goodbye.

"Come back to me, *farang*. We haven't finished," she said.

Thanasis had lost all interest in the war. He said "It's ending. Then I'll come." He left the train station, headed for the Project Whisper helicopters. She watched him until he had disappeared, then looked around to see if anyone watched her. She clutched the Buddha amulet hung around her neck.

The two Hughes helicopters were flown to Pakse 44 at night. Thanasis was fascinated not only by the silence but by the fact the helicopters flew without lights, using instead an infrared floodlight that cast a dull red glow before them as they landed. He set to work the next day with the eight commandoes, teaching them the use of climbing spurs, exiting from hovering helicopters, and wiretapping. He drilled the Lao Theung until all of them could execute the mission skills wearing blindfolds. They practiced flights and insertions from the commando base, using a tree as a practice telephone pole, installing a practice wiretap that sent signals to a radio relay.

The importance to North Vietnam of the telephone line was indicated by the fact NVA squads patrolled the entire length of the 150-mile line, from Vinh south to the demarcation line between North and South, using a bike path. There was only one short section where the line could not be seen from the bike path. Meo ground intelligence had confirmed that interpretation of air reconnaissance photos. About fifteen miles south of Vinh, the bike path followed a westward bend in the river rather than the telephone line as the line, straight and true as is the nature of telephone lines, climbed a bluff, crossed it, and returned down to the river. The patrol never climbed the steep sides of the bluff or checked the telephone line as it crossed the top in a cover of second-growth trees.

Thanasis wanted to inspect the wiretap site. Without looking at the poles and cross-arms and wires in the same proximity as the commandoes he felt he was training the dark-skinned fighters with guesswork. The super-grade CIA agent flown in to supervise the project rejected Thanasis' arguments for a personal inspection of the site.

"The betting line in Udorn on this team actually scorin' is pick'em. We are doin' it once. The Air America pilots for the flight have my entire supply of cyanide capsules. I am not risking an agent so he can touch a telephone pole. Close your eyes and use your imagination." He turned to walk away. He stopped and said "You'll do fine. They'll be OK. They make it up all the time."

It was cold in the quiet black helicopter as it crossed the Ho Chi Minh Trail. It did not attract the usual antiaircraft fire and climbed silently over the Annamite mountains toward the border of Vietnam. There were two armed commandoes and an Air America crew of two on The Quiet One. The remaining six commandoes were on an Air America S-58 Twin Pack helicopter which had turned back as they approached the Trail. It circled west, prepared to carry out a rescue if that was necessary. Thanasis was in the Twin Pack monitoring progress of the insertion and wiretap.

He cursed when the commandoes on the ground reported that the telephone poles were concrete. The commandoes tossed the climbing spurs and shinnied up the concrete poles. "They make it up," he said and punched a Lao Theung commando on the shoulder.

The commandoes spliced into wires of the multiplex line and concealed the tap in a glass insulator. CIA had supplied one identical to those used by the French in building the Vinh telephone line.

The radio relay of the intercepted telephone signals registered clearly at the radio receiver array in Thailand. The Quiet One picked up the two commandoes on the bluff and flew uneventfully to a celebration in a Savannakhet bar. The Secretary of State celebrated with a martini and flirtatious conversation with an intern.

Two months of wiretap boredom was enough for the South Vietnamese. The treaty ending the war in Vietnam was signed. A month later the Agreement on the Restoration of Peace and Reconciliation in

Laos was negotiated and signed by the Pathet Lao and the Royal Lao Government. The CIA Chief of Unit at Long Tieng advised Vang Pao by message the same day that the United States was honoring the Lao agreement and "USAF are under instructions to clear Lao air space by 1200 this date."

CIA case officers at Long Tieng were directed by Chief of Station at Vientiane to disarm the Meo. When the Meo guerillas heard, they left Long Tieng, still armed. All CIA and Air America personnel and planes left Laos.

The beer-fed bears at Long Tieng were killed and eaten.

CHAPTER FORTY-THREE

Four hundred miles to the south, in Bangkok, Thanasis waited for Norris at the Oriental Hotel. They were to have breakfast, and he sat at a table overlooking the Chao Phraya River, reversed by the morning tide carrying seaweed and plastic trash through the bustling downtown, older buildings sinking into its waters. The smell of plumeria blooming around the hotel brought Dao to his thoughts, turned them to their first meeting in Savannakhet.

"When I see smokejumpers lookin' all moony like you I know they're either headin' for Patpong Road with a pocket full of *bhat* or off to a wedding chapel. Which is it, chum?" Norris said as he sat down.

"You're gettin' sneaky comin' up on people. Not attractive in an old man . . . sir. I was actually just thinkin' about Laos."

"Now that's something can make a man look moony. We won our war, Thanasis, but just leaving sure as hell doesn't feel like winning." Norris pulled a newspaper from a folder he was carrying and pushed it across the table. "Then there's this. In case you don't read the *Khaosan Pathet Lao* regularly, today's edition calls for, quote, extermination of the Meo down to the root of the tribe. That's the official Pathet Lao peacetime position. They weren't so tough when the Meo were kickin' their ass. The little guys, what's left of 'em, are about to be wiped out and most everybody in Laos is just fine with that."

"Isn't the king stepping in? He likes the little guys. Hell, why aren't we doin' something?"

"The king admires the Meo from the palace in Luang Prabang, but he can't help 'em. He's busy getting ready to abdicate. Thailand won't take the Meo as refugees, except to inter them in a camp and, when the Thai think they've done that long enough, they'll shove them back across the river. As for us, the United States has taken the lawyer-like position that because it does not recognize the Lao People's Democratic Republic we're not going to talk to the Pathet Lao." Norris motioned a waiter over.

"Thanasis, I've got one more job for you before we're all thrown out of Southeast Asia. If you're interested I'll have breakfast and we can talk. If not, I'll just pay your bill and leave you alone."

Thanasis was still picking through the bad things described by Norris. It was an easy call, but he had to be sure before he talked about anything.

"Norris, this whole deal has a name you haven't mentioned. The name is Charlie Mazzarelli. You haven't said so, but not talkin' to a country holding American POWs sounds like abandoning them. Tell me why I'm wrong about that. Tell me what you're doing to rescue Charlie." Thanasis was working to control himself, not pound the table. He was afraid of the answer.

Norris waved the waiter away. "We're not abandoning Charlie or anyone else. The return of prisoners has to be addressed outside the State Department. We were never in Laos, the Pathet Lao deny they hold any American prisoners, and we deny they are a country. All that makes diplomatic negotiation a non-starter. We know a lot about some prisoners. Where they are, what kind of security they're under, whether they're injured or sick. But for Charlie and some high value people the trail has gone cold. A few years from now we'll recognize the Communist government of Laos and help 'em set up a tourist bureau. But that'll be too late for Charlie, won't it. The Company is about to be gutted at home but we still have the go-ahead to carry out prison raids in Laos to free American POWs. Before we can do that we need intelligence. That's what I want to talk to you about. Are you recommending anything for breakfast or do you just want me to go away?"

At the news about prison raids Thanasis went from fearful to giddy. "Boss, your choice is giant water bugs with chili paste or tapioca with grass jelly. It's a little early in the day for chili paste."

"I'd heard you've gone native." Norris had an omelet while they talked.

"Your day-job will be here in Bangkok. You'll be a State Department employee working on Meo refugee issues. It's a real job, with consequences. There are people in CIA think we'll have blood on our hands forever if we don't do everything we can to get the Meo out of Laos. Casey and I among them."

Thanasis thought about the Meo he had worked with for ten years. *Ten fucking years!* Guerilla fighters, cargo riggers, pilots, backseaters in FAC aircraft, crouching road watch teams, and a general.

"There are probably fifty thousand of 'em at Long Tieng. That's a lot of flights and we don't have airplanes anymore. Where you hidin' 'em, Norris?"

"We don't have any authority to operate flights to relocate Meo out of Laos. They're going to have to walk to Thailand. If they can't get to Thailand we can't help."

"Not much of a job you're offerin' me, boss. Sortin' out wetbacks with a price on their head, even after they've crossed the river and surrendered."

"It's your cover. Take it or leave it." Norris paused. "I have a personal reason for seeing the refugee job is done well."

Thanasis considered a belated comeback to Norris' "gone native" remark but asked instead "May Ly still have family in Long Tieng?"

"Yes."

"Alright, I've got a State Department job, but I haven't heard about my job for the Customer. What kind of intel operation are we talkin' about? I'm not negotiating. I just want to get at it."

Norris looked around, and said in a low voice "It's two things. Both involve the refugee job. You will use your refugee contacts to recruit and communicate with a Meo spy operation to be left behind in Laos. The Meo spies will focus on POWs, locating them and getting the information we need to carry out rescue operations. If they give us other information, that's fine, but that's not their job. They're all about gettin' Charlie and the other guys out of Lao prisons."

Thanasis was excited but he showed only detachment and professional interest. "Have you selected a Meo contact or do I create that?"

"A man you all call Longfellow is a refugee in the Ban Vinai refugee camp. Start with him. Select him and his family for processing to the United States. Move ‘em up the list to right now. After they have left Thailand we will divert him back into Laos, probably from the Philippines. He will be your go-to Meo guy.”

“What’s his game?”

“Total loyalty to Vang Pao. VP has already let him know he should cooperate with us on this. One of your control issues will be to make sure he’s not a dual agent acting for Vang Pao in trying to overthrow the Pathet Lao. We can’t be in that business and it will just muck up our prisoner rescue effort. VP has said he’s cool on leavin’ the Pathet Lao alone but we’re not sure we believe him.”

“I know Longfellow. This will work. What else? You said there were two things.”

“The other thing is you’ve got to keep the refugee pipeline clean.”

Thanasis thought a moment and said “I have no idea what that means, Norris.”

“We have reason to believe the Pathet Lao are using the refugee camps to send agents after the Meo who have worked for us. Most of the first wave of refugees are Meo who soldiered for us and their families. As you know some of the Meo clans were on the PL side. Only the refugees, our Meo, will be able to sort out who’s who inside the refugee rags. You’ll need to set up an organization within Ban Vinai and other camps to finger the bad guys so that we’re not sending assassins to the U.S., exposing Vang Pao and his lieutenants. It’ll be tricky. The Meo will use any process you set up as a way to settle personal scores. They may finger some innocent people. You have any doubt, you don’t let ‘em through. Clean pipeline.”

Norris knew the kind of hard choices Thanasis would have to make, wondered if he would have the stomach to make them.

“Tell me who May’s people are and I can handle the rest. Norris, we’re bringin’ Charlie out.”

“I know you will.”

Norris ordered more coffee and was quiet, except for details about who Thanasis should get in touch with at the State Department refugee office in Bangkok.

Thanasis thought their meeting had ended, but Norris asked another question. “What’s your friend Dao doing in Vientiane this past week?”

Thanasis was surprised, then angry. "Boss, I know you guys spy on everybody works for the Company every day. I don't mind. You can look down my shorts anytime. But you take your goddamn spies off Dao. If she's with me you go ahead and watch. If she's livin' her own life, leave her alone."

"If she's crossing the border into Laos while you're sharin' a bed I can't look the other way. I don't care if she's there to sell onions. Any Pathet Lao contacts are poison. You tell her. She's three hundred miles from home in a Communist country we don't recognize. We were killing them until day before yesterday. Don't be thinkin' the war's over. Don't be thinkin' with your dick."

"Look who's talkin'. The head dickhead."

"Alright. Let's take the emotion out of this. Just tell me what she's doin' in Vientiane and that's my report and the end of it." Norris did not think Thanasis even knew his girlfriend had been in Laos.

Thanasis was slow in responding and spoke deliberately. "She said she was going to Nong Khai to visit an uncle who needed help. Vientiane is pretty much just across the river from Nong Khai. They could have just got in a boat and visited old friends." His speech became rapid, intense. "I don't know, Norris, but she told me she was goin' up there. She wasn't sneaking off. It's not like nobody but Lao goes to Vientiane. Jesus. She isn't some fuckin' Communist. Her brother flew T-28s for us. Got shot down, nobody's heard anything since, probably dead. Jesus, you guys."

"Maybe he's not dead."

Thanasis puzzled at the statement. "What? He's alive like some kind of Manchurian candidate? Sure, and teenage girls think James Dean's alive. Does this business make all you guys nutty?"

"Just ask her what she was doin' in Vientiane."

"I will."

The two agents finished their meeting in hot silence.

Thanasis asked Dao that evening. He reported her response to Norris verbatim. "My uncle has a longtime friend in Vientiane, a woman who makes clothes. Because of the war and the trade embargo she no longer has access to materials for her business. We smuggled some cloth to her by wearing several layers. Her name is Koulavongsa. I don't know what address. Why are you asking me these things?"

He did not tell Norris that she wanted to know who had told him she had been in Vientiane, that her hands shook as she told him about the seamstress, that she did not look at him much of the evening, that they were awkward and ritualistic in making love that night. He did not tell Norris she was lying to him.

CHAPTER FORTY-FOUR

Thanasis processed Longfellow and his extended family out of Ban Vinai internment camp and onto a flight to the United States, one routed through the Philippines. It took CIA less than twenty-four hours to settle the family on the blue earth of Minnesota farmland.

Longfellow did not accompany his family. He spent a week in what he thought a strange Sky compound on the U.S. naval base at Subic Bay, Philippines. Everything was new, soundproof, pre-planned, documented, and without connection to Laos jungle. He prepared there for infiltration into his homeland, learning from the Sky Men what little was known about prisoners held by the Pathet Lao.

Like most Meo, Longfellow was an animist, but a lifetime of war had reduced the number of spirits in his life to those that lived in his rifle and his radio. The night he parachuted back into Laos in a monsoon rain he recognized two new spirits. There was the huge one that occupied the bright skin of the A-26 Onmark and held the roaring airplane aloft. The other was round and soft and big-eyed. It formed a bubble on which his parachute floated.

He dropped through the black hole in the floor of the airplane, feet first, face forward, and shaped himself into the shallow arc of a bird's wing, just as the Sky Men and the spirit in the skin of the A-26 had shown him. Not long after he pulled the ripcord he and the wet parachute crashed through layer after layer of trees. Longfellow laughed because the breaking tree limbs reminded him of the loud excitement of ambush. When the branches, splintered and falling in silence, filled the night air with smells of home and wife and children, he laughed again, a different, softer sound.

The maps the Sky Men had given him draped over his hand with the feeling of skin. He was told the thin rubbery material would not decay or tear in jungle wet. The first thing he did was bury the maps at the base of a great tree and leave them there for all time. He thought about asking the spirit of the tree to protect the maps. He shrugged the thought away. He knew where he was, which clan lived here, who would help and who would harm. He keyed the encrypted radio as he had been told.

"Black Man this is Longfellow. Do you hear me? I am home and moving."

The answering voice was familiar, a Sky friend. "This is Black Man. I read you Longfellow. Go find The Dago. He'll be with others. No further instructions. There is no contact schedule. Make contact as you need. Over and out."

Thanasis thought his radio response was cold, did not like it. Regret stopped immediately. He knew more talk would only expose the Meo to Russian radio direction-finding equipment. *Longfellow wouldn't know about feeling cold and alone. Tough little bastard doesn't need me being warm and supportive.* He thought about Charlie, as he often did, wondered if he was in high country, had enough to eat.

Thanasis turned to the piles of paper on his desk. The paper in the refugee program left him tired and irritated. The good part of days were the interviews. He met and talked with each Meo male seeking relocation to the United States. The first part of the interview was to establish whether the man had fought in Vang Pao's army. Sometimes Thanasis knew the man personally. Other times he did not and the man could not name anyone who would vouch for him, or the one he named was dead.

At those times refugee screening became a game of chess. He would ask the Meo across the table questions about battles that had been fought—or maybe they had not. He asked about Meo who had flown T-28s for Vang Pao. Some of those named had flown and some had not. He asked about Meo who had risen to command in Special Guerilla Units, mixing in names of those who had been trained only as parachute riggers or merely butchered water buffalo. If the Meo interviewee stumbled, he lost a lethal game. Failure to pass Thanasis' interview sent the interviewee back to Ban Vinai or another detention camp. What happened there at the hands of Meo veterans depended on how serious, how indicative, the failure had been. Thanasis would learn what the camp action was, sometimes in detail he did not want to know. There were times when he thought maybe he had been too clever in his screening. He accepted the harsh results of cleverness. He had become convinced there was an organized effort to assassinate leaders of the fleeing Meo and that refugee screening was frustrating it.

Thanasis started getting anonymous phone calls. They were English-speaking voices without other identity, except they were tinged with Meo accent and speech patterns. At first, the voices suggested only that he leave the refugee program. He was doing great harm to the Meo, the voices said, destroying the culture of an ancient people who only wanted to return to their mountains in Laos. Moral coaxing gave way to threats of death. He would be shot like a yellow dog and his heart cut out, a Meo threat more typically made to or about Chinese. Meo leadership in the camps assured him it was the clans that had been with the Pathet Lao in the war. "They are not here. Ignore them," the Meo in the camps said.

When a smokejumper buddy showed up in Bangkok to say goodbye before leaving for Idaho, Thanasis mentioned the threats over a beer.

"Hell, they're phone calls. Just a thing."

"Goddammit, Thanasis, they're real as that Thai woman you're in love with."

"Nobody said I'm in love."

"Course you are. War's over, everybody's goin home, and you're stayin'."

"There's reasons."

"Whatever they are they aren't enough to get yourself killed over. Everybody in Laos and most the rest of Asia hates us. When I was up in Long Tieng gettin' Vang Pao out of Dodge the place was full of huckleberries tryin' to kill him and me."

"That's Long Tieng."

"Don't think they aren't right here in Bangkok. Get to hell out of here. Somebody here wants to kill you, they will."

"We'll go soon as I finish up a job I'm doin' for Norris."

"You gonna marry her?"

Thanasis resented the intrusive question, said only "It's slidin' that way."

"Could do worse."

He and Dao were spending more and more time together. Though living separately they spent their nights with each other, often in the intimate, excited conversation of people making plans for a future neither had fully examined. Some of the talk shared past pain and disappointment. Some was used to spin fanciful ambition. Some was domestic detail. He gave her a telephone number she could call if she needed anything. It was a CIA help number for dependants, code name Michael. "Just ask for Michael. You'll be sharin' him with other CIA wives." She noticed the grouping, though he did not.

Not everything was talked through. He did not speak of the death threats. She told less than all about her continuing trips to the Mekong. Given his warning, she no longer crossed the river. Instead, the Pathet Lao agents came to her, one or two at a time, crossing in a rented pirogue.

At first, they told her only that they knew where her brother was. They would not tell her where. They said she could tell no one about her brother or he would die, that they had agents throughout Thailand and would know everything she said. She demanded proof that Zorro was alive. They responded, in a subsequent meeting, by showing a photograph of her and Zorro together as children, him in the mask of the bandit hero, a photo she knew he carried when he flew.

Recovering from her shock at seeing the photograph she pushed for more. "This is nothing. I want to see him. Take me to him." They gave her instructions for a further meeting, this one across the Mekong River from Savannakhet, in the small Thai town of Mukdahan. She was to go to the river edge at midday, they would find her.

She did not tell Thanasis. She traveled by bus, dressed as a Malay Muslim, a scarf covering her head and shadowing her face. The roads were full of cattle, oxcarts, and pedestrians. The trip seemed endless and left her wrung out. When the Lao agents found her they immediately handed her military field glasses and directed her attention to three men on the opposite river bank. "Look at the man in the middle."

Her anticipation was full of foreboding and made her feel weak. She lifted the heavy glasses awkwardly. In the light of midday, in her own country, she was not afraid of the Lao agents, but her hands shook as she focused the field glasses. The two men on either side of the man in the middle faced away from her. They held the man between them by his arms. She could not see his hands and wondered if they were tied behind him. The glasses finally focused, she recognized the thin man with dark sunken eyes as her brother. He seemed older, his skin yellowed and mottled with sores. She cried out softly, involuntarily.

One of the Lao agents took the field glasses from her. "You can see him again. If you are helpful."

Dao felt a rush of emotions. Relief, gratitude, hope, frustration, anger. She stepped toward the water, would have entered it if the man who had spoken to her had not grabbed an arm and pulled her back. She waved the other arm over her head. She could not tell if her brother saw her. He did not move.

She finally spoke. "What is it you need help with?"

"You will be told that at your next meeting."

She said she could not keep meeting them, that she was probably followed by American agents. She sensed that her brother's release would be tied to whatever it was they would demand and she wanted to accelerate the process, to have Zorro back.

She watched the three men across the river as they began moving away. Her brother appeared to walk with difficulty and would have fallen had the other two not held him up. His legs did not seem to work.

"He is injured," she wailed. "Is he getting medical attention?" Dao's question was urgent.

Instead of answering her question one of the Lao men said "As you can see he has many needs. Your opportunity to assure that his needs are met will be brief. Once it passes, that chance will be gone forever. Your next meeting will be in Bangkok with one of our Thai agents. He will have your instructions." The two agents standing by her turned in unison and walked away. They left her standing on the river bank.

CHAPTER FORTY-FIVE

The Pathet Lao agents turned Channarong from the river and led him away. He was a light cargo but cargo just the same. Awkward, wooden and limp at once. They had practiced how to move him so as not to alarm the observer across the river. She was to be aware of injury and threat to her brother, but left with hope and a glimpse of her power to save him. Close up he was a large puppet being dragged on a muddy street, shaking in pain, but from across the river he should seem an enduring hero owed devotion and deliverance.

The trip to the Mekong had exhausted Zorro. The handling had been rough as soon as they took him from prison. The truck bed, without the support of springs or other suspension, wrenched his injured back around every axis, movement of the truck on the collapsed jungle road sending penetrating pain through his buttocks and legs. When there was fighting there had been painkilling drugs for fighters and prisoners alike. With the end of the war, when only political prisoners and hostages of value remained, nothing was offered for pain. Pain was for wearing down, for control, for information.

On the return trip to the prison, unable to protect himself from the jounce of the truck bed, Zorro distracted himself by thinking about what he had seen at the river. Eyesight dimmed by prison food, he had seen little. People had come to the opposite bank. He had been propped up, held in place near the river edge, facing three figures across the water. He had assumed from how the guards held him in place that he was being offered for view, to establish it was him, that he was alive, here. That anyone would seek such information, value it in any way, took him by surprise. He argued to himself against optimism. He knew hope as false and defeating.

He finally gave in to the notion that being viewed by three people on the opposite bank of the Mekong, people standing in Thailand, was a good thing, good enough to cause a vision of purple and fine linen and let him be, for a moment, the King of Siam.

Who were those people? he wondered. He dug into the thought. Probably two men by their dress. A woman between them, gender indicated again by dress. There were no details, no personal features. The woman's clothing was odd in its configuration, not something a Thai woman would wear.

Focused by his inquiry, his thinking became rapid, elliptic, though short on confirming detail. *Someone from Malaysia? Maybe. Why would a Malay woman come to the Mekong River to view me? A thousand miles from her home?*

Now self-aware, he was absorbed by his fanciful thinking. His subconscious brought memories, pleasure, and knowledge from the past. He thought of Dao.

She had always directed their games. Make believe and disguise. Dao in disguise, hiding her identity. A pirate, a tiger, doctor, fish and fisherman both, fooling him into her fantasy world. They argued only over whose turn it was to be King of Siam.

It came to him. *The Malay woman is a disguise. It is Dao! Dao has been brought to the river to see me. So she can believe I am here.*

Zorro did not question the thin evidence on which his subconscious relied. Nor did he ask himself why someone wanted Dao to believe he was alive. He ignored the questions lying all about him and enjoyed the thought of his courageous sister knowing where he was. His rescue would follow. He was certain.

Returned to the prison camp, he slept fitfully. The pain was less now that he lay still on the dirt floor of his cell, alone, but the emotion of the visit to the river and his thoughts about what it meant interrupted his sleep, kept him from rest. By morning he was irritated, depressed again, given over to the linear thinking of flyers. He thought about the question raised by the previous day's exhaustion. *Was she there, at the river?* He would confront them today, whatever it cost. He had "tradin' goods," as the CIA cowboys at Savannakhet used to say. He would trade it all, just to know.

He asked to talk to the prison commander. He promised information about CIA operations in Thai refugee camps. The offer from solitary confinement in a prison cell far from the Thai camps was not credible but the subject itself won him a meeting with the Pathet Lao officer. Zorro was brought to the man on a litter, further evidence of the importance of the subject he had chosen.

The prison commander offered him water in a bamboo cup and asked "What is it you would tell me for this privileged visit?"

Zorro swallowed some of the water and said "I know the location of the camps."

"Fool. So do we." The commander leaned forward and slapped the cup from Zorro's hands.

"There's more. I know how the CIA finds your camp assassins." Zorro knew nothing of the sort. He only guessed at the existence of Pathet Lao fear of the Meo, and a campaign to wipe the mountain people out. He played to the fear. "Your people cannot penetrate to Vang Pao. He will return, and all his people with him. A guerilla army. They will spare no one who opposes them."

The prison commander colored and was slower to respond this time. The poker-playing fighter pilot coughed into his hand to hide his knowledge. He had his 'tell.' Armed with a tell, Zorro was at liberty to go anywhere he wanted in the prison world in search of Dao. He would just read the man across from him and go through his pockets.

The commander finally said "We already know how the CIA resists the will of the collective. We know who they use in the camps. We are about to end that conspiracy. No one will help them. The CIA will cut their losses and leave. But go ahead, what is it you want to tell me, who in the CIA do you want to save with your chatter?"

"I'm sorry. I'm not here to save the Pathet Lao, or the Meo, or the CIA for that matter. This meeting is for me . . . and for you. What I have for you will take more than you have offered. In a land where the water spirit comes every day no one bows down to a cup of water. What you and I have in common is a need to know things that are kept from us. Those are the things we can give to each other . . . to improve our situations."

"What is it you want to know?"

"Where you keep your strongest painkillers."

"Why?"

"So that I can steal some. They will help me remember."

"What else?"

"The name of the Meo I see bringing you opium."

The commander made a dismissive wave and looked away.

Zorro thought *Another tell.*

The commander turned to him and said "You really think I will treat you like a royal guest, don't you? You are just a visitor here, the king on a white elephant stopping over on the way to his summer house at Hua Hin?"

"I can tell you about the CIA training at Hua Hin. It is your turn to say what you want to know."

The prison commander rubbed his chin as if reflecting. Looking away from Zorro he said "Tell me two things. What does CIA do at Hua Hin, even now after they have lost?"

"And the other thing?"

Color came to the commander's face. "Tell me everything you know about Mavros, the one they call Black Man."

Zorro decided to provoke with an obvious lie, see where it went. He hoped it might lead to Dao. "I know little about him. I knew him at Savannakhet, knew him to be in CIA. Haven't followed him since he left there. He is important to the Pathet Lao?"

He did not anticipate the blow from the commander. It was delivered with the strength of anger, frustration. When he woke Zorro was in his cell, aware that he had been knocked unconscious, the pain in his jaw exceeding the rest of his discomfort. He grinned. He knew he had entered the commander's head. Mere gambler's luck, but the rest would be easy. He waited.

The following day a Meo quietly delivered a colorful woven bag to his cell, leaving without a word. The bag included an unlabeled plastic bottle containing several small white pills, a folded paper holding pea-sized balls of dark, tar-like opium, and a capped bamboo section filled with water. Curious and fatalistic, Zorro immediately took one of the white pills and washed it down with the water. Within minutes he was free of pain.

Morphine? I think camp commander wants to talk.

The drug interfered with his ability to concentrate and think clearly. *Not good for poker nights.* He hid the few remaining pills in a hole he scraped in the dirt of the floor and covered once again with dirt.

He used the opium to counter his pain, ingesting the small pellet and washing it down with water. It was not as effective as the narcotic in the pill, but he remained in control, smarter in his stories about Hua Hin and Mavros. The commander interviewed him every other day on those subjects. Zorro filled his answers with easy to verify truth and impossible to check falsehood, patched together to seem a whole. He made the commander work, in part to make the man an admiring owner of his effort. Ownership would credit the stories. He avoided answering open-ended questions, made the commander cross-examine and badger him.

Crediting his story was only part of Zorro's strategy. Making the commander work at his interrogation would help him intuit in the man's questions what use they wanted to make of him and the woman at the river. *Was it Dao?*

The answer came more quickly than he expected.

"Is your sister a clever woman?"

"She can take a marine engine apart and repair it. Why do you want to know? You have work for her?"

The prison commander thought a moment, smiled. "Yes. Yes, we do. We would like her to take something apart, fix it." He laughed, as if he had told a joke, one the audience would not get. He continued the conceit. "We don't have her complete resume. What are her other strengths?" He was smiling at his cleverness.

Zorro avoided the question. "I have known her all her life. But she is a woman. She remains a mystery to me. She is always in disguise." *Take the bait. Say if it was her.*

"What are her feelings toward you?"

"Hard to tell. Mostly resentment at an older brother who would not introduce her to his friends."

"Then why does she ask to see you again?"

Zorro saw the target slide to the center of the cross-hairs, felt his thumb depress the firing button.

He flattened his voice as he answered, showing no emotion. "Probably so she can tell my parents I am alive and well. It is a daughter's role to comfort parents."

"She will tell no one you are alive."

"If she knows I am alive she will tell our parents."

They sat in silence, the commander wondering if he had said too much, Zorro wondering why the commander was so certain Dao would tell no one about him.

The commander broke the silence. "What are her political loyalties?"

"She has always been loyal to the King of Siam." He did not interpret.

"You mean King of Thailand."

"Sure."

"How loyal? Has she ever killed for the King of Thailand?"

Zorro thought about Dao on a shooting range, taking instruction from him. "She is capable of it."

"Who else?"

"What do you mean 'Who else?'"

"Has she ever killed for the Americans?"

"Don't know."

"Has she ever killed anyone for any reason?"

Zorro hesitated at the strange questions. "I don't know."

"Try to help me on this. Keep in mind you will quickly run out of pills. Can she kill another?"

The effort to see behind the commander's questions, to keep the pain away so that he could see clearly, was disorienting. He could no longer see the cards. He shrugged and said, in simple admiration, "My sister is capable of anything."

"I will see that you receive more pills in the morning."

The Meo brought three more pills the following day. Zorro sensed that the commander was engaged in a plan of addicting him, making him dependant on the small white pills. Addiction would give the commander leverage. It would be easy to give in, go there. Zorro sucked in air as he thought about the pain and his choices. He crawled to the hiding place in the dirt and hid all three pills. In the ensuing weeks, without a plan other than avoiding addiction and leverage, he hid every pill sent him by the commander, used only the opium.

CHAPTER FORTY-SIX

In the days following her trip to the river at Mukdahan, Dao was alternately distant and clinging when she was with Thanasis. He was amused and then annoyed with the behavior.

He finally asked "What the hell's up, Dao?"

She hesitated and said "I see Thai soldiers on the street, airmen who flew for Laos, come back from the war. They make me think of my brother. What if he is alive and imprisoned? How do I help him? Sometimes it is very real and upsetting. That is all."

He hugged her and said "I know how you feel. You've got to let it go. We would have heard if he was a POW. You know that. And we haven't heard a thing."

They made love that night and as she had a quiet orgasm she began crying. He asked what she was crying about and she said it just happens this way sometimes, "you wouldn't understand." He thought *That's for damn sure.*

The next day she was approached on the street by a Thai military officer. He was young, handsome, and in uniform. To passersby it was unremarkable, a young man introducing himself to a pretty woman.

The handsome young officer spoke quietly, saying "I am sent by the men you know in Mukdahan. Your brother needs your assistance. You and I will meet for lunch at noon in Lumpinee Park two days from now and you will be told how you can help your brother. Wait for me by the vendors near the Rama VI statue at the park entrance. Tell no one about this and make sure you are not followed. Any misstep on your part will cause your brother's death." The officer bowed slightly, smiled and said "Good day then."

Dao put her hand to her face, trying to mask the fear and distress the meeting caused her. Those on the street saw only a woman hiding interest in an encounter with a handsome officer, a smile perhaps. Tears welled but did not fall. The renewed threat that she could be the agent of her brother's death made her feel helpless. "Any misstep," the man had said. That could be anything. Telling Thanasis, telling her parents. She could not risk what they might want to do, and they would want to do something. The thing they wanted might be a misstep. She felt herself becoming mute with the fear of a misstep. *I will meet with him and find out what they want.*

She avoided Thanasis and tried off and on to meditate, to pull herself together for the meeting in the park. Her meditation was interrupted and scattered by imaginings of what they would want her to do to earn Zorro's freedom. Everything and nothing was counted in her distraction.

By the time she stood near the food vendors waiting for the Thai officer she had settled into an upbeat mood, anticipating her brother's welcome home. She was hungry and wanted to eat. She was watching the vendors and did not notice the officer when he approached and stood next to her.

He said "Have you selected lunch? I will get it."

His sudden appearance made her start. She said nothing, but indicated a woman slicing duck. He went to the vendor and returned, a small paper package of duck and bread in each hand. He motioned for her to walk with him into the park.

They walked along a wide path through the umbrella shade of large monkeypod trees, moving away from the street. He began to make small talk. She interrupted. "Stop. I will hear nothing from you except news of my brother. You will arrange for me to see him. Captain Channarong and I will meet in a room alone, a hospital room." She had stopped walking and stood, feet set wide and braced in the path.

He looked around, saw an unoccupied bench partly obscured from the artificial lakes and open areas of the park. "Let us sit. I will tell you while you eat."

Sitting on the bench, the officer next to her, she waited for word of her brother, focused only on that, no longer hungry. She did not watch him carefully opening the food packages. He put both of them down between them and said "Eat, please."

She made no move to eat. He said "Given what we are doing, we must look like we are doing something else. In case we are watched, as you have suggested. I will not talk about your brother until you are eating. It is excellent duck. A good choice. Don't waste it. Your brother would not."

In spite of the fact she was no longer hungry, felt suddenly cold in the afternoon heat, and was in fear for her starving brother, she began eating.

"You are right to cooperate." He paused. "The news of your brother is that he has a back injury. It is a result of being shot down while he was bombing the people of Laos. He is not able to walk by himself. If he is to recover he needs surgery. It is not available in Laos."

"Then release him to his family," she pleaded, her voice softening. "We will provide whatever care he needs."

The young Thai officer looked at her sympathetically. "For many the war goes on. Your friend, for example. He continues to fight the common goals of the people in new ways. So it is not simple. Prisoners have value in war, right up until the end. The end is not here."

"What is it you want? What do I have to do to have my brother released? The war is over."

"You must help us remove him from the war," the Thai officer said.

"Who? Remove who? I do not know what war you talk about." Her confusion was not feigned.

"Don't be naïve. The war our brothers, the Pathet Lao, fight against the Meo, the savages with tails, the barbarians who would overthrow the Lao People's Democratic Republic. Your friend, the American they call Black Man, the one who keeps you off the streets at night, Thanasis Mavros. He fights the Meo war for them. He has chosen the wrong side of history, so he must die. He is the price of your brother's release, your brother's life."

Dao was overwhelmed by what she was hearing. She did not believe that Zorro and Thanasis could be threatened this way, that a young Thai man could calmly demand the life of one for the other. She stood to leave and a flood of vertigo took her balance. She quickly sat again.

"Catch your breath and think. You cannot go to the king or to the police or to the military or to the Americans. If you do any of those things your brother will die. Like that." He snapped his fingers softly. "None of them know where he is and none of them can save him. Only you can save him. No one else. And for such a small price. The Black Man takes you to his bed? So what. He goes to other women, to whores. You think 'he loves me and I love him.' So? Many men have loved you and you have loved others. Most of them are dead now, aren't they. What difference have those dead men made in your life? You don't even keep their letters."

Dao was in tears. She could not speak without sobbing. "I am leaving. I won't listen to this." She started again to rise from the bench.

"Only you can keep your brother alive. I have a small package to put in your bag, wrapped in the food vendor's paper. I have substituted something for the duck. It is all you need to save your brother's life. Do you want to hear what it is? Of course you do."

Dao did not move. She listened while he talked, watching as he continued to fold the remains of her lunch in its paper.

He described a small bottle containing an odorless, tasteless powder, and a small inhaler containing a liquid spray. They each contained, he said, saxitoxin, a shellfish toxin. As little as 0.2 milligrams was fatal. The two small containers contained thousands of times that dose, he said.

"Why two containers of poison?" She could not believe she had asked the question, shown any interest. She looked away from him as he answered.

In spite of herself she heard that the powder was easy to administer. It could be mixed into food during preparation and would not be detected. While the powder alone would be fatal, she might want to use the spray. Inhalation would cause death in minutes, while oral ingestion could take as long as an hour and involve distress from paralysis and respiratory failure. She was being provided the inhaler out of consideration for her, at his suggestion. She would have options. He reached over and inserted the small package wrapped in lunch paper into her handbag.

Dao stood up, clutching her handbag, and walked in hurried, chopped steps to a park trash container. She vomited into it convulsively. She wiped her mouth and left the park.

CHAPTER FORTY-SEVEN

Zorro and the prison commander continued to meet. Each thought there was advantage to it. The commander sought to know more about Channarong, seeking leverage. The opium-calmed prisoner wanted to hear more about Dao as killer.

The commander did not return to the subject of killing, no matter how Zorro tried to reintroduce it. Was the prison commander reading him? Zorro became more careful. All he could do was look for the tells as he spun stories, trying to keep track of his own disinformation and the commander's reaction to it.

Zorro talked of women who killed, careful to note the commander's reaction. He set their homicidal feelings, borrowed from Greek mythology, in towns of the American West, walled cities of ancient Thailand, Meo mountain villages. They killed because of despair, jealousy, maternal feelings, ideology, and madness.

Nothing elicited reaction from the commander, until the pilot summarized a memory from Zorro movies of boyhood. "A woman was made to choose between friends, the death of one in order to save the life of the other." The commander's response came in familiar pattern, beginning with facial coloring. Zorro quickly added "Of course the movie ended happily."

That night Zorro wept repeatedly as he imagined the pull between them, a bond that would bring his sister to choose the death of a friend. Whatever the Pathet Lao were planning it meant agony for her. The details did not matter. They were going to turn her into a killer of someone close to her, someone unsuspecting.

He realized his emotional state was interfering with his ability to think about what the Pathet Lao might be planning and what he needed to do to frustrate them, to protect Dao. He swallowed some of the commander's opium to calm himself and clear his head.

When he no longer wept, he focused on his questions.

Why would they need her to do a killing? The Pathet Lao ranks are full of people who would kill to not be killed themselves. *They need her*, he thought in the darkness, because no one else can get close enough to the target. That meant the target was visible, important, protected . . . and that *she has access* behind the screen of security.

Who do they want her to kill? *Their enemy*. He brushed past his generalization in annoyance, knew that he was avoiding something. The war over, the Meo fleeing, who was the Pathet Lao enemy? *Anyone interfering with removal of the Lao royal family, anyone aiding the Meo threat*. "Better," he said aloud of his answer. He thought of the Meo refugee camps and the commander's particular interest in Thanasis Mavros' role protecting the refugees. The Meo were menacing to the Pathet Lao, and the CIA an endless resource for the violence of the mountain people.

The target is The Black Man, my friend, her lover.

How would they conscript her to a killing beyond foul, strange, and unnatural, to assassination of her lover? He parsed it out in slow self-examination. *Dao is a romantic paroled to heroic make believe. They are beginning to read her. Thanasis links us all together—Dao, Meo, CIA, me. She will think she must break the link in order to rescue me. They know she will try to rescue me at all costs.*

It had taken only minutes of solitary, opiate-fed inquiry to convince himself that he was a weapon wielded against his sister, a bargaining chip being used by the commander. He was not a player at all, only the chip. He acted immediately, his head filled with the image of a masked bandit overturning a table, spilling all the chips onto the floor.

He dragged himself across the dirt floor to the buried morphine. He scraped the bottle out of its hole and poured the weeks of hoarded pills into his hand. He worried *Will there be enough?* He counted the pills, moving them from one hand to the other. He did not know the number necessary to end the commander's game, but concluded a fistful would do it. He started, one pill at a time. Without water, his mouth dry with the excitement of a winning hand, he struggled to get the individual pills off his tongue and down his throat. When he realized he was counting, he laughed. *I'm not going to have a use for that number.* The pills seemed to go down more easily when he lost track. He paused in his endgame to wonder what strange and wonderful thing his sister was doing far away in the warm nights of Bangkok. As he swallowed more pills, he pictured dark-haired children playing doctor long ago.

On this night she played another game. She was on the phone with the Thai agent for the Lao People's Democratic Republic. She had called him on the Bangkok telephone number he had given her. She said to him "There are two conditions to my brother's release. You have set one of them. I will now set the other. You must accept my condition or what you want will never happen, whatever the result."

"What is it you want?"

"My brother must be brought to me. We must meet face-to-face on the banks of the Mekong before anything else proceeds. In Thailand, at Mukdahan." Her plan, still vague, included Meo and weapons. She was having trouble with details, but knew she could get both. She kept imagining, however, the soft snap of the Thai agent's fingers.

"He cannot be brought to Thailand. We are not foolish and you should not be. On the other hand, I understand you might need to see him before you proceed. Come once more to Mukdahan and we will take you to him, across the river. A meeting perhaps in Party offices in Savannakhet. You must come alone, of course."

Her rescue fantasy—an image of armed Meo leaping from an ambulance, led by Dao rushing to her brother, screaming "Kill them! Kill them all!"—dissolved in tears of impossibility and loss.

She made her decision and planned its execution, telling no one. She experimented with the poison, killing a starving dog with a plate of food laced with saxitoxin powder. The inhaler spray ended the dog's convulsions immediately. She hid the containers of poison in her house on the canal, rooms full of hiding places from her childhood. Having decided, she was now obsessed with avoiding discovery. Obsession pushed her deep into her recurring fantasy world. As always Zorro was there, trusting her and whatever game was to be played. The difference now, she saw, was that she wore the mask of Death and there was no game. She moved in and out of fantasy, pain and relief trading places throughout the day.

She contacted the Thai officer again, using a public telephone at a hotel in one of the business districts. She was calling to tell him when she would travel to Savannakhet to see her brother, that the time had come. The procedure they had set up was for her to call him posing as a prostitute. They made an appointment for sex, hung up, and he called her back on the public telephone. She confirmed when she would arrive. He told her how she would be transported across the river to Savannakhet and that the meeting place would not be disclosed—all she would be told is that she had arrived. There would be prison guards present throughout the meeting with her brother. She objected to the guards, to which the agent said only "He is a prisoner."

The Thai officer took the opportunity to ask "For purposes of timing the release of your brother, how will I know Mavros is dead?"

"A man identifying himself as Michael will call you at my request to say that Thanasis Mavros is dead, that his body is at his apartment. He will think you are his physician and have been asked to view the body and make burial arrangements. How you handle that is up to you." She had not prepared to say these things. She was surprised at how glib she was about the details of Thanasis' murder, though not at her capacity for deception.

Dao returned to her house on the *klong* and left it not long after, crossing the Chao Phraya in her narrow dugout, dressed in a laborer's jacket, its deep pockets carrying sticks of incense, skimpy clothing, and the inhaler of saxitoxin. She entered the service entrance of a hotel near the river, changed into the revealing skirt and makeup of the sex trade, left the hotel through its main entrance, and took a taxi to Soi Cowboy and a bar specializing in trysts with transsexuals. She struck up a conversation with a sex worker and, with little effort, persuaded her to trade clothing. This caused admiring giggles and requests from the *kathoeys,* the transsexuals, for her surgeon's name. They gladly helped her shave her head, could not touch her enough. Though she thought of it as disguise the shaved head was not that as much as it was an effort by her subconscious to disappear, to hide from the thoughts of death and madness that sought her out. When those thoughts nevertheless came, she embraced the loss of her hair as surrender of all that was feminine, intimate and alive about her, surrender of the man she loved. Tears came when she thought of him removing the pins from her hair, his hands in her hair, his least touch felt.

She left Bangkok in another taxi. A night's travel brought her once again, disguised and unfollowed, to the Mekong.

While she waited on the river bank, hands in her jacket pockets, she held the inhaler, imagining what was to come, praying aloud to Buddha for strength. "In your death, my source of good and happiness, may you be reborn in a heavenly realm." She touched the three sticks of incense in her pockets.

The appointed hour came and went. The pirogue did not appear out of the river mists. The sun rose and she waited for word of some unforeseen delay. None came.

Dao began running through the possibilities. The arrangement, the communication with the Thai agent, had been clear. There was no confusion as to time and place. *There has been no failure of will,* she thought. *They are in control and want Thanasis' death. I can give them that. They know I will do anything—anything—to rescue my brother. As long as Zorro is alive they are sure they control my will.*

She was shocked by the next possibility her logic suggested. They did not come for her because she could not help Zorro. Her will was no longer relevant.

When they did not come for her, to show her helpless Zorro, she knew it was because she was no longer needed. Not by Zorro, not by the Pathet Lao. Her brother was dead. Buddha had provided.

She set the incense sticks upright in the muddy sand of the river beach and lighted them, poured water on the ground, the ritual honoring death. *Walk with me, Zorro, in the mountain paradise, be my guide once again. To Buddha abiding in the heavenly realm, I humbly prostate.* She waited by the smoldering incense sticks until they were ash.

When she returned to Bangkok she left a telephone message at Thanasis' office asking him to join her at the house on the *klong*. She had information about Zorro, she said. In a note to Thanasis she described her Pathet Lao contacts and that she had seen Zorro, held a prisoner somewhere near Savannakhet. She wrote "I had thought to rescue Zorro to end their use of him. If I failed in that, my resort was to take his life and then my own. In the end, Buddha and Zorro made their own arrangement. Ask your Meo to bring his body out. Bury him beside me."

Dao squeezed the inhaler and breathed. She quickly felt numbness and tingling in her lips. The feeling moved to her fingertips, then her neck and throat. The muscle paralysis that left her flaccid was rapid. Her last thought was about how war gives us meaning. She did not have time to finish the thought, comprehend it.

The bald and absurdly made up figure, half naked in her bed, her mouth in gaping rictus, left Thanasis unable to imagine how Dao had spent her last days. He imagined instead his slim lover kneeling over him, removing pale jade pins from her long black hair, the hair falling to her shoulders, to his hands. When the poison in the inhaler was identified he realized its source and thought over and over of her weeks of pain.

He included her note in his report to Norris, along with transcription of an encrypted radio message from Longfellow. The Meo spy said "The prison commander comes to the pilot's cell in the day. He smokes opium and kicks the dead man again. They do not bury him."

Norris authorized a raid to bring the body out.

CHAPTER FORTY-EIGHT

"How's he doing?" Norris asked.

The young Army captain had not met Norris before. "Are you part of Mr. Mavros' family?"

"No. As far as I know, he has no family. I'm his boss. He works for me."

The captain looked at Norris, as if deciding something about him. "You are a civilian in a secure area of Tripler Army Medical Center, Honolulu. I assume you are a spook and that you were cleared at the reception area. I'm Dr. Dunn. Mr. Mavros is my patient." He paused. "Just what the hell is it you are boss of? My patient is a mess."

"I know where I am, and I'm head of Aerial Delivery Service Research and Development, a government organization associated with the State Department. How is Thanasis? I would like to visit with him if he's available."

"Let's go to my office and talk about his situation. Then you can see him." They sat down in Dr. Dunn's office and the captain began talking, paraphrasing a single-page report he held in his lap.

"Apparently, Thanasis walked onto a Thai military base, showed his U.S. State Department credentials and entered the Officers Club, asked someone if he knew people by the name of Dao or Zorro, and, when the man said he did not, proceeded to beat the shit out of him. Thai military police then arrested Thanasis and beat the shit out of him." The doctor looked up from the report and asked "Do you know why they stabbed him?"

"The military police didn't do that. That happened earlier in the evening when Thanasis asked the same question of a series of taxi drivers lined up at the airport, and assaulted each of them when they answered in the negative." Norris added "He was drunk."

"Of course." Dr. Dunn picked up a pad of paper and pen. "Tell me what you can about this incident and events leading up to it. I have been asked to provide psychotherapeutic intervention for this patient on the assumption he is suffering from Dissociative Identity Disorder or Post-traumatic Stress Disorder or some mishmash of the two. He is severely depressed and not talking. It would help if I knew what the hell is going on."

Norris spent the next two hours telling the doctor Thanasis' history in Laos and about the deaths of smokejumper friends in the war, the violent death of his father, and, within the week, the deaths of Dao and Zorro. There were many questions from the doctor.

"We will likely need to talk some more, Mr. Wright, but I think I know where we are for now. You can drop the State Department stuff." He pushed away from his desk and stood, ending the conference with a prognosis.

"We can be optimistic about Thanasis' recovery, but only if he engages in the prescribed course of counseling and therapy. There is no drug treatment for either Post-traumatic Stress Disorder or Dissociative Identity Disorder. We can manage symptoms—aggression, flashbacks, nightmares, and so on—with drugs. But to recover he has got to want it and participate in the therapy. The standard of care for PTSD in the Department of Defense is cognitive behavioral therapy. We've got to change the way he feels and acts. It is important that he go into counseling and group therapy. If you want to bring someone into this from CIA Office of Medical Services, that is OK with me. But he is my patient and if CIA Medical chooses another course of treatment or messes him up in any way I will throw everybody but Thanasis to hell out of Tripler. The generals will back me because they worry about what their wives tell me."

Dr. Dunn stopped talking and held up his hand. "Sorry. This has nothing to do with you, personally. You have been very helpful. What needs to be said is that Thanasis must go into treatment with something that commits him to the future. A reason to recover. If you have any ideas, anything that would help identify such a commitment, that would be a real contribution. As I say, he isn't talking."

Norris thought a moment. "Charlie."

"Charlie?"

"Charlie is a buddy of Thanasis. He may be able to help. Let me talk to Thanasis," Norris said. *Thanasis would die trying for somebody in trouble. Charlie is in trouble and needs Thanasis. Thanasis will respond.* "I will report to you everything we cover, what we say. You probably bug the generals' wives. Why not me?"

Norris visited Thanasis daily over the next week. At some point Norris said something about the need they both had, if they were to move forward, to "take responsibility for the pain." Thanasis wept for all those he had caused pain, and he began talking about his pain and that of Dao, standing by herself and protecting him. When he spoke about Charlie, he became agitated and revisited his own failures. He focused on rescue, on mission. He could not sleep and when he did he woke up screaming from nightmares.

Dr. Dunn provided drugs and told Norris "I'll take it from here. The buddy Charlie is definitely a way forward, the kind of commitment by Thanasis to the future we want to see. But missions, or whatever you call them, are out of the question. Don't think for a minute you can put this man back in the bush, leading prison raids. Charlie is going to rescue Thanasis, not vice versa."

"I'm not nearly as much into killing my own men as you may think," Norris said. "What occurs to me is that the CIA needs representation on the National League of Families of American Prisoners and Missing in Southeast Asia. Maybe we could do a little funding. Anonymously, of course. Maybe Thanasis could even start his own POW/MIA group, something with a name that evokes the reason we have a prisoner mess in the first place. Something like . . . Rolling Thunder. We'll get Charlie out, and Thanasis will be a part of that, but not in the bush."

As Norris left the hospital he thought *Might happen that way. It's pretty to think so.*

M.I.A.

A guard brushed against a bamboo pole the POW had spent a week untying. Movement of the pole caused the guards to investigate further. The attempted escape threatened the guards with beatings. They beat the prisoner stroke for imagined stroke. They stopped only when they were exhausted and no longer saw threat in the thin, dirty man who stared at them, never moving, never crying out.

The guards tied the POW's feet together and ran the rope from his feet, behind him, up to his hands. They left him bleeding in his cage, unable to sit up. He fell asleep in spite of his restraints and dreamt he was in a fight. A man was holding him down, tearing his face with a broken beer bottle, and he could not raise his arms to protect himself. When he threw his head from side to side to escape the attack, the rat picking at the edge of his wounds panicked and scurried from his face, dragging its thick tail into the surrounding grass.

The POW, chilled with fever, longed for a blanket even more than he longed for food. His head, limbs, and trunk were scabbed with tick and flea bites, his legs and feet swollen with beriberi.

The bounds of his world were the bamboo cage and the elephant grass. The grass and his failing eyesight merged in a blur beyond which nothing existed. Even the sound of airplanes had disappeared.

The guards woke him and took him as usual to the stream and had him empty his waste bucket. In a departure from routine, they gave him a blanket and, instead of returning him to his cage, walked him into the compound where the other prisoners had been confined. The fenced enclosure and huts struck the POW as boundless and the open space made him fearful, weak. The compound was silent. He looked around for another prisoner, cautious, unsure what was happening to him. Then he saw the compound was empty. He sank to the ground.

A Vietnamese intelligence officer walked up. The POW did not try to stand and the officer did not react to the indifference.

The Vietnamese spoke in a rehearsed tone. "Lao prisoners have been released pursuant to the terms of the Lao Agreement of Peace and Reconciliation. Your country is not a signatory and the Pathet Lao is not releasing American prisoners until there is formal agreement ending hostilities between Laos and the United States addressing the prisoner issue." He stopped looking at the POW and continued. "You are not my responsibility. You are being moved to another Pathet Lao prison."

What the POW felt was a great draining, and nothing replaced what left him. He lay on his side, holding himself, and gave up being Charlie.

Arms tied behind his back, he was walked, feverish and dehydrated, to another prison in caves at the base of the Annamite mountains. He was cold beneath the blanket draped over his head. He would not move without it.

AUTHOR'S NOTE

Tex and Yogi—John Lewis and Darrell Eubanks—were the first smokejumpers to die in the Laos war. High school buddies from Lampasas, Texas, they died in an air crash while kicking cargo to the Meo. Seven other jumpers died in the war out of the ninety-two recruited by the CIA. The death of one-in-ten, drawn by an unseen lot, is decimation.

In the years that followed the end of the Laos war, Vang Pao and thousands of Meo, properly called Hmong, were relocated to the United States. Lulu closed her house in Vientiane and moved back to Paris. ARVN officers Lieutenant Phan and Captain Tien were identified as North Vietnamese agents. The king of Laos and his family were imprisoned and died in a jungle prison camp. The smokejumper participants in Operation COLDFEET received medals and commendations from the CIA for the successful intelligence mission. Congressman Morris Udall of Arizona blew the whistle on the CIA airbase at Marana in *Newsweek* magazine and the base was closed.

There are those who say Marana never closed. They say it still exists, in south Texas, on ranchland leased from a private citizen for a case of Wild Turkey a year. The ranch in Texas is where the boat drop used to kill the Somali pirates was developed by an old smokejumper rigger. "Oh yeh," they drawl, "CIA still uses smokejumpers. Because they hang."

The POW/MIA organizations of the Southeast Asia wars still exist. Their offices are not far from CIA facilities in northern Virginia.

ACKNOWLEDGEMENTS

Without lunch with my friend Charlie, I would not have known where to turn with my book about smokejumpers and the CIA. Charles Brandt is a master of the true-crime genre and knows a lot of people in witness protection. His book *I Heard You Paint Houses* will soon be available to us through a Scorsese/De Niro movie, *The Irishman.*

What Charlie did was deliver me into the hands of publishing icon Bill Thompson. William G. Thompson is the editor of the first seven Stephen King books and the first two John Grisham novels. Bill agreed to be my editor. No bones about it, he agreed because Charlie called him.

In our first conversation, Bill asked "What do you want your book to be?" This is pretty much what I answered: "The story is a tragedy in a little-known historical setting. It is told *in memoriam* for those who are recruited to die in wars. The book rewards the reader with new information about strange things—secret war, wilderness smoke jumping, CIA use of surrogate fighters. The characters are a little chipped but likeable enough that, hopefully, the reader will miss them when they finish the read." Whether that was helpful to him, I don't know. I do know that he made me write what I wanted. I hope he is there for me next time. I am working on it, Bill.

There are three other groups of people to whom I owe thanks for this book. They are the smokejumpers who populated *Kickers* with characters and events when I interviewed them about the Laos war from fifty years ago; the writers in my writing group who risked giving offense in order to save me from myself; and the numerous family members and friends who read my drafts and encouraged me just because they wanted me to tell this story.

The Laos smokejumpers I interviewed include guys with whom I jumped out of fabulous old airplanes: Ray Beasley, Dick Graham, Glenn Hale, Ken Hessel, Shep Johnson, Larry Moore, Toby Scott, Woody Spence, Rocky Stone, and T.J. Thompson (who rigged the boat drop used by Delta Force in taking out the Somali pirates).

The writers who made up my loosely associated writing group and talked me out of the trees include my brother-in-law Ray Blomgren, my brother-in-law Jerry McGovern, my daughter Jennifer Lee (nominee for the Pushcart Prize for her short stories), and my longtime friends Barbara Bares and Barbara Mathias Riegel.

My family and friends who encouraged me, to the point of identifying authors I might usefully steal from, are too many to name. No greater support was given than what I received from my wife Janis. She knows there is no money in this business and goes unblinkered in our life together, yet supports my cabined, silent efforts to tell stories. Remarkable.

AUTHOR BIOGRAPHY

Patrick Lee is a former smokejumper who made twenty-five parachute jumps into the Idaho Primitive Area fighting forest fires. After leaving jumping to study law, he began to hear of smokejumper deaths in Laos, including those of men who had been his jump partners.

Interviews of surviving smokejumpers about their CIA experiences in Laos convinced Lee their stories needed to be told. He incorporated core elements of their recollections in *Kickers*. In 2012, he was awarded a writer's residency by the Jentel Artist Residency Program based on the *Kickers* manuscript.

After forty-five years practicing law in Washington, D.C., Lee now lives and writes on a ranch in the Sawtooth Mountains of Central Idaho with his wife Janis.

Patrick Lee

Made in the USA
Charleston, SC
12 June 2014